Raves
**THE KIL**
and for the new
master of unrel
**GREGG**

"*The Kill Clause* is a bullet-fast ride** through a landscape
of high tension and sudden death—but it's also a moving
story of real human beings negotiating the gray areas of
the world. Hurwitz draws you into the mind of a top-flight
U.S. marshal and then shows you how and why such a
good man might cross the line. It's strong stuff, exciting on
every page."

Andrew Klavan, author of *Don't Say a Word*

"**Hurwitz really excels.** His action scenes rival those of
Stephen Hunter and, especially, Lee Child. And his command of cutting-edge weapons and surveillance technology is second to none . . . [*The Kill Clause*] packs the kind of
wallop thriller fans thirst for and find all too infrequently."

*Providence Journal-Bulletin*

"Gregg Hurwitz perfectly realizes the gritty, hair-trigger
world of the U.S. marshal's elite Arrest Response Team
with some of the most intense action scenes I have ever
read, counterpointed beautifully by the **heart-wrenching
story** of a father's horrifying loss."

Robert Crais, author of *The Last Detective*

"A tough, engaging, and morally complex work that grabs
you early and never lets you go. Hurwitz knows a cop's
world inside and out. **Every page bristles with authenticity.** I highly recommend it."

Christopher Reich, author of *The First Billion*

BY GREGG HURWITZ

THE KILL CLAUSE
DO NO HARM
MINUTES TO BURN
THE TOWER

AVAILABLE IN HARDCOVER

THE PROGRAM

# GREGG HURWITZ

## THE
## KILL
## CLAUSE

HarperTorch
*An Imprint of* HarperCollins*Publishers*

This is a work of fiction. Names, characters, places, and incidents are products of the author's imagination or are used fictitiously and are not to be construed as real. Any resemblance to actual events, locales, organizations, or persons, living or dead, is entirely coincidental.

HARPERTORCH
*An Imprint of* HarperCollins*Publishers*
195 Broadway
New York, NY 10007

Copyright © 2003 by Gregg Hurwitz
Excerpt from *The Program* copyright © 2004 by Gregg Hurwitz
ISBN 0-06-053039-1

First HarperTorch paperback printing: September 2004
First William Morrow hardcover printing: August 2003

HarperCollins®, HarperTorch™, and ❦™ are trademarks of Harper-Collins Publishers Inc.

Printed in the United States of America

Visit HarperTorch on the World Wide Web at www.harpercollins.com

12

*For Melissa Hurwitz, M.D.*

*My first reader*
*Ever, and each time out*

**There is no justice. There is only the law.**

—Old judicial proverb of obscure origin,
loosely attributed to Oliver Wendell Holmes

# THE
# KILL
# CLAUSE

**1** WHEN BEAR CAME TO TELL HIM THAT GINNY'S BODY HAD been found raped and dismembered in a creek six miles from his house, that her remains had required three biohazard bags to depart the scene, that they were currently sprawled on a pathologist's slab awaiting further probing, Tim's first reaction was not what he would have expected of himself. He went ice cold. There was no grief—grief, he'd learn, takes perspective, recollection, time to unfurl. There was just the news slapping him, dense and jarring like face pain. And, inexplicably, there was embarrassment, though for whom or what, he was not sure. The heel of his hand lowered, searching out the butt of his Smith & Wesson, which of course he wasn't wearing at home at 6:37 in the evening.

To his right Dray fell to her knees, one hand clutching the door frame, fingers curling between the jamb and hinges as if seeking pain. Beneath the razor edge of blond hair, sweat sparkled on the band of her neck.

For an instant everything was frozen. Rain-heavy February air. The draft guttering the seven candles on the pink-and-white-frosted birthday cake that Judy Hartley held poised for revelation in the living room. Bear's boots, distressingly carrying the crime-scene mud, blotting the aggregate porch, the pebbles of which Tim had meticulously smoothed on his hands and knees last fall with a square trowel.

Bear said, "Maybe you want to sit down." His eyes held

the same guilt and attempted empathy Tim himself had used in countless situations, and Tim hated him unjustly for it. The anger dissolved quickly, leaving behind a dizzying emptiness.

The small gathering in the living room, mirroring the dread emanating from the hushed doorway conversation, gave off a breath-held tension. One of the little girls resumed recounting Harry Potter Quidditch rules and was hushed violently. A mother leaned over and blew out the candles Dray had lit in eager anticipation after the knock on the front door.

"I thought you were her," Dray said. "I just finished frosting her . . ." Her voice wavered hard.

Hearing her, Tim registered an aching remorse that he'd pressed Bear so hard for details right here at the door. His only way to grasp the information had been to try to contain it in questions and facts, to muscle it into pieces small enough for him to digest. Now that he'd taken it in, he had too much of it. But he'd knocked on enough doors himself—as had Dray—to know that it would have been only a matter of time until they'd known it all anyway. Better to wade in fast and steady and brace against the cold, because the chill wasn't going to leave their bones anytime soon, or maybe ever.

"Andrea," he said. His trembling hand felt the air, searching for her shoulder and not finding it. He couldn't move, couldn't so much as turn his head.

Dray bent her head and started to weep. The sound was one Tim had never heard. Inside, one of Ginny's schoolmates matched her crying—confused, instinctive mimicry.

Bear crouched, both knees cracking, his form broad but huddled on the porch, his nylon raid jacket sweeping low like a cape. The yellow lettering, pale and faded, announced U.S. DEPUTY MARSHAL in case someone cared. "Darlin', hold on there," he said. "Hold on."

His immense hands encircled her biceps—no small feat—and drew her in so her face pressed against his chest. Her hands clawed the air, as if afraid to set down on something for fear of what they might do.

He raised his head sheepishly. "We're gonna need you to . . ."

Tim reached down, stroked his wife's head. "I'll go."

The three-foot tires of Bear's chipped-silver Dodge Ram hiccupped over seams on the roadway, shifting the broken-glass dread in Tim's gut.

Composed of twelve square miles of houses and tree-lined streets about fifty miles northwest of downtown L.A., Moorpark was renowned for little more than the fact that it housed the state's largest concentration of law-enforcement residents. It was a low-rent country club for the straight arrows, a post-shift refuge from the streets of the off-kilter city they probed and fought for most of their waking hours. Moorpark radiated an artificial fifties-TV-show feel—no tattoo parlors, no homeless people, no drive-bys. A Secret Service agent, two FBI families, and a postal inspector lived on Tim and Dray's cul-de-sac. Burglary, in Moorpark, was a zero-growth industry.

Bear stared dead ahead at the yellow reflectors lining the center of the road, each one materializing, then floating downward in the darkness. He'd forgone his usual slouch, driving attentively, seeming grateful for something to do.

Tim sifted through the mound of remaining questions and tried to find one to serve as a starting point. "Why did you . . . why were you there? Not exactly a federal case."

"Sheriff's department took prints from her hand. . . ."

From her hand. A separate entity. Not *from her*. Through his sickening horror, Tim wondered which of the three bags had carried away her hand, her arm, her torso. One of Bear's knuckles was smudged with dried mud.

". . . the face was tough, I guess. Jesus, Rack, I'm sorry." Bear heaved a sigh that bounced off the dash and came back at Tim in the passenger seat. "Anyways, Bill Fowler was in the handling unit. He firmed the ID—" He stopped, catching himself, then reworded. "He recognized Ginny. Put in a call to me, since he knows how I am with you and Dray."

"Why didn't *he* do the advise next of kin? He was Dray's first partner out of the academy. He just ate barbecue at our house last month." Tim's voice rose, grew accusatory. In its heightened pitch he recognized his desperate need to lay blame.

"Some people aren't cut out for telling parents that—" Bear laid off the rest of the sentence, evidently finding it as displeasing as Tim did.

The truck exited and hammered over bumps in the off-ramp, making them bounce in their seats.

Tim exhaled hard, trying to rid himself of the blackness that had filled his body, cruelly and methodically, somewhere between the porch and now. "I'm glad it was you that came." His voice sounded far away. It betrayed little of the chaos he was fighting to control, to categorize. "Leads?"

"Distinctive tire imprints heading out of the creek's slope. It was pretty muddy. The deputies are on it. I didn't really . . . that's not really where my head was at." Bear's stubble glimmered with dried sweat. His kind, too-wide features looked hopelessly weary.

Tim flashed on him setting Ginny up on his shoulders at Disneyland last June, hoisting her fifty-three pounds like a bag of feathers. Bear was orphaned young, never married.

The Rackleys were, for all intents and purposes, his surrogate family.

Tim had investigated warrants with Bear for three years on the Escape Team out of the district office downtown, ever since Tim's eleven-year stint in the Army Rangers. They also served together on the Arrest Response Team, the Marshals' SWAT-like tactical strike force that kicked doors and hooked and hauled as many of the twenty-five hundred federal fugitives hidden in the sprawling L.A. metropolis as they could get cuffs on.

Though still fifteen years from the mandatory retirement age of fifty-seven, Bear had recently begun referring to the date grudgingly, as if it were imminent. To ensure he'd have some conflict in his life after retirement, Bear had completed night law school at the SouthWest Los Angeles Legal Training Academy and, after failing the bar twice, had finally wrung a pass out of it last July. He'd had Chance Andrews—a judge he used to work court duty for regularly—swear him in at Federal downtown, and he, Dray, and Tim had celebrated in the lobby afterward, drinking Cook's out of Dixie cups. Bear's license sat in the bottom drawer of his office file cabinet, gathering dust, preventive medicine for future tedium. He had nine years on Tim, currently apparent in the lines etching his face. Tim, who'd gone enlisted at the age of nineteen, had had the benefit of opposing stress with youthfulness when learning to operate; he'd emerged from the Rangers seasoned but not weathered.

"Tire tracks," Tim said. "If the guy's that disorganized, something'll break."

"Yeah," Bear said. "Yeah, it will."

He slowed and pulled into a parking lot, easing past the squat sign reading VENTURA COUNTY MORGUE. He parked in a handicap spot up front, threw his marshal's placard on the dash. They sat in silence. Tim pressed his hands together, flat-palmed, and crushed them between his knees.

Bear reached across to the glove box and tugged out a pint of Wild Turkey. He took two gulps, sending air gurgling up through the bottle, then offered it to Tim. Tim took a half mouthful, feeling it wash smoky and burning down his throat before losing itself in the morass of his stomach. He screwed on the lid, then untwisted it and took another pull. He set it down on the dash, kicked open his door a little harder than necessary, and faced Bear across the uninterrupted stretch of the vinyl front seat.

Now—just now—grief was beginning to set in. Bear's eyelids were puffy and red-rimmed, and it occurred to Tim that he may have pulled over on his way to their house, sat in his rig, and cried a bit.

For a moment Tim thought he might come apart altogether, start screaming and never stop. He thought of the task before him—what awaited him behind the double glass doors—and wrestled a piece of strength from a place he didn't know he had inside him. His stomach roiled audibly, and he fought his lips still.

"You ready?" Bear asked.

"No."

Tim got out and Bear followed.

The fluorescent lighting was otherworldly harsh, shining off the polished floor tile and the stainless-steel cadaver drawers set into the walls. A broken lump lay inert beneath a hospital-blue sheet on the center embalming table, awaiting them.

The coroner, a short man with a horseshoe of hair and a stereotype-reinforcing pair of round spectacles, fussed nervously with the mask that dangled around his neck. Tim swayed on his feet, his eyes on the blue sheet. The draped form was distressingly small and unnaturally proportioned. The smell reached him quickly, something rank and earthy beneath the sharp tang of metal and disinfectant. The whiskey leapt and jumped in his stomach, as if trying to get out.

The coroner rubbed his hands like a solicitous and slightly apprehensive waiter. "Timothy Rackley, father of Virginia Rackley?"

"That's right."

"If you'd like, ah, you could go into the adjoining room and I could roll the table over before the window so you could, ah, ID her."

"I'd like to be alone with the body."

"Well, there's still, ah, forensic considerations, so I can't really—"

Tim flipped open his wallet and let his five-point marshal's star dangle. The coroner nodded weightily and left the room. Mourning, like most things, gets more deference with a little authority behind it.

Tim turned to Bear. "Okay, pal."

Bear studied Tim a few moments, eyes darting back and forth across his face. He must have trusted something he saw, because he backed up and exited, easing the door closed discreetly so the latch bolt made only the slightest click.

Tim studied the form on the embalming table before drawing near. He wasn't sure which end of the sheet to peel back; he was accustomed to body bags. He didn't want to turn aside the wrong edge and see more than he absolutely had to. In his line of work he'd learned that some memories were impossible to purge.

He ventured that the coroner would have left Ginny with her head facing the door, and he pressed gently on the edge of the lump, discerning the bump of her nose, the sockets of her eyes. He wasn't sure if they'd cleaned up her face, nor was he sure he would prefer that, or whether he'd rather see it as it was left so he could feel closer to the horror she'd lived in her final moments.

He flipped back the sheet. His breath left him in a gut-punch gasp, but he didn't bend over, didn't flinch, didn't turn away. Anguish raged inside him, sharp-edged and bent on destruction; he watched her bloodless, broken face until it died down.

With a trembling hand he removed a pen from his pocket and used it to pull a wisp of Ginny's hair—the same straight blond as Dray's—from the corner of her mouth. This one thing he wanted to set straight, despite all the damage and violation stamped on her face. Even if he'd wanted to, he wouldn't have touched her. She was evidence now.

He found a single ray of thankfulness, that Dray wouldn't have to carry the memory of this sight with her.

He pulled the sheet tenderly back over Ginny's face and walked out. Bear sprang up from the row of cheap, puke-green waiting chairs, and the coroner scurried over, sipping from a paper cone filled with water from the cooler.

Tim started to speak but had to stop. When he found his voice, he said, "That's her."

**2** THEY HEADED BACK TO DRAY IN SILENCE, THE BOTTLE sliding empty on the dash. Tim wiped his mouth, then wiped it again.

"She was supposed to be just around the corner at Tess's. You know, the redhead—pigtails? Two blocks away from school, right on Ginny's way home. Dray told her to go there after school, so we'd have a chance, you know, her other friends, the presents. To surprise her."

A sob swelled in his throat, and he swallowed it, swallowed it hard.

"Tess goes to private school. We have an arrangement, us and her mom. The kids can stop by for play dates unannounced. There was no one expecting Ginny, no one to miss her. This is Moorpark, Bear." His voice cracked. "It's *Moorpark*. You're not supposed to know your kid's not okay when she's four hundred yards away." Tim faded off into a space between agonizing thoughts, a momentary respite from the distinct pain of having failed—as a father, as a deputy U.S. marshal, as a man—to protect his sole child's existence.

Bear drove on and didn't talk, and Tim appreciated him greatly for it.

Bear's cell phone rang. He picked it up and spoke into it, a string of words and numbers that Tim barely registered. Bear flipped the unit shut and pulled to the curb. Tim didn't notice for several minutes that they were stopped, that Bear was studying him. When he looked over, Bear's eyes were startlingly severe.

Tim spoke through the sluggishness of his exhaustion. "What?"

"That was Fowler. They caught him."

Tim felt a rush of emotions, dark and hateful and intertwined. "Where?"

"Off Grimes Canyon. About a half mile from here."

"We're going."

"Ain't gonna be nothing to see but yellow tape and aftermath. We don't want to contaminate the arrest, fuck up the crime scene. I thought I'd take you to Dray—"

"We're going."

Bear picked up the empty bottle, jiggled it, then set it back on the dash. "I know."

They pulled down the long, isolated drive, gravel popping beneath the tires, winding their way into the heart of the small canyon. A converted stand-alone garage to a house that had long since burned down sat dark and slanted along a crescent of eucalyptus. The smudged side windows diffused a single spot of yellow interior light. Rain and wear had lifted the plywood from the walls, and the swing-down door was rotting in fat patches. To the side a rusting white pickup rose from the weeds, fresh mud caked in the tire treads and thrown up around the wheel wells.

A police vehicle sat diagonally across the overgrown concrete foundation of the extinct house, lights blinking. Like the other cars in the fleet, it was labeled MOORPARK POLICE, though all two-man crews were, like Dray, sheriff's deputies contracted from Ventura County. Parked beside it was an unmarked, lights flashing from the sun visor. Without the accompanying scream of the sirens, the strobe action was disorienting.

Fowler met them at the truck, his mouth pursed over a lipful of tobacco. He was breathing hard, his eyes sharp and gleaming, his face flushed with excitement. He unsnapped his holster, then snapped it again. The detectives were not in sight. No yellow tape, no perimeter, no crime-lab guys working up forensics.

Before Tim could get out of the truck, Fowler was talking. "Gutierez and Harrison—they rolled from Homicide Bureau—they got a read off the tire tracks at the riverbank. I guess they're factory-issue radials for Toyotas '87 to '89 or some shit. Crime lab found a fingernail at the scene—"

Tim buckled, and Bear laid a supporting hand across the small of his back, out of Fowler's view.

"—chip of white paint under it. Automobile paint. Gutierez what-the-fucked it, ran it through for a ten-mile radius, only got twenty-seven hits, if you can believe it. We split up the addresses. This was our third stop. There's hardcore evidence. The guy spilled in seconds. Cases just don't work out like this." He coughed out a single note of a laugh, then went pale. His hand dipped to his holster again, and he unsnapped and snapped the thumb break. "Jesus Christ, Rack, I'm sorry. I've just been . . . I should have come over myself, but I wanted to get my head down and help bust the piece of shit."

"Why isn't there a perimeter up?" Tim said.

"We, uh . . . we still have him. He's inside."

Tim's mouth went dry. His fury narrowed, gathering like a parachute pulled through a napkin ring; with focus it seemed less likely to bleed into sorrow. Bear slid up next to him like a revving car at a stoplight.

"What about CSU? Did you even call them?"

Fowler grew suddenly interested in the ground. "We called you." He toed a desiccated weed, which gave off a good crackle. "I know if *my* little girl—" He shook off the thought. "The boys and I just weren't gonna let this one fly." He unsnapped the thumb break again, slid his Beretta from the holster, and held the pistol out to Tim, butt first. "For you and Dray."

The three men stared at the pistol. Bear made a noise deep in his throat that didn't quite shape itself into a judgment one way or the other. Fowler's face was still flushed and intense, a lightning bolt of a vein forking his forehead. Somewhere in his jumble of thoughts, Tim grasped why Fowler had contacted Bear on his cell phone, not the radio.

Bear shifted so he was close to Tim, beside him but facing opposite, his back to Fowler, his eyes staring out at the dark of the canyon. "What do you want here, Rack?" His fingers spread, then clenched into fists. "As a father? As a representative of the law?"

Tim took the pistol. He walked toward the garage, and neither Bear nor Fowler followed. He heard sounds issuing through the warped door. Murmuring voices.

He knocked twice, the ragged wood biting his knuckles.

"Hang on." The voice belonged to Mac, Fowler's partner and another of Dray's deputy colleagues. Some shuffling. "Stand back!"

The garage door swung up on screeching springs. With inadvertent theatricality, Mac moved his large frame out of Tim's way, revealing Gutierez and Harrison standing on either side of a scrawny man on a torn couch. Tim recognized the detectives now—local boys. Dray had worked with them when they were still patrolmen out of Moorpark Station; Homicide had assigned them the area, no doubt, because of their familiarity with it.

Tim's eyes swept the interior, taking in a heap of blood-moist rags, a pair of little girl's fingerprint-muddied cotton panties plugging a draft in the far wall, a bent hacksaw with the teeth worn down to nubs. He fought to get his mind around these objects, these inconceivabilities.

He stepped forward, his shoes slippery on the oil-stained concrete. The man was clean-shaven, his face razor-nicked at the jaw. He hunched over his legs, elbows tucked into his crotch, hands cuffed before him. His boots, like Bear's, were caked with mud. The two detectives stepped away as Tim approached, straightening their poly wool suits.

Mac's deep voice issued over Tim's shoulder. "Meet Roger Kindell."

"You see him, you puke?" Gutierez said. "This is that little girl's father."

The man's eyes, focused on Tim, showed neither comprehension nor remorse.

"That this could happen in *our* fucking town," Harrison said, as if continuing some previous conversation. "The animals are drifting north. Invading."

Tim stepped forward again, until his shadow fell across Kindell's face, blocking the dim light from the bare lamp bulb. Kindell sucked his teeth, then bent his face into the bowl of his hands, his fingers massaging the line of his scalp. His voice was loose, vowel-heavy at the ends of his words, and a touch guttural.

"I already tole you I did it. Lee me alone."

Tim felt his heartbeat hammering in his temples, his throat. Controlled rage.

Kindell kept his face turned down into his hands. Black crescents stood out beneath his fingernails—dried blood.

Harrison uncrossed his arms, sweat shining on his ebony face. "Look at him. You look at him, son." Still no response. In a flash the detective was on top of Kindell, hands digging into his throat and cheeks, knee riding his gut, bending his head back and up so he faced Tim. Kindell's breathing flared his nostrils; his eyes were sharply defiant.

Gutierez turned to Tim. "I got a throw-down." Tim glanced at the proffered bulge at the detective's ankle beneath his pant leg, a crappy gun to be left on the scene clutched in Kindell's dead hand. Gutierez nodded. "See no evil, hear no evil, speak no evil, my friend."

Harrison pulled himself off Kindell, shoved his head to the side, and nodded at Tim. "You do what you need to do."

Mac was playing lookout at the wide opening of the

garage door, his head swiveling back and forth, checking the darkness despite the fact that Bear and Fowler were less than twenty yards away with a clear line of sight to the main road.

Tim turned back to Kindell. "Leave me."

"You got it, brother," Gutierez said. He paused beside Tim and slipped him the handcuff key. "We already frisked the piece of shit. Just don't leave any of the wrong kind of marks on him."

Mac squeezed Tim's shoulder, then followed the two detectives out. Tim reached up, grabbed the dangling rope handle on the garage door, and tugged. The door creaked again, gained momentum fast, and slammed shut. Kindell didn't so much as blink. Cool as a blade.

He took note of the Beretta in Tim's hand, pointed down at the floor, and turned his head to the wall, as if expressing vague uninterest. His hair was cropped short, a grown-out buzz cut that resembled fur.

The question came out before Tim considered it. "Did you kill my daughter?"

The lightbulb in the lamp emitted an odd humming noise. The air wrapped around Tim, dank and tinted with the odor of paint thinner.

Kindell turned back to face him. His even features were set off by an unusually flat and elongated forehead. His hands rested together in his lap. He didn't look as though he planned to answer the question.

"Did you kill my daughter?" Tim asked again.

After a thoughtful pause, Kindell nodded slowly, once.

Tim waited for his breathing to even out. He felt his lips trembling, fought them still. "Why?"

Same sluggish cadence to the words, as though they'd been slowed down. "Cuz she was so beautiful."

Tim racked the Beretta's slide, chambering a round.

Kindell emitted a muffled sob, his eyes starting to stream. The first sign of any emotion. He glared at Tim defiantly, even as snot ran from his nose and forded his upper lip.

Tim raised the pistol. His hands were shaking with rage, so it took a moment for him to line the sights on the tall target of Kindell's forehead.

Bear leaned against his truck, massive arms crossed, eyeing the other four men.

"You don't motherfuck around with a deputy's family," Gutierez was saying. A deferential nod to Bear. "Or a marshal's."

Bear didn't nod back.

Fowler weighed in. "They don't give a shit anymore. No sense of anything."

"Amen to that," Gutierez said.

"It's like that guy who walked the sarin nerve-gas bomb into the day-care center. Ezekiel or Jedediah or whatever." Harrison shook his head. "Nothing makes sense anymore. Nothing."

"How's Dray doing?" Mac asked. "She all right?"

"She's tough," Bear said.

"Ain't that the fuckin' truth," Fowler said.

Gutierez again—"She's gonna be better once Rack brings her back a little news."

"You know Tim well?" Bear asked.

The detective shifted his weight from one shoe to the other. "Know *of* him."

"Why don't you leave his nickname to those of us who do?"

"Hey, come on Jowalski," Mac said. "Tito don't mean no harm. We're on the same side, us out here."

"Are we?" Bear said.

They waited, glancing at the closed garage door, bracing

themselves for a gunshot in the silence. The crickets were at it, filling the air with nervous chirping.

Mac wiped his brow with a forearm, though the night was cool. "Wonder what he's doing in there."

"He's not gonna kill him," Bear said.

The others' heads swiveled toward Bear, surprised. Fowler wore a shit-eating grin. "You don't think?"

Bear shifted uncomfortably, then crossed his arms as if to lock down his posture.

"Why wouldn't he?" Gutierez said.

Bear regarded him with unadulterated disdain. "For one, he's not gonna want to be yoked to you jackasses for the rest of his life."

Gutierez started to say something but took note of Bear's flexed forearms and closed his mouth. The crickets continued to shrill. They all did their best to avoid eye contact.

"Fuck this. I'm gonna get him." Bear drew himself up off his truck. Beside him even Mac looked small. Bear took a step toward the garage, then stopped abruptly. He lowered his head, eyes on the dirt, frozen between advance and retreat.

Tim kept the Beretta trained on Kindell's head, his body still and rigid, a shooter's outline cut from steel. After a moment his gun arm began to quake. His eyes moistened; two jerking breaths racked his shoulders. With a sudden, stunning certainty, he knew that he would not kill Kindell. His thoughts, absent the focus of the task, pulled back to his daughter. He was overtaken with a sadness so stark and selfish and crushing that it seemed to defy the limits of his heart. It came on fierce and full-powered, like nothing he'd ever confronted. He lowered the gun and bent, fists on thighs, as it throttled through him.

When he regained awareness that he was still drawing breath, he straightened as best he could. "Were you alone?"

The same roll of the head, up, down, up.

Unremitting cramps in Tim's chest kept him curled into an old man's arthritic hunch. His voice rasped, weak and uncomprehending, "You just decided . . . decided to kill her?"

Kindell blinked hard and drew his bound hands over his face like a squirrel grooming. "I wasn't supposed to kill her."

Tim's body snapped upright, his posture firming. "What does 'supposed to' mean?" No answer. "Was someone in on this with you?"

"He didn't—" Kindell stopped, closed his eyes.

"*He* who? He didn't *what?* Someone else helped you kill my girl?" His voice was shaking with fury and desperation. "Answer me, goddamnit. *Answer me!*"

Kindell remained still, impervious to Tim's questions, the smooth ovals of his closed eyelids like veined eggs.

The garage door flew up with a bang, spilling light across the weed-dense grounds. Kindell stumbled out, propelled by Tim's shove, his hands now cuffed behind him. Tim caught up to him quickly, fisting the chain between the cuffs and pulling it up so Kindell's arms locked straight behind him. Kindell grimaced but didn't cry out.

Bear and the others silently watched them approach. As Tim neared, Kindell tripped and went down, his knees and chest taking the shock of the ground. His grunt sounded like a bark.

Kindell struggled to stand up. He bore no bruises or signs of punishment. "You asshoe. You uckin' asshoe."

"Better watch your mouth," Tim said. "I'm your best friend right about now."

Bear exhaled in a low, cheek-puffing rumble.

Fowler glowered at Tim like a woman scorned. Gutierez and Harrison looked equally displeased.

"Can we have a second here?" Fowler said, the skin tight around his jaw.

Tim nodded, then followed the three men a few paces away from Mac and Bear.

"He's a piece-of-shit motherfucker," Fowler hissed.

Tim said, "No argument here."

Fowler spit a brown stream into the brush. "You're gonna let pieces of shit like this run loose in our town?"

Tim looked at him with a steady gaze until he turned away.

"What the fuck, Rackley? We were doing you a favor here."

Gutierez smoothed his mustache with a thumb and forefinger. "This guy just killed your daughter. How can you not want to cap his ass?"

"I'm not a jury."

"I bet Dray would have another opinion on the matter."

"You're probably right."

"Juries suck," Fowler said. "I don't trust the courts."

"Then move to Sierra Leone."

"Listen, Rackley—"

"No, *you* listen." Ten yards away Bear's and Mac's heads snapped to attention. "There's an ongoing investigation here that you may have just fucked up in your eagerness to tie things up neatly."

Harrison weighed in from above crossed arms. "It's an open-and-shut."

"He didn't kill her alone."

Gutierez blew air out through clenched teeth. "What the fuck is this?"

"Someone else was in on it." Tim's hand was jiggling back and forth, thumb tapping his thigh.

"He didn't tell us that."

"Well, then, it looks like you've exhausted your bag of detective tricks."

Bear walked over, his boots creaking, leaving Mac with Kindell. He scowled at the others, standing protectively at Tim's side. "Everything all right?"

"Your boy here is looking to complicate matters that aren't complicated." Gutierez glared at Tim. "You're being emotional."

"That's for sure."

"How do you know there was someone else involved?" Gutierez jerked his head at Kindell, still lying prone on the ground. "What did he say?"

"He didn't say anything outright—"

"Nothing outright," Harrison said. "A hunch, huh?"

Bear's voice issued so low Tim felt it in his bones. "You'd better mind your *fucking* mouth after what he's been through tonight."

Harrison's smirk vanished instantly.

"This is precisely why we don't kill people without a trial." Tim regarded the three men. "Call CSU. Start your investigation. Gather evidence."

Fowler was shaking his head. "This is a fucking mess. Kindell heard us talking. Planning this out."

Gutierez made a leveling gesture with his hands. "It's fine. We'll move forward with standard procedure. If the scumsuck wants to whine to the public defender, it'll be his word against ours." He glared at Tim and Bear. "All of ours."

Tim debated informing Gutierez that the last thing he intended to expend energy on this night was Gutierez's anxiety, but he didn't want to give anything up to him.

Behind them Mac helped Kindell to his feet.

"You were never here," Harrison said. "We stick together on this, no matter what."

Bear gave a cough of disgust. They walked back to the vehicles, their breath visible in the cold air.

"You're a lucky little motherfucker," Gutierez said to Kindell, who'd finally found his feet. He poked him hard where his chest met his shoulder. "Did you hear me? I said you're a lucky motherfucker."

"Lee me alone."

Bear circled his truck, climbed in, and turned over the engine.

Mac cleared his throat. "Tim, man, I am so sorry about . . . everything. You send Dray my condolences. I'm really sorry."

"Thanks, Mac," Tim said. "I'll tell her."

He climbed into the truck and they drove off, leaving the four deputies and Kindell behind them, standing out from the night in carnival flashes of watery blue.

 **BEAR PULLED UP TO THE CURB, AND TIM MOVED TO GET** out, but Bear grabbed his shoulder. It had been a silent ride home.

"I should have stopped you. Stepped in. You were in no shape to make that kind of decision." He squeezed the wheel.

"It wasn't your responsibility," Tim said.

"It's my responsibility to do more than stand around while my partner maybe kills some mutt in a moment of justifiable rage. You're a federal agent, not some yokel deputy."

"The boys just got a little fired up."

Bear struck the steering wheel hard with the heels of his hands, a rare display of anger. "Stupid pricks." His cheeks were wet. "Stupid, stupid pricks. They shouldn't have dragged you into it. They shouldn't have jeopardized the investigation."

Tim knew Bear was turning his grief to anger and throwing it at the nearest target, but he also knew he was right. Tim spoke to the words, because he knew if he touched the grief right now, he'd come apart. "Nothing happened."

"It's not done happening yet." Bear wiped his cheeks roughly. "And we don't know what those idiots did before we got there, how well they secured the scene. They weren't looking for accomplices. They weren't looking to build a case. It's not like they were dotting their i's and crossing their t's for the DA. It's not like they were expecting a trial."

"They're gonna have to be aboveboard now. After we've been there."

"Great. So in addition to the case being tied to their competence or tremendous lack thereof, we are, too." Bear shuddered hard, like a dog shaking off water. "Sorry, I'm sorry. You got enough on your plate."

Tim managed a faint smile. "I better go check on my yokel-deputy wife."

"Shit, I didn't mean that."

Tim laughed, and then Bear joined him, both of them still wiping their cheeks.

"Do you want me to . . . Can I come in?"

"No," Tim said. "Not yet."

Bear was still idling at the curb when Tim closed the front door behind him. The house was dark and empty. Two holes had been kicked through the living room wall, leaving jagged edges in the drywall. Though Tim had left Dray with two of her friends who'd come over to help with Ginny's party, he was not surprised to find the house silent. When Dray was upset, she handled it alone. Another trait she'd learned from four older brothers and six years and counting on the job.

He passed through the small living room into the kitchen. The simple interior had been improved upon over the years by Tim's meticulous attention. He'd torn up the floors and laid down hardwood in the halls and bedrooms and replaced the brass-plated and faux-crystal chandeliers with recessed lighting.

On the counter sat Ginny's cake, uncut, the top puddled with wax. Dray had insisted on baking it herself despite her lack of prowess in the kitchen. It was uneven, sloping left, and the frosting had been applied and reapplied in a failed attempt at smoothness. Judy Hartley, their next-door neighbor and a recent empty-nester, had offered to assume baking duties, but Dray had refused. As she did each year on Ginny's birthday, she'd taken the day off work to pore over borrowed cookbooks, determined and stubborn, pulling cake after cake out of the oven until she'd produced one she deemed acceptable.

Dray wasn't there, though the cabinet where they kept the liquor stood open. The handle of store-brand vodka was missing.

Tim walked quietly down the hall to their bedroom. The bed, neatly made, stared back at him. He checked the bathroom—also no luck. He tried Ginny's room next, across the hall. Dray was sitting in the darkness, the half-gallon bottle between her legs, the glow of a Pocahontas night-light discoloring one side of her face. On the carpet before her sat the cordless phone and her PalmPilot, the backlight still glowing.

Her face was gaunt, drawn in by grief. Three years ago she'd red-handed a fifteen-year-old kid fleeing a Ventura office building with an armload of laptops. He'd tried to throw down with a nickel-plated .22, and she'd double-tapped him; when she got home, her face looked not quite so bad as it did now. Her head was bowed slightly, in thought or drunkenness.

Tim closed the door behind him, crossed the room, and slid down the wall beside her. He took her hand; it was sweaty and feverish. She didn't look up, but she squeezed his fingers as if she'd been barely holding on for his touch.

He stared at Ginny's twin bed. The wallpaper, unrestrained yellow and pink flowers now muted by the darkness, had been perfectly aligned so it didn't mess up the repeat at the room's corners.

Tim thought about Ginny's last few minutes of life, then about where he might have been at the corresponding times. Putting his weapon away in the gun safe when she was snatched from the street. Driving to the store for pink candles when the dismemberment began.

That he couldn't give Kindell's partner a face was an added torment, another mockery of his imagined control over his world. The notion of kinship to this end was beyond sickening—two men bent on the destruction of a child, two men joined in ripping apart a young body. He pictured Kindell's dopey face and wondered if there was a special place in hell for child-killers. He indulged himself in imagined tortures. He had never been a religious man, but the thoughts found their way out from the darker recesses of his mind, the shadowed corners hidden from the light of reason.

Dray's voice, calm, but hoarse from crying, forced him from his thoughts. "I was here alone tonight, this night, sitting with Trina and Joan and Judy fucking Hartley, getting the other kids off home, waiting to hear about the positive ID, calling our relatives so they wouldn't have to hear it from . . . or read about it in . . ." She raised her head sluggishly, bangs sweeping over her eyes. She took another slug from the bottle. "Fowler called."

"Dray—"

"Why didn't you come to me?"

He wouldn't have thought his grief would have left room for shame, but there it was, undiminished. "I'm sorry."

The distance between them he registered as an aching in his stomach. He remembered how they'd fallen in love, hard and terrifyingly fast. Neither of them had ever learned to *need* as adults—both had endured childhoods that had disappointed them, punishingly, for relying on anyone— yet there they were, fixed on each other with an unyielding, constant focus, staying up all hours talking and pressing against each other in the flickering blue glow of the muted TV, driving across town to meet for lunch because they couldn't make it from morning to evening without each other's touch. Every detail of the first months shone with clarity—how he'd steer *and* shift with his left hand so he wouldn't have to let go of hers with his right in the car after dinner, a movie, a night walk on the beach; the soft noise she made when she smiled, just short of a laugh; the way her face hurt when she blushed after a compliment— pins and needles, she claimed—and she'd have to massage out the bunched cheeks above the grin with her fingertips until he finally started doing it for her. Just last week he'd pulled her in for a slow dance when Elvis came crooning on late-night reruns; Ginny had alleged nausea and retreated to her bedroom.

And now he was in the same room with his wife but could barely sense her through the darkness, which had grown soupy, infused with hurt and foulness and stopped-up grief.

He struggled to find words, to reconnect. "I got the call. We were three miles away. I had to go, to see."

"Okay. So you went."

He took a deep breath. "And he confessed."

She was trying to soften her voice, but he could hear the frustration in it. "Tim, you're the father of the victim. You were illegally called to the crime scene to commit a vengeance killing. Explain to me how him confessing to you is the least bit useful." She lowered the bottle to the floor with a thunk. "That man took our daughter and *violated* her. *Took her apart.* And you went to him, you risked the crime scene and the arrest, and then you let him walk away."

"I think he had an accomplice."

Her eyebrows rose and spread. "Fowler didn't mention that."

"Kindell said he wasn't *supposed* to kill her, as if there had been some previous understanding between him and someone else."

"He could have just been saying he didn't *mean* to kill her. Or that he knew it was illegal."

"Maybe. But then he started to refer to someone else—a *he*—but he caught himself."

"So why aren't Gutierez and Harrison looking into *that?*"

"They weren't aware of it, obviously."

"Are they looking into it now?"

"They'd better be."

Ginny's bedside clock emitted a soft chime, announcing the hour; the sound struck Tim sharp and unexpected, a stab to the heart. Dray's face seemed to crumble. She quickly took another pull off the bottle. For a moment they'd indulged the illusion that they'd set aside the personal, that they'd been two cops talking.

Dray wiped tears from her cheeks with her sweatshirt cuff, which she'd pulled over her hand like a girl. "So the crime scene is muddled up, and now there's a possibility that the killer isn't the only killer."

"That's about right, unfortunately."

"You're not even angry."

"I am. But anger is useless."

"What isn't?"

"I'm trying to figure that out." He wasn't looking at her, but he heard her take another gulp from the bottle.

"All your training—Spec Ops and Combat Engineering and FLETC—you should have known to prioritize under pressure. You should've known not to go there, Timmy."

"*Don't* call me Timmy." He stood and wiped his palms on his pants. "Look, Dray, we're both wrecked right now. If we keep this up, it's not gonna go anywhere we want it to."

Tim opened the door and stepped out. Dray's voice followed him out into the cool hall. "How can you be so calm right now? Like she's just another victim, someone you never knew."

Tim halted in the hall and stood, his back to the open door. He turned and walked back in. Dray's hand was over her mouth.

He ran his tongue across the points of his teeth and back, waiting for his breath to stop hitching in his chest. When he spoke, his voice was so quiet it was barely audible. "I understand how upset—how destroyed you are. I am, too. But don't ever fucking say that."

She lowered her hand. Her eyes were shell-shocked. "I'm sorry," she said.

He nodded and withdrew gently from the room.

In the bedroom Tim spun the dial on his gun safe, then removed a Spec Ops–issue p226 nine mil, his favored .357 Smith & Wesson, a hefty Ruger .44 mag, and two fifty-round boxes of nine-mil and .44. He kept a broader ammo range on hand for his .357, as it was his duty weapon; he opted for the wad cutters over the copper-jacketed rounds and the duty 110-grain hollow-points. The service issued the S&Ws with three-inch barrels, as they were often carried concealed.

When he entered Ginny's room, Dray still had not moved. "I'm so sorry," she said again. "What a fucking thing to say."

He knelt, placed his hands on her knees, and kissed her on the forehead. It was damp. The sharp smell of alcohol lingered about her face. "It's okay. What's that they say about rocks and glass houses?"

Her lips pursed, not quite a smile. "Don't throw glass houses if you live in a rock."

"Something like that."

"You need to go shoot." She wasn't asking; she was offering.

He nodded. "Come with me?"

"I need to sit here for a while and look at nothing."

He moved to kiss her forehead again, but she tilted back her head and caught his lips with hers. The kiss was hot and dry and edged with vodka. If he could have crawled into it and lived there, he would have.

The garage housed Tim's silver M3 BMW—a car confiscated by the service under the National Asset Seizure and Forfeiture Program—and his workbench. Tim threw his ordnance in the trunk and backed out, careful to dodge Dray's Blazer, parked in the driveway. He drove to the outskirts of town, then turned onto a dirt road and followed it up a few hundred yards.

He pulled the car onto a flat dirt apron and left it running, angling the high beams downrange, where a cable stretched between two stakes, about five feet off the ground. Tim removed a stack of targets, a mix of color-coded Transtars and old B-27s, and strung them along the cable. Then he sat in the dirt, jammed the Sig mags, and readied the speedloaders for the wheel guns. Six bullets locked into the cylindrical base of each speedloader, tips sticking up like fangs, spaced to correspond with the caliber holes in the wheel.

He was left-eye dominant but right-handed, so he drew from a high-ride right-hip holster. Shoulder holsters were discouraged by the service because the cross-draw presented a hazard on the firing line, but Tim preferred the up-and-out anyway, not liking the time given up on a cross-draw. They didn't call shoulder holsters widow-makers for nothing. He started with the Sig, doing some quick-draw plinking at three yards to warm up his reactive shooting. Then he moved to seven yards. Then ten.

His shooting was remarkably precise, having been learned in urban-warfare courses and perfected in Malibu's Maze at Glynco. The aptly named shooting course features pop-up and swinging targets that prospective deputies attack with live ammo through a confusion of strobing lights, blaring music, and amplified screams. The vibe is so invasive, the surroundings so surreal, that grown men have emerged weeping. Once outside, deputies subdue actors playing felons; a Juilliard dropout had once gotten a little too method with Tim, jawing off and sinking his teeth into Tim's forearm, and Tim had knocked him cold.

His breath misting in the sharp February cold of the higher altitude, Tim shot and shot. When he'd burned through the nine-mil ammo, he switched to his .357 and toed the concrete ledge at twenty-five yards.

He struck a modified Weaver, a forward-leaning fighting stance, his feet shoulder width with his left leg forward. The landscape reflected his mood—the barren stretch of dirt and rocks, the twinning cones of the headlights boring through the night, brief throws of light in a vast, dismal universe. The paper targets alone picked up the glow, floating rectangles of white, bobbing like fruit on a tree. The emptiness of the dark opened him up like a gutted beast, and he stared into the void. All that stared back was a row of eyeless, two-dimensional combat silhouettes, fluttering on the cable.

His right hand shot down, breaking his perfect stillness, and grabbed the pistol. As soon as the barrel cleared leather, he rotated it, punching it forward, his left hand already coming, grabbing his right at its junction with the butt. He lined the sights even as his arms were extending. His right arm locked, his left staying slightly canted. The trigger split the precise middle of the pad of his right index finger so he wouldn't group high and right or low and left, and he applied quick, steady pressure through the double action, not anticipating recoil, not flexing too hard. The gun barked and a hole punched through the thoracic region of the Transtar, center mass. He fired five more times in rapid succession, regaining front sight focus between each shot almost instantly. The cordite still rising, he thumbed the left-side lever forward, releasing the well-lubed wheel. His left hand dug for the speedloader in his belt pouch as he tilted the gun back, the casings spinning to the dirt like brass hail. In a single smooth gesture, he angled the gun down and filled the wheel, the six new bullets sliding neatly into place. He got off six more rounds, Swiss-cheesing the five-ring of the Transtar before the empty speedloader hit dirt.

The wad cutters, ideal for paper punching, left behind satisfying gashes.

Mindlessly he repeated the routine, losing himself in it, distilling his rage into concise bursts of bullets and sending it outward. The anger departed slowly, like water leaving a tub; when it was gone, he tried to shape and fire away the residual sorrow in similar fashion but found he could not. He alternated static shooting with lateral-movement drills, firing until his wrists were aching, until the pads of his hands were chaffed from recoil.

Then he loaded the Ruger with long, slender .44s and shot it until his thumb webbing bled.

He came home a little after midnight to an empty house. The handle of vodka sitting on Ginny's floor, significantly depleted, was the only trace of Dray. Her Blazer was still parked in the driveway, the hood cool.

Tim drove the six blocks to McLane's, the semiauthentic Irish pub owned by Mac's father, and parked among the Crown Vics and Buicks in the lot. The heavy oak door gave with a shove. Aside from a few hangers-on and the cluster of deputies and detectives in the back by the pool tables, the place was empty. Myriad mustaches. Antique police light bar mounted above the shelves of booze. Typical cop hangout. The bartender, a dandy with cuffed sleeves and a bristling Tom Selleck, looked up from drying glasses. "Sorry, pal, we're closed."

Tim ignored him, walking the length of the bar toward the circle of men in the back. Mac, Fowler, Gutierez, Harrison, and about five others. Dray was standing over them, bent at the waist, forearm cocked back ending in the accusatory point of her finger. For some reason she'd put on her uniform, even though policy was not to drink in the monkey suit. Enhanced with alcohol, voices were carrying.

"—*dare* you put my husband into that situation. Or at

least you could have given me—your *colleague*—the courtesy of a phone call."

"We thought he'd be able to handle it," Fowler said.

"Because he's a male?"

"No, because of, you know, the military stuff."

"Military stuff, right. So he's got no feelings." She pivoted to face the detectives, swaying drunkenly. "What'd you find on the accomplice lead?"

Gutierez, the front man, addressed her like a politician—hands spread and calming, condescension masquerading as avuncular reassurance. "We're looking into it. But we don't think it's as strong an angle as your husband does."

"The conspiracy theorist," someone muttered.

Fowler took note of Tim's approach first, and then the others turned as well, everyone except Dray. "Let me tell you something." Dray was slurring now. "You can throw shit at *me* all you want. But you say one more thing about my husband, I'll knock your teeth down your goddamn throat."

The bartender was out from behind the bar, following Tim, but Mac waved him off. "It's okay, Danny. He's with us."

"Is he?" Gutierez said quietly. Two of the deputies eyed Tim and whispered something back and forth.

Tim addressed only his wife. "C'mon, Dray. Let's get you home."

Finally noticing him, Dray took a step and, losing her balance, sat down abruptly. Mac put an arm across her back to stabilize her, his hand resting on her shoulder. The others flanked her in their chairs protectively.

Mac's free hand fluttered in a calming gesture. "Hey, Tim. No offense, huh? We thought it would be good for her to be out right now, given—"

"Shut up, Mac." Tim's eyes didn't leave Dray. Her head was tilting. The others looked not many drinks behind her. Her eyes closed, she tilted her head into the cup of her hand. Tim bit down, the corners of his jaw flexing. "Andrea. Please let's go."

She moved to rise but only got so far as to lean heavily on the table.

Fowler picked up an empty shot glass, held it up like a scope, and eyed Tim through it. "Next time someone goes out on a limb for you, you might want to respect that," he said, slurring slightly. "Me and Tito went out for you, man."

Mac removed his arm from around Dray and stood up. Mac possessed effortless good looks, his hair tousled just so, day-old stubble touching his cheeks—Tim was all exertion and discipline by comparison.

"Listen guys, we've all had a long night here," Mac said. "Let's just take it easy."

"Yeah, let's go easy on the Medal of Valor winner," Harrison said.

Gutierez snickered. Tim's eyes shot over in his direction. Steeled by the others' expectations and the row of empties on the table before him, Gutierez stared back. "Take a hint, pal. Your wife's fine here. We take care of our own."

Dray mumbled something angrily.

Tim turned and headed for the door. Behind him he heard a chorus of murmurs.

"—good at walking away—"

"—better keep moving—"

Tim reached the door and threw the dead bolt, which gave off a metallic clank. The bar fell silent. He walked back down the length of the bar, the few remaining drunks watching him from their stools.

He reached the cluster of deputies and turned to the bar,

facing away from them. He removed his Smith & Wesson, still encased in its belt holster, and set it on the bar. His badge-heavy wallet followed. His jacket he hung neatly on a high-backed stool. He cuffed his sleeves neatly, two folds each.

When he turned, the deputies had sobered a few notches. He walked over to Gutierez. "Stand up."

Gutierez shifted in his chair, leaning back, trying to look tough and unworried, and not succeeding at either. Tim waited. No one spoke. Another deputy took a sip of beer, set his bottle down on the table with a soft thud. Gutierez finally looked away.

Tim put his jacket back on, grabbed his gun and badge. He stepped around the table, but Dray was already rising to meet him. She leaned heavily on him, 135 pounds of muscle and gear.

He hooked an arm around her waist and navigated her to the door.

He undressed her like a child, crouching to pull off her boots while she leaned on his shoulders. When he tucked her in, she threw the sheets back, sweating. He kissed her on her moist forehead.

She looked up at him, her face unlined and youthful in the dark. Her voice quavered. "What did he look like?"

Tim told her.

He wiped her tears, one cheek with one thumb, then the other.

"Tell me what happened. In the shack. Every detail."

He told her, fighting back his own tears at times, wiping hers throughout.

"I wish you'd killed him," she said.

"Then we would have lost our chance at the truth."

"But he'd be dead. Gone from this planet. Eradicated."

More tears than Tim could keep up with. She took his hand, squeezing it in both of hers, letting her tears streak down her temples to the pillow. "I'm angry. So angry. At everything. Everyone."

His throat was closing, so he cleared it once, hard.

"Are you gonna go to sleep?" she asked.

"I don't think so."

She drifted off for a moment, then opened her eyes. "Me neither." She smiled sleepily.

"I'm gonna go watch a little TV. I don't want to thrash around and keep you up." He smoothed the hair gently out of her eyes. "At least one of us should get some sleep."

She nodded. "Okay."

He lay on the living room couch as if in a coffin, fully dressed, hands laced across his chest. He stared at the ceiling, trying to grasp the new realities of his life. He couldn't get his mind around the monumentality of his loss. He was falling into darkness, with no idea of its depth. Canned laughter emanated from Nick at Nite at hypnotic intervals. He tuned out everything but its sound. Laughter still exists, he thought. If I need to remember that, I can turn on the little box and there it is.

Sometime around 3:00 A.M. Dray awakened him, trudging to the couch, trailing the comforter. She crawled on top of him and burrowed into his neck.

"Timothy Rackley," she said, her voice soft and sleep-heavy.

He stroked her hair gently, then pulled it up and rubbed the soft nape of her neck. They slept entwined in a restless embrace.

**4** TIM OPENED HIS EYES AND FELT DREAD DESCEND ON HIM before he could even put a name to it. He swung his legs off the couch and set his feet on the floor. Dray was in the kitchen, rustling.

He didn't just remember his grief, he relearned it. For several minutes he sat on the couch, slumped forward, arms angled out in anticipation of his rise. Paralyzed with sorrow. Unable to bear a single movement. He focused on his breathing. If he could draw three breaths, then he'd be able to draw three more, and life could go on as such, in three-breath increments.

Finally he mustered the strength to stand. Walking back to the shower, he tried not to think about his daughter's theatrical heaviness when he carried her along this same path from TV to bedroom at night. Her head tilted back, eyes squeezed shut, tongue stuck out the side of her mouth like a drunk cartoon character's. Trying to steal a few extra minutes of tube time by feigning sleep.

In daylight her death had taken on a reality. It lived in the house with them, in the dust on the floors, the blankness of the ceilings, the soft, unanswered noises of his movement past her room.

After a scorching shower, he dressed and walked back to the kitchen.

Dray sat at the table, sipping coffee, her eyes swollen, her hair flat on one side. The cordless phone sat on the table beside her. "Well," she said, "I just got off the phone with the DA. It looks like you guys didn't screw up the case against Kindell."

"Good. That's good."

They studied each other for a moment. She held her arms out like a child wanting to be hugged, and Tim walked into her embrace. She buried her head in his stomach, and he scrunched her hair in the back. She groaned.

He slid down into the chair next to her.

Black half-moons stood out beneath her eyes. "Mother-fucking asshole prick cocksucking goddamned fucked-up pile of miserable shit," she said.

"Yeah," Tim said.

"They have Kindell at county. He's got three priors—a weenie wagger and two lewd acts with a minor. All girls under the age of ten. Three slaps on the wrist. Last time out he pled. Judge found him not guilty by reason of insanity. NGI bought him a year and a half at Patton, padded walls and warm food." She spoke quickly, getting it out.

"And the case?"

"He completely clammed up at the station—wouldn't talk no matter how hard they pressed—but there's evidence all over his little shack. They got a blood match this A.M. from the . . . from the hacksaw. . . ." She leaned over and gagged, her spine arching through two dry heaves.

Tim held her hair back gently, but she brought nothing up. She shoved herself upright in her chair, wiped her mouth, gave a great, halting exhale, then it was back to business. "The DA's hammering him, filing special circumstances. The arraignment's tomorrow." She spun her coffee mug, then spun it again.

"We still have an accomplice out there who they need to track down."

"Someone in on the kill who knew how to cover his tracks in ways Kindell didn't."

"Or a partnership gone bad, or a double-cross."

"Or, as the DA seems to think, it was just Kindell in his

truck, Ginny walking to Tess's, and bad goddamned timing."

"He's not looking into this?"

"*She* assured me personally her office would continue to explore the possibility, but she doesn't seem hot on it."

"Why not?"

"A high-visibility case, a neat little package as it stands. And I'm sure Gutierez and Harrison are none too eager to spend sweat probing your leads."

Tim considered the dried weeds outside Kindell's, the soft dirt that could have borne footprints or the marks of a second set of tire tracks. He thought of all the traffic through there—him and Bear included—before CSU was called, obscuring evidence, polluting the scene. Guilt felt weightier heaped on top of intense sorrow.

"I keep thinking I'll have to make arrangements. Like they always say." Her face contorted as if she were going to sob, though she didn't.

Tim poured himself a cup of coffee, focusing on the task, trying for a numb moment.

"Remember at the department picnic, when she was four?"

"Don't," Tim said.

"She was wearing that yellow-checked dress your aunt sent. A plane went overhead. She asked what it was. And you told her it was an airplane, and that people were up there flying in it."

"Don't."

"And she looked up at it, gauged its size with a chubby little thumb, and do you remember what she said? 'No way,' she said. 'They'd never fit.'" A tear tracked down Dray's cheek. "Her hair was curly back then. I remember it like I could touch it."

The doorbell rang, and Tim rose to answer it, grateful

for the disruption. On the doorstep stood Mac, Fowler, Gutierez, Harrison, and a few other deputies from the bar last night. They all had their hats off, like salesmen feigning deference.

"Uh, Rack, we . . ." Fowler cleared his throat hard. He smelled of coffee and stale booze. He seemed to catch himself. "Is Dray here, too?"

Tim felt a tug at the back belt loop of his jeans. Dray went up on tiptoe and rested her chin on his shoulder.

Fowler nodded at her, then continued. "We all wanted to apologize. For in the bar. And earlier, too. It was a, uh, a real tough night for us all—not near as hard as for you, I know, but we're also not used to . . . Anyways, we were way out of line at a time when you least needed it, and uh, well . . ."

Gutierez picked up for him. "We're ashamed."

"We're on it now," Harrison said. "The case. Full force."

"If there's anything we can do . . ." Mac said.

"Thank you," Tim said. "I appreciate you coming by."

They shuffled around a bit, then moved forward one at a time to shake Tim's hand. It was a foolish, formal little ceremony, but Tim found it a moving one nonetheless. Dray held him from behind, trembling slightly.

The deputies headed back down the walk, and then the patrol cars pulled out one after the other. Tim and Dray watched the procession until the last car faded from sight.

The next forty-eight hours passed tediously and painfully, like a jagged kidney stone. Every action was weighty and frightful, full of hidden turns and dark corners. Calling family members and friends. Trying to get Ginny's body released from the coroner. Receiving updates on the case the DA was preparing against Kindell. Even the smallest tasks left Tim and Dray drenched in exhaustion.

Kindell, understandably reticent about staying in custody, refused to waive time, demanding a prompt prelim. Dray learned that the public defender had filed a 1538 motion to suppress evidence. She hit the roof and called the DA's office but was assured that the motion was not meritorious, that PDs filed them prophylactically all the time to keep appellate lawyers off their asses down the line. It wasn't the worst thing that the PD was touching all the bases; he had a reputation for being a loose cannon, and the last thing they wanted was Kindell filing an Ineffective Assistance of Counsel Writ after the trial.

The phone rang constantly with calls from investigators, well-wishers, press, its jangle an unnerving marching-band tune for the parade of tin-foil-covered plates and eyes crinkled with sympathy. But despite the traumatizing details and petty tortures, the days were defined by a maddening eventlessness, all sound and fury and little advancement, like running on ice.

The incessant hammering of grief and stress left Tim and Dray with tattered and few resources. Though they tried to comfort each other, to embrace, to mourn together, their pain seemed amplified by the other's distress and their own uselessness in the face of it. They both found themselves increasingly wrapped in their own private pain, unable to muster the strength to pull themselves out of it.

They began keeping a respectful distance from each other, like roommates. They napped frequently, though always separately, and they rarely ate, despite the array of filled Tupperware that packed their refrigerator, replenished almost hourly by neighbors and friends. When they did interact, it was in brief, overpolite exchanges, parodies of domesticity. The sight of Dray elicited in Tim a piercing shame that he was unable to be more for her right now. He knew that in his face Dray saw reflected back only the same devastation that weighed down hers.

The DA's office was respectful about keeping them in the loop about the case, though also cautious about releasing many specifics. In conversations with her colleagues, Dray managed to piece together fragments of information about Gutierez and Harrison's investigation, enough to grasp that they'd jettisoned the accomplice theory to focus their full energies on shoring up the case against Kindell.

Tim's mind returned to Kindell's shack with obsessive regularity, replaying each detail, from the slipperiness of the oil-stained floor to the sharp scent of paint thinner.

*I wasn't supposed to kill her.*

*He didn't—*

Eight words had opened up a chasm of doubt. The pain of not knowing almost equaled the pain of loss, because it played carnival-mirror tricks with Tim's grief, magnifying it one moment, reshaping it the next. He was mourning without knowing the exact parameters of what he was mourning—Ginny was dead, but what she had gone through and who was responsible for it were blank canvases awaiting the latest incarnation, the latest projection of rage or horror. Kindell had proved enough to sate the appetite of the detectives and the DA, but Tim knew there were additional gutters to be flushed. The progression of atrocious events that had filled his daughter's last hours remained out there, frozen in history, waiting to be reconstructed.

Wednesday night he and Dray went for a drive, their first outing together since Ginny's death. They sat awkwardly in silence, trying to let the movement and crisp night air lull them back to compatibility. On their way home they passed McLane's. Dray craned her neck, checking out the vehicles in the dark lot. "Gutierez's rig," she murmured.

Tim flipped a U-turn and pulled in the lot. Dray turned in her seat to watch him, more curious than surprised.

They found Gutierez in the back, shooting stick with Harrison. Gutierez nodded in greeting, then spoke in the same softened voice everyone used with them now. "You guys holding up okay?"

"Fine, thanks. Can we have a minute?"

"Sure thing, Rack."

The detectives followed Tim and Dray out to the back parking lot.

"Word is you're dropping the accomplice angle," Tim said.

Harrison stiffened. Gutierez cocked his head slightly. "It didn't yield."

"Have you checked Kindell's priors? Did he work with an accomplice on those?"

"We're working very closely with the DA, and we've turned up no evidence of other people's involvement. We've looked into everything. Now, you're well aware that we can't involve parents of victims in our cases—"

"A little late for that," Dray threw in.

"You've got no distance from the case. No perspective. And to say you're biased is something of an understatement. Now, I know what you *thought* you heard in there—"

"How did you find Ginny's body?" Tim said. "So quickly. I mean, that creek bed is pretty remote."

Harrison blew out a breath that clouded in the cool air. "Anonymous call."

"Man or woman?"

"Look, we don't have to—"

"Was it a man's or a woman's voice?"

Gutierez folded his arms, irritation starting to shift to anger. "A man's."

"Did you trace it? Was it recorded?"

"No, it went to the private line of the deputy working the desk."

"Not 911? Not dispatch?" Dray said. "Who would know the private number?"

"Someone making sure their ass was covered," Tim said. "Someone afraid to be implicated or ID'd. Like an accomplice."

Harrison stepped forward, getting in Tim's space. "Listen, Fox Mulder, I don't think you have any idea how many anonymous tips we get. It doesn't mean the guy was in on a murder. I mean, odds are a guy drifting through an out-of-the-way creek bed is up to something other than selling Girl Scout cookies. It could have been a guy with a rap sheet, a scared kid who didn't want to get tangled up in a murder case. It could've been a bum sniffing glue."

"Because bums whacked out on glue fumes are in possession of private phone numbers into the Moorpark Police Station," Dray said.

"It's listed."

"A bum with a phone book," Tim said.

"Hey, man, you missed your chance to take care of business. We gave it to you. And guess what? You wanted everything aboveboard. Well, fine. We can respect that. But that means it's out of your hands now. You're a biased party, the parents of the vic, and you're to go nowhere near this case or we'll slap you with obstruction. There's no shooter on the grassy knoll. Your daughter died, and we got the sick fuck who did it. Case closed. Go home to each other. Grieve."

"Thanks," Dray said. "We'll take that under advisement."

They walked back to Tim's car silently, climbed in, and sat.

"He's right." Tim's voice was soft, cracked, defeated. "We can't get involved. There's no way we could go about this investigation fairly, objectively. Let's hope Kindell sweats it and tries to talk for a plea. Or chokes on the stand

and spills. Or that his PD trots out the accomplice theory as part of the defense. Something. Anything."

"I feel useless," Dray said.

A cop car pulled in swiftly and parked across the lot. Mac and Fowler got out, joking and chuckling, and headed into the bar.

Tim and Dray sat in the afterwash of the laughter, eyes on the dash.

When Tim entered the kitchen Thursday morning, Dray looked up from the latest batch of thank-yous and condolence-card replies she was writing. Her eyes went to the pager in his hand, then to his Smith & Wesson, clipped to his belt. "You're going to the office? Already?"

"Bear needs me."

Light glowed yellow through the drawn blinds, falling across her face. "I need you. Bear'll be just fine."

The phone rang, but she shook her head. "Press," she said. "All morning. They want a sobbing mother, a stoic father. Which do you want to play?"

He waited for the phone to quiet before speaking. "A tip came in from one of our CIs this morning. We're planning a hot takedown. I have to go in."

One of Bear and Tim's confidential informants had caught wind of a deal going down that had Gary Heidel's smell all over it. The Escape Team had been tracking Heidel, a Top 15, for the better part of five months. After being convicted for one count of first-degree murder and two counts of drug trafficking, Heidel had escaped during his transport from courthouse to prison. Two Hispanic accomplices in a pickup had pinned the sedan against a tree, shot both deputy marshals, and extracted Heidel.

Tim had known that Heidel would need money quickly, and so he'd turn to the one place guys like him got money quickly. Since Heidel's MO was a distinctive one—he acquired diluted cocaine from Chihuahua and had mules drive it across the border hidden in wine bottles—it had been easier for Tim and Bear to press the street for related information. Finally their vigilance had paid off. If their CI had given Bear reliable intel, a forty-key deal was going down sometime that afternoon or night.

"You sure you're ready to work?"

Tim's eye flicked to the scattering of cards on the wood tabletop. Garlands in muted inks on taupe paper. "I don't know what else to do. I'm going out of my mind. If I don't work, I might do something stupid."

Dray dropped her eyes. He knew she sensed his eagerness to get out of the house. "You should go, then. I think I'm just upset that *I'm* not ready yet."

"You sure you're okay? I could call Bear—"

She waved him off. "It's like what you said to me that first awful night." She mustered a faint grin. "At least one of us should get some sleep."

He paused for a moment in the doorway before leaving. Dray leaned over the card she was writing, her jaw set just slightly as it got when she concentrated. Early sunlight shone through the window, turning the edges of her hair pale gold.

"Of course I remember that day at the picnic, with her and the airplane," Tim said. "I remember everything about her. Especially when she was bad—for some reason those memories bring her the closest. Like when she drew on the new wallpaper in the living room with crayons—"

Dray's face lightened. "And then denied it."

"Like *I* might have done it. Or you. Or that time she put the thermometer against the lightbulb to get out of going to school—"

She matched his smile. "I came back in the room, and the mercury was redlined at a hundred six degrees."

"The princess tyrant."

"The little shit." Dray's voice, loving and soft, cracked, and she pressed a fist to her mouth.

Tim watched her fighting tears, and he looked down until his own vision cleared. "That's why I can't . . . why I avoid it. When we talk about her, it's too . . . vivid . . . and it . . ."

"I need to talk about her," Dray said. "I need to remember."

Tim made a gesture with his hand, but even he wasn't sure what it was meant to convey. He was again struck by the ineffectiveness of language, his inability to digest his feelings and shape them into words.

"She's a part of our lives, Tim."

His vision grew watery again. "Not anymore."

Dray studied him until he looked away. "Go to work," she said.

**5** TIM SPED DOWNTOWN, REACHING THE CLUSTER OF FEDeral and courthouse buildings surrounding Fletcher Bowron Square. The squat cement and glass structure that passed for the Federal Building housed the warrant squad's offices. Embedded in the front wall was a mosaic mural of women with square heads, which Tim had never quite grasped. The few times he'd taken Ginny to the office, she'd found the seemingly inoffensive mural unsettling; she'd keep her face turned into his side as they passed. Tim had always had a tough time deciphering her fears; also on her list were movie theaters, people over seventy, crickets, and Elmer Fudd.

He badged himself at the entrance, took the stairs to the second floor, and headed down a white-tiled corridor with spotty patchwork on the walls.

The office itself wasn't much to look at, a haphazard throw of cubicles with metal schoolboy desks and fabric walls the color of Pepto-Bismol-laced vomit. For months admin had been promising the deputies a move to the more upscale Roybal Building next door, and for months it had been delayed. The bitching had reached a daytime-talk-show high, but it did little good; the deputies weren't the first to note that federal bureaucracy moved like an arthritic tortoise, and, to be fair, shoddy office space had never been an impediment for deputies who preferred the street anyway. The walls were covered with newspaper clippings, crime stats, and most-wanted mug shots. John Ashcroft peered out from a portrait, all beady eyes and weak chin.

As Tim threaded through the cubicle labyrinth to his desk, the other deputies mumbled condolences and averted their eyes, precisely the type of reaction he'd come to work to avoid.

Bear approached him at a half sprint, filling the narrow space between desks. He was geared up—ballistic helmet under an arm, goggles around his neck, thin cotton gloves, a mike-mounted portable radio, two sets of matte black cuffs, a gaggle of hard plastic flex-cuffs fanning back off his shoulder, black steel-plate boots, a Beretta in a hip holster, a can of Mace, extra mags dangling from a shoulder rig on his right side, and a Level III tactical vest, more flexible than the old Christmas-platter trauma-plate specials, but still able to stop most rounds. Forty-plus pounds, not counting his primary entry weapon, a cut-down twelve-gauge pump-action smoothbore Remington, charged with double-aught buck and fitted with a fourteen-inch barrel and pistol-grip stock. Because of its absence of a shoulder stock, the shotgun kicked back thirty-five pounds of recoil to be absorbed by the arms; this was nothing for Bear, but Tim had seen more slender deputies get knocked ass over teakettle.

Like the rest of the Arrest Response Team members, Tim preferred the shoulder-mounted MP-5, which could better pinpoint targets. He thought Bear's shotgun an unwise choice because it tied up both hands and presented penetration problems in a confined area, but Bear had grown partial to the Remington in his Witness Security days, and the *shuck* it gave when he racked a round could up a fugitive's pucker factor considerably.

ART was composed of the best-trained deputy marshals. When the bell rang, they came off regular duty, threw on Kevlar, and enacted precision strikes to extract fugitives. Because of Tim's Spec Ops background and his early record working up warrants, he'd been fortunate to make ART almost immediately after graduating the academy. During one fugitive roundup in his second month, his team had been hitting as many as fifteen hideouts a day, guns drawn on each entry. They kicked in the door half the time, and more than half the arrests were of armed men.

Bear hardly slowed as he reached Tim, and Tim turned and moved with him to keep from getting run over.

"We're waiting on you. Downstairs. Now. We'll have our pre-op briefing on the way over."

"What happened?"

"Our CI dropped dime on a buddy who was supposed to mule a shipment of imported wine, clear it through customs, port of entry San Diego. His meet is with a guy who fits Heidel's description."

"Where?"

Bear's gold marshal's star flashed on its leather belt clip as he walked. "Martía Domez Hotel. Pico and Paloma."

The mule would probably leave the drugs in a truck in the parking lot to eliminate the risk of getting caught with them in the room. At the motel he'd receive his first payment and get directed to the stash house, where the water would be extracted from the "wine," leaving behind cocaine.

"How'd you pin location?"

"ESU. Heidel's a smart bastard, been phone-swapping about every other day, but the CI coughed up his new number and it tripped a cell site right at Paloma and Twelfth."

The Electronic Surveillance Unit had a unique set of tricks at its disposal when it came to tracking fugitives. Every cell phone emits a locating burst in its own distinct radio frequency, identifying itself to its network. If a top-clearance government agency like the Marshals Service or NSA is willing to commit outrageous resources, a nationwide cellular system can be programmed to pinpoint that burst to a local cell-system coverage area within a radius of less than three hundred yards. Because of the expense—a live cell-phone trace requires men and cars and global positioning satellite handsets—the obvious problems gaining legal clearance, and the reliance on private-sector telecommunication cooperation, the technology is used sparingly. They were going all out for Heidel.

"Martía Domez is the only hotel on the block, and the CI knew the meet was in a hotel Room 9," Bear continued. "The meet wasn't supposed to be until six P.M., but Thomas and Freed did a drive-by about twenty minutes ago and said someone's already in the room. Two more men just showed up."

"Either of them fit Heidel's description?"

"No, but they look like the spicks who helped spring

him. Thomas and Freed are sitting surveillance with the ESU geeks—I told them not to get eye-fucked, that we'd hot-ass over and take the mutts before Elvis leaves the building."

Bear knocked the door open so hard it left a dent in the wall. The other deputies watched them with some envy as they headed out.

The Beast waited for them downstairs. An old, retrofitted military ambulance, the Beast fitted twelve people on two opposing benches. Huge white letters stood out from the black paint—POLICE U.S. MARSHALS—almost exactly matching the T-shirts of the ART members. On all U.S. marshal–issue clothing and gear, POLICE appears in text larger than that proclaiming the agency name, because if given the choice in a high-heat situation, a deputy marshal doesn't want to wait for the Average Citizen to remember what a deputy U.S. marshal is, and because POLICE is the international language for CAN SHOOT STRAIGHTER THAN YOU. The yellow lettering and embroidered badges also cut the odds considerably that the ART squad would be mistaken for a stickup crew.

Tim grabbed his gear from the trunk of his car, swung up into the back of the Beast, slapped a few fives, and sat between Bear and Brian Miller, the supervisory deputy in charge of ART and the Explosive Detection Canine Team. Miller's best bitch, a black Lab named Precious after Jame Gumb's poodle, nuzzled up to Tim's crotch before Miller snapped her back into place.

Tim regarded the eight other men on the benches. He was not surprised to see both Mexican ART members present; knowing that Heidel's two deputy-killing accomplices were Latino, Miller had pulled in the Hispanic talent as a preemptive strike against claims of racial retribution. A

Cuban kid named Guerrera was sitting in for their regular number-three man, who was the brother-in-law of one of the deputies whom Heidel's men had shot. Miller had taken every precaution to ensure a fair, lawful takedown and to make sure his men would survive the post-op hernia-check scrutiny of the Los Angeles media.

There was some uneasy shifting on the bench opposite Tim. "Do me a favor. Don't tell me how bad you feel about my daughter. I know you all do, and I appreciate it."

Assorted nods and mumbles. Bear broke the awkwardness, pointing to Tim's holstered .357. "Hey, Wyatt Earp. When are you gonna get an auto and enter the twenty-first century?"

Bear's little drill to show the others Tim wasn't fragile. Appreciative, Tim played along. "The average gunfight lasts seven seconds, occurs within a range of fewer than ten feet. Do you know how many rounds are typically exchanged?"

Bear smiled at Tim's mock-formal tone, and a few of the others joined him. "No, sir, I do not."

"Four." Tim removed the pistol and spun the wheel. "So the way I see it, I'm actually packing two spare bullets."

The vehicle lumbered out of the parking lot, passing the Roybal Building's metal sculpture composed of four immense human outlines that looked as though they'd been aerated by the crew that took down Bonnie and Clyde. The perforated men and the women with square heads left Tim with the strong impression that the government should stick to issuing budgets, not art.

Frankie Palton stretched his arm back over his head, grimacing, and Jim Denley snorted. "Your pimp beat you up?"

"No, the old lady brought home this goddamn Commie Sutra book, you know, all the sexual positions—"

Tim noticed that Guerrera's MP-5 was set to three-round

bursts, and he gestured with his middle and index fingers to his own eyes, then pointed at the gun's knob. Guerrera nodded and clicked it to safety mode.

"—and she had me going in this goddamned Congress of the Cow last night, I shit you not, I thought I was gonna blow out my rotator cuff."

Ted Maybeck leaned over and searched the floor at his feet. "Goddamnit. God*dam*nit."

"What's the fucking problem, Maybeck?" Miller said.

"I forgot my ram."

"We have two battering rams and a sledge up front."

"But not *my* ram. I brought that ram from St. Louis. It's good lu—"

"Don't say it, Maybeck," Bear growled, looking up from loading his five-shot. "Don't you fuckin' say it."

Tim turned to Miller. "What do we got?"

"Thomas and Freed are reconnoitering as we speak, getting the lay. ESU's keeping an eye on the cell-phone signal, making sure it stays put. As we all know, Heidel is considered armed and extremely dangerous. If the four firearms he's chosen to register are any indication, he prefers wheel guns. When we get him, don't order him to put his hands behind him—he'll probably have a pistol shoved in the back of his jeans. We want his hands on his head. According to witnesses, the two Hispanic males—"

"You mean Jose and Hose B?" Denley said.

"You fucking white guys," Guerrera said. "Always an inferiority complex with your little glowworm dicks."

"Big enough to fill *your* mouth."

The two men extended their fists and bumped knuckles. If tactical precision was an ART requirement, the ability to generate repartee was not.

Miller's voice rose to warning pitch. "The two Hispanic males have some gang insignia on the backs of their necks, and one might have a barbed-wire tattoo encircling his biceps. We don't know for sure, but we're counting on four men in the hotel room—Heidel, the two Hispanics, and the mule. Heidel's got a common-law wife—fat bitch with limited English and several weapons violations. We couldn't flip her last year, so she might be along for the ride. We have numerous statements from Heidel that he's not going back to prison, so we can interpret that pretty easily."

Heidel, like the majority of postconviction fugitives they tracked, had nothing to lose. He'd already had his day in court. If captured, he'd spend the rest of his life in prison, and that wouldn't make him or his two deputy-killing buddies particularly docile takedowns. Once again the deputies would have to play by the rules even when the mutts did not. Mutts had no departmental guidelines, no deadly-force policy, no concern for bystanders or passersby. To fire they didn't have to wait to get threatened with a gun or be in fear for their lives.

"We're gonna go with an eight-man stealth, no-knock entry. No flash-bangs. Usual order through the door. LAPD'll set a secondary perimeter, give us a nice visible uniformed presence, and we'll have some cover rifles across the street. Guerrera, this ain't Miami—the doors open in here, not out. Denley, remember you're in Los Angeles. Through the door and straight back. Forget those vertical Brooklyn entrances."

"Try to lose the Bobby De Niro accent while you're at it," Palton said. "No one buys that shit anyway."

Denley jerked a thumb toward his chest. "You talkin' to me?"

Tim cracked a smile, his first in days. He realized he hadn't thought about Ginny in nearly five minutes—his first free five minutes since the incident. His return to the memory was jarring, but he felt steeled with the first bracings of hope. Maybe tomorrow he'd manage six minutes free and clear.

The Beast screeched over a curb and pulled into the back lot of a 7-Eleven. Two LAPD officers at his side, Freed crossed to them in a crouched under-fire run, though the motel was nearly two blocks away. One of the ESU geeks—matted hair, thick glasses, the whole nine yards— was right behind him, eyes glued to a handheld GPS unit, the faintly glowing readout showing that the locating RF pulse from Heidel's mobile phone was not moving.

The ART squad exchanged greetings with the cops, and Miller thanked them for their presence and discussed where to set the perimeter. With ART huddled around, Freed unfurled a thick sheet of butcher paper across the hood of a nearby Volvo. On it he'd sketched a rough diagram of the hotel room's interior based on a conversation with the manager and his own assessment of the lay of the roof and the locations of various vents and external pipes. They didn't want to risk the visibility of taking a tour through a similar room. The blueprint was oddly elongated; a hallway led back from the front room to a bedroom and bathroom.

"The mule just showed up in a hoopty," Freed said. His command of slang disguised the fact that he came from money, but his crisp enunciation still betrayed a private school education. "A kitted-up '91 Explorer. Chrome rims, running boards, brush guards, curb feelers, air dam—the whole street-scum package. The back looks to be filled with boxes, but the windows are tinted, so we can't ID if they're wine crates or not. He's been in there about five minutes. The two Hispanic males arrived in a Chevy, and we think whoever was waiting for them in the room came in a green Mustang. Plates check out to a Lydia Ramirez,

Heidel's girlfriend, so that's a pretty good confirm."

Maybeck was fondling the new battering ram, getting a feel for it like a pitcher with a new glove. "What do we got on the door?"

"It's a circa-1920s building, so probably a metal door with a wood core. There's no security screen to pop or anything."

Tim took a look around. Empty 40s in brown paper bags. Weedy front yards. Broken windows. "They might've sold the doors when the neighborhood went to shit and the hotel switched ownership."

"Double-check in case they're hollow-core," Bear said. "The last thing we need is you putting the ram through the goddamn door again."

"Relax, Jowalski. That happened once, six fucking months ago."

"Once was enough."

Freed cleared his throat. "It's a two-story building, room is center first floor, number nine. It's got sliding-door access to a shitty pool in the back, and a back-facing bedroom window. Me and Thomas'll cover the rear."

Tim turned down the volume on his portable radio so he wouldn't have to remember to do it on the approach. "Is the unit connected to the rooms on either side?"

"No."

The adrenaline started to hammer pretty hard. The men had instinctively paired into their two-man cells, and they were bristling like fillies in the gate. Precious strained a bit on her leash.

Miller finished with the police officer and turned to his men. "All right, boys. Let's Pearl Harbor his ass."

They shuffled along the outdoor walkway, stacked tight, guns low-ready across their chests, approaching from the hinge side of the door. Miller led with Precious, Maybeck hauling his ram close behind. Tim was in his customary position as the number one; Bear, his cell partner, would be through the doorway right after him. The other cells were pressed behind them. All black gear and weapons, their eyes bugged out with goggles, helmets low and sleek. More than a few fugitives had wet themselves after being surprised by a kick-in.

Bear was sweating heavy, holding the action back on the Remington, the ejection port empty and ready for when he wanted to jack the pump and make some noise.

Miller crept forward and tapped the far edge of the door frame. Precious went up on her hind legs, holding her paws back from the door, then followed Miller's hand down across the bottom of the door and back up to the knob. If she smelled any explosive materials booby-trapping the door, she would have sat, but she just stood there panting. Miller took her off in a fast trot, clearing the way.

The door was particleboard, probably hollow, with cheap, white-metal hinges. Maybeck rested his hand on it, feeling its vibe. Deputy marshals and doors have a long-standing respect for one another.

Maybeck drew back the battering ram. A perfect moment of quiet. Then he swung it down, striking the locking mechanism. The dead bolt tore through the frame, the door banging in with a jagged Pac-Man bite missing at the knob. Maybeck flattened himself against the outside wall, and Tim swept past him, kicking through into the unknown, the heat of seven more bodies following him, all yelling.

"U.S. Marshals!"

"Down! Everybody down on the ground!"

*"Policía! Policía!"*

"Hands up! Get your fucking hands up!"

The mule's head snapped up. He'd been counting hundreds into a wrinkled brown paper bag. Three cell phones lay on the dinged-up wood table beside the cash, one of them silently emitting the telltale burst.

Tim was aware of the shirtless male to his right—a *Joaquín y Leticia* tattoo inked across his left pectoral—but he went for the first immediate threat, shoving the mule over and getting him proned out. "Spread your arms! Spread your arms!"

The room shook with thundering boots and commands as the other ART members poured in, moving threat to threat. Tim frisked the mule quickly around the waist and sides to make sure he couldn't get to a weapon immediately, then stepped over him and let Bear move up to take custody. Tim's head pivoted with the MP-5, cheek mashed to the shoulder stock, sighting down the dark hall.

Two deputies were on Joaquin, four more spreading along the walls, MP-5s raised. One of them took over the mule for Bear, then Bear was at Tim's back, one hand touching his shoulder, stutter-stepping after him into the dark hall. Behind them Joaquin struggled and cursed as the others finished clearing the front room.

"U.S. Marshals!" Tim yelled down the hall. "You're surrounded! Step out into the hall! Step out into the hall!"

Two more men waited behind Tim and Bear, eager to penetrate the rear rooms. The hall stood dim and silent, a fifteen-yard stretch back to the open opposing doors of the bedroom and bathroom. No closets or corners behind which to seek cover—reasons veterans sometimes balked at hallways and called them fatal funnels.

Tim moved swiftly down the hall, men stacking up behind, still shouting commands. The place smelled of rotting carpet and dust. As Tim neared the two open doors, Heidel and Lydia Ramirez leaned barely out from either side, pistols lowered at Tim's head. It was an impeccably timed move; Tim couldn't get a shot off on one without the other's opening up on him. The narrowness of the hall cut off Bear's angle behind him.

Heidel's face was pressed hard against the inside jamb of the bedroom door, so his voice came out slurred. "That's right, motherfucker! Keep moving!" The gun flicked to Bear, still behind Tim. "You! Big guy! Back the fuck off."

Heidel was sporting what appeared to be a Sig Sauer. He carried a wheel gun, a Ruger from the looks of it, in a shoulder holster under his left armpit.

"Come here, come here!" Heidel's greedy hand bunched Tim's shirt.

Bear chambered a round, his massive fists encompassing the shotgun like a pool cue. "Release that federal officer! I said *release that federal officer!*"

Without raising the MP-5, Tim thumbed the release, dropping the clip on the floor just before Heidel whipped him around the corner into the bedroom. Heidel slammed Tim against the wall and pressed the Sig into his cheek so hard it crushed his flesh against the bone. Heidel wore a Philly Blunt skullcap pulled low over his eyebrows. A wispy goatee, light blond, barely stood out from his pasty white skin. Another man, a big Hispanic male with a snake tattoo encircling his biceps, snatched the MP-5 from Tim with one hand and lifted Tim's Smith & Wesson from the holster with the other. He looked at the MP-5's empty receiver and threw the gun to the side in disgust, though it still housed a round in the chamber.

More shouting farther down the hall. Heidel stuck his arm out and fired blindly into the hall until the Sig's slide locked to the rear. He threw the empty gun aside, drew his Ruger, then gestured for Tim's Smith & Wesson, which he jammed into his empty shoulder holster as a backup. He shoved the Ruger up against Tim's face.

"Anybody fucking moves, I'm wasting your guy!" Heidel yelled. "Come on, baby. Come on." His girlfriend stepped across the hall into the bedroom, and Heidel slammed and locked the door. Tim rotated slightly into the grinding pain of the pistol to get the lay of the room and noticed the fire door connecting to the hotel room next door. Faulty intel.

Heidel yelled at the closed door, "Anyone comes through here, I shoot the fed! I'm not fucking around." He turned, panicky, and shoved the big man toward the fire door. "Move it, Carlos."

Carlos flung open the fire door and stepped through. Another bedroom, another long hall. Heidel pushed Tim forward, following Carlos's trail. The big man had a revolver tucked in the back of his jeans, the pearl handle glimmering. Tim slowed a bit, falling back. Heidel and his girlfriend fired idiotically at the walls behind them.

"Move it, *cabrón*," Lydia screamed. She shoved him, and Tim faked a fall.

Carlos kept running, disappearing around the corner.

"Get up! Get the fuck up!" Lydia stood over Tim, unbound breasts swaying fat and free beneath a stretched-out man's undershirt. Heidel was behind her, providing rear cover.

Tim pushed up onto his hands and knees, then rose. His holster hung empty from his belt. "Get him the hell up and moving!" Heidel shouted.

Tim crossed his arms, his left hand high on his biceps. When Heidel raised the Ruger to his forehead, as Tim knew he would, he snapped his hand over, grabbing the wheel tightly so it couldn't rotate, and kicked the girlfriend in the stomach as hard as he could. She grunted loudly and dropped, maintaining her clutch on the pistol.

Heidel was yanking the trigger, not yet realizing that the

cylinder couldn't turn, the barrel digging into the middle of Tim's forehead. With his right hand Tim reached across and pulled his own Smith & Wesson from its limp dangle in Heidel's shoulder holster, then calmly fired a shot into Heidel's chest. The back-spray of blood misted Tim's face, and Heidel fell away, arms spreading out and up like a kid's first pass at a snow angel. Tim kept his grip on the Ruger, still held up and backward, aimed at his own head. He pivoted quickly, saw that Lydia had found her feet, and he fired a shot through her chest and one through her face before her upswinging pistol arm reached horizontal.

She collapsed with a gurgle, a shudder of flesh and ripped cotton jersey.

Tim spun the Ruger and holstered it, keeping his Smith & Wesson at the ready. He ran down the hall, shoulder scraping a wall, and entered the front room just as Carlos banged through the sliding door onto the hotel's pool deck. With the exception of Freed and Thomas, all the cover rifles were out front, and the LAPD's secondary perimeter was a block away. Tim sprinted through the sliding door in pursuit, but Carlos was gone. Thomas was running toward Tim, shotgun at his side, while Freed kept rear cover by the pool. Having unexpectedly moved the length of four rooms and two hallways, Carlos had caught them off guard.

Without slowing, Thomas gestured to a still-swinging gate to Tim's left. "Come on!"

Tim followed after him into a narrow alley. Puffs of smoke rose from the window of a restaurant kitchen, clinging to the walls. Carlos was halfway down the alley in a dead sprint for the traffic-heavy street ahead. Tim passed Thomas quickly. Carlos burst out onto the street and saw the LAPD vehicle at the far curb, the small crowd of bums and passersby drawn to the police perimeter, now pointing and shouting. Twenty yards behind, Tim cleared the alley just as Carlos froze up in surprise. The two young cops at the perimeter looked more shocked than Carlos.

Carlos reached for the revolver tucked in the small of his back, and Tim stopped running, raised his Smith & Wesson, and sighted on center mass. He double-tapped Carlos between the shoulder blades, then put his last bullet through the back of his head in case he was wearing a bulletproof vest.

When Carlos slapped the pavement, what was left of his head sent out a spray like a dropped melon.

**6** **WHEN TIM ARRIVED BACK AT ROOM 9, TWO DEPUTIES** were hauling Joaquin out. They'd hoisted him by his ankle and wrist cuffs and were carrying him horizontally, facedown. A length of nylon cord cuff ran around his ankles and back up to his arms. He continued to resist violently, jerking and trying to bite the deputies' legs. The mule evidently had gone more peacefully.

Five LAPD patrol cars cordoned off the area, lights flashing. A sizable crowd had gathered; in the distance Tim spotted the panning dishes atop the first news vans to pick up the story. The chop of a copter was audible, though the visible sky was empty.

Bear sat propped against the outside wall, clutching his ribs, Miller and a paramedic bent over him. Tim felt his pulse quicken once again. "Everything all right?"

Miller opened a fist dramatically, revealing the flattened slug he'd just picked out of Bear's vest. Tim exhaled hard and slid down the wall to plunk beside Bear.

"You've got nine lives, Bear."

"Only seven left. The first I owe to you, this one to Kevlar."

Freed, Thomas, and a cop milled around the hoopty, peering hungrily through the tinted windows. Sweat stains on Freed's T-shirt outlined the pattern of a bulletproof vest.

"What are they doing?" Tim asked.

"Waiting for the U.S. Attorney's office to call back," Miller said. "She's tracking down a judge at home so they can get a telephonic search warrant for the car."

"We stumble in on a Top 15 exchanging cash with convicted drug traffickers who then try to kill us, and that doesn't constitute probable cause to search the fucking car?" Bear deteriorated into a coughing fit.

"I guess not anymore," Miller said.

"You mean my night classes at the SouthWest LA Legal Training Academy weren't wellsprings of infallibility? How 'bout that?"

Tim shrugged. "We have the guys, we have the vehicle. Nothing's going anywhere. They might as well wait another twenty minutes and cover their asses."

They sat watching the commotion in the parking lot and the street beyond, a windstorm trying to quiet. The younger deputies were circled up by the door to Room 9, trying to joke off the bitter aftertaste of mortality.

"You could toss a cat through Motherfucker's chest cavity."

"Nice hit, nice hit."

"Rack shot that fuck, he was DRT: Dead Right There."

A few of them swapped high fives. Tim noticed that Guerrera was gripping his wrist hard to keep his arms from shaking.

"That's the way to do it, Rack," someone called out. "Fuckin'-A yeah."

Tim raised a hand in a half wave, but his eyes were on the marshal's Bronco, just pulling through the police perimeter. Marshal Tannino hopped out and approached in a jog. A stocky, muscular man who'd come up through the ranks, Marco Tannino had joined the service at twenty-one. His recommendation last spring by Senator Feinstein paved the way to his marshalship, one of the few appointments made on genuine merit. The majority of the ninety-four marshals were big contributors to Senate campaigns, trust-fund babies whose dads rubbed elbows with Beltway brass, or sycophantic bureaucrats from other government agencies. Much to the chagrin of the street deputies, one of the marshals out of Florida was a former professional clown. Tannino, on the other hand, had logged plenty of trigger time in his distinguished career, so he was respected from bottom to top in the district office and elsewhere.

He wore a focused expression, running a hand through his coiffed salt-and-pepper hair as Freed filled him in.

Miller squeezed Tim's shoulder. "We need to get you a paramedic?"

Tim shook his head. The aftermath of the adrenaline kick had left his mouth dry and sour. The area smelled of sweat and cordite.

One of the police officers crouched over Tim and flipped open his black notebook. He started to talk, but Tim cut him off. "I have no statement."

Tannino stepped in hard, his knee brushing against the cop so he had to stand to regain his balance. "Get out of here," he said. "You know better than that."

"Just doing my job, Marshal."

"Do it elsewhere."

The cop retreated inside the hotel room.

"How are you doing?" Tannino asked. He was looking

Hill Street hip in his Harvey Woods sport coat, polyester slacks, and Nunn Bush wingtips.

"Okay." Tim unholstered his Smith & Wesson, double-checked that the wheel was empty save the six casings, and handed it over to Tannino, not wanting to make him ask for it. The weapon was no longer his; it was federal evidence.

"We'll get you a fresh one soon."

"I'd appreciate that."

"Let's get you out of this mess. The media monkeys are banging the bars, and the scene's gonna heat up."

"Thanks, Marshal. I fired si—"

The marshal held up his hand. "Not now, not here. Nothing oral, ever. You know the game. You'll make one statement one time, and it'll be in writing. You did your job and did it well—now let's jump the hoops and make sure you're protected." He offered his hand and pulled Tim up off the wall. "Let's go."

The room was small and painfully bright. Tim shifted on the examination table, and the stiff paper beneath him crinkled. Bear and the other ART members had also been cleared to County USC Hospital and set up in separate rooms to simmer down.

A polite knock on the door, then Marshal Tannino stepped in. "Rackley. You left quite a trail back there." He cocked his head, regarding Tim with his dark brown eyes. "The doctor told me you refused sedatives. Why's that?"

"I don't need to be sedated."

"You're not upset?"

"Not about this."

"You've been through this before. With the Rangers, too."

"Yeah. Yeah, I have. I'd like to say just a few times."

"There's an Employee Assistance Intervention Team

coming out. They're available to talk to you, the other guys, your wife, whatever you want."

"The Hug Squad, huh? I might take a pass."

"You can do that. But you might want to consider it."

"To be honest, Marshal, this doesn't bother me very much. I had little choice. I abided by regulations. They tried to kill me. I shot them justly." Tim moistened his lips. "There are other things I need to tend to. Things closer to home."

"I wanted to talk to you about that, too. Your daughter. There's that guy who specializes in this kind of stuff—that high-profile shrink over at UCLA. . . ."

"William Rayner."

"He's expensive, but I'm sure I could get admin to spring for—"

"We're gonna feel our way through this one on our own, thanks."

"Okay." Tannino clicked his teeth a few times, watching Tim with concern. "How are you two doing with that stuff?"

Tim pursed his lips, then unpursed them. "I don't know."

Tannino cleared his throat, studied the floor. "Yeah. I'd imagine that's just about right."

"Is there any way . . . ?"

"What, son?"

"Is there any way we could have one of our guys look into my daughter's case? The sheriff's detectives on it aren't . . ." He stopped again, unable to meet Tannino's eyes.

"We can't put this office's resources on the line for a personal case, Rackley. That's not how we play. You know better than to ask that."

Tim's face reddened. "Yes. I do. I'm sorry." He slid off the table. "I'm okay to go?"

"I'd like to buy you a little more time from the media. Three dead, a public shooting—it's gonna be a circus. We'll have to do things very methodically." He looked at Tim as if unsure he was registering this. "Plus, your FLEOA lawyer is on his way over. He'll help you with your statement, make sure you're all lined out."

"Okay," Tim said. "Thanks."

"I'm sorry about this crap. This is just the way things go down these days. But we'll cover all our bases. You can't turn a bad shooting into a good shooting, but you can turn a good shooting into a bad one."

"It was a good shooting."

"Then let's make sure it stays that way."

Dray was curled up on the couch in the gloom of the living room when Tim returned. The blinds were drawn, as they'd been when Tim had left that morning, and he wondered if she'd bothered to open them all day. She was wearing ripped jeans and a sweatshirt from the academy and looked as though she hadn't gotten around to a shower. At arm's length from her repose sat a half-eaten bowl of cereal, beside two empty Coke cans that had been knocked over.

It was too dark for Tim to see whether she was asleep, though he sensed she wasn't. He checked the clock on the VCR: almost eleven. "Sorry I'm so late. I got—"

"I know. I watched the news. I thought you might've been able to find a phone."

"Not the way things went."

With effort Dray propped herself up on her elbows, her face rising into visibility. "How'd it go down?"

He told her. A thoughtful frown appeared on her face halfway through.

"Come here," she said when he was done. He crossed to

her, and she made room on the couch between her legs. He sat, leaning against her, her body sleep-warm and firm. She'd been working her triceps last month, and they stood out like prongs on the backs of her arms. She played with his hair. She pressed his head to her chest, and he let her. As he relinquished control, it became clear how much he'd retreated into protective rigidity to drag himself through the past few days. He lay back, breathing Dray in, relishing her touch.

After a few minutes he turned and kissed her. They broke apart, hesitated, then kissed again.

Dray brushed his bangs back from his forehead, running a finger over the thin scar at his scalp line where he'd been struck by a rifle butt outside of Kandahar. He kept his hair combed down on the right side to hide it; Dray alone could study it without making him uncomfortable. "Maybe we could, I don't know, go back to the bedroom," she said.

"Are you hitting on me?"

"I think so."

Tim stood and leaned over her, sliding his hands under her knees and shoulders. She let out an anomalous giggle and looped her arms around his neck. He exaggerated his trouble picking her up, groaned, and dropped her back on the couch. "You're gonna have to lay off the weights."

He'd intended it as a joke, but it came out sharply. Her smile dimmed, and he felt his insult bank and come back a vicious self-loathing. He crouched and cupped her face with both his hands, letting her read the remorse in his eyes.

"Come with me," he said.

She stood, and they regarded each other. They hadn't made love since Ginny was killed. Though it had been only six days, the fact hung disproportionately heavy between them. Maybe they were punishing themselves, denying themselves intimacy, or maybe they feared the closeness itself.

Tim felt first-date nervous, and he thought how odd to be so fragile at his age, in his house, with his wife. She was breathing hard, her neck sparkling with remembered sweat, and she reached out and took his hand, a touch awkwardly.

They walked back to the bedroom, pulled off their shirts, and began to kiss, tentatively, tenderly. She lay back on the bed, and he moved gently above her, but then her noises shifted direction and gained edge. He stopped, realizing she was weeping. Her fingers splayed, her palms finding the balls of his shoulders, and she pushed him back and off. He sat on the bed, naked and confused as she grappled with the sheets to pull them over herself. Ginny's empty room across the hall silently made itself known, like a deep vibration.

Dray tucked one arm across her stomach and pressed her other hand to her trembling lips until they stopped. "I'm sorry. I thought I might be ready."

"Don't be sorry." He reached out and stroked her hair, but she didn't respond. He put on his clothes quietly, unsure whether she perceived his dressing as an insult or as his move to gather his pride; he'd intended neither.

"I guess I just need some space."

"Maybe I should go back to . . . ?" He pointed down the hall, then retreated slowly across the room. He paused for a moment at the door, but she didn't stop him.

Tim slept lurchingly through a tangle of nightmares and awoke in a sweaty haze a mere hour later, his intake of dream images somehow affirming his suspicion that Ginny had died at the hands of two killers—one still an enigma.

He couldn't trust the detectives' competence. He didn't

agree with the DA's take on the case. He couldn't use the service. He couldn't investigate the case himself.

He was desperate.

Desperate enough to look for help in the one place he swore he never would.

He glanced at the clock—11:37 P.M.

He jotted Dray a note in case she woke up, left the house quietly, and drove swiftly to Pasadena. He headed through the clean suburban neighborhood, his heartbeat and anxiety increasing with his proximity. He parked at the end of an aggregate concrete walk, the stones perfectly smoothed as they were on Tim's porch. The windows sparkled—not a single smudge. The lawn was dead level and precisely trimmed, the sides lined to perfection by an edger or maybe even shears.

Tim headed up the walk and stood for a moment, taking note of the coat of paint on the front door, untainted by even one brush mark. He rang the bell and waited.

The footsteps approached evenly, as if timed.

His father opened the door.

"Timmy."

"Dad."

His father stood, as always, wedged between the door and the jamb, as if protecting the house from a Bible salesman's assault. His gray suit was cheap but well pressed, the knot of his tie seated high and hard against his throat despite the hour. "How are you holding up? Haven't talked to you since the news."

The news. An engagement. A business deal. A daughter's death.

"May I come in?"

His father inhaled deeply and held his breath for a moment, indicating the inconvenience. Finally, he stepped back and let the door swing open. "Would you mind taking off your shoes?"

Tim sat on the couch in the living room, facing the La-Z-Boy upon which he knew his father would eventually settle. His father stood over him for a moment, arms crossed. "Drink?"

"Water would be good."

His father leaned over, plucked a coaster off the coffee table, and handed it to him before disappearing into the kitchen.

Tim looked around the familiar room, unchanged since his childhood. A scattering of picture frames covered the mantel, displaying the sun-faded stock photographs that had come with them. A woman at the beach. Three babies in a kiddie pool. A generic couple having a picnic. Tim was unsure if the frames had ever housed personal photos. He tried to remember if a picture of his mother, who'd wisely left them when he was three, had ever been on display in the house. He could not.

Ginny was the last of the Rackleys, the end of the lineage.

His father returned, gave Tim the glass, and offered his hand. They shook.

Easing into the La-Z-Boy, his father shoved the wood lever on the side and leaned back, the footrest kicking up beneath his legs. Tim realized he hadn't seen his father since Ginny's fourth birthday. His father had aged, not drastically but significantly—a faint net of wrinkles beneath each eye, a slight pucker cupping the points of his mouth, coarse white hairs threaded in his eyebrows. It distressed Tim. Another stark glance at death's encroachment—slow this time, but equally unrelenting.

It struck him that when he was little, he hadn't understood death. Or he'd understood it better. It had seduced him. He'd played war, he'd played cops and robbers, he'd played cowboys and Indians, but he'd played no game in which death had not been a participant. When his first Ranger buddies had died, he'd worn his uniform and sunglasses to the funerals and observed stoically, dark and tough. And he hadn't been mourning for his friends, not really, because they'd just beaten him to it. First one to get a license, first one to get laid, first one to get killed. But with falling in love, losing a daughter, that had all changed. Death wasn't seductive anymore. When Ginny died, he'd felt a part of himself break off and spiral down a void. The damage had lessened him. And left him more exposed to dread.

He found he had less and less stomach for death.

To steel himself he reached for the reliable joist of aggression. "You been shooting straight?" he asked.

"Absolutely."

"No fraudulent checks, no running fake credit-card numbers?"

"Not a one. It *has* been four years now. My parole officer is quite proud, even if my son is not." His father tilted his head for emphasis, then let his smile drop.

He leaned forward, the footrest sucking into the cheap fabric and disappearing. Crossing his legs, he laced his hands across his knee. He'd always exhibited an elegance that far outpaced the people and objects with which he surrounded himself. It was hard to square his well-filed nails with a life patched together from second-rate cons.

What he said next surprised Tim more than anything he'd ever said.

"I miss Virginia."

Tim took a sip of water, more to stall for time than anything else. "You never saw her much."

His father nodded, again with his head slightly tilted, as if he were listening to distant music. "I know. But I miss the idea of her."

Tim found himself gazing at the photographs on the mantel. "She wasn't just an idea."

"I didn't say she was."

It took some effort for Tim to get the words out. "I need help."

"Don't we all." His father uncrossed his legs and leaned back, his hands gripping the armrest, like Lincoln at the monument. "Money?"

"No. Information."

His father gave a grave nod, that of a judge who'd seen it all before.

"I was wondering if you could put the word out about Ginny's death. To your guys. You know people in all walks—maybe someone's heard something."

His father stood, removing a handkerchief from the breast pocket of his jacket. He wiped the condensation from Tim's glass, wiped the coaster, replaced them on the coffee table, and sat back down. Tim wondered if his own impeccable neatness was an attempt to satisfy some deep-buried urge to please his father or simply a learned need to hold in order those matters in which order could be held. The house conveyed not a loving custodianship but the rigidity of the not deeply secure. His father had built it plank by plank, or so he'd always claimed.

"It was my understanding from the newspapers that there's a clear suspect. This Kindell."

"He is. But I have a feeling there's more to the story."

"It sounds like you're being a bit emotional." He regarded Tim, waiting for a response. When it became clear he wasn't going to get one, he said, "Why don't *you* dig around? You have confidential informants, colleagues. You deal with people on the wrong side of the tracks, I'd imagine. Aside from your father, I mean."

"I'm reluctant to put myself too close to the case, given my clear bias. And I can't use the service for a personal cause."

"Ah. The superego speaks." His father pursed his lips; he had a pronounced Cupid's bow, a more handsome face than Tim's. "So you'll put me on the line, call in my contacts but not your own."

"I'm compromised here, for obvious reasons. I thought if you came across something hard, a strong lead, we could turn it over to the authorities."

"I don't like the authorities much, Timmy."

Tim forged through thirty-three years of hard-built instinct, opening himself up to the intense vulnerability that came in expecting something, anything from his father. "I've never come to you before. Ever. For a job, for money, for a personal favor. Please."

His father sighed, affecting regretfulness. "Well, Timmy, things have been tight lately, and I only have so many favors to call in. I gotta spend them wisely."

Tim's mouth had gone dry. "I wouldn't be asking if it wasn't important."

"But *your* important, you see, isn't necessarily *my* important right now. It's not that I don't want to help you out, Timmy, it's just that I have some problems of my own and some priorities of my own. I'm afraid I don't have any extra favors to call in right now."

"*Any* or any *extra?*"

"Any extra, I suppose."

Tim bit the inside of his lip, took it to the verge of pain for a few moments. "I understand."

His father traced the edges of his mouth with his thumb and forefinger, as if smoothing a goatee. "The lawman come to the con man for help. I believe that's what they call irony."

"I believe you're correct."

His father stood up, smoothing his pant legs. Tim followed suit.

"Give my regards to Andrea."

"I'll do that."

At the door his father straightened his arms, showing off his jacket. "Like my new church suit, Timmy?"

"I didn't know you went to church."

He winked. "Hedging my bets."

**ALL THE MEDICAL EXAMINER'S ROOTING THROUGH** Ginny's body produced no essential physical evidence. There was extensive vaginal tearing, but no signs of semen. A condom had been used—identified as a Durex Gold Coin from the lab workup of the lubricant residue—but no matching or discarded condoms had been logged at Kindell's house or at the crime scene. On the seventh day the medical examiner finally released the body. Because of the severity of Ginny's assault and the ME's thoroughness, Tim and Dray had no choice but to arrange a closed-casket service, which suited them anyway.

They paid for the funeral from Ginny's incipient college fund.

The service was mercifully brief. Dray's four brothers

showed early, tall and refrigerator-wide, packing flasks of
bourbon. They circled up like a football huddle in the par-
lor, shot Tim criminating looks, and wept. Bear sat alone in
the last pew, his head lowered. Mac came with Fowler and
didn't miss a single opportunity to be at Dray's side. They
kept their distance from Bear.

Dray wore a gray coat over a black dress, and carried
herself gracefully despite her visible exhaustion.

Tim's father appeared late, slender, well groomed, and
smelling conspicuously of aftershave. He kissed Dray on
the cheek—she received him warmly for once, clutching
his hand—then nodded somberly at Tim. "I'm very sorry
for your loss."

"Thank you," Tim said.

After awkwardly reaching and rereaching for each other,
they managed a dour embrace. Tim did his best to avoid his
father for the rest of the service, and his father seemed to
find the unspoken arrangement equally acceptable.

The burial itself took place at the Bardsdale Cemetery in
a wet breeze that left the mourners' clothes damp and uncomfortable. The mud collecting around the base of Tim's
dress shoes reminded him of that on Kindell's boots—the
stain of guilt. Tim contemplated whether he wore it now for
withholding retribution against his daughter's murderer.

His father left midway through the ceremony. Tim
watched his solitary form make its way down the grassy
hill, shoulders not squared with the resoluteness that ordi-
narily so defined his father's posture, and his father.

On the drive home Tim jerked the car to the side of the
road and hunched over the wheel, his breath hammering
through him. He used to wake up this way a few times a
month upon his return from Croatia, flooded with images
of mass graves, but he'd not before experienced such
claustrophia in the daylight. Dray reached over, rubbed

his neck lovingly, patiently. The sensation of constriction departed as suddenly as it had started. He sat staring numbly at the road, the rise and fall of his shoulders still pronounced.

"I wanted to give her things I never had. A stable home. Support. I wanted to teach her ethics, respect for society—things I was never shown, things I had to find on my own. Now that's gone. I lost the future." He blew out a shaky breath. "What's the point now? To make another mortgage payment? To get up for work another day, go to sleep another night?"

Dray watched him, wiping her cheeks. "I don't know."

They sat until Tim's breathing returned to normal, then drove home in silence.

Waiting for them on the doorstep was the morning paper, still unread. The cover photo featured Maybeck and Denley throwing high fives outside Room 9 of the Martía Domez Hotel as two cops carried off a body bag on a stretcher. Both deputies were smiling, and Denley's glove was smudged with blood, probably from checking Heidel's pulse inside. The headline read: U.S. MARSHALS CELEBRATE DOWNTOWN BLOODBATH. Without a word Dray walked the paper to the curb and dumped it in the recycling bin.

In the middle of the night, Dray's keening from the bedroom awakened Tim on the couch. He walked back to the bedroom and found the door locked. She answered his soft knock between sobs. "I just n-need . . . to do this alone for a while."

He returned to the couch and sat, her sobs reaching him muffled through the walls.

To respect Dray's need for space, Tim took to brushing his teeth and showering in the other bathroom, near the garage, entering the bedroom only to get clean clothes. On the coffee table beside the couch, he put an alarm clock and a reading lamp. Marshal Tannino had asked him to take a few days while things cooled down, so Tim tried to keep busy, working out, doing small repairs around the house, trying to limit the time each day he spent feeling sorry for himself or basking in his unrequited hatred of Kindell.

He and Dray ate at different times so as not to overlap in the kitchen, and when they passed each other, their eye contact was short and uncomfortable. Ginny's absence loomed large in the house, a growing shadow that fell between them.

If Tim had bothered to turn on the TV or read the newspaper, he would have seen that the Heidel shooting had captured that hottest spotlight of all, the attention of the L.A. media. Highlights from the trial of Jedediah Lane—the right-wing extremist thought responsible for releasing sarin nerve gas at the regional office of the Census Bureau—occasionally bumped the shootings from the front page, but Tim's story proved to have surprising staying power. Phone calls from the press trickled in at first, then reached a fevered pitch. Soon Tim could glean whether it was a press call based on how firmly Dray put the phone down. Tim raised the issue of getting a new number, but Dray, unwilling to concede another change no matter how small, wouldn't have it. Mercifully, no media made the trek to their house.

Tim was to give a statement for the shooting review board the day before Kindell's preliminary hearing. He awakened early and showered. When he entered the bedroom, Dray was sitting on the bed, her hands in her lap. They exchanged polite greetings.

Tim walked to his closet and gazed inside. His three suit jackets were center-vented so his pistol would never be exposed at his hip. All his shoes were lace-up; he'd learned the hard way about loafers his first time walking the fenders on a Protective Services detail on a muddy afternoon.

He dressed quickly, then sat on the bed opposite Dray to pull on his shoes.

"Nervous?" she asked.

He tied his shoelaces and crossed to the gun safe before remembering that he no longer had a service-issued weapon. "Yes. More about the prelim tomorrow."

"He's gonna be sitting there. In the same room as us." She shook her head, mouth firmed with anger. "He's all we have on this. Kindell. No accomplice, nothing else." She stood up, as if sitting left her in too vulnerable a position. "What if they let him plea-bargain? Or if the jury doesn't believe he did it?"

"It won't happen. The DA will never let him plead out, and there's enough evidence to convict him six times over. It'll go smoothly, we'll have ringside seats at the lethal injection, and then we can get on with things."

"Like what?"

"Like finding the right place for Ginny. Like figuring out what parts of all this to let go. Like learning to live in this house together again." His voice was soft and held longing. He could see his words working on Dray, cutting through some of the calluses the friction of the past days had built up between them.

"Two weeks ago we were a family," Dray said. "I mean, we were so close, we were the ones they were jealous of. The other ones, with the bad marriages. And now, when I need you the most, I don't even recognize you." She sat back down on the bed. "I don't even recognize myself."

Tim thumbed the snap on his empty holster. "I don't recognize us either."

They shifted and waited, studying everything but each other. Tim searched for what he wanted to say but found

nothing except confusion and an intense, unfamiliar need
for assurance that unsettled him further.

Finally Dray said, "Good luck with the shooting board."

**8** REPORTERS CLUNG TO THE COURTHOUSE STEPS LIKE PI-
geons, trailing cords and setting up their field
lead-ins. Tim drove past unnoticed and pulled
through a gated entrance into the lot. Marshal Tannino's
office and those of his chiefs were arrayed along a quiet,
carpeted hall behind the courthouse that felt more East
Coast library than West Coast lowest bidder. The administrative offices were farther down the hall, past an immense
antique safe from a late-nineteenth-century marshal's stage-
coach escort team.

Bear was sitting on a chair in the small lounge, flirting
with the marshal's assistant and, from her weary expression of forbearance, doing a bad job of it. He stood quickly
when Tim entered and ushered him into the hall.

"I've got to make a statement in three minutes, Bear."

"I've been trying to reach you."

"We had to take the phones off the hook. Too many—"

"I drove over to your house two nights ago. Dray said
you were out shooting." Bear studied Tim's face. "She
didn't tell you I stopped by?"

"We haven't been talking so much lately."

"Jesus Christ, Rack. Why the hell not?"

A flare of anger that Tim smothered. "Look, I need to
focus on my shooting statement right now."

"That's why I'm here." Bear took a deep breath, held it
for a moment. "You're getting ambushed."

"What do you mean?"

"Have you been watching the news?"

"No, Bear. I've been dealing with more important stuff. Like burying my daughter." Bear took a step back, and Tim inhaled deeply, then squeezed his eyes hard with his thumb and index finger. "I didn't mean it to come out that way."

"The coverage has been pretty ugly. There's this high-five picture—"

"I saw it."

Bear lowered his voice as a couple of DOJ suits walked by. "It's getting play like the shot of the INS agent with the MP-5 in Elián González's face. On top of that, some Mexican Al Sharpton out of Texas has been beating the drum—"

"That's ridiculous. Heidel was white, and half our team was Hispanic."

"But the photograph is of Denley and Maybeck, and they're both white. And all that matters is that fucking photo, not the facts behind it."

Tim held up his hands, a gesture of patience and capitulation. "I can't control press coverage."

"Well, you're not just repeating your statement in there. A few shooting review board members flew out from HQ. You're gonna get the full-court press."

"Fair enough. It was a high-profile shooting. There's a process. I get it."

"Listen, Rack, this thing gets out of hand, goes civil or criminal, I'm gonna represent you. I don't care if I have to resign—I got your back."

"I knew law school would turn you paranoid."

"This is serious stuff, Rack. Now, I know I'm just a dumb-ass who took a few night classes, but I can rep you for free and get you a real attorney to cover the hard shit."

"I appreciate that, Bear. Thank you. But it's gonna be fine."

The marshal's assistant stuck her head into the hall. "They're ready for you, Deputy Rackley." She withdrew without acknowledging Bear.

" 'Deputy Rackley,' " Tim repeated, troubled by her formality.

"I just wanted to warn you."

"Thank you." Tim tapped Bear on the ribs. "How's the bruising?"

Bear tried not to wince. "Don't hurt at all."

Tim started back for the lounge. When he turned around, Bear was still watching him.

The big brick of a tape recorder shushed hypnotically in the center of the elongated table. Tim's chair, with its middling size and cheap upholstery, was no match for the high-backed black leather numbers his interviewers commanded on the opposing side. Tim jiggled the handle beneath his seat inconspicuously, trying to elevate it.

With painstaking detail they'd covered every inch of Tim's account of his shooting of Gary Heidel and Lydia Ramirez. The Internal Affairs guy wasn't so bad, but the woman from Investigative Services and the gunner from Legal were attack dogs in knockoff suits. Tim's forehead felt moist, but he refrained from wiping it.

The woman uncrossed her legs and leaned forward, her finger tracing something in the file before her. "You claim you emerged from the alley and saw Carlos Mendez reaching for his weapon?"

"Yes."

"Did you issue a warning to Mr. Mendez?"

"The firing of warning shots is against agency regulation."

"As is firing at fleeing suspects, Deputy Rackley."

The Internal Affairs inspector shot her a look of irritation. He was an older guy, probably switched over to IA to log a few more years of service before retirement. Tim remembered he'd introduced himself as Dennis Reed. "This was not merely a fleeing suspect, Deborah. He was armed and intent on firing."

She made a calming gesture with her hands. "Did you issue an *oral* warning to Mr. Mendez?"

"We'd been issuing oral warnings for the preceding seven minutes to no avail. Two people were already dead as a result of the fugitives' failure to heed those warnings."

"Did you issue another oral warning immediately before you fired on Mr. Mendez?"

"No."

"Why not?"

"There was no time."

"There was no time for you to issue a final command of any sort?"

"I believe that's what I just said."

"But there was enough time for you to draw your weapon and fire three shots?"

"The final two shots were irrelevant."

If Reed's smirk was any indication, he liked Tim's answer.

"Let me rephrase my question. There was enough time for you to draw your weapon and fire the first shot but not to issue an oral warning of any kind?"

"Yes."

She feigned immense puzzlement. "How is that possible, Deputy Rackley?"

"I'm a very quick draw, ma'am."

"I see. And were you concerned that Mr. Mendez was going to fire at you?"

"My primary concern was for the safety of others. We were on a street filled with civilians."

"So I can take that to mean that you weren't concerned he was going to fire at you?"

"I thought he was probably going to shoot one of the police officers in front of him."

" 'Thought,' " the lawyer said. " 'Probably.' "

"That's right," Tim said. "Only I used them in a complete sentence."

"There's no need to get defensive, Deputy Rackley. We're all on the same side here."

"Right," Tim said.

The woman flipped through the file, then frowned, as if she'd just discovered something. "The crime-scene report indicates that Mr. Mendez's weapon was still tucked into the back of his jeans when they assessed the body."

"Then we should be grateful he wasn't given the opportunity to draw it."

"So he wasn't trying to draw the weapon?"

Tim watched the wheels of the tape recorder spin their lethargic circles. "I said he wasn't given the *opportunity* to draw it. He was, in fact, *attempting* to draw it."

"We have mixed eyewitness reports regarding that fact."

"I was the only one behind him."

"Uh-huh. On the alley side."

"That's right." Tim let out his breath through his teeth. "As I said, he was a clear—"

"Threat to the safety of others," she said. His textbook recitation of the deadly-force policy inspired a note of disdain, almost parody.

The lawyer perked up in his chair, evidently sighting a lead-in. "Let's talk about the 'safety of others.' Did you have target acquisition?"

Reed grimaced. "I'd say from the looks of the body, he had pretty damn good target acquisition, Pat."

Pat ignored him, continuing to address Tim. "Are you aware that there were civilians in the backdrop when you took that shot? A whole crowd, in fact?"

"Yes. Those civilians were my concern. That's why I elected to use deadly force."

"If you had missed, your round would almost definitely have struck one of those civilians."

"That's highly debatable."

"But what if you had missed?"

"Our pre-op briefing made clear the fugitives had nothing to lose, as it made clear their unwillingness to be taken alive. Mendez's behavior, from the time he aided in taking me hostage, only reinforced this intel. He, like Heidel and Ramirez, was willing to kill *any number* of people to evade capture. It was a clear calculation: My chances of taking him out were vastly greater than the chances of his not killing someone once he got his weapon free and clear."

"You still haven't answered my question, Deputy Rackley." Pat slid his pen behind his ear and crossed his arms. "What if you had missed?"

"I shot a consistent twenty out of twenty on the pistol qual course as a Ranger, and I'm a six-time qualified three-hundred shooter as a deputy marshal. I wasn't planning on missing."

"Well, bravo. But a deputy marshal in the field has to be willing to consider *every* potentiality."

Reed rocked forward and thumped his elbows on the table. "Just because he agreed to submit to questioning does not give you the right to drag him over the coals. There's a subjective element to every decision to engage with deadly force. If you'd ever toted a gun, you'd be aware of that."

"Excellent point, Dennis. I've heard packing heat greatly enhances one's interpretation of the law."

Reed pointed at Pat. "Watch your step. I'm not having you harass a good deputy. Not in my presence."

"Moving on," the woman said. "I understand you've had a recent trauma in your personal life?"

Tim waited several seconds to answer. "Yes."

"Your daughter was killed?"

"Yes." Despite his efforts, some of his fury crept into his voice.

"Do you think this event may have influenced any of your actions during these shootings?"

He felt the heat rise to his face. "This 'event' has influenced every single moment of my life since. But it hasn't altered my professional judgment."

"You don't think that you may have been feeling . . . aggressive or . . . retaliatory?"

"Had I not been in fear for my life or concerned for the lives of others, I would have done everything in my power to bring those fugitives in alive. Everything in my power."

Pat tilted back in his chair and made a little temple with his pudgy fingers. "Really?"

Tim stood up and placed both his hands palm down on the table. "I am a deputy U.S. marshal. Do I look like a soldier of fortune to you?"

"Listen—"

"I'm not talking to you, ma'am." Tim didn't remove his eyes from Pat. Pat remained tilted back in his chair, fingers pressed together. When it became clear he wasn't going to respond, Tim reached over and turned off the tape recorder. "I'm done answering questions. Anything further, you can talk to my FLEOA rep."

Reed rose as Tim exited, but Pat and the woman remained seated. As Tim walked away, he could hear Reed start laying into them. The marshal's assistant stood as he passed her, heading for Tannino's office.

"Tim, he's in with someone right now. You can't just—"

Tim knocked on the marshal's door, then opened it. Tannino sat behind an immense wood desk. An overweight man in a dark suit was sprawled on the couch opposite, smoking a brown cigarette.

"Marshal Tannino, I'm very sorry to interrupt you, but I really need a moment."

"Of course." Tannino exchanged a few words of Italian with the man as he showed him out. He closed the door, then waved a hand at the cigarette smoke, shaking his head. "Diplomats." He gestured to the couch. "Please, sit."

Though he didn't want to, Tim sat. His dress shirt was pinching him at the shoulders.

"I'm not gonna lie to you, Rackley. The press is bad. Now, I understand you weren't one of the knuckleheads throwing high fives, but you were the shooter, and we both know shooters take the scrutiny. Deserved or not, the service got a black eye on this one. Here's the good news: The shooting review board is convening next week at headquarters, and they're going to clear you."

"They don't seem like they're going to clear me. They seem like they're looking for a scapegoat for a situation that doesn't demand one."

"They will clear you. All the written statements are in and check out. They just sent out a few board members to run your statement through the ringer in-house so steps won't have to be taken out of house. We don't want any FBI involvement here. Or some state DA looking to make a name."

"What's the bad news?"

Tannino puffed out his cheeks in a sigh. "We're gonna put you on light duty for a while, get you off the street until the press calms down. In a couple of months, we'll get you qualified on a fresh service pistol."

At first Tim was not sure he'd heard Tannino correctly. "A couple of *months?*"

"No big deal—you'll just do analytical work rather than fieldwork."

"And while I'm putting my training to use making schedules at the operations desk, what is the unparalleled service PR machine going to be putting out about me?"

Tannino walked over and examined a Walker .44 cap-and-ball six-gun that hung on the wall, encased in Lucite. A black plastic comb protruded from the back pocket of his suit pants. "That you've quite responsibly elected to enroll in an anger-management course."

"Absolutely not."

"That's it. It's a nothing thing. Then headquarters can stand behind your decision to engage with deadly force, and we're a big happy family again."

"What does this have to do with Maybeck and Denley high-fiving?"

"Absolutely nothing. But this is a bullshit perception game, as you'll see if you're ever so unfortunate as to reach my level. And the bullshit perception, because of that goddamn photograph, is that we're a bunch of bloodthirsty, gung ho loose cannons. If we indicate the shooter is acquiring a heightened sensitivity to anger issues, we cut some of that perception, and the paper pushers at the Puzzle Palace can go back to their normal job, which is doing exactly nothing. In the meantime I get the pleasure of dealing with this on all fronts and of having to ask one of my best deputies—unjustly—to take some shit for us." His grimace showed more regret than disgust. "The system at work."

Tim stood up. "It was a good shooting."

"Good shootings are relative. I know that what they're asking is difficult, Rackley, but you have your whole career ahead of you."

"Maybe not with the U.S. Marshals Service." Tim unhooked his leather badge clip from his belt and laid it on Tannino's desk.

In a rare display of anger, Tannino grabbed it and hurled it at Tim. Tim trapped it against his chest. "I am not going to accept your resignation, goddamnit. Not considering what you've been dealing with. Take some more time—administrative leave—hell, a few weeks. Don't make a decision now, in these circumstances." His face looked tired and old, and Tim realized how much it must have pained him to take the kind of company line Tannino himself had always despised and thought cowardly.

"I'm not going to do it."

Tannino spoke softly now. "I'm afraid you're going to have to. Everything else I'll protect you on. *Everything.*"

"It was a good shooting."

This time Tannino met his eyes. "I know."

Respectfully, Tim laid his badge back on Tannino's desk, then walked out.

**9** ON TIM'S WAY HOME A WHITE CAMRY EMERGED FROM the crush of midday traffic to inch alongside him. A flurry of movement drew his attention to the car's backseat. A young girl wearing a yellow dress was pressing her face to the window in an attempt to horrify nearby drivers.

Tim watched her. She mashed her nose against the glass, pigging it upward. She crossed her eyes and stuck out her tongue. She feigned picking her nose. Her mother looked over at Tim apologetically.

The car stayed more or less at his side, lurching and braking in time with him. He tried to focus on the road, but the girl's movement and bright dress pulled his gaze back to her. Realizing she had Tim's eye again, the girl fisted her straight blond hair out in Pippi Longstocking pigtails. She laughed openmouthed and unencumbered, as only children can. As she looked for a reaction in Tim's face, her expression suddenly changed. Her smile faded, then vanished, replaced with uneasiness. She slid down in her seat, disappearing from Tim's view, save for the top of her head.

By the time he got home, Tim's shirt was spotted through with sweat. He entered the house and slung his jacket over one of the kitchen chairs. Dray was sitting on his couch, watching the news. She turned, regarded him, and said, "Oh, no."

Tim walked over and sat beside her. Not surprisingly, the chirpy KCOM news anchor, Melissa Yueh, had taken up the shooting. A graphic of a gun appeared in the upper right corner of the screen, in front of a shadowy outline of two hands high-fiving. Tim's own personal logo. Beneath it stretched SLAUGHTER AT THE MARTÍA DOMEZ HOTEL in block letters.

"Did it go as bad as you look?" Dray asked.

"They want to let drop I've enrolled in an anger-management course, then desk-jockey me till the storm blows over. It lets them cover their asses without admitting to liability or guilt."

Dray reached over and laid a hand on his cheek. It felt warm and immensely comforting. "Screw them."

"I resigned."

"Of course. I'm glad."

An attractive African-American reporter came on-screen, soliciting the takes of passersby on the shooting. An obese man with a skimpy goatee and a backward Dodgers cap—the archetypal Man on the Street for the market and time slot—offered his opinion gladly. "The way I see it, a guy's running from the cops like that, he deserves to get shot. Drug dealers, cop killers, man, I say we execute 'em before the judge's gavel drops. That U.S. Marshal guy, I hope he gets away with it."

Great, Tim thought.

Next a woman with vivid green eyeliner added, "Our children are safer with drug dealers like that out of the picture. I don't care how the police get them off the streets, as long as they're gone."

"Look at those people," Tim said. "No idea what issues are in play." The bitterness in his voice surprised him.

Dray looked over at him. "At least you have a few allies."

"Allies like that are more dangerous than enemies."

"They may not be the most well spoken bunch, but they seem to have a grasp of justice."

"And no grasp of the law."

She shifted on the couch, arms weaving together across her chest. "You think the law adds up to justice, but it doesn't. There are cracks and fissures, loopholes and spin. There's PR, perception, personal favors, and cluster fucks. Look at what just happened to you. Was that justice? Hell no. That was a big, self-cleaning machine clanking forward, squashing you beneath it. Look at how the investigation went into Ginny's death. We'll never know what really happened, who was involved."

"So you're mad at me because . . . ?"

"Because my daughter got killed—"

"*Our* daughter."

"—and you were in a position—a unique position—to see justice served. And instead, you served the law."

"Justice will be served. Tomorrow."

"What if he's not executed?"

"Then he'll rot in prison the rest of his life."

Dray's face was flushed, frighteningly intense. She ground a fist into an open hand. "I want him *dead*."

"And I want him to talk. To cough out what really happened when he's on the stand. So we can know if there's someone else out there, someone else responsible for our daughter's death."

"If you had just shot him, instead of asking him, then we'd never have been burdened with this *mystery*. This *unknown*. It's awful. It's awful not knowing and thinking someone out there, someone who we could know or could see on the street and not ever guess . . ."

Her face creased, and Tim moved over to embrace her, but she pushed him away. She rose to head back to the bedroom but paused in the doorway. Her voice was cracked and husky. "I'm sorry about your job."

He nodded.

"And I know it was more than a job."

The early-morning rain had vanished, leaving behind a moist, stifling heat that permeated the courthouse. Tim's head throbbed with exhaustion and stress. He'd spent the night fidgeting on the couch in a kind of unsleep, sweating off his frustration about the shooting review board and obsessing about the upcoming hearing. He pictured the little girl in the Camry, her arms pale and thin. Ginny's face at the morgue when he'd drawn back the sheet. The wisp of hair trapped in the corner of her mouth. Her fingernail they'd found at the crime scene, loosed in some desperate act of clawing or crawling.

His own mind had become hostile, a treacherous terrain. There was less and less of it he could inhabit peacefully.

Dray sat beside him, rigidly forward, her arms crossed on the bench back in front of them. They'd arrived early and sat in the last row, awash in an unspoken dread. When Kindell had been led in by a young sheriff's deputy and the shoddily dressed public defender, he'd looked neither as menacing nor repugnant as Tim had remembered. This disappointed him. Like most Americans, he preferred to see evil embodied unequivocally.

The DA, a sharp, well-put-together woman in her early thirties, had sat with Tim and Dray for a few moments before the preliminary hearing had begun, offering further condolences and assurances. No, she wasn't making a case for an accomplice, since that could open up the door to a reduced sentence for Kindell. Yes, she was going to nail Kindell's ass to the wall.

Despite her prudish name—Constance Delaney—she was a tiger of a prosecutor, with a stellar track record. She opened strong, fending off the defense's motion to reduce the high bail set at arraignment. She artfully examined Deputy Fowler, working to establish probable cause to bind the case over to trial, while trotting out as little of her case strategy as possible. Fowler spoke clearly, without sounding coached. He left out Tim and Bear's presence at Kindell's dwelling without committing anything to the record that could be contradicted. CSU's delayed arrival to the crime scene did not arise.

Kindell sat erect, attentively watching all the proceedings, his head swinging back and forth from Delaney to Fowler.

It wasn't until the cross that things came unwound.

"And of course you had a warrant to search Mr. Kindell's property . . . ?" The public defender shuffled closer to the witness stand, the sheaf of yellow legal-pad pages swaying in his hand. Delaney propped her chin on her fist, jotting notes.

"No. We knocked and introduced ourselves, asked him if we could take a look around. He clearly gave oral consent for us to search the area."

"I see. And that's when you discovered"—a few moments as the PD shuffled through the sheets of paper—"the hacksaw, the rags stained with what was later identified to be the victim's blood, and the truck tires with tread that matched that at the scene of the crime?"

"Yes."

"You discovered all of these things *after* he gave you consent to search the property?"

"Yes."

"With no search warrant?"

"As I said—"

"Just yes or no, please, Deputy Fowler."

"Yes."

"At which point you began arrest procedures?"

"Yes."

"You're entirely certain, Deputy Fowler, that you Mirandized Mr. Kindell?"

"One hundred percent."

"Was this before or after you cuffed Mr. Kindell?"

"I suppose during."

"You suppose?" The public defender dropped a few of the sheets and crouched to pick them up. Tim was beginning to suspect that his bumbling-lawyer routine was just that.

"I read him his Miranda rights as I was cuffing him."

"So he wasn't facing you?"

"Not through all of it. He was turned around. We generally handcuff suspects from behind."

"Uh-huh." The PD's pencil poked at his upper lip. "Are you aware, Deputy Fowler, that my client is legally deaf?"

Delaney's hand slipped from her face, slapping the table and breaking the perfect silence of the superior court. Judge Everston, a small, pucker-faced woman in her late sixties, bristled in her black robes as if she'd been shocked. Dray's hand pressed over her mouth so hard her nails left red imprints in her cheek.

Fowler stiffened. "No. He's not. He understood everything we said to him."

His stomach churning, Tim recalled Kindell's uneven voice, its lopsided cadence. Kindell had responded only when spoken to directly and when he'd been watching his questioner. Tim's chest tightened painfully, a vise closing.

The PD turned to Judge Everston. "Mr. Kindell lost his hearing nine months ago in an industrial explosion. I have his treating physician in the hallway, who I'm prepared to call as a witness to testify that he is legally deaf, and two independent complete audiology reports showing bilateral deafness here." He raised a manila folder, promptly scattering the papers it held, then retrieved them and handed them to the judge.

Delaney's voice lacked its usual confidence. "Objection, Your Honor. The reports are hearsay."

"Your Honor, as those records were produced directly to the court from USC County Medical pursuant to a subpoena duces tecum, they are exceptions to the hearsay rule as official records."

Delaney sat down. With a stern frown, Judge Everston reviewed the file.

"Mr. Kindell is able to read lips, Your Honor, though only minimally—he's never received professional instruction in this area. If he was being cuffed during the admonishment, he would have been facing away from Deputy

Fowler's mouth. Any questionable chance he might have had to comprehend his Miranda rights was surely eliminated. His confession was made without any clear knowledge of his rights."

Delaney broke in. "Your Honor, if these officers made a good-fai—"

Judge Everston cut her off with a wave of her hand. "You know better than to come at me with 'good-faith effort,' Ms. Delaney." Judge Everston's mouth tightened, wrinkles ringing her lips. "If Mr. Kindell is really deaf, as counsel has indicated, there would seem to be a clear Miranda problem."

The public defender rocked forward on his shoes. "Further, the defense requests that all physical evidence found at my client's house be suppressed, as the search was in violation of the Fourth Amendment."

Dray's voice, small and strained, escaped from beneath the hand she held cupped over her mouth. "Oh, God."

Delaney was on her feet. "Even if the defendant is legally deaf, he can still give legally binding consent to search, and the evidence should *not* be suppressed."

"My client is deaf, Your Honor. How on earth could he give knowing and voluntary consent for a search-and-seizure request *he didn't even hear?*"

Kindell turned, craning his neck to locate Tim and Dray. His smile was not malicious or gloating, rather the pleased grin of a child allowed to keep something he'd just stolen. Dray's face was drawn and bloodless and, Tim was fairly certain, a match of his own.

"What other physical evidence do you have, Ms. Delaney, linking Mr. Kindell to the crime scene and the crime?" Judge Everston's bony finger emerged from the folds of her robes, pointing at Kindell with thinly veiled disdain.

"Aside from what we recovered at his residence?" Delaney's nostrils flared. Her skin had reddened in blotches spreading down her neck to the high reaches of her chest. "None, Your Honor."

Something escaped Judge Everston that sounded remarkably like "Goddamnit." She glowered at the PD. "I'm calling a half-hour recess." She exited, taking the audiology reports with her, not seeming to notice that half the courtroom forgot to rise.

Dray leaned over as though she were going to vomit, digging her elbows into her stomach. Tim's shock was so heightened it actually set his ears humming and pinched his vision at the sides.

The recess seemed to stretch on for decades. Delaney glanced back at them from time to time, her pen tapping nervously on her pad. Tim sat numbly until the bailiff entered and called for order.

Judge Everston hoisted her robes as she took the bench, her short stature apparent until she settled into position. She studied some papers for a few moments, as if mustering the strength to proceed. When she spoke, her tone was heavy, and Tim knew immediately she was about to impart bad news.

"There are times when our system, with its protections of individual rights, seems almost to conspire against us. Times when the ends justify the sordid means, and we must shut our eyes and take our medicine, despite the fact that we know it will kill a little part of us to serve a greater health. This is such a case. This is one of the sacrifices we make to live with liberty, and it is a sacrifice paid unjustly and by an unfortunate few." She tilted her head regretfully toward Tim and Dray in the back row. "I cannot in good faith allow evidence which will clearly be overturned in an appellate court. As the audiology reports are unequivocal about Mr. Kindell's bilateral deafness, it strains my credibility to believe that a deaf man with no formal training in lip-reading comprehended the intricacies of his Miranda rights or the oral consent he was asked to grant. It is not without considerable despondency that I hereby grant the motion to suppress evidence, with respect to the alleged confession and any and all physical evidence recovered from Mr. Kindell's residence."

Delaney shakily found her feet. Her voice quavered slightly. "Your Honor, in light of the court's rulings suppressing the confession and the evidence, the People are unable to proceed."

Everston spoke in a low tone of disgust. "Case dismissed."

Kindell grinned sloppily and raised his hands for his cuffs to be removed.

**10** THE RAIN HAD RESUMED, AS IF TO MATCH TIM'S MOOD, and around dusk it had kicked up fairy-tale strong, battering the screen doors and palm fronds in the backyard. The windows rattled from occasional thunder. Tim sat quietly on the couch, staring at the blank TV that reflected back only the raindrops streaking down the glass sliding doors to his side. Dray worked on a scrapbook at the kitchen table behind him, trimming and inserting pictures of Ginny in a fury of scissors and pages.

Moving only his thumb, Tim clicked the remote, and the picture bloomed. William Rayner, UCLA's ubiquitous social psychologist, appeared in the left box of a split-screen news interview with KCOM's anchor, Melissa Yueh. The live feed featured him seated in a somber library, legs crossed. His silver hair and well-manicured white mustache added to his slightly dated but handsome appearance. On the bookshelves behind him stretched rows of his latest nonfiction bestseller, *When the Law Fails*. A consummate performer with as many enemies as admirers, Rayner was a Men Are from Mars cultural critic, in a camp with Dominick Dunne and Gerry Spence. ". . . excruciating feeling of impotence when someone like Roger Kindell is not brought to justice. As you know, such cases strike a personal chord with me. When my son was murdered and his killer set free, I fell into a terrible depression."

Yueh gazed on with an expression of fudge-thick empathy.

"And that's when my interest veered in this direction," Rayner continued. "I conducted countless interviews, countless studies. I began speaking to others about how they view these shortcomings in the law and about how these shortcomings undermine efficacy and fairness. Unfortunately, there are no easy solutions. But I do know that when the law fails, the very fabric of our society is threatened. If we don't believe that the cops and courts will see to justice, what alternative does it leave us with?"

Tim pressed the remote, and the TV blinked off. He sat in silence for a few minutes, then hit the button again. Yueh had now turned her attentions to Delaney, who looked uncharacteristically flustered. Tim hit the "on/off" button again and watched the raindrop shadows play across the blank screen.

"How could Delaney not have found out the guy was deaf?" Dray said. "I mean, he was *deaf*. It's not like overlooking his eye color."

"She was working off his old case file. He wasn't deaf then."

Another angry snip of the scissors sent a strip of paper fluttering to the floor. "He's been arrested four times. You don't think he knows his rights? He's an expert on his rights. And why didn't Fowler wait for a warrant? What am I saying?—of course he didn't wait for a warrant. Of course he wasn't careful about reading the rights or getting oral consent. He never thought Kindell was going to *make it* to trial. The case wasn't dismissed because Kindell was deaf—it was dismissed because the last thing on any of your minds at the crime scene was securing the arrest properly, taking things slow and right." She slammed the scissors down on the table. "Damn that judge. She could have done something. She didn't have to throw everything out."

Tim still did not turn to face her. "Right. Because the Constitution works selectively."

"Don't be smug and detached, Timmy."

"*Don't* call me Timmy." He set the remote on the coffee table. "Come on, Dray—this isn't productive."

"Productive?" She laughed, a one-note bark. "I'm entitled to be unproductive for a day or two, don't you think?"

"Well, I don't feel like being in your line of fire right now."

"Then leave me."

He was glad he'd stayed turned away, so she couldn't see his face. It took a moment for him to respond. "That's not what I'm—"

"If you were going to go to Kindell's house that night, then you should have killed him. Killed him when you had the chance."

"Yeah, if only I'd snuffed Kindell, then our mourning process would be complete."

Dray's face tightened. "At least we'd have a little closure."

"Closure's a sham invented by talk-show hosts and self-help authors. Besides, Dray, you have a gun of your own. If you're so unhappy with my decision, why don't *you* go kill him?"

"Because I can't now. There's no opportunity. Plus, I'd be the first suspect. It's not like how Fowler silver-plattered it for you. His weapon, at the scene. You plant a gun, claim things got violent, and that's it. No phantom accomplices to plague us, no Kindell out there *for the rest of our lives.*" She slammed the scrapbook closed. "Justice served."

Tim's voice came low and even, and it held a stunning cruelty. "Maybe if you'd picked Ginny up from school on her birthday, you wouldn't have so much blame to throw around."

He didn't see the strike until the fist was closing from the right. The blow knocked him off the couch, then Dray was on him, throwing wild punches. He kicked her away and rolled to his feet, but she bounced off her soft landing on the couch and charged him again. She led with a right, but he hooked her wrist with his left hand, locking her elbow with his right. Her momentum slammed her into the bookcase. Books and picture frames rained down on them. Something shattered.

Dray found her feet quickly and came at him. She fought like a well-trained deputy, which was, of course, logical, though this particular capability of hers had never before occurred to him. He tied her up in a wrist-lock hug so as not to inflict real damage on her, pinning her arms between them. They stumbled back, smashing him into the wall. He felt his shoulder blade punch through the drywall but held on. He pressed her backward, hooking her ankle with a foot and bringing her down hard on her back on the carpet. She struggled and cried out as he lay on top of her, his hips twisted to protect his groin, head lowered and pressed to hers so she couldn't bite his face or head-butt him. He was an ice-cold fighter, all logic and strategy, against which blind rage didn't stand a chance.

Dray was thrashing and cursing a blue streak, but he kept his head lowered, repeating her full name like a chant, urging her softly to calm herself, to breathe deep, to stop struggling so he could release her. Her face was hot, sticky with sweat and tears of rage.

The storm had subsided, giving way to a shower. Only Tim's murmuring, punctuated by Dray's expletives, broke the soft pattering on the roof. Five minutes passed, or twenty. Finally, convinced her anger had spent itself, he released her. She stood. He gingerly touched the skin around his eye, swollen from the sharp blow she'd dealt him. Breathing hard, they faced each other across a wash of shattered glass and fallen books.

The doorbell rang. And again.

"I'll get it," Tim said. Not taking his eyes from Dray, he backed slowly to the door and opened it.

Mac and Fowler stood on the doorstep, arms crossed. Mac was wearing Fowler's smaller deputy hat perched atop his head like a beanie, and Fowler wore Mac's, the brim down over his eyes. An old trick for responding to domestic-violence calls—get 'em laughing.

Fowler tilted back the hat and saw that no one was amused. The cast of his face changed as he regarded the damage in the house. "We, uh, got a complaint from Hartley next door. You guys fighting?"

"Yeah," Dray said. She wiped the blood from her nose. "I was winning."

"We have everything under control now," Tim said. "Thanks for stopping by." He started to swing the door closed, but Fowler got a foot in.

Mac peered past him at Dray. "Are you okay?"

She made a limp gesture with her arm. "Dandy."

"I'm serious, Dray. Are you all right?"

"Yes."

"None of us wants a report filed," Fowler said. "Can we leave you two without you going at it again?"

"Yes," Dray said. "Absolutely."

"All right." Fowler looked from Dray's face to Tim's. "I know you're going through some hard-core shit right now, but don't make us come back here."

Mac's gaze shifted to Tim, his expression changing from concern to anger. The scene didn't look good, Tim knew, but he couldn't help resenting the accusatory edge in Mac's eyes.

"We're not kidding, Rack," Mac said. "If we hear so much as a yelp out of this house, I'm hauling you in myself."

They shuffled back to their car, hunching in the rain. Tim closed the door.

"It's not my fault I didn't pick her up." Dray's voice cracked. "Don't fucking lay that on me. There's no way I could have known."

"You're right," Tim said. "I'm sorry."

She wiped her nose again, leaving a dark stain on her sweatshirt sleeve, then walked past him out the front door. Standing out in the rain, she turned to face him. Her hair was pasted to her cheeks, her chin smeared with blood, and her eyes were the most exquisite shade of green they'd ever been. "I still love you, Timothy."

She slammed the door so hard that a painting slipped from the wall at Tim's side, the frame breaking on the hard tiles of the entry.

He walked back through the wrecked living room, grabbed a chair from the kitchen table, and spun it around to face the rain splattering against the sliding doors. He sat, leaning forward until his forehead pressed against the cool glass. The storm had resumed with added fury. Stray palm fronds littered the backyard. Ginny's bicycle lay on its side on the lawn, one of the training wheels spinning listlessly in the wind. The darkness seemed to have a malignant consistency, drawing itself around the house like a shroud, but Tim recognized the perception as little more than his own self-flagellating need for gloomy, second-rate imagery.

The wheel continued to spin, its rusty shrilling audible even over the sound of the rain. Its banshee cry underscored each betrayal of the past two weeks. It was as though an altered light had been cast across Tim's life, revealing its order for precisely what it was: scaffolding lending false form to chaos. He had no daughter to assure him a future, no vocation to moor him, no wife to confirm his humanity. The stark unjustness of his losses struck him. He'd done everything to uphold his contracts with the world, and yet he'd been set adrift.

He lowered his face into his hands, inhaling the moisture of his breath. The chair made a screech when he shoved back. He drew in a deep lungful of air, and it hitched twice, caught on the raised edge of a sob.

The doorbell rang.

He felt an overwhelming relief. "Andrea," he said. He jogged across the living room, almost slipping on a book.

He threw open the front door. A man's shadowy form stood at the far edge of the porch, rain tapping down on his slicker. A dark green southwester curled down around his face, hiding it in darkness. His posture was slightly stooped, almost indiscernibly so, an indication of age or the dawn of some illness. A strobe of light flickered across him, illumination lent by an unseen lightning bolt, but it revealed only the band of his mouth and chin. A rush of thunder permeated the air, sending its vibration up through Tim's feet.

"Who are you?"

The man looked up, water falling in tendrils from the sloped brim of his vinyl hat. "The answer," he said.

**11** "I'M NOT BIG ON PRANKSTERS, WELL-WISHERS, OR RUB-berneckers," Tim said. "Take your pick—the grieving father, the bloodthirsty deputy marshal. You've seen him now. Go back to your news station, your Rotary Club, your church, and tell them you gave it the college try."

He moved to shut the door. The man raised a fist, ungloved and callused with age, and coughed into it. There was an immense fragility in the gesture that made Tim pause.

The man said, "I share your disdain for those types. And for many more."

Despite the rain and the fluttering of his clothing around him, the man remained still, standing there like a PI cut from a dime novel. Tim knew he should close the door, but something stirred within him, akin to curiosity and compulsion, and he heard himself saying, "Why don't you come in and dry off before you get on your way?"

The man nodded and followed Tim in, stepping over the fallen books and pictures without comment. Tim sat on the couch, the man on the facing love seat. The man took off his hat, rolled it like a newspaper, and held it in both hands.

His face was textured with age and sharply intelligent. Two vivid blue eyes stood out as the only points of softness in his rugged features. His hair, black given over to steel, he wore short and well trimmed. He displayed the kind of gaunt, confused musculature of a man whose body had changed rapidly with age; Tim imagined he'd once been a hulking presence. His hands rasped when he rubbed them together, trying to work some of the cold out of his broad fingers. Tim put him in his late fifties.

"Well?"

"Ah, yes. Why am I here? I'm here to ask you a question." He paused from rubbing his hands and looked up. "How would you like ten minutes alone with Roger Kindell?"

Tim felt his heartbeat notch up a few levels. "What's your name?"

"That's not important right now."

"I don't know what kind of games you're playing, but I'm a federal deputy."

"Ex–federal deputy. And that's beside the point. This"— his hands flared, indicating the room around them—"is just speculative talk. No more. You're not plotting a crime or even commissioning one. The question is hypothetical. I have neither the means nor the intention to carry anything through."

"Don't con me. I don't mind cruelty, but I hate a con. And believe me, I know every one in the book."

"Roger Kindell. Ten minutes."

"I think you'd better leave."

"Ten minutes alone with him. Now that you've had time to think. Your marriage is on the rocks—"

"How do you know that?"

The man glanced at the sheets and bed pillows heaped beside Tim on the couch, then continued. "You've lost your job—"

"How long have you been watching me?"

"—and the man who murdered your daughter has been set free. Say you could get your hands on him now. Roger Kindell. What do you think?"

Tim felt something within him yield, giving way to anger. "What do I think? I think I would love to beat Kindell's face into an unrecognizable pulp, but I'm not some jackass cop bent on street justice or a backwater deputy who can't see farther than the end of his gun. I think I want the truth about what happened to my daughter, not just reckless vengeance. I think I'm tired of seeing individual rights trampled by people who are supposed to be upholding the law on the one side, and seeing mutts and pukes hide behind those rights on the other. I think I'm furious watching a system I spent my life fighting for fall apart on me and knowing there's no better alternative out there. I think I'm tired of people like you who poke and pry and criticize and offer nothing."

The man didn't quite smile, but his face rearranged itself to show he was pleased with Tim's response. He deposited a business card on the coffee table between them and slid it over to Tim with two fingers, like a poker chip. When Tim picked it up, the man rose from his seat. There was no name on the business card, just a Hancock Park address in plain black type.

Tim set it back down. "What is this?"

"If you're interested, be at this address tomorrow evening at six o'clock."

The man headed for the door, and Tim hastened to keep up. "If I'm interested in what?"

"In being empowered."

"Is this some sort of self-help crap? A cult?"

"Christ, no." The man coughed into a white handkerchief, and when he lowered his hand, Tim noticed specks of blood on the cloth. The man crumpled it back into his pocket quickly. He reached the front door, turned, and offered Tim his hand. "It's been quite a pleasure, Mr. Rackley."

When Tim didn't shake his hand, the man shrugged, stepped out into the rain, and quickly disappeared into the haze.

Tim did his best to straighten up the living room. He realigned the books, repaired one of the broken shelves with wood glue and C-clamps, then patched the holes in the walls with squares of drywall, which he fastidiously sized and inserted. His back felt out of whack from his fight with Dray, so he hung upside down a few moments from his gravity boots in the garage, arms folded across his chest like a bat, wishing he had a cityscape view rather than one of the oil-spotted garage floor. He unhooked himself from Dray's pull-up bar, cracked his back, then returned inside and vacuumed up the shattered glass, going over the area twice to make sure he picked up all the slivers. Though he tried to ignore the business card on the coffee table, he was aware of it the entire time.

Finally he returned to the table and stood over it, studying the card. He ripped it in half and tossed it into the garbage can beneath the kitchen sink. Then he flicked off the lights and sat staring out at the rain working on the backyard, turning the neat garden to mud, scattering leaves across the lawn, pooling in black puddles.

Dray didn't acknowledge him when she returned home hours later, and he didn't turn around. He wasn't even sure she saw him in the darkness. Her steps were heavy and uneven down the hall.

Tim sat a few minutes more, then rose and retrieved the ripped business card from the trash.

**12** TIM DID A DRIVE-BY WITHOUT SLOWING. A LARGE TUDOR house, not quite a mansion, loomed behind a wrought-iron fence. Beside the detached three-car garage, a Toyota truck, a Lincoln Town Car, and a Crown Vic were parked next to a Lexus and a Mercedes. Two of the three chimneys issued smoke, and light seeped around the drawn curtains of the downstairs windows. A gathering. And a demographically mixed one at that. The luxury cars had been there when Tim had taken his last drive-by a few hours ago, but the American metal had arrived more recently.

The house had checked out as belonging to the Spenser Trust, and further digging, predictably, had yielded little. Trusts are notoriously difficult to trace, as they aren't filed anywhere—the paperwork exists only in a lawyer's or accountant's file cabinet. The trustee, Philip Huvane, Esq., was a partner in an offshore law firm on the Isle of Man. Tim's contact with the IRS had said he couldn't get back to him with more specific information until tomorrow, and he wasn't optimistic he'd have anything useful even then.

Tim turned the corner and drove around the block. A conservative, moneyed community located south of Hollywood and west of downtown, Hancock Park is Los Angeles's best stab at East Coast sophistication. The enormous houses Tim watched fading into the dusk had been built mostly in the 1920s by rich WASPs, after the infiltration of the middle class had made Pasadena less palatable. Despite the imperious brick mailboxes and staid English exteriors, the houses still feel a touch gritty and oddly free-spirited, like a nun smoking a cigarette. In Los Angeles there's a new twist to every habit.

When Tim came up to the house again, he pulled into the drive. He pushed a button on the call box, and the large gates swung open. He put the Beemer in park, preferring to leave it outside the gates in case he needed to make a hasty retreat, slung a black bag over one shoulder, and walked to the front door. Oak, solid core. Doorknob probably weighed ten pounds.

Tim adjusted his Sig, ensuring that it remained snugly tucked into his jeans over his right kidney, handle flared outward to precipitate a fast draw. He'd looped a few rubber bands around the fore end of the grip just below the hammer so the pistol couldn't slip beneath his waistband. It didn't sit on him as well as his .357.

He raised the knocker, a brass rabbit that looked uncomfortably elongated, and let it fall. It sent an echo into the house, and the murmur of conversation inside ceased.

The door swung open, revealing William Rayner. Tim covered his surprise quickly. Rayner wore an expensively tailored suit, much like the one he'd had on in the television interview last night, and he held a gin and tonic, from the smell of it.

"Mr. Rackley, so glad you decided to come." The man offered his hand. In person his face had a decidedly mischievous cast. "William Rayner."

Tim pulled the proffered hand aside with his left and tapped Rayner's chest and stomach with the knuckles of his right, checking for a wire.

Rayner regarded him with amusement. "Good, good. We value caution." He stepped back, letting the door swing with him, but Tim didn't move from the porch. "Come now, Mr. Rackley, we certainly didn't invite you all this way to beat you with pipes."

Tim entered the foyer warily. It was a dim room, heavy with original oils and dark wood. An ornately carved newel post marked the base of a curving staircase carpeted with a brass-pinned runner. Without another glance at Tim, Rayner walked ahead into an adjoining room. Tim circled the foyer before following.

Five men—including Rayner—and a woman awaited him, sitting in elaborate armchairs and on a seasoned leather club sofa. Two of the men were twins in their late thirties with hard blue eyes, thick blond mustaches, and Popeye forearm bulges covered with reddish-blond hair. They were unbelievably sturdy, with action-figure bulk, barrel chests, and sharp-tapering lats. About average height—maybe five-ten. Though they were nearly identical, some ineffable quality gave one a harder, more focused orientation. He was holding a glass of water but sipping it like a scotch. Probably spoke fluent Twelve-Step.

A slight man with too-thick eyeglasses in fat black frames sat perched on the couch. His features were rounded and yielding, like those of a cloth doll. His *Magnum, PI*, shirt screamed out in the muted furnishings, as did the sheen of light from his bald, pointed head. He had no chin to speak of and an extremely slight nose. His upper lip bore the signs of a repaired cleft palate. His small hand swept up from between the cushions of the couch, knuckling his glasses back up the almost nonexistent bridge of his nose. Beside him sat Tim's visitor from last night.

The woman sat in one of the armchairs directly facing Tim, framed perfectly by the fireplace behind her. She was primly attractive; a thin button-up sweater showed off a lean, feminine build, and her glasses looked as if they'd been plucked off the face of a 1950s secretary. She wore her hair up, neatly styled and fixed in place by a pair of black chopsticks. The youngest of the group, she looked to be in her late twenties.

All around them rose bookcases, stretching from the floor to the twenty-foot ceiling. A sliding library ladder hooked onto a brass bar that ran the length of the far wall. The books were organized by set and series—law publications, sociology journals, psych texts. When Tim saw the rows of Rayner's own books, he recognized this as the library from which KCOM had broadcast Rayner's interview last night—it only looked like a set. His books all bore titles reminiscent of network movies from the eighties—*Violent Loss, Thwarted Vengeance, Beyond the Abyss.*

A honey-hued writing desk occupied the far corner; on it stood a sculpture of Blind Justice with her scales. This hokey prop seemed a cut below the other furnishings, perhaps because it was placed for TV. Or for Tim.

The woman smiled curtly. "What happened to your eye?"

"I fell down the stairs." Tim dropped his bag on the Persian rug. "I would like to state for the record that I have not consented to anything, that I am only here regarding a meeting about which, at present, I know nothing. Are we agreed?"

The men and the woman nodded.

"Please respond orally."

"Yes," Rayner said. "We are agreed." He had a con man's easy charm and quick grin, qualities Tim recognized all too well.

As Rayner slid behind Tim to close the door, the woman said, "Before anything else, we'd like to offer our condolences for your daughter." Her tone rang genuine, and it seemed to include some personal sadness. Had the circumstances been otherwise, Tim might have found it moving.

The man whom Tim recognized from last night rose from his chair. "I knew you'd show up, Mr. Rackley." He crossed the room and took Tim's hand. "Franklin Dumone."

Tim felt him for a wire. Dumone gestured to the others, who unbuttoned or pulled up their shirts, exposing their chests. The twins' compact, gym-tempered torsos struck a contrast to the formless flesh of the man in the loud shirt. Even the woman followed suit, pulling aside her sweater and white blouse and exposing a lace bra. She met Tim's glance unflinchingly, mild amusement playing across her lips.

Tim removed an RF emitter from his bag and walked the perimeter of the room, scanning the wand across the walls to check for any radio frequencies that indicated the presence of a digital transmitter. He paid particular attention to the electrical outlets and a grandfather clock beside the window. The others watched him with interest.

The device emitted no tones suggesting they were being recorded.

Rayner had been watching Tim with a little grin. "Are you done?"

When Tim did not respond, Rayner nodded to the severe-looking twin. With a quick flick of his hand, the twin removed Tim's G-Shock from his wrist. He tossed it to his brother, who dug in his shirt pocket, came up with a tiny screwdriver, and removed the watch's backing. With tweezers he extracted a minuscule digital transmitter, which he pocketed.

The man in the bright shirt spoke in a high-pitched, wheezy voice complicated by a number of minor speech defects. "I turned off the signal when you pulled through the gate—that's why you didn't pick it up just now."

"How long have you been listening to me?"

"Since the day of your daughter's funeral."

"We apologize for the intrusion into your privacy," Dumone said, "but we had to be sure."

They'd been party to his shooting review board, his confrontation with Tannino, and his and Dray's intimate exchange of blows last night. Tim fought to regain his focus. "Sure of what?"

"Why don't you sit down?"

Tim made no move to the couch. "Who are you, and why have you been gathering intel on me?"

The twin tightened the final screw and tossed the watch back at Tim, hard. Tim caught it in front of his face.

"I assume you know of William Rayner," Dumone said. "Social psychologist, expert on psychology and the law, and notorious cultural pundit."

Rayner raised his glass with mock solemnity. "I prefer *celebrated* cultural pundit."

"This is his teaching assistant and protégé, Jenna Ananberg. I myself am a retired sergeant from Boston PD, Major Crimes Unit. These two are Robert and Mitchell Masterson, former detectives and task-force members out of Detroit. Robert was a precision marksman, one of SWAT's top snipers, and Mitchell worked as a bomb tech in explosive ordnance disposal." After a reluctant pause, Mitchell nodded, but Robert, who'd snatched the watch from Tim's wrist, just stared at him.

Robert's aggressive bearing and the sharpness of his face reminded Tim of the Green Beret who had trained him in hand-to-hand. He'd taught Tim a close-quarters front-move, a downthrusting punch to the opponent's groin, tight and viciously hard, timed with the twisting sink of the hips to give it more force. It could shatter the pelvis like a dropped dinner plate. The Beret claimed that if the punch was correctly aligned so the knuckles struck the top of the pubic bone, it could knock a man's dick clean off. His smile when he'd related the fact had a particular gleam that told of strange appetites and vivid memories.

Robert and his brother were dangerous men, not because they gave off anger but because they exuded a fearlessness that years of training and combat had attuned Tim to distinguish. They shared a graveyard gleam in the eyes.

Dumone continued, "And this is Eddie Davis, aka the Stork. He's a former sound agent and forensic locksmith for the FBI."

The little man waved awkwardly before rewedging his hand between the couch cushions. Given the weather, the sunburn on his nose was as mystifying as his nickname.

Dumone paced behind Tim, and Tim pivoted slightly to keep him in view. "And this, fellow members of the Commission, is Timothy Rackley, a former platoon sergeant who used to wear the Rangers tab. His military training includes Close Quarter Combat School, Night Movement School, SERE School, HALO School, Jumpmaster School, Pathfinder School, Land Nav, Sniper School, Demo School, SCUBA, Urban Warfare, Mountain Warfare, Jungle Warfare. Did I leave any schools out?"

"A few." Tim noticed an antique mirror hanging on the far wall, and he crossed to it, taking a letter opener from the desk on his way.

"Would you like to name them?"

Tim touched the tip of the letter opener to the mirror. The gap between the point and the reflection indicated all was normal; a one-way would have showed none. He returned the letter opener to the desk. "I've always thought credentials are overrated."

"Oh? Why's that?"

Tim bit the inside of his lip, his impatience growing.

"When it comes down to it, everyone bleeds just about the same."

Robert, who'd risen to lean cross-armed against a bookcase, snickered. Dimpled finger marks on his T-shirt sleeves showed he'd stretched them first to get his biceps through. Neither twin had spoken yet; they were busy posturing and exuding menace. Their intensity was displayed in the flush of their cheeks. Tim knew their type from his Ranger days: competent, vigorous, and fiercely loyal to what they thought their ideals were. Not afraid to get mean.

Dumone turned back to the others and continued, "In his three years with the U.S. Marshals Service, Mr. Rackley has received three Outstanding Performance Ratings, two Distinguished Service Awards, and the Forsyth Medal of Valor for saving a fellow deputy's life, one Mr. George 'Bear' Jowalski. The September before last, Mr. Rackley kicked through the wall of a crack house, retrieved Mr. Jowalski's injured body while taking fire, and carried him to safety. Isn't that right, Mr. Rackley?"

"That's the Hollywood version, yes."

"Why didn't you stay in Spec Ops for the army?" Dumone asked. "Bump up to Delta?"

"I wanted to spend more time with—" Tim bit his lip. Rayner started to say something, but Tim held up his hand. "Listen to me carefully. I will leave if you don't tell me why I'm here. Right now."

The men and Ananberg exchanged looks, seeming to reconcile themselves to something. Dumone settled heavily into a chair. Rayner took off his jacket, revealing an elegant shirt with flared sleeves and gold cuff links, then hung it across the back of an armchair. He stepped in front of Tim, ice jiggling in his glass.

"There is one thing we all share, Mr. Rackley. Everyone in this room, including you. We all have loved ones who have been victimized by perpetrators who managed to evade justice due to loopholes in the law. Procedural defects, chain-of-possession mishaps, warrant irregularities. The courts of this country, at times, have trouble functioning. They're backed up, choked with statutes and new case law. Because of this we're forming the Commission. The Commission will operate within the strictest legal guidelines. Our criteria will be the Constitution of the United States and the Penal Code for the state of California. We'll review capital cases in which defendants have gotten off due to technicalities. The three responsibilities with which we will be concerned are those of judge, jury, and executioner. We're all judge and jury." His eyebrows drew together, forming a single silver line. "We'd like you to be our executioner."

Dumone used both arms to help himself out of the chair. He headed over to a collection of bottles on a shelf behind the desk. "Can I get you a drink, Mr. Rackley? Christ knows, I need one." He winked.

Tim looked from face to face, searching for some hint of levity. "This is not a joke." He realized his remark sounded closer to a statement than a question.

"It would certainly be an elaborate one and a considerable waste of time if it were," Rayner said. "Suffice it to say, none of us have a lot of time on our hands."

The ticktock of the grandfather clock was slightly unnerving.

"So, Mr. Rackley," Dumone said, "what do you think?"

"I think you've all been watching too many Dirty Harry movies." Tim dropped the RF emitter wand into his bag and zipped it up. "I want nothing to do with vigilante retribution."

"Of course not," Ananberg said. "We would never ask you to engage in such activities. Vigilantes are outside the law. We're an adjunct to it." She crossed her legs, lacing her hands over a knee. Her voice was soothing and had the practiced cadence of a newscaster's. "You see, Mr. Rackley, we have an immense luxury here. We can concern ourselves exclusively with the merits of a given case and the culpability of the defendant. We needn't stand on procedural formalities or permit them to get in the way of justice. Courts regularly have to make rulings irrelevant to the merits. They're not always ruling on the case itself—they're ruling preemptively to deter illegal or improper government conduct in the future. They know that if they overlook warrant limitations or Miranda rights even once, it can set a precedent that will open the way for the government to act without regard for individual rights. And that is a valid and compelling concern." She spread her hands. "For them."

"Constitutional guarantees will still function," Dumone said. "We're not in conflict with them. We're not the state."

"You understand firsthand how complex Fourth Amendment search-and-seizure issues have grown," Rayner said. "It's gotten to the point that good-faith efforts by the police fall short. The system's rough patches aren't due to crooked cops who feel they're above the law, or bleeding-heart knee-jerk judges. These are men and women like you and me, of good conscience and fair temperament, who are seeking to uphold a system that's increasingly undercut by its neurotic fear of victimizing the accused."

Robert finally chimed in with a smoker's voice, his hands flaring in disgust. "An honest cop can't even fire a shot without being waylaid by an internal investigation, shooting board . . ."

"Maybe a criminal and civil case on top of that," Mitchell said.

Dumone spoke coolly, mitigating some of the twins'

sharpness. "We need those people, and we need the system. We also need something else."

"We'll be tied not to the letter of the law but the spirit." Rayner gestured to the sculpture of Blind Justice on the desk. Their prop.

Tim noted how carefully orchestrated the presentation was. The affluent milieu, designed to impress and intimidate him, the arguments laid out succinctly, the language heavy on law and logic—Tim's language. The speakers hadn't so much as interrupted one another. Yet despite their skillful maneuvering, they also evinced circumspection and righteousness. Tim felt like a buyer annoyed with the salesman's pitch but still interested in the car.

"You're not a jury of their peers," Tim said.

"That's right," Rayner said. "We're a jury of intelligent, discerning citizens."

Robert said, "I don't know if you've ever seen a jury, but lemme tell you—they ain't your peers. They're a group of sorry-ass individuals with nothing better to do on a workday and no brains to fabricate an excuse to duck duty."

"But you'd be lying to say you don't have biases. Your system is flawed, too."

"Isn't everything?" Rayner said. "The question is, is our system *less* flawed?"

Tim took this in silently.

"Why don't you sit down, Mr. Rackley?" Ananberg said.

Tim didn't budge. "Do you have an investigative arm?"

"That's the beauty of our system," Rayner said. "We'll address only those cases that have already gone to court—cases in which suspects were let off due to procedural technicalities. These cases tend to have exhaustive evidence and reports already in the dockets, court transcripts, and case binders."

"And if they don't?"

"If they don't, we won't touch them. We're aware of our limitations—we don't consider ourselves equipped to deal with more complex investigation and evidence gathering. If the proof isn't all there, we happily defer to the court's decision."

"How do you get the court files and case binders?"

"The court files are public record. But I have several judges—close friends—who send me materials relevant to my research. They enjoy seeing their names in the acknowledgments of my books." He worked something off one of his cuff links with a fingernail. "Never underestimate vanity." A self-aware grin. "And we have certain arrangements—untraceable arrangements—with temps, mail-room workers, clerks, and the like, positioned advantageously in DA and PD offices. We get our hands on what we need our hands on."

"Why do you only review capital cases?"

"Because our capabilities for punitive action are limited. We can impose either a death sentence or nothing at all. Because of this we don't concern ourselves with lesser charges."

Robert settled back against the wall and flexed his crossed arms. "Our rehabilitation program is not yet under development." He ignored Dumone's unamused glance, his eyes on Tim, dark stones in the leathery flesh of his face.

Ananberg said, "An added benefit is, we serve as a corrective for all those death-penalty biases. The majority of those sent to death row by America's traditional courts are underprivileged minorities who can't afford proper representation—"

"Whereas we're an equal-opportunity exterminator," Mitchell said.

"Do you know, Mr. Rackley, one of the overlooked benefits of legal punishment?" Tim found Rayner's rhetorical questions to be another indication of his not-so-subtle condescension. "It removes from the victims and victims' families the moral obligation of retaliation. In doing so it prevents society from deteriorating into feuds. But when the state defaults on its ability to inflict punishment for you, you still feel it, don't you? The moral necessity to see justice done for your daughter? You'll *always* feel it—believe me. The twitch of a phantom limb."

Tim walked over, got in Rayner's space just enough to imply aggression. Robert pushed himself up off his incline against the wall, but Dumone backed him down from across the room with the briefest flutter of his hand. Tim took note of all these dynamics and plugged them in to the dominance hierarchy he was evolving in his head. Rayner didn't give the slightest indication of being intimidated.

Tim gestured at the others. "And you collected them through your work?"

"Yes. I conduct extensive subject analysis in the course of my research. It's helped me determine who would be responsive to my ideas."

"And you took an interest in me when my daughter was killed."

"Virginia's case caught our eye, yes," Ananberg said.

Tim was impressed by her decision to refrain from euphemism and refer to Ginny by name. This small, knowing touch also added credibility to Rayner's claim that everybody present had lost a family member.

"We were having a hard time finding candidates," Rayner said. "Your particular set of skills and ethics is *remarkably* rare. And the other remotely similar candidates we were considering fell too much into the rule-follower camp, which made them unlikely to partake in a venture such as this. We started looking at candidates whose lives had been marred by some personal tragedy. Especially those who'd had loved ones killed or raped by assailants who navigated through a faulty system to find their way back onto the streets. So when Ginny's story hit the news, we thought, here is someone who understands our pain."

"We didn't know, of course, that Kindell would get off *again*," Ananberg said, "but when that happened, it pretty much sealed our decision to approach you."

"We'd hoped to recruit you as a deputy marshal, when you still had access to your tracking resources," Rayner confided. "We were disappointed by your resignation."

"I never would have done anything to undermine the service," Tim said. "I still wouldn't."

Robert scowled. "Even after they betrayed you?"

"Yes." Tim turned back to Rayner. "Tell me how it started. This . . . idea."

"I met Franklin when I was in Boston for a law and psychology conference about three years ago," Rayner said. "We were on the same panel—I had lost a boy, Franklin his wife—and we had an immediate affinity for each other. We went out to a meal afterward, found ourselves a few drinks in and theorizing openly, and the idea of the Commission was hatched. The next morning, of course, we dismissed our conversation as hypothetical banter. The conference ended, and I came back to L.A. A few weeks later I had one of those nights—you know the kind of night to which I'm referring, Mr. Rackley? The kind of night when grief and vengeance take on a life of their own? They become tangible, electric." Rayner's eyes drifted.

"Yes."

"And so I called Franklin who, as fate would have it, was having a night similar to mine. We revisited the idea of the Commission, again in the safety of the night, but this time it took. It seemed less frightful in the cold light of the next morning." His eyes regained their sharp focus, and his tone became more brisk. "I had tremendous resources at hand for selecting members of the Commission. In my studies I looked for law-enforcement officers with unusually high IQs, who were sensitive to authority and policy but were also independent thinkers. Now and then someone would strike me as particularly right for the Commission. And Franklin could run background checks, contact them, bring them into our circle." He flashed a pleased little smile. "The hesitation you're displaying now, Mr. Rackley, affirms our opinion that we want you on board."

"Think of the collective experience and knowledge we have assembled in this room," Ananberg said. "All the different ways we've spent time with the law, learning its curves and contours, flaws and strengths."

"What if you disagree on a verdict?"

Rayner said, "Then we'll throw out the case and move on. Only a unanimous verdict will stand in the Commission. Unanimity is required for any policy shift as well. That way, if any of us grows uncomfortable with *anything*, we have veto power."

"Is this the entire Commission?"

"You will be the seventh and final member," Dumone said. "If you elect to join."

"And how is this little enterprise funded?"

Rayner's mustache shifted with his grin. "The books have been good to me."

"You'll draw a humble paycheck," Dumone said. "And, of course, all expenses will be covered."

"Now we'd like to clarify one point," Ananberg said. "We do not advocate cruel and unusual punishment. The executions are to be swift and painless."

"I don't go in for torture," Tim said.

Ananberg's lipsticked mouth pulled to one side in a smirk, the first break in her icy façade. Everyone seemed comfortable with letting silence fill the study for a few moments.

Tim asked, "What's the status of your *personal* cases?"

"Franklin's wife's killer disappeared after being acquitted," Rayner said. "The last reports of him were from Argentina. The man who killed the Stork's mother is currently incarcerated for a later offense. Robert and Mitchell's sister's murderer was later shot and killed in an unrelated incident, and Jenna's mother's killer was beaten to death in a gang killing over a decade ago. That's the status of our—how did you put it?—personal cases."

"And the man who killed your son?"

Bitterness passed through Rayner's eyes, then vanished. "He's still out there, my son's killer. Walking the streets. Somewhere in New York—Buffalo when last I heard."

"I bet you just can't wait to vote him guilty."

"I wouldn't touch my own case, actually." Rayner looked offended at Tim's expression of disbelief. "This is not a vengeance service." His face firmed with a stalwart pride common to maudlin World War II movies. "I could never be objective. However . . ."

"What?"

"We're going to call upon you to be. I've selected Kindell's case for the Commission. It'll be the seventh and final one we examine in our first phase."

Tim felt himself flush at the thought of another crack at Kindell. He hoped his longing wasn't too clear on his face. He gestured at the others. "How about theirs?"

Rayner shook his head. "Yours is the only personal case we're going to examine."

"Why'd I get so lucky?"

"It's the only case that precisely fits our profile. An L.A.

crime, a lot of media heat, the trial botched due to a procedural violation."

"L.A. is key from an operational perspective," Dumone
said. "We're only comfortable dealing with cases in this
area. Our strongest contacts are here."

"We've spent a lot of time here, me and Mitch," Robert
said, "smelling the street, figuring out how to operate—operate invisibly. You know the drill. Well-placed contacts.
Phone lines. Car rentals. Back routes around town."

"You must have well-placed contacts in Detroit," Tim
said.

"We're known there. In Hell-A nobody's anybody until
they're somebody."

"Once we start traveling, dealing with other court systems and police bureaus, it really opens us up," Dumone
said. "Not to mention the trail it leaves. Airline tickets, ho-
tels." His eyes twinkled. "We dislike trails."

"Something tells me there's another angle," Tim said.
"Like Ginny's case being a carrot you can dangle in front
of me. That's why it's the 'seventh and final' one."

Rayner seemed pleased—Tim was talking his language.
"Yes, of course. No need to pretend. We do need an insurance policy of sorts, to make sure you're not doing this just
for revenge. We want to ensure that you stick around, that
you're committed to our cause. We're not here merely to
serve your agenda—there's a greater social good at stake."

"What if I don't think the other executions are justified?"

"Then vote against all six of them, and we move to
Kindell."

"How do you know I won't do precisely that?"

Dumone's head was tilted back at such an angle to suggest authority and mild amusement. "We know you'll be
fair."

"And if you're not *equally* fair, just, and competent when

we're deliberating the Kindell case," Ananberg said, "we'll ask you to recuse yourself or I'll personally vote against execution. You won't muscle a guilty past us."

Dumone settled back in his chair. "It serves you, too. To delay Kindell's case until last."

"How do you figure?"

Rayner said, "If we ruled to execute Kindell first, you'd be the most obvious suspect."

"But if we rule to kill him after two or three other high-profile executions, the suspicion will be shifted off you," Dumone said.

Tim reflected for a moment, silently. Rayner watched him with shiny eyes, seeming to enjoy this all a bit too much.

"We know about your accomplice theory," Rayner said. "And rest assured—I can obtain information that you can't get access to—from all sides of the case. The public defender's notes from his interview with Kindell, media investigator reports, maybe even police logs. We'll get to the bottom of your daughter's murder. You'll get her the fair trial she never received."

Tim studied Rayner for a moment, his stomach knotting with anxiety and excitement. Despite his aversion to Rayner, he couldn't deny that some connection existed—to another father who had lost a child. To someone who actually took Tim's accomplice theory seriously because he understood what it meant to be plagued.

Tim finally crossed to one of the armchairs and sat. On the low table before him was an American Psychological Association journal titled *Psychology, Public Policy, and Law*. On the light brown cover, Rayner was listed as the principal author of two articles.

Keeping his eyes on the journal, Tim said quietly, "I just need to know who killed my daughter. Why she was

killed." Hearing himself express this deep-rooted impera-
tive so starkly—as a plea directed out at the unfair universe—gave it a sudden reality and pitifulness. His eyes
moistened. Quickly following came a stab of self-disdain
for revealing emotion here, in front of these hardened
strangers. The childhood lesson his father had drummed
into his head: Never give up the personal—it will return as
a weapon wielded against you.

He waited until his face felt less heavy before raising it.
He was surprised to see how uneasy his grief made Robert
and Mitchell. They'd grown fidgety, uncomfortable, suddenly real—their own remembered pain cutting through
the barriers, washing the aggression right out of them.

"We understand," Dumone said.

Robert said, "You get to serve your personal cause—
pursuing your daughter's killer or killers—and the bigger
legal issues . . ."

"—illuminated—" Mitchell said.

"—by the hell you went through. The rest of us don't get
that."

"Why did you choose L.A.?" Tim asked.

"Because this city has no notion of accountability, of responsibility," Rayner said. "As you're aware, L.A.'s court
rulings, especially for media-intensive cases, seem to go to
the highest bidder. Justice isn't administered by the courts
here, it's administered by box-office grosses and a well-
oiled press."

"O.J. Simpson just bought a one-point-five-million-
dollar house in Florida," Mitchell said. "Kevin Mitnick
hacked in to the Pentagon, now he's got a talk radio show
out of Hollywood. LAPD's got a scandal a week. Cop
killers and drug dealers land record deals. Hookers marry
studio moguls. It's got no memory, Los Angeles. There's
no logic here. No rhyme. No reason. No justice."

"The cops here," Robert said, with surprising vehemence, "they don't give a shit. There's so many murders, so much indifference. This town just chews people up."

"It's seductive, and, like most things seductive, it burns you with indifference. Kills you with apathy."

"That's why this city." Robert crossed his thick arms again. "L.A. deserves it."

"We want the executions to serve as crime deterrents," Rayner added, "so they'll have to be high-profile."

"So that's what this is?" Tim glanced around the room. "A grand experiment. Sociology in action. You're gonna bring justice to the big city?"

"Nothing quite so grandiose," Ananberg said. "The death penalty has never been a proven deterrent."

"But it's never been deployed in this fashion." Mitchell was standing now, gesturing concisely with flattened hands. "Courts are clean and safe, and—due to the appeals process—their rulings lack a sense of threatening immediacy. Courts don't scare criminals. The thought of someone coming unexpectedly in the night will. I know there are certainly methodological complications with our plan, but there's no denying that murderers and rapists will be aware there's another level of the law they may have to answer to—it's not just the court game. They might hop through a loophole, but we'll be out there, waiting."

Mitchell demonstrated the commonsense logic and unaffected eloquence of a self-taught thinker; Tim realized he'd underestimated the man's intelligence at first glance, probably due to his intimidating physical presence.

Robert was nodding emphatically, in aggressive agreement with his brother. "The streets of Singapore look pretty graffiti-free to me."

Rayner's chuckle drew a sharp look from Ananberg.

"Correlation is not causation." Ananberg wove her hands over a knee. "My point is simply that we shouldn't expect some sort of drastic social impact. We're acting as the mortar between the cracks in the law. No more, no less. Let's be frank about what we're doing. We're not saving the world. In a few specific cases, we're serving justice."

Robert set down his glass with a thunk. "All me and Mitch are saying is, we're here to kick a little ass and dispense a little justice. And if it trickles back to the motherfuckers that there's a new sheriff in town . . . well, hell, that won't break our hearts either."

"It beats whining and building memorials," Mitchell added.

The playfulness gone from his eyes, Dumone turned to Tim. "The twins and the Stork will be your operational team. They're there merely to provide you support. Use them as you see fit, or not at all."

Now, finally, Tim understood the hostility he'd elicited in the twins from the first moment, their blatant jockeying with Tim before the others. "Why would I be in charge?"

"We lack the operating skills that someone with your unusual combination of training and field experience brings to the table. We lack a subtlety of execution needed for this first phase of, uh, executions."

Rayner said, "We need a primary operator who's extraordinarily levelheaded on the front line." One of his hands circled, then settled in his pocket. "These executions need to be carefully orchestrated so the occasion of a shoot-out with law enforcement never arises. Ever."

Dumone freshened his glass at the small bar behind the desk. "As I'm sure you're aware, there are a truckload of ways things can go south. And if they do, we need a man who'll keep his head, who won't gun his way out of trouble. The Stork is not a tactical operator."

The Stork's smile was flat and generically curved, like a slice of watermelon. "No, sir."

"And Rob and Mitch are good aggressive cops, like I was when the sap was still rising." Dumone's smile held some sadness; something was hidden beneath it, perhaps the blood-spotted handkerchief. He tipped his head toward Tim deferentially. "But we haven't been trained to kill, and we're not Spec Ops–cool under fire."

"It's been a long, frustrating haul closing in on a viable and receptive candidate," Rayner said wearily.

Tim took a moment with this, and they let him. Rayner's eyebrows were raised, anticipating Tim's next question. "How do you protect against someone breaking all these elaborate rules you've set up? There's no controlling authority."

Rayner held up a hand in a calming gesture, though no one was particularly agitated. "That is one of our primary concerns. Which is why we have a no-tolerance policy."

"Our contract is exclusively oral, of course," Ananberg said, "as we don't want to set anything incriminating down in writing. And this contract includes a kill clause."

"A kill clause?"

"Legally speaking, a kill clause sets forth prenegotiated conditions detailing what will occur should a contract be terminated. Ours goes into effect the instant any member of the Commission breaks any of our protocols."

"And what are those prenegotiated conditions?"

"The kill clause dictates that the Commission be immediately dissolved. All remaining documentation—which we go to every effort to keep to a minimum—will be destroyed. With the exception of tying up loose ends, there

will be no future Commission activity of any kind."
Rayner's face hardened. "Zero tolerance."

"We're well aware that the Commission places us on a
slippery slope," Ananberg said. "So we're anxious to ensure that there will be no sliding."

"And if someone withdraws?"

"Go with God," Rayner said. "We presume that what
passes here remains here, as it is equally incriminating to
whoever elects to leave." He grinned a smirky grin. "Mutual assured destruction makes for a nifty little insurance
policy."

Tim did not return the grin but studied the practiced
lines around Rayner's mouth. William Rayner, vehement
proponent of the insurance policy.

Ananberg said, "The Commission would go on brief
hiatus until we found an appropriate replacement."

Tim leaned back in the armchair so he could feel his Sig
pressing into the small of his back. He gauged his angle to
the door—not good. "And if I decide against joining?"

"We would hope that, as someone who's lost a daughter,
you would appreciate our perspective and leave us to our
work," Rayner said. "If you were to contact the authorities,
be advised there is no incriminating evidence on site. We
will deny ever having had this conversation. And to say our
collective words are greatly respected in the legal community is something of an understatement."

All eyes were suddenly on Tim. The ticking of the
grandfather clock punctuated the silence. Ananberg went
to the desk, turned a key, then removed a dark cherry box
from one of the drawers. Tilting it, she opened the hinged
lid, revealing a gleaming Smith & Wesson .357—service
make—nestled in the felt interior. She closed the box and
set it on the desktop.

Rayner lowered his voice so it seemed he was addressing only Tim. "When people endure such a . . . bureaucratic betrayal as the one the courts handed you, as the one the U.S. Marshals Service handed you, they contend with it in different ways, most of them bad. Some get angry, some get depressed, some find God." One of his eyebrows drew up, almost disappearing beneath the line of his hair. "What will you do, Mr. Rackley?"

Tim decided he'd had his fill of questions, so he kept his eyes on Dumone. "How do they feel about taking a backseat? Operationally?"

Dumone's and Robert's fidgeting broadcast that this was well-covered ground.

The Stork shrugged and adjusted his glasses. "I got no problem," he said, though no one had asked him.

"They'll deal with it," Dumone said.

"That's not what I asked."

"They understand the necessity of bringing in a high-demand operator, and they're reconciling themselves to the change." Dumone's voice gathered edge, and Tim could hear the tough Boston cop in it.

Tim looked at Mitchell, then Robert. "Is that true?"

Mitchell looked away, studying the wall. Robert had a slight upper lip, so when he smiled, his mouth was a sheen of teeth and hair. His voice came slick and sharp, like a scalpel. "You're the boss."

Tim turned back to Dumone. "Call me when they're reconciled."

Dumone's shoes shushed across the rug as he approached. He stood over Tim, gazing down at him. His face, a blend of wear and texture, held in it a dark-tinted element of calm that Tim thought might be wisdom. "We'd like an answer now."

"We *need* an answer now," Robert said. "Either this proposal strikes a chord with you or it doesn't. There's no thinking about it."

"This isn't a gym membership," Tim said.

"Our offer terminates the minute you walk out that door," Rayner said.

"I don't negotiate like this."

Now Mitchell—"Those are our terms."

"All right, then." Tim stood and walked out.

Rayner caught him outside near the gate. "Mr. Rackley. Mr. Rackley!"

Tim turned, keys in his hand.

Rayner's face was red with the cold, and his breath was visible. His shirt had come untucked. He looked less smug out here, away from his first-among-equals reign in the library. "I apologize for that. I can be a little . . . firm sometimes. We're just eager to begin our work." He moved to rest his hand on the trunk of Tim's car but stopped, his fingertips hovering an inch off the metal. He seemed to have a tough time manufacturing his next words. "You are our top choice. Our sole choice. We took a great deal of care in selecting you. If you don't sign on, we have to start the search over—a long process. Take more time if you need it."

"I intend to."

Tim pulled out into the street. When he glanced into his rearview mirror, Rayner was still standing in front of the house, watching him drive off.

**13** AS TIM TURNED INTO HIS CUL-DE-SAC, HE SPOTTED DU-
mone leaning against a parked Lincoln Town
Car at the far curb, arms crossed, like a waiting
chauffeur. Tim pulled up beside him and rolled down his
window.

Dumone winked. "Touché."

Tim glanced around to see if any of the neighbors had
taken note of them. "Touché yourself."

Dumone gestured to the backseat with a tilt of his head.
"Why don't you come for a ride?"

"Why don't you get off my street?"

"I wanted to apologize."

"For being rude?"

Dumone's laugh was worn, and it crackled around the
edges like an old LP. "Christ no. For underestimating you.
That hard-sell, tough-cop bit. At my age I should know
better."

Tim's lips pressed together in a half grin.

Dumone jerked his head again. "Come on. Hop in."

"If it's just the same, why don't you take a ride with me?"

"Fair enough." When Dumone pulled his frame into
Tim's passenger seat, he let out a textured groan like a bel-
lows collapsing. He removed a Remington from his hip and
a small .22 from an ankle holster and set them in the center
console. "Just so you can listen without being distracted."

Tim drove a few blocks, pulled into the deserted back
parking lot of Ginny's old elementary school, and killed
the lights. Dumone's chest jerked with a held-in cough.

Tim gazed out the windshield so he could pretend for Dumone's sake he didn't notice.

"This that school where those three teenagers went on that shooting spree?"

"No," Tim said. "That was at the other Warren, a high school south of downtown."

"Kids shooting kids." Dumone shook his head, grunted, then shook his head again.

For a while they watched the unlit school in silence.

"When you get on in life," Dumone said, "you start viewing the world a bit differently. Your idealism doesn't die, but it's mitigated. You start thinking, hell, maybe life's just what we make it, and maybe our job is to leave this place a little better than it was when we came in. I don't know. Could be all old-man disconnect. Maybe that poet was right, that youth holds knowledge and everything we learn as we get older takes us away from it."

"I don't read poetry."

"Yeah. Neither do I. The wife . . ." Even in the dark his eyes shone jarringly blue, the blue of newborns and summer skies and other things discordant and mawkish. He worked at a hangnail, his head down-bent, skin texturing in rough folds beneath his chin. He reminded Tim of an old lion. "You see, Tim—is it all right if I call you Tim?"

"Of course."

"To try to find meaning, give meaning, to shape things and people for the better, you have to navigate through a gray zone. And to do so you need ethics. You need to be even and just. You are both."

"What about the others?"

"Rayner is vain, and dumb in the ways vanity makes you, but he's also brilliant. And he's extremely competent at reading people and cases."

"And Robert?"

"You have a problem with Robert?"

"He just seems a little"—Tim searched for the most displeasing adjective he could conjure—"nonlinear."

"He's a great operator. Loyal to a fault. Some of his connections are a touch loose, but he always falls in."

"He and his brother don't seem particularly eager to play betas to my alpha."

"They need to learn from you, Tim. They just don't know it yet. They felt their operating skills were sufficient. They didn't see a need for you, but me, Rayner, and Ananberg made clear we weren't willing to free them up or even review cases without someone like you in place. We need this thing to run not just well but seamlessly. And you're really the only candidate within our reach who has the skill set to make that happen."

"How did you determine that?"

Dumone's lips set in a manner to suggest mild annoyance. "Rayner found you after Ginny's death—he'd been putting together profiles of all-stars in the L.A. law-enforcement community. Running psych assessments and whatever other mad-scientist crap he gets up to at that office of his. Once he zeroed in, the boys went to work gathering intel as best they could. The more we saw, the more we liked."

"Who's to say 'the boys' will fall in under my command?"

"Because I'll tell them to."

"They're afraid of you."

"No. Respectful. Intimidated, maybe. I met them right after their sister's death, helped them find a way through some of their grief. Not the grief-group couch-lay crap, but the real deal. How I handled it. Cops. How cops deal. You help someone when they're raw like that, they never forget. They're always grateful. And they might look up to me a bit more than I deserve. They're different from you, different from me, even. They need guidance. I keep them close at hand, keep an eye on them."

"Sounds like a case of keeping your enemies nearer."

"An overstatement," Dumone said. "They're solid men."

"For what you're proposing, they need to be more than that."

"No. They need a leader." He coughed again, moistly, into a fist. "A new leader."

"That might not be a role I want." Tim reached for the keys and turned the engine over.

"I know. That's why I chose you." Dumone sighed heavily but without theatricality. "What none of the others understand is that joining the Commission for you would be a sacrifice, not a release. You'd have to be willing to renounce your values, your righteousness. You'd be vilified by precisely the kinds of organizations and individuals you've always valued." He reached over and tapped two knobby fingers against Tim's chest. "And even worse, you'd feel a hypocrite in your own heart. But in calmer moments, when flag waving and slogans no longer seem quite so weighty, you'll also realize that you took direct action that had direct results. It's tough to lead the way when you're standing on a soapbox, even if that soapbox is platinum or sterling or made of the wood of the True Cross." He shifted noisily to face Tim, bearing his weight on his hip. "If you do this, there will be fewer girls raped, fewer people murdered. And maybe at twilight, in our final reckoning, that's all we'll really have to hold on to."

It struck Tim that in the respect Dumone so naturally commanded, in his gravity and acumen, resided a deep moral authority, and that any hope for justice apart from and beyond the law resided precisely in such integrity embodied in like individuals.

"When someone is mugged, raped, killed, *society* is the victim," Dumone continued. "*Society* has a right to assert its position. We don't represent the victims, we represent our community. We can be that voice. What you want to try to accomplish, it can be done here." He smiled, warmly, and it attenuated the pain in his eyes. "Something to think about at least."

"Are you out of your fucking mind?" Dray leaned over the table, her eyes the same cornered-cat intensity they were when she lifted weights or ran. A piece of popcorn fell from the fold in her sweatshirt; she'd just gotten back from a Meg Ryan movie with Trina, the most girlie of her friends and the only one with whom she indulged her occasional appetite for maudlin movies and pedicures and other things she thought unbefitting a POST-certified female range master with a hundred-fifty-pound bench press.

"I don't know. Maybe." Tim leaned back in the chair, crossing his arms.

The wind kicked up outside, whooshing off the east side of the house, making the dimly lit kitchen seem a small and quiet place of shelter.

"Have you talked to Bear about this?"

"Absolutely not. I'm not talking to anybody."

"Why me?"

Tim felt a sudden pressure in his face. "Because you're my wife."

Dray grabbed his hand. "Then listen to me. These people are preying on your pain. Like a cult. Like some screwed-up self-help group. Don't let them make your decisions. Make your own." Her tone held an anomalous note of pleading.

"I am making my own. But I'd rather act within some context. With some element of order. Of law."

"No. The institutions we're part of are the law. What they're creating, in there, is not."

"And what you and Fowler were advocating? That was lawful?"

"At least it was authentic. At least I don't need a roomful of fat men to tell me what to do."

Tim pursed his lips. "They're not *all* fat."

But Dray's face held no levity. "I never told you this, because you're vain enough already. And even though I love it, your vanity, I don't think it needs any help. But the pride you took in being a deputy marshal, it was infectious. I love the way you talked about it, like a calling, like you were a priest or something. And I bought into it, that energy. The marshals who have no hidden agenda, not like the Feebs or the Company. The marshals who are there for the raw enforcement of federal law. Upholding individual constitutional rights. Keeping abortion clinics open. Escorting black first-graders to school in desegregated New Orleans." Her face held an atypical note of shyness before it returned to a harder cast. "And so this thing with this house in Hancock Park, I just can't believe that you, who swore to uphold and protect the courts, would consider it."

"I'm not a deputy anymore."

"Maybe not, but this . . . *Commission*"—she nearly spat the word out—"it has no checks and balances. If you want some outlet for your rage, at—at Kindell, at Ginny, at yourself, I understand that. Believe me, I do. But take a real one. Go shoot Kindell and face the music. Why build all this . . . scaffolding around it?"

"It's not scaffolding. It's justice. And order."

Dray's expression shifted to a weary exasperation, a look he had grown to anticipate and dread. "Tim, don't be

impressed with straw ethics and ten-cent words." She bit
the inside of her cheek. "So if no accomplice pops up and
you rule against Kindell, you get to kill him."

"Justly. He'll have had a trial—one that focuses only on
his guilt, not procedure. And if we uncover evidence that an
accomplice *was* involved, I could always elect to leak that
information into the right hands and have Kindell and the
accomplice prosecuted. Remember, there's no double jeopardy, since Kindell never went to trial. It's not about getting
him killed, it's about having Ginny's murder *addressed*."

"And where will this magical evidence come from?"

"I'll have access to the PD and DA investigative reports.
And Kindell probably shared with his PD what went down
that night. Let's just hope it's indicated somewhere in the
notes."

"Why not go to the PD directly?"

"There's no way a PD would betray confidentiality to
me. But Rayner's got the inside line on that file. And that
file might get us closer to the accomplice."

"It sure as hell isn't the straightest distance between two
points."

"We never had the option to take the straightest distance.
Not judiciously."

"Well, I've been poking around the case a bit already.
Peeks took the anonymous call the night of Ginny's
death—he was the deputy working the desk. And he said
the caller sounded highly agitated, really upset. It was his
gut that it wasn't an accomplice or someone who could be
in on it. Just a hunch, but Peeks is pretty buttoned-down."

"Any description of the voice?"

"Nothing helpful. You know, male adult. No accent or
lisp or anything. Might've just been what it was."

"Might've been a good performance." Not until he felt
the wave of disillusionment did he realize how much he'd

been hanging on his accomplice theory. "Or maybe I was wrong. Maybe I misinterpreted. Maybe it *was* just Kindell."

Dray took a deep breath and held it before exhaling. "I've been debating having a little chat with Kindell."

"Come on, Dray. The PD would have advised him strenuously not to say a word about the case—a new confession could open him up again."

"Maybe I could get him to talk."

"What, are you gonna beat it out of him?" He was all reason and circumspection right now, but the thought had occurred to him with alarming frequency.

"I wish." She grimaced. "No. Of course not."

"All talking to Kindell will do is alert his accomplice—if there is one—that we're looking. And then the accomplice will know we're coming, and he'll cover his tracks or disappear. And you'll wind up with a restraining order slapped on you. What we have going for us is the fact that no one knows we're exploring this."

"You're right. Plus, if you idiots end up taking him out, I'd be a key suspect if word leaked I'd visited him." She laced her fingers and reverse-cracked her knuckles. "I ordered the preliminary-hearing transcripts from Kindell's previous cases."

"How did you do that?"

"As a citizen. They're public record. Evidently the stenographer doesn't type up the actual trial transcripts unless the case gets appealed, but the prelim hearings should be enough for me to get a handle on the specifics. I debated contacting the LAPD detectives who worked the cases, seeing what they had in their logs, but there's no way they'd talk to me. Not after interfacing with Gutierez and Harrison, and not given who I am."

"How long will it take to get the transcripts?"

"Tomorrow. Court clerks don't quite snap to when it's not an official request."

"It looks like we're both being unofficial."

"You can't put this in a category with what you're considering. Don't even try."

"Everything's imperfect, Dray. But maybe the Commission can be closer to justice than what we've gotten. Maybe it can be that voice."

"You really want to rededicate your life to this? To hate?"

"I'm not doing it because of hate. The opposite, actually."

She drummed her fingers on the table, hard. Her hands were small and feminine; her delicate nails recalled the girl she had been before she put on a sheath of muscle and enrolled in the academy. Tim had met her only after she'd become a deputy. At his first Thanksgiving with her family, when her older brothers had proudly and with some silent element of warning shown him Dray's high-school yearbook, he'd hardly recognized the pixie face in the photos. She was now bigger and more powerful, and she'd taken on a toughened sexuality. The first time they'd gone to the range together, Tim had watched her from the shade of the overhang, her hips cocked, holster high-riding her hip, a squint drawing her cheek high and tight beneath a water-blue eye, and he'd thought for not the first time that she'd been spun from the daydream of some sugar-buzzed, comic-book-gorged adolescent.

Her lips were pursed, perfectly shaped, and chapped. Gazing at them, he realized that he wanted them not to be dry from crying, and in that he felt the depth of his continued love for her. He had told her about Rayner's proposal because she was the second leg on which he moved forward through life, and that reality, that trust that had been forged and built upon through eight solid years of their marriage, held true regardless of circumstance or even estrangement.

"Come here," he said.

She stood and trudged around the table as he scooted his chair back. She sat in his lap, and he leaned forward, pressing his face to the bare fan of skin revealed beneath the back collar of her stretched T-shirt. Warmth.

"I know you feel like you've lost so much so quickly. I do, too." Dray shifted in his lap so she was looking down at him across the bulge of her shoulder. "But there's more we can lose."

Tim ached with an uncharacteristic fatigue. "I'm tired of sleeping on the couch, Dray. We're not helping each other here."

She stood abruptly and walked a half turn around the kitchen. "I know. I've got all this . . . all this *anger*. When I pass the bathroom, I see her on her stool brushing her teeth, and in the backyard I see her trying to get that damn kite untangled, the yellow one we got her in Laguna, and every time I get that ache, I've got a need to blame someone. And I don't want us to keep on tearing at each other in the middle of all this. Or worse, I don't want us to go numb around each other."

Tim rose and rubbed his hands. A childish urge gripped him—to scream, to yell, to sob and plead. Instead he said, "I understand." His throat was closing, distorting his voice. "We shouldn't stay on top of each other if we're winding up hurting each other in small, spiteful ways."

"But a part of me feels like we should. I mean, maybe that's something we need to do. Hate each other. Slug it out. Fight and scream until the blame's gone and there's just . . . us."

He could see in her eyes that she knew otherwise, that

she was just trying to convince herself. "I can't fight that kind of fight," he said. "Not against you."

"I can't either." She shook her head, roughly, like a child. The chair creaked when she sat again. She dipped her head and let out a sigh. "If you're gonna do this thing, with those men, you're gonna need a safe house. Because I'm not getting implicated in it."

"I know."

"That crew sounds pretty geared up on surveillance."

"They are. And I don't want their eyes on you or this house. I'm gonna be in it pretty good with the criminal element, too, and I won't put you one inch at risk if one of my targets catches wind of me coming."

She sighed, the heel of her hand sliding from cheek to forehead. "So where's that leave us?"

They faced each other across the kitchen, both of them knowing the answer. Tim finally mustered the courage to say it. "We need some time off anyway."

A tear arced down her cheek. "Uh-huh."

"I'll get my things together."

"Not permanently. It's not permanent."

"Just enough for us to catch our breath. Get some perspective back on each other."

"And for you to kill some people." She looked away when he tried to meet her eyes.

He packed in twenty minutes, amazed at how little he had amassed over the years that he held to be essential. His laptop, some clothes, a few toiletries. Dray followed him silently from room to room like a heartsick dog, but neither of them spoke. With a stack of shirts draped over his arm, he stood in the threshold of Ginny's room. Moving out of the house where his murdered daughter grew up seemed to constitute some formal trespass, and he feared the unknown emotional consequences it might bring.

As he loaded up his car, Dray watched him from the porch in her bare feet, shivering. The after-scent of a neighbor's barbecue lingered in the air, smoky and domestic. He finished and walked over and kissed her. Her mouth felt both moist and dry.

"Where are you going?" she asked.

"I'm not sure." He cleared his throat once, hard. "We have a little over twenty grand in our savings account. I'm gonna take out five probably, soon. But don't worry, I'll leave the rest until we figure out what to do."

"Of course. Whatever."

He got in his car and shut the door. The clock on the dash read 12:01. Dray knocked on the window. She was shivering hard now, her whole body shaking.

He rolled down the window.

"Damn it, Timothy." She was crying now, openly. "Damn it."

She leaned over, and they kissed again, a quick one on the mouth.

He rolled up the window and backed out into the street. It wasn't until he turned the corner that he remembered it was Valentine's Day.

**14** **TIM WAS WAITING IN HIS CAR ACROSS THE STREET** with a brick of hundreds in his lap when the manager shuffled inside the four-story building on the corner of Second and Traction, holding a cluster of keys on a jail-style ring and a steaming double-cupped coffee bearing the ubiquitous Starbucks logo. As part of the rejuvenation push for downtown, the civic promoters had given a face-lift to economy housing. This area of Little Tokyo housed artists, recovering druggies, and other people at the fringe of economic sanity. In a building like this, Tim could pay cash up front without raising any eyebrows. Plus, since it was a subsidized property, all utilities would be included with the rent; that would leave him fewer paper trails with which to contend.

The plates on his car—good through September—he'd pulled from a smashed-to-hell Infiniti at Doug Kay's salvage yard. During his years in the service, Tim had been particularly good about routing seized and totaled vehicles to Kay, precisely so he could cash in on a favor like this if the shit hit. His tires had been replaced by the previous owner—they were a widely used Firestone brand, nothing factory-specific and traceable.

A new Nokia cell phone bulged in his shirt pocket. He'd rented it just up the street, in a shop where little English was spoken. He'd plopped down a healthy security deposit and paid out two hundred in cash for a month of unlimited domestic minutes, and because of this, the wizened, diminutive store owner had been less meticulous about eyeing the false name with which Tim had signed the contract. International calling was restricted. Tim selected the option to block Caller ID on outgoing calls.

The J-town crowd was mixed, Caucasian and East Asian, with a few blacks thrown in for good measure. Tim could dissolve right into the melting pot here and benefit from the kind of who-gives-a-shit anonymity to be found only on downscale city blocks.

Tim crossed the street in a jog, lugging his first load of clothing, and slipped through the building's front door. The manager—gay, going by his right-ear pierce and JOSIE AND THE PUSSYCATS T-shirt—an ex–aspiring actor from his upright carriage and stagy comportment, fussed with the locks to the manager's office while juggling his coffee and pinching a stack of mail between his elbow and love handle. He finally found the correct key, shoved open the door with a knee, dumped the mail on the desk, and collapsed into a stuffing-exposed office chair as if he'd just braved Everest's north face without oxygen.

He mustered a smile when Tim entered, turning down the volume on a small-screen TV that took up half his desk. A KCOM Menendez brothers retrospective flickered on silently. "Can't *resist* true-crime stories," he stage-whispered.

"Neither can I."

The drab room, in all likelihood a converted janitor's office, had been livened up with a few framed headshots on the walls. Beside a toothy Linda Evans, John Ritter gazed out with woeful earnestness. Next to them hung a few more posed eight-by-tens of actors Tim did not recognize, but who he guessed were former stars by their exuberant use of exclamation points and trite exhortations about following dreams and staying real. The photos were all signed with Sharpie pens, the inscriptions made out to Joshua.

Joshua followed Tim's eyes to the photos and shrugged, feigning dismissiveness. "A few colleagues of mine. From my days on the stage." He flared his arms, theatrically but with an element of self-deprecation that Tim appreciated. "I bowled them over at the Ahmanson with my Sancho Panza." He seemed disappointed by Tim's blank look. "It's a supporting role in a musical. Never mind. What can I help you with?"

Tim adjusted his armload of shirts and the bag slung over his shoulder. His coiled laptop cable was sticking out of his back pocket. "I saw from your sign outside you have apartment availability."

"Apartment availability. Yes, well. So formal." When Joshua smiled, Tim realized he was wearing lip gloss. "I can rent you a single on the fourth floor for four twenty-five a month. To be honest, it could use some freshening up, maybe a throw rug or two—let's make it four even." He shook a jeweled finger in Tim's direction jokingly. "But I'm not going any lower."

"That'll be fine." Tim set down his things and counted twelve hundreds on the desk between them. "I assume this will cover the first and last months and the security deposit. Fair?"

"Fairer than springtime. I'll get the paperwork together—we can deal with it later." Joshua slid out from behind the desk as Tim gathered up his possessions. "I'll show you the apartment."

"The key's fine. I can't imagine the place has got too many bells and whistles that need explaining."

"No, no, it doesn't." Joshua cocked his head. "What happened to your eye?"

"I walked into a door."

Joshua returned Tim's gentle smile, then grabbed a key from a pegboard hook behind him and offered it across his desk. "You're in 407."

Tim shifted his shirts so he could take the key. "Thank you."

Joshua leaned back in his chair, knocking the John Ritter frame askew. He adjusted it quickly, then stopped, embarrassed. A can of shaving cream fell from Tim's unzipped bag and rolled across the floor. Weighed down with his things, Tim made no move to pick it up.

Joshua smiled sadly at him. "It wasn't supposed to work out like this, was it?"

"No," Tim said. "I suppose not."

The key fit a Schlage single-cylinder knob lock. There was no dead bolt, but Tim didn't mind, since the door was solid-core with a steel frame.

The square of the room had a single large window that overlooked a fire-escape platform, bright red and yellow Japanese signs, and a busy street. Aside from a few worn patches, the carpet was in surprisingly good shape, and the alcove kitchen came equipped with a narrow refrigerator and chipped green tile. All in all, the place was bare and a touch depressing, but clean. Tim hung his four shirts in the closet and dropped his bag on the floor. He removed his Sig from the back of his pants and placed it on the kitchen counter, then pulled a small tool kit from his bag.

With a few twists of a Phillips-head screwdriver, he removed the entire doorknob. He drew out the Schlage cylinder from its housing and replaced it with a Medeco—another item he'd scrounged up at Kay's salvage yard. Because of their six tumblers and the uneven spacing, angled cuts, and altered depth of the keys, Medecos were Tim's locks of choice. Virtually impossible to pick. The new cylinder came with only a single key, which Tim slipped into his pocket.

Next he connected his PowerBook to the Nokia and accessed the Internet through his home account. He'd leave the apartment's phone jack dormant, thereby avoiding any records linked to a landline and an address. He was not surprised to see that his password no longer worked at the Department of Justice Web site, but he wouldn't have used the site extensively anyway, as he knew that all traffic was closely monitored and recorded. Instead he ran Rayner's name through a Google search and came up with a smattering of articles and promotional Web sites for Rayner's books and research.

In clicking around he discovered that Rayner had grown up in Los Angeles, gone to college at Princeton, and received his Ph.D. in psychology from UCLA. He'd been involved in a number of progressive experiments, for which he'd been widely praised and criticized. In one of them, a group dynamics study he'd run with students at UCLA over spring break in 1978, he'd separated his subjects into hostages and captors. The pseudo captors had grown so identified with their roles that they'd begun abusing the hostages, both emotionally and physically, and the study had been called off amid a storm of controversy.

Rayner's son, Spenser, was murdered in 1986, his body dumped off Highway 5. The FBI, monitoring a truck-stop pay phone as part of a mob sting, inadvertently recorded a panicked trucker, Willie McCabe, describing the murder to his brother in the course of seeking advice on whether he should turn himself in. The wiretap warrant, of course, did not extend to McCabe, so his incriminating comments were deemed inadmissible in court.

It occurred to Tim that Rayner had strong secondary motivations for not now focusing his vigilante energies on McCabe—having his son's killer on the loose elevated his cause and gave it a sales hook. Plus, Rayner, and his connection with McCabe, was too public. He'd be a leading suspect in the event of foul play.

After McCabe's case was dismissed, Rayner had begun to focus on the legal aspects of social psychology. One journalist went so far as to refer to him as a constitutional expert. Rayner and his wife, like an alarming majority of couples who lose a child, split within the first year after their son's death. Tim couldn't deny the sense of distress provoked by the possibility of his and Dray's bolstering the divorce statistic further.

Rayner had really come into his own after his son's death, publishing his first bestseller—a social-psychology study packaged as a self-help book. Tim found a review in *Psychology Today* bemoaning the fact that Rayner's books had grown thinner and more anecdotal each time out. It certainly hadn't hurt his sales. Another article stated that Rayner had become less involved with his teaching, though it did not make clear whether that had been his decision or the university's. He was now an adjunct professor who taught two occasional yet wildly popular undergraduate courses.

Tim logged on to the *Boston Globe* Web site next and ran a check on Franklin Dumone. He was not surprised to find that in his thirty-one years on the job, Dumone had been an extremely capable detective, then sergeant. Because of the arrest record of the Major Crimes Unit under his tenure, Dumone had grown to become something of a local legend. He'd retired after he'd arrived home one evening to find his wife beaten and strangled. Her alleged killer had been someone who'd just gotten out of a fifteen-year stint in the pen; Dumone had been his original arresting officer, catching up to him with a still-alive five-year-old girl in the trunk of his car. The killer's prison sentence, like so many others, had merely provided time for notions of revenge to evolve.

The *Detroit Free Press*'s Web archives housed only a few articles involving the Masterson twins, most of them fluff pieces on twins or siblings in law enforcement. They'd been top-notch dicks and solid operators within their specialty units but had maintained a fairly low media profile until their sister's rigor mortis–ed body had been found pressed into the sand beneath the Santa Monica Pier. She'd moved to L.A. just a few weeks previous. In interviews Robert and Mitchell were quite outspoken about their belief that the Santa Monica police had handled the investigation incompetently. When her accused killer's case was dismissed after evidence was tainted by sloppy chain of custody, their responses grew even more vitriolic. The fuel behind their antagonism toward L.A., which they'd expressed so vehemently at Rayner's, was glaringly evident.

Another burst of newspaper articles followed several months later, when they won a $2 million settlement against a tabloid for going to press with illegally obtained—and gruesome—crime-scene photos.

Tim called trusted contacts at six different government agencies and had them each run a member of the Commission. The background checks came back clean—no wants, no warrants, no past felony charges, no one currently under investigation. He was amused to find that Ananberg had been arrested during high school on a marijuana-possession charge. Because of his technological prowess, the Stork had been accepted into the FBI despite his failure to meet physical qualifications. Deteriorating health had forced him into an early retirement eight years ago, at the age of thirty-six. A buddy at the IRS told Tim that Rayner had paid seven figures in federal taxes each year for the past decade.

No one, aside from Tim, was currently married—that would leave matters less complicated. Dumone, the Stork, and the twins had no current addresses, which didn't surprise Tim. Like him, they'd dug themselves in somewhere, safe and protected, before embarking on a project like the Commission.

At a discount furniture store up the street, Tim purchased a mattress and a flimsy dresser and desk. The store owner's son helped him unload the items from the delivery truck and get them upstairs. The kid moved gingerly, clearly having strained his shoulder on a recent delivery, so Tim tipped him handsomely. Then he bought a few more essentials, like sheets, pots, and a nineteen-inch Zenith TV, and unpacked what little he'd brought.

Flipping through the *L.A. Times* obits, he found a Caucasian male, thirty-six, who'd just died of pancreatic cancer. Tom Altman. That was a name Tim could live with. He cross-indexed the name with a phonebook he borrowed from Joshua, and found a West L.A. address. On his way over he stopped at a Home Depot and bought some heavy-duty gloves and a long-sleeved rain slicker. Dumpster diving could be a messy affair.

His concerns proved unnecessary, however. The house was empty, and the trash cans, hidden behind a gate in the side yard, weren't too filthy. He found a stack of medical bills under a used coffee filter, Altman's Blue Cross subscriber number—the same as his Social Security number—featured prominently on each form. As Tim had fortuitously hit the cans just after the midmonth billing cycle, further digging revealed a utilities bill, a phone bill, and a few canceled checks, all of them presentable. On his way to Bank of L.A., he stopped at the post office and retrieved a change-of-address form, useless in its own right, but official-looking when filled out and presented atop a stack of other documents.

The woman at the bank was pleasant enough when he explained he'd misplaced his driver's license. His Social Security number and current bills sufficed, and, feeling grateful that Altman had been considerate enough to leave behind a solid credit rating, he left with paperwork confirming his new checking and savings accounts and a rush-processed ATM card that doubled as a Visa.

These he took with him on a pleasant late-morning drive to Parker, Arizona, a grenade toss from the border, where he presented his information and explained to the peevish DMV clerk that he'd misplaced his California license but had been looking into getting an Arizona one anyway, as he summered in Phoenix. He spent the four-hour drive back marveling at the massive emptiness composing the majority of California and thinking how the sun-cracked barrens were a pretty damn good metaphor for what his insides felt like since Bear had showed up on his doorstep eleven days earlier.

Nightfall found Tim sitting on the floor of his apartment with his back to the front door, watching the neon lights blink through the wide window and throw patterns on the ceiling. He attuned himself to a cacophony of new sensations—thin, susceptible walls, conversations in foreign tongues, the back-kitchen stench of day-old fowl. He missed his simple, well-tended house in Moorpark and, more glaringly, he missed his wife and daughter. His first night in this new place confirmed what he'd already known: that nothing would be the same. He'd fallen into a new life, like a second birth, like a death, and with it came a sensation of suspended numbness, of underwater drifting. In this small womb of a room, linked to the outside world by no record, no trail, no necessity to leave, he felt at last safe from whatever corrosiveness the outside world was brewing and preparing to hurl in his face. From here he felt strong enough to begin his counterassault.

He gazed at the three major items he'd purchased—mattress, desk, dresser. There was no comfort in their arrangement, no lessening of what they were, things-in-themselves, rectangular practicalities that sat on carpeting. He thought of the gentler touches a woman—even Dray with her tomboy sensibilities—could bring to a room. Some softening of the lines, some notion that a space was to be lived with, not merely in.

He thought of Ginny's head-thrown-back hysterics at the Rugrats, the sense of joyful—yes, joyful—anticipation he got when he could sneak off work early to pick her up at school, like a date, and how he'd sit in his car and watch her for a few appreciative moments before getting out and claiming her. Ginny painted the world with child excesses—openmouthed smiles, floor-shaking tantrums, vividly colored candy and clothing. He realized how gray and inert she'd left the world with her departure, and how he was all abstinence and temperance—he was all lesser shades.

He was unsure he could abide a world that weathered her absence so easily.

He blinked hard, and tears beaded his eyelashes. Loneliness crushed in on him.

He found himself holding his phone, found himself dialing his house.

Dray picked up on a half ring. "Hello? Hello?"

"It's me."

"I thought you would've checked in last night. Not today."

"I'm sorry. I haven't stopped moving."

"Where are you?"

"I got a little place downtown."

He heard the air go out of her. "Jesus," she said. "A place." The line hummed, then hummed some more.

He opened his mouth twice during the ensuing silence but could not figure out what needed to be said. Finally he asked, "Are you okay?"

"Not really. Are you?"

"Not really."

"Where do I get you if I need you?"

"This is my new cell-phone number. Memorize it. Don't give it to anyone: 323-471-1213. I'll have it on twenty-four/seven, Dray. I'm ten digits away."

He heard the receiver rustle against her cheek and wondered what expression she was wearing. He thought about the phone nuzzled in close to her face, then about him here in this cold apartment.

"I already talked to some of our friends," she said. "But we should tell Bear together. I thought we could have him over tomorrow. At the house. One o'clock?"

"Okay."

"Timothy? I, uh . . . I . . ."

"I know. I do, too."

She clicked off. He snapped the phone shut and pressed it to his mouth. He sat, dumbly inert, phone against his mouth for the better part of twenty minutes, trying to figure out if he was actually going to follow through with the preparations he'd been laying.

He rose and turned on the TV to cut his lonesomeness, and Melissa Yueh's familiar voice filled the room.

"—Jedediah Lane, the alleged fringe terrorist, was released today to much fanfare. He was standing trial on charges of releasing sarin nerve gas at the Census Bureau, a terrorist act which claimed eighty-six lives. The Census Bureau attack was the biggest act of terrorism on U.S. soil since 9/11, and the largest perpetrated by a U.S. citizen since Timothy McVeigh's 1995 assault on Oklahoma City's Murrah Federal Building. Despite the fact that his courtroom antics provoked the judge on several occasions, Lane was found not guilty by the jury. The prosecutor claimed that Lane benefited from having had much of the physical evidence against him suppressed. Lane's post-trial comments have unleashed a whirlwind of anger in the community."

The screen cut away to a shot of Lane being escorted through a crush of news reporters, ducking lenses and mikes. "I'm not saying I did it," he mumbled in a quiet, almost affable, voice. "But if I did, it was to assert the rights upon which this nation was founded."

Back to Yueh's expression of barely concealed disgust. "Tune in Wednesday at nine when, in a KCOM special event, I'll be interviewing this controversial figure live. Watch it as it happens.

"In related news, construction continues on the memorial honoring victims of the Census Bureau attack. A one-hundred-foot metallic sculpture of a tree, the monument was designed by renowned African artist Nyaze Ghartey. Located on Monument Hill overlooking downtown Los Angeles, the tree will be lit at night, each branch representing a child who died, each leaf an adult victim."

An architect's sketch showed the tree looming large on the federal park, light emanating in the trunk's interior sending beams out through myriad holes in the metal hide. It was Christmas-tree hopeful. Very gaudy, very over-the-top, very L.A.

"Ghartey, who generated some controversy during the trial as an outspoken opponent of the death penalty, is the uncle of one of the seventeen child victims of the sarin nerve-gas attack, eight-year-old Damion LaTrell."

A school photo of a boy wearing overalls and a forced smile flashed on the screen.

Tim turned off the TV and grabbed his Sig from the kitchen counter. The door closing behind him sent a hollow echo down the hall.

He parked around the corner from Rayner's. The wrought-iron gates were more show than security; Tim slipped over them easily due to a vanity break to accommodate the dipping bough of a venerable oak. The front doors and windows were well secured, but the back door had only a simple wafer lock that he picked easily with a tension wrench and a half-diamond pick.

He prowled the downstairs, keeping his Sig tucked into his pants. Beside the stairs was an impressive conference room, complete with banker's lamps and leather chairs arrayed around an obnoxiously long table. A solemnly rendered oil of a boy roughly the age Spenser, Rayner's son, had been when he was killed, hung on the far wall. The portrait had an eerily posthumous affect, as if it had been done from a photo. A TV was suspended from the ceiling in the far corner of the room.

After getting the lay of the other first-floor rooms, Tim entered the library. He found the cherry box in the desk and claimed the .357 nestled within.

He headed upstairs.

Tim clicked on his Mag-Lite and shone the harsh beam on the two lumps beneath the covers of Rayner's bed. The Mag-Lite, which packed four D cells in its hefty metal shaft, provided one part illumination, three parts intimidation. Tim sat backward on a chair he'd moved silently from its place in front of the bathroom vanity, his feet on the plush velvet seat, his ass atop the back. His Sig and the .357 flared out from either side of his jeans like linebacker hip pads.

The larger form shifted and raised an arm to the light. Rayner's squinting face appeared when the expensive sheets slid down to his pajamaed chest. Confusion predictably turned to panic, then he was fumbling in his nightstand drawer and pointing a shaking revolver in Tim's direction.

Tim clicked off the flashlight. A silence. Rayner reached over and turned on the lamp, illuminating the nightstand telephone with a sleek accompanying recording device Tim had seen previously only in the homes of Secret Service acquaintances. Rayner's face, sweaty and tense, relaxed. "Jesus, you scared the hell out of me. I thought you'd call."

Tim's eyes went to the recording device by the phone,

positioned to capture his acceptance call. If Tim ever got inconvenient, Rayner could edit the recording however he pleased and drop it in the wrong hands. Not-so-mutual assured destruction.

At Rayner's voice the bulge in the bed beside him wriggled up out of the sheets. Her face was sleepy and full, her dark hair lank and down across her eyes. Though Rayner's face was colored to the ears, she didn't look the least bit scared or embarrassed. A bit pleased, maybe, which didn't surprise Tim from what he knew of her. Rayner was still frozen with shock, gun clutched in both hands like an unruly garden hose.

"These are my conditions," Tim said. "Number one: I get uncomfortable—the least bit uncomfortable—and the deal is off. I walk. Number two: I have full operational control. If anyone on my team starts stretching their britches, I reserve the right to slap them back into place. Number three: Stop pointing that gun at my head." He waited for Rayner to comply, then continued. "Number four: My privacy is to be respected. As you can see, it doesn't feel so nice when the shoe's on the other foot. Number five: I've already taken the .357 you tempted me with the other night, and I'm keeping it. Number six: First meeting of the Commission will be in the conference room downstairs, tomorrow night at twenty hundred hours. Inform the others."

He slid off the chair.

"I could've . . . could've shot you," Rayner said.

Tim walked over to the foot of the bed and opened his fist. Six bullets plinked down on the comforter at Rayner's feet.

Heading back down the stairs in the darkness, he couldn't help but crack a smile.

**15** PULLING INTO THE DRIVEWAY OF HIS—DRAY'S—HOUSE
felt like a return to comfort. Tim threw the car
into park and sat for a moment, admiring the
perfect alignment of shingles he'd hammered row by row
onto the roof, the uncracked concrete blocks of the walkway that he'd reset and resmoothed after last year's
tremors. Tad Hartley, mowing his lawn next door in jeans
and his trademark FBI windbreaker, raised a hand in silent
greeting, and Tim felt like a liar when he waved back.

He got out of the car, walked up the front path, and rang
his own doorbell—a weird sensation.

Dray's voice came with her footsteps before she opened
the door. "Shoot, Bear, you're early. I wanted to—"

She pulled the door open and did a poor job blinking
back an upset expression. "What are you doing, Timothy?
You've been entering this house through the garage every
day for the last eight years."

He had a difficult time deciding where to look. "I'm
sorry. I didn't want to . . . I didn't know what to do."

She stepped back. She was wearing her uniform—probably working a P.M., which meant she'd report to briefing
at three. "Very well, Mr. Rackley. Won't you please come
in?" She moved quickly back to the kitchen, leaving him to
trail. Once she was out of sight, he tidied up the newspaper
sections strewn across the couch.

"Can I get you a drink, Mr. Rackley?"

"Dray. Point taken. And yes, water."

She entered, bearing the glass on a plate she held up like

a cocktail tray, a dishtowel over her arm like a waiter's service napkin. They both started laughing.

Their smiles faded. Tim rubbed his hands together, though he wasn't cold.

Dray handed him the water and sat opposite him on the love seat. "I got Kindell's court transcripts yesterday. They're fat as hell—I was up half the night reviewing them."

"And?"

"Nothing of interest on the weenie wagger. But both of his lewd acts were with an accomplice—rare for child molesters, from what I know—so that puts a bit of fuel behind your theory."

"The previous accomplices?"

"Both in the clink. They didn't get to cop out with the cuckoo plea. They were the brains both times out—there to arrange and watch the show. Both white-collar—one guy was an accountant. Kindell's the freak, not a capable planner."

"So we have an accomplice who wanted in on the fun, but Kindell took it too far." Hearing his own words brought on a wave of nausea, which he fought away.

"Right. Which might explain why the guy sounded so upset when he made the anonymous call. He was in for a show, not a murder."

"An ethicist."

"And calling the private line to the station, covering his ass on the call—that matches a planner profile. More organized."

They sat with their respective thoughts for a few moments. Tim still hadn't adjusted to the seesawing emotion that each new development in Ginny's case brought. It occurred to him he might not ever.

When he looked up, Dray's face had shifted to sadness. "I know we agreed to take some time apart, but I didn't sign on for this," she said. "The vanishing act. The secret phone number. The move downtown. We went through this kind of stuff enough when you were a Ranger."

"This isn't us having to be apart because I'm deployed somewhere. This is us saving this marriage by taking a break from it."

He could tell from the set of her mouth that she knew he was right. She'd put on the faintest touches of makeup, something she normally reserved for weekend evenings, and Tim found it delightful and desperate all at once. Especially since he knew she'd wipe it off before heading to the station.

"Being alone in this house." She shook off a chill. "And the quiet. And the nighttime." She had a tendency to tick off on her fingers points she wasn't listing by number, an endearing break from the usual precision of her demeanor.

"It'll get easier," he said gently. "You'll get used to it."

"What if I don't want to?"

"Don't want to what?"

"Get used to living without you. And . . ." She wedged her legs beneath her. "Maybe I don't want to get used to Ginny being gone. A part of me wants to carry that . . . that pain all the time, because it keeps her with me at least. And if it fades, then what do I have? Last night I couldn't sleep because I couldn't remember what color her school shoes were. Those stupid Keds she wanted so bad. So I was up at four in the morning, digging through her closet, her things." She pursed her lips. "Red. They were red. Someday I won't remember that anymore. Then I won't remember what her favorite cartoon is, or what size pants she wore, and then I won't be able to remember what her eyes

looked like when she smiled, and then I won't have anything left of her."

"There's got to be a middle ground. Between comfort
and disregard."

"But where is it?"

"I think we each have to find that for ourselves."

Across the five-foot stretch of carpet, they studied each
other.

The doorbell rang. After the second ring, Dray broke off
her gaze and answered the door. Bear gathered her up in an
immense hug. She tapped his ribs. "How's the side?"

"It's nothing. But you two . . ." Bear thunked into Tim
with a hug. Tim braced himself for the double back pat,
which came like a tank cannon firing. Bear shoved him
away. "Where the hell have you been? I left you two messages yesterday."

"We've . . . we've been having some problems."

Bear's body seemed to settle like an old piece of machinery shuddering off. "Oh, no."

He trudged over to the love seat, which left Dray
nowhere to sit but beside Tim on the couch. Tim and Dray
took each other's hand, nervously, then released it. Bear
watched these proceedings with dread.

"We're . . . uh, separating, Bear. For a while."

Bear blanched. "Oh, for fuck's sake." He slapped the
side of his leg, then crossed his arms, fixing them with a
ponderous stare. He seemed to take note of Tim's black
eye, but he didn't comment. "I leave you two alone for a
few days and this is what you get yourselves into. Separating. That's great. That's just great." He stood, agitated,
then sat back down again. "Is there anything to drink in
this house?"

"No," Dray said. "We're . . . we're out."

"Fine. Fine." His big hands rose, then clapped to his knees. "So maybe you can explain this to me. What does 'separated' mean? I've never understood it. You're either married, or you're divorced. What is 'separated'?"

"Well," Dray said. "I—"

"How do you get out of 'separated'? It's not like 'separated' people suddenly find themselves together again. Do they? It seems like 'separated' is chicken-shit terminology for 'divorced.' Is that what this is?" Red blotches were starting to bloom beneath his stubble-dense face and throat.

"Listen, Bear, when you lose a child—"

"Don't you throw statistics at me, Dray. I don't give a shit about statistics. You're Dray and you're Tim and you're my friends and you get along as good as any husband and wife I've ever seen." He was breathing hard, pointing hard. "If you think you don't need each other now more than ever, you're crazy."

"Bear," Tim said. "Calm down."

"I'm not going to—"

"Calm. Down."

Bear took a few deep breaths, then tilted his head and flared his hands as if to evince a newfound tranquillity. "All right," he said. "All right. Who am I to tell you what to do? I guess you guys would know if you need . . . whatever. I guess you would know."

Tim took a deep breath and held it before exhaling. "A thing like this, with Ginny, it comes in, and it changes the fabric of things. And you feel like there's a tear or a crack and you try and smooth it over but you can't. And the more you work on it, the more it unravels or fissures and you can't keep working on it because it's just ruining what you had before." He moistened his lips, then snuck a quick look at Dray. "What you had before, it's this beautiful thing that you don't want to see defiled, and so maybe you'd rather walk away while there's still some of it intact because you can't stand to see it . . ."

Dray had her fist pushed up against her mouth, holding something in. Bear, stuffed into the too-small love seat, looked utterly crestfallen.

Tim rose and rested a hand on Dray's soft blond hair, let it drift until he touched the edge of her cheek.

As Tim headed back down the walk to his car, shoulders aching as if some great weight had been lowered or lifted, Tad Hartley paused from trimming his shrubs to offer another wave.

Sitting at his flimsy, window-facing desk with little to do beside wait for his eight o'clock meeting, Tim studied the foreign street scene below, losing himself further in grief's endless folds and wrinkles.

A C-section delivery with a complicated post-op course had left Dray horizontal for the first three weeks of Ginny's life. Tim had been the one up in the night, rocking Ginny back to sleep or preparing her bottle when she cried. He'd explained away the tree monster outside her window when she was three. He'd negotiated with a kindergarten bully, crouched on one knee beside his trembling daughter.

He'd made the world a safe place for Ginny. He'd taught her to trust it.

And she shouldn't have.

Every time he thought he'd familiarized himself with its contours, grief surprised him; it was ever bountiful, ever yielding. He released himself to it, letting it spread through him, noxious and painful and—finally—deadening.

After forty-five minutes he condemned himself as self-indulgent and useless, so he hauled himself out for a jog. Unaccustomed to the smog and exhaust, he wound up on a street corner, bent at the waist, hacking like a coal miner with a three-pack habit. It was with immense relief that he showered and headed over to Rayner's. The Commission, he realized with equal parts happiness and disquiet, gave him something to look forward to.

It gave him purpose.

Rayner was back to his usual socially lubricated self when he met Tim at the door. No hint of resentment about Tim's intrusion last night. After receiving Tim warmly, he led him into the conference room where the others waited. Ananberg spun in her chair to face him, legs crossed beneath a short but professional navy blue skirt.

Wearing another tropical shirt, this one a blend of greens and blues, the Stork rose to greet Tim. His hand was puffy and moist, his grip limp, and his pate and nose were peeling, despite the fact that it hadn't been sunburn weather for months. "I'd like to welcome you to the Commission, Mr. Rackley." Up close he looked even more odd, with his tiny chin, soft features, and twisted upper lip.

Mitchell was leaning back in the big leather chair, his Nikes resting on the edge of the table's marble surface. Robert mirrored him on the other side.

Dumone walked over and regarded Tim with a surprising expression of pride. For a moment Tim thought he might embrace him and was relieved when he offered his hand. He gripped Tim's right arm at the elbow when they shook. "I knew I could count on you, Tim."

Two garbage-can paper shredders stood at either side of the door like footmen. The confetti visible through their clear basins displayed that the machine cross-cut vertically and horizontally. No square of paper was bigger than a thumbnail.

Two pitchers of water and a set of glasses waited on the sidebar.

Tim's eyes went to the table, where framed pictures had been set in front of seven of the chairs. An old black-and-white of a woman with a seventies-style haircut was propped in front of the seat in which Dumone had been sitting. The same photo sat before Mitchell and Robert, that of a stunning blonde in her late teens on horseback. Tim walked around until he arrived at what he assumed was his own chair. Ginny looked out from within the thin silver frame with a goofy, slightly uncomfortable grin. Her second-grade photo, the one the *L.A. Times* had run. Seeing it in this new and unrelated setting was jarring. Tim picked it up, regarding it as if he'd never seen it before.

"We took the liberty," Dumone said.

Tim acquiesced to the manipulation, letting his sorrow re-form as anger; this provided him more traction. His mind went to Kindell, awakening each morning in the garage shack marked with Ginny's blood, cooking dinner for himself, breathing the air with impunity. He thought about having ten minutes alone in a room with him, and the stains he'd like to leave on the walls.

Robert nodded at Ginny's picture. "I know it seems a little weird and . . ."

"—ritualistic—" Mitchell said.

"—but the pictures are good to have around. They help us keep our eye on the ball." Robert's eyes were drawn back to Ginny's photo, and his face relaxed into an expression of bitter sadness, the first break in his rock-hard façade.

"We are very sorry about your daughter," Mitchell said. "It was an awful thing."

Grief shared, grief compounded. "Thank you," Tim said quietly.

Rayner signaled Dumone. "Why don't you swear him in?"

Dumone cleared his throat uncomfortably and began reading from a yellow legal pad. The oath was a brief encapsulation of the points they'd already covered in their conversation two days ago in Rayner's library. Tim repeated each point after Dumone, ending with the kill clause, then sat and pulled his chair in to the table. "Let's get to work."

With a shudder the paper shredder devoured Dumone's sheet of paper. Dumone pulled his hands back from the feeder, a humorously chary motion. "Hungry little bastard."

Rayner removed the creepy portrait of his son from the wall, revealing a Gardall safe with an electronic keypad on a circular dial and an inset baffle near the top that allowed items to be deposited when the door was locked.

Blocking the others' view with his body, Rayner punched in the code and tugged the steel handle. He stepped aside, revealing a weighty stack of black three-ring binders within.

A charge moved through Tim, quickening his heart.

One of the binders was Kindell's. One potentially held the key to the accomplice. A name. The secret of Ginny's fate.

Rayner gestured to the open safe. "These are the relevant case binders I've compiled, the cases of the past five years that have generated the hottest debate in legal circles. I'm culling more for our next phase, but for now we'll focus on these seven. Feel free to jot notes as we review the cases"— he nodded to the paper shredders by the door—"but no documents are to leave this room. Each binder is magnesium-lined, so in the event the authorities come, I can drop a lit match through the safe's baffle and we're evidence free. The safe has a three-hundred-fifty-degree, one-hour fire label, so it'll contain the blaze until it's burned itself out. If anyone tries to hacksaw his way in, the handle shears off."

Ananberg said, "Now, before we start, I want to explain the process—"

Robert inhaled deeply, a half-joking show of exasperation. "The procedure hound howls again."

Ananberg turned to address Tim. "Before you joined, Franklin and I moved that we come up with a procedure—nothing rigid, but a floor plan for our meetings. By acclamation we agreed I'd work out a rough idea of how we're going to comprehensively review each case. In place of arraignment, we'll first discuss what crime the defendant is alleged to have committed. Rayner and Dumone will lead the discussion. Since we already have to give up any pretense of being unbiased from the media, we'll talk through the case in broad strokes and lay out major arguments. If it looks like a guilty vote is a reasonable possibility, we'll return and move systematically through the files. Since William has managed to obtain files from both the DA and the PD, we have access to everything from discovery, whether it was eventually ruled admissible or not."

Tim tore his eyes from the bottom binder in the safe, focusing on Ananberg's words.

"We'll move through the police investigation, then to the interview reports with investigators from both the DA's and PD's offices so we'll be familiar with all angles both sides were considering in forming their respective arguments. From there we hit the forensic reports, then we assess evidence that came out in trial, including eyewitness testimonies. Everyone reviews every document before we vote—doesn't matter how long it takes. Since I'm the procedure hound, as Robert so ingeniously dubbed me, I'll be in charge of researching case precedent, which we'll use as a touchstone."

"Thank you, Jenna." Rayner nodded once, slowly, with the proud air of a father at his daughter's piano recital. He removed the top binder from the safe and sat, resting a spread hand on the cover. "We'll start with Thomas Black Bear."

"The gardener who slaughtered the family up in the Hollywood Hills last year?" Tim asked.

"*Allegedly,* Mr. Rackley." Ananberg tapped a pencil against the arm of her glasses.

"Get off his dick, Jenna," Robert said. Sitting beside Tim, he smelled faintly of bourbon and cigarettes. His face was more textured than his brother's, a trellis of wrinkles supporting his eyes. The nails of his left-hand thumb and forefinger were yellowed from nicotine, the knuckles stained.

"What's the evidence?" Tim asked.

The crime-scene diagram and evidence reports went around the table. An eyewitness had placed Black Bear, an immense Sioux, at the house earlier that morning, overseeing the removal of a dead sycamore from the front yard. Black Bear had no alibi for the two-hour span during which the crimes had been committed. He said he'd been home watching TV, a dubious claim given the detectives' discovery that his set was broken. Motive was hazy; nothing had been stolen from the house, and the victims hadn't been assaulted in a fashion suggesting a sexual predator or thrill killer. The parents and the two children—eleven and thirteen years old—had been murdered with gunshot wounds to the head, execution style.

After intensive questioning, Black Bear had signed a confession.

"Reads to me like some kind of drug hit," Robert said, flipping through the file. "The father's Colombian."

"Because all Colombians are drug lords," Ananberg said.

"Black Bear's got a colorful rap sheet, but no drug or assault charges," Dumone said. "Mostly small-time. Stolen cars, B and E, public drunkenness."

"Public drunkenness?" Robert kept an eye on Ananberg. "Damn Injuns."

The forensic report at his elbow, the Stork jotted a few notes, then stopped and worked a cramp out of his hand. A pill appeared magically in his palm, and he popped it without water and kept writing.

"How'd he get off?" Tim asked.

"The prosecution's whole case rode on the confession," Rayner said. "It was thrown out after it was determined that Black Bear was illiterate and spoke little English."

Dumone added, "They sweated him in the interrogation room for nearly three hours, and he finally signed. The defense argued he didn't understand what he was doing, that he was worn down and just wanted to get out."

"Wonder if they turned the heat up," Robert said. "In the room. We used to do that. Get 'em cooking at around eighty-five degrees."

"Or the coffee," Mitchell said. "Gallons of coffee and no bathroom breaks."

The Stork placed his plump hands flat on the table. "Nothing conclusive in the forensics."

Ananberg asked, "No prints, no DNA?"

"No blood was found on his person or property. A few prints were picked up around the exterior of the house, but that doesn't mean much, since he was their gardener." The Stork's hand darted to the bridge of his nose, pushing his glasses back into place. "No fibers, no footprints in the house."

"He did disappear after the trial," Mitchell said. "That hardly bespeaks innocence."

"Hardly establishes guilt either," Ananberg said.

Tim flipped through the pictures of the family members. The shot of the mother—a candid—had caught her standing in a garden, bent at the waist, laughing. Attractive, well-defined features, layered hair thrown back in a pony-tail, bare feet in the grass. Her husband had probably taken the shot—the woman's expression and the camera's atti-tude toward her made it clear that the photographer had adored her.

Tim slid the picture down the table to Robert and waited for his reaction, anticipating he'd comment about her looks. But when Robert raised the photo from the table, his face eased into an expression of sorrow and tenderness so genuine that Tim felt a stab of guilt for estimating him so cheaply. The photo trembled slightly in Robert's grasp, blocking his face, and when it lowered, his eyes were edged with a cold resentment.

They reviewed the rest of the binder, and then, at Anan-berg's behest, they returned and moved systematically through the entire case, examining the documents and ar-guing the merits. Finally they voted: Five to two not guilty.

Robert and Mitchell cast the dissenting votes.

Rayner rubbed his hands together. "It seems the shadow of reasonable doubt falls protectively over the defendant."

The razor edge working Tim's nerves eased, leaving him with either a keen disappointment or a clammy relief—he was unsure how to interpret the moisture left on his back and neck from the anticipation.

Rayner replaced the binder in the safe. Robert expressed his frustration at the verdict with a not-so-subtle sigh and strenuous reshuffling of paperwork.

Tim checked his watch—it was nearing midnight.

"Next case." Rayner flipped open an immense binder overflowing with scraps of paper and newspaper articles and announced, "This is a case with which we're all famil-iar, I'm sure. Jedediah Lane."

"The militia terrorist," Ananberg said.

Robert smoothed his mustache with a cupped hand. "The *alleged* militia terrorist."

Ananberg scowled at him, and he threw a wink in Tim's direction.

The Stork ran a hand over his bald head. "I'm something of a media hermit, so I—I'm afraid I'm not familiar with the case."

"The guy who walked a briefcase of sarin nerve gas into the Census Bureau downtown," Robert said.

"Oh. Oh, yes."

"Know where he left it?" Robert's eyes were past angry, almost gleeful. "Near the main AC duct on the first floor. Eighty-six deaths. Including a bunch of second-graders on a civics field trip. He just walked in, walked out without a trace." His flattened hand drifted in a gesture of evanescence, of stealthy malice.

"One of our own goddamned citizens," Mitchell said. "After 9/11."

Dumone flipped through the arrest report. "FBI obtained a search warrant for his house after a neighbor came forward and reported seeing Lane exit his residence that morning with a similar metal briefcase."

"That was enough for a search warrant?" Ananberg asked.

"That and Lane's history of membership in fringe organizations. The judge went for it, issued FBI a warrant, but wouldn't grant night-service authorization. The problem was, the investigators were shaking a list of other leads. Everyone and their aunt was calling in with sightings, suspects, theories. They got hung up with a militia guy in Anaheim who was stockpiling M16 ammo. When they finally got back to serve Lane's warrant, they received no response to their knock and notice. The door was double-barred from the inside. When they went through the door with a battering ram, they knocked over a table in the entry, breaking, among other things, a clock. Do you know what time the broken clock showed?" Dumone set down the binder, flipped it closed. "Seven-oh-three."

Mitchell grimaced. "Three minutes late."

"That's right. Night-service authorization kicks in on the hour. Sharp."

"Foolish," the Stork muttered. "Why didn't they wait till morning?"

"They never checked the warrant. Probably assumed it was standard. Keep in mind, they had a handful of them."

"What did they find in the house?" Tim asked.

"Maps, charts, diagrams, notebooks, pressure containers holding traces of what was later determined to be sarin gas, lab equipment consistent with the generation of chemical weaponry."

"Thrown out?"

"All of it. The prosecutor tried to convict based on the eyewitness report and a few beakers later found in Lane's vehicle, under a valid warrant. It wasn't enough."

"Did he take the stand?" Ananberg asked.

"No," Rayner said.

"Since the acquittal he's received a number of death threats, so he's gone underground," Dumone said. "Some of his fringe buddies packed him off to a safe house."

"Then he's probably on a ranch somewhere, barricaded behind a bunch of militia wackjobs," Mitchell said. "Those boys don't tend to be short on ammo."

"Endless civil claims are brewing, but since there's no way to hold someone in custody on civil charges, there's a lot of speculation Lane might just Osama bin Laden his ass off into a secret desert enclave."

"Oh, Lane's planning to resurface. On his way out of town, he had this to offer the press." Rayner aimed a remote control at the suspended TV, and the screen blinked to life. Wearing a starched button-up shirt and a sharply pressed pair of slacks, surrounded with a cadre of bodyguards, Lane addressed a pack of reporters on a browning lawn outside his house. He kept his hair military-short and precisely side-parted. Stubble curled from his sideburns, pronounced and patchy on his sallow cheeks, a lapse in his otherwise clean grooming.

"Whoever committed that terrorist act against the government's totalitarian socialistic agenda is a patriot and a hero," Lane said. "I'd be proud to have released the sarin gas, because in doing so I would have been championing American freedom and sovereignty against a fascist citizen list—the same kind of list used by Hitler to carry out raids and round up citizens, the same kind of list that propelled him to power. The blood of those eighty-six federal workers will save countless lives and protect the American way of life. While I'm not saying I was or was not involved, I will say that such actions are not at odds with my mission as a citizen of this nation under God against the New World Order."

A reporter's adrenaline-high voice cut in as Lane's men pushed a path through the crowd toward an awaiting convoy of trucks at the curb. "Does that mean your mission will continue?"

Lane paused, his jaw cocked. "If you'd like to know more, watch my interview Wednesday night on KCOM."

Rayner clicked off the TV.

"He left out the fact that seventeen of those eighty-six 'federal workers' were children under the age of nine," Tim said.

Robert said, "If Motherfucker's gone underground, at least the interview gives us a when and where we can find him."

"If the when and where aren't security cover smoke," Tim said.

"For someone who claims to loathe the biased, leftist press, he does get his face time," Dumone said.

"Like most intelligent people seeking to change public policy or make a political statement, he's a press whore," Ananberg said. "Even if he wouldn't admit it."

Rayner rested a hand on his chest and bowed his head, a self-deprecating grin touching his lips. "Guilty."

"Lane has already sold his book rights to Simon & Schuster for a quarter million dollars, and I believe several stations are vying for TV-movie-of-the-week rights," Dumone said. "Thus the expert plug for his interview."

Robert grimaced. "The City of Angels."

"The money could provide Lane ulterior motive to allude to committing the crimes, even if he didn't." Ananberg's voice lacked conviction, but Tim respected her for raising the point.

She ceded under a barrage of facts and evidence.

After several more hours of discussion, Ananberg led them through the case from arraignment to verdict. By the time they finished, the morning sun was creeping across the hardwood floor of the foyer.

The vote went much more smoothly this time around.

**16** THE STORK BOBBED IN THE DRIVER'S SEAT OF THE OVER-heated Chevy rental van, peering across at the KCOM building at Roxbury and Wilshire. He'd toned down his shirt for the low-profile drive-by, but Tim still wasn't pleased about having his distinctive mug pointed out the window. The Stork fidgeted continuously, shifting in the seat, polishing his watch face, one knuckle or another endlessly assisting his glasses on their Sisyphean climb up the barely existent bridge of his nose. He was an incessant mouth-breather, and he smelled like stale potato chips. Tim contemplated how he'd come to be here with this bald, lisping man prone to peeling sunburns and too-bright shirts.

They stared at the fifteen-story building, rising up in planes of concrete and glass to shade a bustling stretch of Beverly Hills. A window washer hung suspended from cables about a hundred feet off the ground, swaying and wiping, his silhouette standing out from the late-morning sun's brilliant reflection off the panes. An enormous front window on the ground floor housed a panoply of plasma-screen televisions broadcasting KCOM's current offering, a talk show exhibiting couches, ferns, and women of various ethnic backgrounds sharing a common unpleasantly vigorous demeanor. Since the TVs ran on closed circuit, showing the sets even during commercial breaks, they drew a small crowd of voyeurs and Rodeo Drive tourists hungering for table scraps of behind-the-scenes showbiz.

"If the new metal detectors at the entrance are any indication," the Stork said, "they're gearing up to turn this place into a high-tech funland by the Wednesday interview. Entry control points, IR sensors, metal-detector wands. The whole ten yards."

"Nine yards."

"Yes, well." He shifted his weight deliberately from one side to the other, as if breaking wind. "Heck of a lotta security."

"News orgs are all about confidentiality and scoop. They're notoriously difficult to penetrate. CNN used to come in with stories ahead of Army intel."

"What's CNN?" the Stork asked.

Tim studied him to see if he was joking. "A news station."

"I see. I can help you more if you tell me what you're planning here."

"I appreciate that, but I don't need more help. I just need you all to do your respective jobs."

"Okeydokey."

As they pulled past the building, Tim armed some sweat off his forehead. "Listen . . . Stork—"

"No origin."

"Excuse me?"

"My name has no origin. At least none that's exciting. Everyone asks, everyone wants a story, but there isn't one. One day, third or fourth grade, a kid on the playground remarked that I looked like a stork. Perhaps he intended it to be hurtful, but I don't believe I look like a stork—I mean, *truly resemble* a stork—so I took it as neutral. The name stuck. That's it."

"That's not what I was going to ask."

"Oh." The Stork strummed the padded wheel with the heels of his hands. "Fine, then. That. Okay, not that it's any of your business, but it's called Stickler's syndrome." His voice slipped into a drone as he launched into a rehearsed speech. "A connective-tissue disorder that affects the tissue surrounding the bones, heart, eyes, and ears. Among other things it can cause nearsightedness, astigmatism, cataracts, glaucoma, hearing loss, deafness, vertebrae abnormality, hunchback, flattening of the nasal bridge, palate abnormalities, valve prolapse, and vicious arthritis. As you can see, I have a relatively mild case. I can't type, I can't shuffle cards, and I'm nearsighted to twenty over four hundred, but I could be curled in a wheelchair deaf and blind, so I try not to bitch. Does that satiate your curiosity, Mr. Rackley?"

"Actually," Tim said, "I was just going to ask if you could turn down the heat."

The Stork made a soft popping sound with his mouth. He reached over and rotated the dial. "Righto."

They finished their turn around the block and came up on the building again. Tim tracked a bike courier at the crosswalk, heading for the shipping and receiving dock at the northeast corner of the ground floor. She had a KCOM decal on her helmet and a Cheesecake Factory bag in the bike's front basket.

"Slow down," Tim said.

The courier biked up the ramp and flashed an ID card at an obese security guard with a clipboard, who lazily wanded her down with a metal detector, then tugged open the roll-up gate. Heading back into the dock interior, she slotted her front wheel into a bike rack by the service elevator, yanked the bike seat free of the frame, and tucked it protectively under an arm. Just before the guard slid the rolling gate down, Tim saw the courier punch a code into a numeric keypad beside the elevator. An extended metal frame shielded the pad from view; her hand disappeared to the wrist by the time her fingers reached the keys.

The Stork eased the van over to the curb in front of a pharmacy and medical-supplies store that displayed a wheelchair and a bevy of aluminum walkers in the front window. They sat watching the closed, corrugated dock gate and the security officer rolling something he'd dug out from his nose between his thumb and index finger.

"Do you think the bike-courier cards are strictly ID, or do they double-function as access-control cards for movement within the interior?"

"They'd be strictly ID, I'd bet," the Stork said. "Access-control cards are usually only issued to high-clearance people, not mailroom gofers. Corporations are very strict about them. If they're reported missing, they're immediately deactivated."

"Fine," Tim said. "Forget the access-control cards. If I gave you a prototype of a regular ID, could you manufacture a fake one?"

The Stork snorted and flopped his hand in a dismissive wave. "I engineered a microphone that could fit in a pen cap and pick up a whisper at a hundred yards. I think I can deal with duplicating an overglorified library card."

Tim indicated the dock gate with a slight tilt of his head. "The bike rack's just past the checkpoint, near the service elevator."

"Probably a Beverly Hills zoning law—they don't want the sidewalks cluttered up." The Stork popped a pill into his mouth and swallowed it effortlessly without water. "If you want to get a pistol through, smuggle in a dismantled Glock. They're mostly plastic. Only the barrel has enough ping to set off a detector—make a key chain out of it and stuff the rest down your shorts. The firing pin doesn't have enough metal to get picked up." He studied Tim curiously, awaiting confirmation.

Instead Tim said, "We need to get a better angle on that keypad."

The Stork pointed at the narrow street running parallel to the north edge of the building. "A window on that side would look directly in on it."

"Give a drive by."

The Stork pulled out and eased down the street. There was indeed a window, but it was largely blocked by a decrepit truck.

Tim barely turned his head. "Keep moving, keep moving."

The Stork drove down the block and pulled over again.

"The truck's in the way, and it's a narrow sidewalk. The only way we could see in would be to press up against the glass, which would be more than conspicuous."

The Stork said, "Then we wait for the truck to move."

"It's a parking-permit street—no meters in need of refreshing—and the truck has a permit dangling from the rearview. There are reservoirs of leaves collected around the front wheels from the last rain four nights ago. I'd bet that's the resting place for someone's old rig."

"I'll get it moved."

"How?"

The Stork grinned. "I just will."

"Even if you get that truck moved and we get binocs on the window, there's no clear sight line to the keypad. It'll be blocked by the courier's body when he's punching in the code."

The Stork's mouth shifted and clamped. "Let me work on that."

"Also work on getting into the security phone lines—tap in to however many phone junctions it takes. I'd like you to monitor all developments." Tim had already asked Rayner to nose around his media contacts to get a read on the security politics, but the more information sources he had, the better.

"How many minutes to pickup?"

Tim glanced at his G-Shock. "Seven."

The Stork dug an eyedropper out of his pocket, removed his immense glasses, and applied the drops. When he put his glasses back on, still blinking against the liquid, his eyes looked like those of an agitated turtle. Tim felt the pull of empathy, followed quickly by an urge for comradeship, for unity in their common cause.

"It hit you hard?" Tim asked. "When your mother was killed?"

The Stork shrugged. "I've learned not to expect much from life. If you never expect things to go right, you're less upset when they go wrong."

"Then why are you doing this? The Commission?"

"Honestly? For the money. A nice little salary on top of my FBI pension. That may sound awful to you, but I don't have anything in this life but money. I've never had many friends. I've never played baseball. I've never had sex with a woman. I'm just an outsider, looking in at this other life I see in movies and advertisements. After a while I just checked out. I don't watch TV anymore, any of that stuff. I read. Mostly older stuff. Now and then I'll rent black-and-white movies when I can't sleep. I have trouble sleeping. My breathing . . ." He gestured to the knot of scar tissue beneath his nose, then folded his hands peacefully in his lap. "The zeitgeist alarms me because it reminds me of all the things I'm missing."

He removed his glasses again and rubbed his eyes. The lenses were concave, thick at the edges. "There's a reasonable chance I may be blind someday. I don't mind having extra money to buy books, to travel around and see things. Different oceans. Arctic snow. I took a helicopter ride around the Grand Canyon last May, and it was divine." He tapped his chest gently with his fingertips. "It's all more than I should do, given my heart condition, but it's my one pleasure." The glasses slid back on again, and his turtle eyes blinked at Tim. "I like money. It doesn't make me a bad person."

"No, I don't think it does."

They sat awkwardly for a moment.

"I'm sorry, Mr. Rackley. I don't have much occasion to talk to people, so when I start . . ." He cleared his throat moistly. "Perhaps we should get moving."

Tim reached into the backseat and removed two mag-

"Tomorrow, before we throw you back up there as a window washer, we'll figure out a way to slide you past security—as a maintenance guy, maybe—to breach the interior. I'll need those IR strobes made bad-operating. Stork?"

"I've dealt with SafetyMan before," the Stork said. "I'll size some mirror fragments to fit the casings. Robert can get 'em in tomorrow during working hours when the strobes are deactivated. When they reactivate at night, the mirrors'll bounce the IR beam back on itself and you'll be able to do the lindy hop down the hall."

"The lindy hop?"

"It's a lively swing dance, Mr. Rackley. Named after Charles Lindbergh."

"Right. Thanks for your help." Tim's eyes flicked to the door, in case the Stork didn't catch the hint.

The Stork tossed Robert a tiny, flat camera, which he slid into his T-shirt pocket, and then the Stork hopped out, climbed into a second rental van parked at the curb, and motored off.

In the back Robert was changing out of his overalls, throwing on a pair of jeans. "Weird dude," he said, jerking his head in the direction of the departing van. "He's a solid operator, but you don't exactly want to drink beers with the guy."

"He's all right," Tim said. "A little soft, but he's had a tough time, I'd guess."

Robert stuck a pencil behind his ear and slid a clipboard into a copy of *Newsweek*. He bent over to relace his sneakers, the Lee insignia popping out on its leather tag in the back of his fitted true-blue jeans. "So why'd you send him packing? Who cares if he overhears?"

"Give me the intel dump."

Robert stared at him, irritated, then inhaled sharply so

netic logos the size of garbage-can lids. He stepped out
stuck one on either side of the Chevy, where they p
claimed PERFECT TINT WINDOW WASHING.

The Stork pulled back down the narrow street, past the
loading dock, and looped around the front of the building.
Tim's watch blinked from 12:59 to 1:00 precisely as
Robert stepped out the maintenance door on the west side,
rags hanging from the pockets of his overalls, baseball cap
askew.

It took him fifteen steps to reach the van—already Tim
had the side door rolling open—and he ducked in as the
Stork pulled away. They rode in silence for several blocks.
The Stork stopped the car on a deserted street, just behind
Tim's parked Beemer.

Robert coughed into a fist, then spit out the window. He
tapped a cigarette out of a crumpled pack he pulled from
his shirt pocket. He snapped open the lid of a Zippo with
an American-flag decal. "Mind if I smoke?"

"Yes," the Stork said.

Robert lit up and blew a gust of smoke up at the driver's
seat. It wreathed the head of the displeased Stork like a
laurel. The Stork tried to hold in a cough, but it hiccupped
out of him.

Tim looped his arm around the headrest so he was facing Robert. "The fourth and tenth floors are empty,
right?"

"Yeah, they are. The dot-coms that used to rent them
went the way of the dodo."

"Are there still infrared-strobe motion detectors in
place?"

"Both floors are rife with 'em—SafetyMan casings.
They're off during the day because of the occasional maintenance guy or mover, but I'd imagine they go hot after
five, six o'clock."

the cigarette's cherry flared. "You didn't answer my question."

"I don't have to answer your questions."

"Look, I've done everything you asked, like a good little soldier. Now I'm not giving you shit until you tell me what the plan is."

"Fine. Then I drive off right now and you can explain my absence to Dumone and Rayner and carry out the mission by yourself."

Robert leaned back and tapped ash out the window with a flick of his thumb, a sharp, efficient gesture. His movements were uniformly tense, anger simmering, violence barely contained. Tim didn't know or trust his steadiness or that of the other operators—no small part of why—on a high-risk mission that carried the potential for collateral damage and civilian injury; he preferred to keep them focused on specific, isolated tasks.

Finally Robert said, "Maybe you should show a little respect. I got the shit you asked for. And then some."

"So give it to me."

Robert shot a jet of smoke in Tim's direction and began. "The skeleton is steel, walls are concrete with plaster overlay, the floors are twenty feet high and supported by metal ceiling joists and metal posts, twelve to a floor. Each floor is a rebar-reinforced poured-concrete slab base, nine inches thick, with a polished finish. The roof is plywood and tar, and it houses twenty-one air diffusers with fans and fifteen three-by-seven skylights with metal bars securing entry. Gas-fed AC and heat-pump units with shutoff valves located in the ground-floor maintenance area. Electrical power enters the building from the southwest corner, heads into an electrical closet through a main disconnect, and gets routed from there. The closet wiring's a mess—more fucked up than a nigger's checkbook."

"Lovely," Tim said, but Robert had already moved on.

"Each floor has roughly five electrical-distribution pan-els around the interior perimeters, rated from two- to three-hundred-amp service. Emergency power is provided by battery, but there are two high-capacity backup generators. Fire enunciator is located at the northeast point on each floor—zoned single-partition system, monitored locally via phone line, FireKing–manufactured panel. Extensive smoke- and flame-detection devices, fire extinguishers, fire hoses in the stairwell. The elevator *does* go down to the un-derground garage—my guess is they bring Lane in there in an armored car. The building core is very well protected—no outside windows into the inner rooms, so we have dick on a sniper angle if that's what you're thinking . . . ?" Cocked eyebrow, pause. "Windows don't open. Garbage chutes located to the right of the service elevator on each floor. The doors on the way to the stairwells are metal, push-handle, and they all have mag strikes. Flip-style light switches are to the left of each door, interior side. Stair-well's vacuum-sealed, no floor-to-floor access—you get locked out there, you're going all the way down to the first floor. The stairwell door locks are single-cylinder handle-turns that autolock, and they open into a rear kitchen on odd floors, a conference room on evens. Interview record-ing usually takes place on the third floor, but—clever fuck-ers—they're building a replica of Yueh's set on the eleventh floor. The switched locale is a secret security pre-caution—I spotted construction workers with bulges at their hips moving set backdrops across the floor."

Tim made a mental note to confirm that.

"They've started installing metal detectors on several floors today, I assume to have them good to go by the time Lane arrives. Access-control-card checkpoints on every floor to breach the inner rooms, guard booths to boot before the editing and interview suites. And there's a brunette on the seventh floor with an ass like Jennifer Lopez who almost made me plummet to my death when she dropped her keys."

"All right," Tim said. "Good job."

"I don't need you to tell me that." Robert hopped out and slammed the door behind him.

Mitchell was just leaving Rayner's house when Tim drove through the gates in the rental van and parked beside his own car. Mitchell ignored him, climbing into his truck. He was backing up fast when Tim knocked the side panel with a fist. Mitchell hit the brakes.

"What?"

Tim pulled a pencil from behind his ear and pointed at the eraser. "Can you make me a contained explosive charge this size?"

"What for?"

"I need something I can hide inside a small item."

"Like in a watch?"

"Right, like in a watch."

Mitchell's mouth shifted and clamped. "It'll be tricky. I'd have to build a minuscule, custom-made detonator."

"What'll you use? C4?"

"C4? And why don't we throw around a few sticks of dynamite or fire off an ACME cannon while we're at it?" He shook his head. "Leave the pyrotechnics to me. We'll need a sensitive primary explosive, like mercury fulminate or DDNT."

"And you're thinking an electronically initiated receiver?"

"Yeah, but that'll be the problem. There's not much space—especially if you're wiring this shit into the existing circuitry of a watch—so I doubt I can fit anything that'll pick up a specialized electrical transmission from any sort of distance. Maybe I can get you a couple hundred yards' range on a remote-control device."

"A couple hundred yards would be fine. And the charge can't send out shrapnel. We can't hurt any bystanders with the explosion."

Mitchell ground his teeth. "Ya think?" He started the truck rolling again, and Tim had to step back so the tire wouldn't run over his foot.

Tim drove to the Moorpark firing range to break in the .357, practicing his draw, getting a sense of the new metal. It felt like home.

When he left, he inadvertently drove several blocks toward his and Dray's house before realizing his mistake and turning around. Passing a park where he used to take Ginny, he broke out in a clammy sweat. He detoured, heading past the long drive leading to Kindell's garage. The .357 fit snugly in his old hip holster. He removed it and pressed it to his thigh, felt its heat even through his jeans. The fact that he had again moved from grief to anger was not lost on him.

Anger was easier.

After driving downtown, showering, and cleaning his gun, he stretched out on his bed and finally checked the Nokia's messages. Two, both from Dray, over the past couple hours.

She sounded discouraged on the first. "I've been hitting walls in every direction on the accomplice angle. I finally caved and called the LAPD detectives who worked Kindell's priors—they were actually really kind, had heard about Ginny. . . ." She cleared her throat, hard. "They still wouldn't give me specifics, but they took a turn through their case logs and assured me there weren't any trails or red flags. Almost all of what they had, they said, would be in the court transcripts, which I already have. I played the guilt card with Gutierez and Harrison, pressed them pretty hard, and they rousted Kindell for us one last time. Said he's not talking—his lawyer made real clear that keeping his mouth shut is what's gonna keep him out of jail. He's a regular constitutional expert now, even ordered them off his property unless they were gonna press charges. We're not gonna get anything from him. Ever." A deep sigh. "I hope things are panning out better on your end."

The sadness expressed in her voice on the first message gave way to irritation on the second, since Tim hadn't gotten back to her. He tried her first at the office, then at home, finally leaving a vague message saying he had nothing to report on his end and explaining he'd wanted to wait until he was alone to talk to her. Hearing her voice, even on a recording, set the hook of his grief more firmly.

He took a moment to consider how lucky he was to have so much to do.

He relieved Robert at four o'clock. Robert slid out of the coffee-shop booth, leaving a clipboard full of notes and charts on the table, hidden in the *Newsweek*. Tim sat and glanced through his jottings. Calendar of movements, times the trash went out, security positions. It was impossible to deny Robert's proficiency.

Tim sipped coffee and watched who came out of which exits and when. Just before five he crossed the street, passing the immense window full of suspended TVs, and entered the lobby—a large marble cavern with a grotesquely baroque chandelier, oddly dated given the building's exterior. Just inside, a newly positioned guard directed a perfunctory glance at Tim's license—thank you, Tom Altman, RIP—before letting him pass. A huge screen, composed of sixteen close-set TVs, formed the west wall. No side doors, no open stairs, no pillars behind which to hide. About twenty yards in from the revolving doors, a massive security console greeted visitors.

Tim took note of the cameras at each corner of the ceiling before acknowledging the security guard with a nervous smile. "Yeah, hi, I, uh, I was wondering if I could fill out a job application form. For, you know, maintenance or whatever."

"Sorry, sir, there's a hiring freeze right now. You might want to try ABC. I've heard they're looking."

Tim leaned forward on the counter for a moment, taking in the bank of bluish-white screens the guard was monitoring. The angles were largely south-facing, capturing the faces of visitors as they entered. Tim searched them for blind spots. "Thanks anyways."

"No problem, sir."

Tim turned and headed out. The security lenses above the revolving doors represented the sole cameras devoted to recording people as they exited. Tim kept his head lowered when he pushed through onto the sidewalk.

He took a new post in the window booth of a deli next door to Lipson's Pharmacy and Medical Supplies. Munching on pastrami, he recorded the order of the office lights blinking out on the eleventh floor.

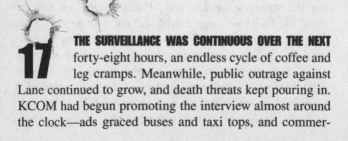

**THE SURVEILLANCE WAS CONTINUOUS OVER THE NEXT** forty-eight hours, an endless cycle of coffee and leg cramps. Meanwhile, public outrage against Lane continued to grow, and death threats kept pouring in. KCOM had begun promoting the interview almost around the clock—ads graced buses and taxi tops, and commercials launched on KCOM's affiliated radio station supplemented the aggressive TV campaign.

The entire city seemed to be holding its breath, awaiting the event.

Tim observed the intensifying circus atmosphere with equal parts awe and concern—the security machinations, gleaned through the Stork's wiretapping and Rayner's rooting, were ever shifting. Tim's plan nearly had to be scrapped several times, the first when KCOM's legal department started making noises about retracting the live aspect of the interview, wanting to prerecord Lane at an unspecified time as a security precaution. Next Lane wanted to shift the meeting to a secret location, for his own safety and cachet, but Yueh was understandably uncomfortable with this, given Lane's history and notorious hatred of the media. With the support of the brass, KCOM security finally threw down a veto, preferring to deal with variables contained in-plant rather than opening up a new locale. For this concession Lane extracted the promise that the interview would remain live, so his gospel couldn't get misrepresented or chopped up in edit. KCOM marketing and Yueh herself were more than happy to comply— putting a live spin on Event TV had already served to up the PR ante. To exploit the hype further, an added fifteen-minute viewer-call-in segment at the end ensured that Lane could respond to the Angry Public.

The next dogfight predictably involved jurisdiction— LAPD, KCOM security, and Lane's crackpot bodyguard team were locked in a protracted and bellicose set of negotiations over everything from employee- and public-safety concerns to personnel screening. LAPD predictably forbade nearly half of Lane's crew from entering the building; the hired replacements, once selected by Lane, would be vetted extensively.

Tuesday night found Tim in the Chevy van's passenger seat, parked on the narrow street on the north side of the KCOM building, staring at the still-lit window that would have provided a view of the service elevator and the numeric keypad had the run-down truck not remained, infuriatingly unbudged, blocking any useful vantage. The last courier usually arrived between 7:57 and 8:01 P.M.; Tim's watch showed 6:45.

In his lap he held a stack of photographs, each containing a shot of a KCOM employee, identified by name on the back. Black-op flash cards.

Humming the theme to *The Roy Rogers Show*, the Stork continued to fuss over what appeared to be a parabolic microphone attached to a small calculator. He fiddled with some wiring, set it down, and pulled a can of red spray paint from the center console.

"What are you doing?" Tim asked for perhaps the fifth time.

The Stork slid out from the driver's seat. He darted across the street in an approximation of a crouch that he probably thought inconspicuous, but that in reality made him look like a constipated hunchback. He disappeared behind the dilapidated truck and moments later emerged on the far side, bent down, spraying the curb fire-engine red.

He dashed back to the van, leapt in, and sat, recovering his breath. He removed a cell phone from his pocket—yesterday Dumone had brought them all matching Nextels so they'd be operating on the same network—and flipped it open. He dialed 411 and at the prompt asked for Fredo's Towing.

He spoke in a deepened voice. "Yes, hello. This is KCOM security, over at Wilshire and Roxbury. I have a truck parked here in a red zone we need moved ASAP. Yeah, okay. Thanks."

He closed the phone and leaned back in his seat, pleased with himself.

"Smart idea, but even if the truck's moved, we're not gonna be able to see through the courier's back to read the code he's punching in."

The Stork raised the cone-shaped piece of equipment he'd been tinkering with earlier. "That's why I brought Betty."

"Betty?"

"Betty trains a laser on the windowpane. She can pick up every vibration in the glass."

Tim shook his head, still not understanding.

"Every number on a keypad emits a slightly different frequency. These frequencies will cause a windowpane to vibrate almost undetectably. Betty reads these vibrations and translates them back to numbers for me."

"How about other, stronger vibrations? Won't they interfere?"

"It's pretty quiet now," the Stork said. "That's why we're doing this at eight o'clock. No gates rolling up, no loading going on at the dock."

Tim gestured at the piece of equipment. "And you . . . you designed it?"

"Her. And I wrote the computer program she utilizes." The Stork sniffed, and his glasses slid a notch down his nose. "Let's just say they didn't let me in the FBI for my bench press."

The tow truck arrived twenty minutes later and hauled off the truck, leaving the Stork a clear angle to the window. The courier arrived earlier than expected—7:53—but the Stork had Betty propped against his door and locked on the glass before the courier entered the code on the keypad. By the time the service-elevator doors slammed shut behind the courier, Betty's small screen had rendered the code: 78564.

The Stork stroked the top of the parabola and whispered something to it.

"I have to say, Stork, pretty impressive."

The Stork put the van back in drive and eased out from the curb. "If my aim was to impress you, Mr. Rackley, I would have brought Donna."

Rayner pulled Tim inside as soon as he opened the front door. "Good, good. You're back. Come—we got the tapes you asked for."

When Tim entered the conference room, Mitchell's head snapped up from his work. His hair looked slightly frayed; he needed a haircut. Hunched over a phone book, he was tinkering with the explosive device. It lay dissected on the yellow cover, its tiny components spread beside it like electronic innards. Breaching reports were scattered across the table, the pages sporting Mitchell's chicken-scratch calculations for determining overpressure. Mumbling to himself, Mitchell pried open a coil with the tip of a screwdriver.

Robert and the Stork were still out on surveillance, but the others were present.

Ananberg, cat-languid and smug, arched an eyebrow at Tim by way of greeting. She pointed to a stack of tapes with her pencil. "There's the rest. View 'em at your leisure."

"Thank you."

Dumone tossed Tim the remote. Tim aimed it at the TV, and the video unfroze—a Melissa Yueh interview with Arnold Schwarzenegger from last April, about the prospects of his running for mayor.

One of Tim's cell phones vibrated—the Nokia, left pocket, not the Nextel supplied by Dumone. He checked

Caller ID and turned it off—for Dray's protection he didn't want anyone to hear him talking to her.

But Ananberg took note of his expression, pressing a pencil against her lips. "Trouble on the home front?"

Tim ignored her, shifting the tape into slo-mo with another click of the remote. Arnie's laugh, viewed at eight frames per second, made him look like a man seeking to devour something. He slapped his knee, turned his head, revealing a shaving nick and the tan plug of the earpiece. The lighting made his skin look glossy.

Mitchell watched the screen, trying to figure out what Tim was looking for, tapping his tweezers against the phone book.

Rayner smoothed his mustache with his thumb and forefinger. "Now that we've done all the legwork, why don't you let us in on your plan? We don't know anything at this point. How are we even supposed to know when it happens?"

"Oh, believe me," Tim said, eyes still on the screen, "you'll know when it happens."

Parked in the driveway, Tim stared at the house numbers nailed just beneath the porch light, beside the front door: 96775. Years ago he'd pencil-sketched their placement before nailing them to the wall, using a framing square turned at an angle to calculate the slant. The 9 had lost its bottom nail and had swung upside down; it was now a misaligned 6.

He replayed Dray's last message on his cell phone.

"Well, since you're too hard to get right now, I'm leaving this on your voice mail. Don't think you can disappear and work things out at the same time. Since I don't know where you live, I can't stop by and try to talk some sense into you, but I'm only gonna wait so long. Come over and let's talk. I'm working a full schedule again, so call first to make sure I'm around."

Her voice, hurt veiled thinly with anger, matched his mood. One part of her message in particular stuck in his head: *I'm only gonna wait so long*. Before she moved on? Before she came looking for him? Because of the demands of the operation, he'd put himself out of touch with her at the worst time. He could hardly be surprised that his remoteness had raised resentment in her.

He slid his wedding band off and eyed the house through it, telescope style. A succinct composition of all he'd allowed to get fucked up. His hand felt naked without the ring, so he put it back on.

He rang the doorbell twice. No answer. He'd sneaked away from Commission duties to come here. The empty house confronted him with just how much he missed his wife and how large a hole her absence left. He was angry with himself for not taking more care to make sure she was home.

He entered through the garage and wandered through the house, not quite sure what he was looking for. He stared at Dray's bottles arrayed on the counter of the master bathroom. Sitting on their bed, he picked up her pillow and inhaled her scent—lotion and hair conditioner. He painted over the new drywall he'd patched into the living room walls. He found his hammer in the garage and fixed the house number out front, swinging the *9* back into proper position and tapping the nail lightly until it came flush with the metal. When he returned to the kitchen, his head was buzzing.

He left Dray a Post-it on the fridge saying he loved her. He was almost to the door when he turned around and left another on the bathroom mirror telling her the same thing.

**18** "MY NAME IS JED. USING MY FULL NAME, JEDEDIAH, AN antiquated name, is an attempt by the government-controlled leftist media to distance me further from the average American, to make me a zealot." On the cluster of closed-circuit TVs suspended in KCOM's ground-floor window, seventeen televised Jed Lanes folded seventeen sets of hands and leaned back in seventeen plush interviewee chairs. An eighteenth screen reflected back the crowd itself, an array of irate and perversely curious faces.

Rolling his bike before him to split the crowd, Tim shouldered his way through the onlookers and picketers glued to the building's immense front window. Melissa Yueh had Lane on set upstairs and was warming him up to go live inside the half hour. As a publicity stunt, KCOM programmers had elected to air the pre-interview banter on a closed-circuit network to the crowds gathered outside the building. Another link in the chain trailing back to the limited broadcast of Tim McVeigh's execution.

The chants had only just quieted down, so Lane's words could be heard, but disdain and outrage emanated from the crowd like heat. LAPD kept up a strong but unintimidating presence, the dark blue uniforms interspersed among the viewers and protesters at regular intervals. Just inside the lobby, KCOM security guards were checking IDs closely before moving visitors and employees through two airport-style metal detectors.

The minuscule detonator was wedged up beneath Tim's

bike seat. He had stuck nine flat magnets to the side of the chain stay and secured a tubular remote device the size of a lighter to the right pedal's toe clip, disguised as a reflector. In addition to wearing eyeglasses, he'd let his scruff grow into a short beard and mustache, and he'd wedged a piece of Big Red at the gum line behind his bottom lip to alter the shape of his chin. A backpack slung over one shoulder, fake ID card flapping from the waist of his khakis, gold cross dangling from a necklace, he turned the corner and headed for shipping and receiving. A flick of his arm brought his watch out from cover: 8:31.

He picked out Robert's picket sign among the others across the street: CHILD KILLER FANATIC. Something was wrong—the sign's flip side, the slogan reversed, was to serve as the go-ahead. Robert continued to chant and follow the circling picket line, but Tim noted his tension in the thick cords of his neck.

Robert tilted his sign toward the shipping and receiving dock. Two new security guards had taken over in the wake of Lane's posse's entry. One patted down a courier at the base of the ramp, the other holding the bike to the side. They waved the courier through but kept his bike outside, despite his protests.

Plan A aborted.

Tim crossed the street and ditched the bike up against a garbage can after removing the hidden devices. He stood still for a moment, mind racing. On the ground by the trash can was a discarded guest pass, dated today. He smoothed it against his thigh. Joseph Cooper. That would do. New guards, after all, provided as many opportunities as disadvantages. Readjusting the backpack on his shoulder, he walked down the street and ducked into Lipson's Pharmacy and Medical Supplies. The sole worker rustled with boxes in the back. "Be there in a minute!"

Seconds later Tim rolled out in the wheelchair previously displayed in the window, his backpack hooked over the seat back. His full-fingered biking gloves, which he'd worn down on a belt sander last night to give them a tatty authenticity, doubled nicely as protective padding against the fast-turning wheels. They also ensured a print-free entry.

Tim zipped over the crosswalk and headed straight at the new guards, flashing the guest pass when the taller one raised a meaty traffic-cop hand. "Hey, guys. I'm consulting with some editors up on eleven this week. I tried to get in at the entrance, but they told me to come around here today. Couldn't get me through the metal detector with this baby"—he patted the side of the wheelchair lovingly—"but they said you could wand me down here."

After shooting his colleague a quick, uncomfortable glance, the guard waved the wand near Tim, but the detector went apoplectic with all the metal from the wheelchair. Tim kept his hands on the tops of the wheels, hiding the detonator and remote wedged into the spokes. The other guard searched Tim's backpack, digging through the clothes inside as if kneading dough. Tim was thankful for their awkwardness and evident fear of offending him— they hadn't even asked him about his outfit.

He smiled shyly at the detector's frenzied beeping. "It happens, man. You should see me at an airport. They practically call in the national guard." He shot a wink. "Would you mind givin' me a roll up the ramp?"

To his credit the guard patted him down first—and well—checking the small of his back and running his hands down the lengths of Tim's legs. In his thoroughness he even removed a silver dollar from Tim's pocket and studied it before returning it. Tim's long-sleeved Lycra biking shirt hugged his chest, making him acutely aware of the thin layer of perspiration covering his body. The intensity reminded him of spinning up for a live op or kicking doors with the service.

Finally the guard nodded and shoved him brusquely up the ramp. "Elevator code's the first five numerals of your floor-access code. They gave you that, right?"

"Yup. Thanks, bro. Appreciate it." Tim eased his way over to the service elevator, punched in the code Betty had retrieved, and forced a smile at the guards while he waited. His muscles relaxed a notch when a ding announced the doors' opening. He didn't realize he'd been holding his breath until he rolled inside and threw a sigh after the doors banged shut.

The elevator was a typical service cattle car—mesh walls, high ceiling, bolted hatch. A TV monitor pointed down from the right corner. "—any idea the crap the Clinton-Gore regime left us to sort through," Lane was saying. "Them and their fuckdamned socialist associates, subverting and destroying our cultural institutions." He had a booted foot up on the edge of the news table.

"When the interview goes live," Yueh said, "you're going to have to watch your language."

"Of course I will," Lane said. "I don't expect I live in a free country."

Tim hit the button for the tenth floor, then removed the detonator and remote from the spokes and collected the flat magnets from where he'd stuck them behind the seat back. The wheelchair accordioned neatly, and he leaned it against the wall. He tugged off his Lycra shirt and replaced it with a nondescript blue button-up, then removed a dry-cleaned shirt from the backpack, the wire hanger slightly bent from the guard's groping.

He stepped out onto the empty tenth floor and shit-canned the folded wheelchair and backpack down the garbage chute to his right. As the elevator doors slid closed, he pulled the silver dollar from his pocket and held it out into the narrowing gap, trapped between his index and middle fingers. The doors slammed shut on it and stopped, the connectors just shy of engaging. He checked his watch again: 8:37. The service elevator wasn't due for use again until the graveyard janitorial shift rode up to the sixth floor, around 9:15. In case there was an emergency response before then, he preferred to have the car out of commission.

Slinging the dry-cleaned shirt over his shoulder, the plastic wrap rustling against him, he poked his head out in the back hall. Infrared motion strobes every ten yards along the ceiling, virtually no blind spots. A perfect opportunity for Robert to hang Tim out—if he hadn't rendered the strobes bad-operating as promised, Tim would be trapped by a screaming alarm on the tenth floor of a building stuffed with cops, guards, and private-militia goons. Taking a deep breath, he stepped out into the line of the first two lenses. The green pinpoint dots atop the units shone steady—no blinking to indicate either strobe had been tripped.

The first door he encountered was a facing push-handle as Robert had reported; the floor had been designed to protect mostly against inward-moving intrusions. Tim removed the stack of flat magnets from his pocket and worked the top one off with his thumbnail. It was thin and silver, shaped like a stick of Wrigley's. He went up on tiptoe and located the mag strikes by the intruding shadow that interrupted the lit seam at the top of the door. He slid the magnet between the two mag strikes until he felt it pulled; when he released it, it snapped into place, covering the top strike.

He pushed the door open and passed through the jamb, glancing up at the magnet clinging to the top mag strike, ensuring that the connection hadn't been broken. He moved from the hall through an enormous room filled with partially dismantled cubicles; they rose shadowed from the darkness like an elephant graveyard, a requiem odeum for the dot-com bubble burst. It turned out he encountered only five more doors; the three leftover magnets he stuck behind the print tray of a discarded Hewlett-Packard.

He leaned against the stairwell door, listening for the footsteps of Susie-Take-The-Stairs, the exercise-minded receptionist from eleven. 8:42. She was running late for her nine o'clock shrink appointment five blocks over; she'd called this afternoon to confirm. Tim waited, controlled his breathing, faked patience. He had an 8:49 checkpoint upstairs, needing to pass Craig Macmanus in the west-east-running hall as Macmanus headed back to his office to answer the emergency page the Stork was going to send his way. By 8:45 Tim figured Susie-Take-the-Stairs had either canceled her appointment, decided to stay on site for Lane's interview, or taken the elevator.

Whistling casually, he popped open the door to the stairwell and stepped on the tenth-floor landing. The door swung shut behind him and locked. As if on cue, the door opened one floor up, and he heard the cushioned tap of Reeboks heading down the stairs. He hugged the railing, raising the dry-cleaned shirt high on his shoulder so it blocked half his face.

Susie swept by, a blur of curls and nylon. "Hi! Bye!"

Tim murmured a greeting and kept moving. By the time he reached the eleventh-floor landing, he had the hanger out from the shirt and untwisted, bent into an L terminating with the hook. He slid the hook beneath the narrow gap at the bottom of the door and rotated it until he felt it grab the handle inside. He tugged and got a satisfying click. Easing the door open, he entered the empty back kitchen.

The TV on the counter showed Melissa Yueh leaning over Lane as a tech affixed a mike clip to his shirt. "Just relax and make eye contact with me, not the camera. We're gonna get you your earpiece in a few minutes here so the producer can talk to you while we're live."

Several of Lane's militia groupies stood in the background, bodyguards with oversize arms and no idea where to put them. They were working hard at looking tough, trying to ignore the cameras and doing a bad job of it. A feisty production assistant moved them out of the shot, and they shuffled clumsily under his command, cattle driven by a sheepdog.

Tim triple-folded the hanger and stuffed it and the shirt into the trash bin beneath the sink. He pulled a Baggie, a plastic earpiece, and a single thread of dental floss from his back pocket. He pried open the earpiece, nestled the tiny detonator within the wiring, and snapped it shut. Dropping the earpiece into the Baggie, he then sealed the bag, knotted the top, and tied the dental floss around it. He swallowed the Baggie, holding the end of the floss. The floss pulled taut, holding the Baggie midway down his throat. He waited for his gag reflex to cease, then strung the floss between two of his molars.

Grabbing two small bottles of Evian from the fridge, he stuffed them into his back pockets and stepped into the hall. 8:46.

A stiff-postured LAPD cop and a tired KCOM guard sat on stools in front of a metal detector that led into the main corridors. Tim nodded and stepped through. The detector beeped loudly.

"You carrying a cell phone, keys?"

Tim shook his head.

The guard slid off his stool and wanded Tim, starting at his feet. When the wand reached his throat, it gave off an intense beeping. The guard stared at the gold cross resting on Tim's Adam's apple, rolled his eyes at the cop, and waved Tim through.

Tim turned into the men's room just past the guard station and ducked into a stall. Plucking the dental floss from between his molars, he gagged up the Baggie. It slid out, slick with saliva. He removed the earpiece, dropped it into his pocket, and flushed the Baggie. He stepped back out into the hall at precisely 8:49.

Craig Macmanus, all jaw and toothy grin, was barreling down the hall with a coworker, glancing at his beeper and winding up a joke about bicycling nuns. Tim timed the lowering of his head to fake-check his watch and brushed against Macmanus's side, lifting the ID and access-control cards clipped to his leather-weave belt.

"Oops. Sorry, Craig." Tim kept moving, not turning for a face-to-face. His hands worked quickly to remove Craig's ID card from the clip and replace it with his fake. The hall was completely empty, save three TVs suspended at intervals from the ceiling. Tim reached the forbidding double doors at the hall's end and flashed Macmanus's access-control card at the pad. The red light blinked green, and he stepped into the inner sanctum.

Here in the interview suite, impervious to binoculars and the probing eyes of window washers, Tim was on his own. Lane and Yueh were positioned at an immense wooden table, Charlie Rose style, and PAs were scurrying about, adjusting lighting and wincing under Yueh's orders. A black digital clock suspended above Yueh's head counted down to airtime—less than five minutes. The guard in the small booth to Tim's right was munching a powdered doughnut without apparent appreciation for caricature. Tim flashed his ID card, and the guard gave it a cursory glance, leaving a sugary thumb whorl over Tim's dour photo.

A tech wearing headphones fussed with a control board, the cables and wires threading back beneath a folding table to his side. Tim headed in his direction, brandishing one of the Evian bottles.

"Someone called over for water?"

The sound tech waved him off, barely looking up. Tim spotted an open metal briefcase on the table, a few pieces of gear nestled within its gray foam filling, including Lane's earpiece; as he'd guessed, Lane's men, extensively experienced with death threats, had brought all their own equipment for Lane's use.

"I'll just leave it here."

Another arm wave, this one vicious.

As Tim set the bottles on the counter, he quickly swapped earpieces.

"Live in two," someone shouted.

"Diffuse the fill light!" Yueh shrieked. "You'll have my pores looking like potholes."

One of Lane's no-neckers, his forearm decorated with a bald eagle tattoo, swept past Tim, heading for the metal briefcase. As Tim walked toward the door, he gestured for the guard to wipe powdery residue from his chin. Back in the sterile hall, he got Yueh screaming commands in stereo, her voice moving through the walls and shrilling from the monitors overhead. The first note of the KCOM jingle announced the show's start, granting the building blissful respite from her stridency.

By the time Tim reached the front elevator, this one smooth and slick with a TV screen embedded in the brushed-stainless-steel panel, Yueh's on-air honeyed tone was pinch-hitting. ". . . haven't seemed to express much remorse over those children and men and women who died." Her brow furrowed slightly, approximating genuine puzzlement.

Tim stood to the front of the car, in the security camera's blind spot. The interior was exclusively metal—no mirroring through which a second camera could be monitoring.

"Those people were working for a fascist, tyrannical cause. The Census intrusion is a communitarian strike against principled individualism, against the free, independent, constitutional republic that men like me are fighting to reestablish. A list of our citizens, available to whoever digs through a federal filing cabinet . . ." Lane snickered, his fingers rasping across his patchy beard. "Do you think our Founding Fathers had this in mind? How much we make? What ethnicity we are? Where we live? There's a war going on in this country, in case you haven't noticed, and the Census is more ammunition for our so-called leaders. They're launching a full-scale offensive against American sovereignty and rights—*God-given* rights, not *government-granted* rights."

"Census data isn't available to other branches of the government, Mr. Lane. Surely you're exaggerating the—"

"Did you know, Ms. Yueh, that the Census list was used in 1942 to round up Japanese-Americans and throw them in internment camps?"

Her smile clicked on like a flashlight, but the split-second delay showed she'd been caught flat-footed. Tim couldn't resist a smirk. Score one for the bad guy.

He slid his thumb along the silver remote device in his pocket. It had a flip top like a lighter, which hid a single black button. He'd estimated its range conservatively—it would extend at least ten strides from the building's front doors.

Lane continued imparting gems of wisdom. "Democracy is four wolves and one sheep voting on what's for dinner. Liberty is the sheep with an M-60 telling the wolves where to stick it. The government is impinging on us, our rights, nibbling away at us, nibbling away. That attack on the Census Bureau was justice being administered."

The elevator doors dinged open in the lobby. From janitors to bean counters, KCOM workers were gathered together, watching the interview on the massive screen on the west wall. One woman stood frozen in place, Jamba Juice straw inches from her open mouth. Scanning the lobby crowd were four uniformed LAPD officers and—from the preponderance of fanny packs—quite a few undercovers.

Tim walked the path he'd mentally charted out, keeping to the edges of the cameras' fields of vision.

Lane's voice boomed off the marble floor and bare walls. "At its least harmless, the Census is an apparatus to serve the expansion of the welfare state. In this country, today, we pay a higher percentage of our earnings in taxes than serfs once did."

"Serfs didn't *have* inco—"

"And the federal bank is an even bigger perpetration of treason by our usurping government."

Yueh's face hardened into her trademark expression, the one used in commercials describing her as "hard-hitting." "You've done everything here but answer the first question I asked. Are you at all sorry that seventeen little boys and girls are dead, that sixty-nine men and women are dead?"

Lane's smile sprang up fast and crooked. " 'The tree of liberty must be refreshed from time to time with the blood of tyrants.' "

Tim crossed the lobby, hand jammed in his pocket, thumb working the lid of the remote device like a rabbit's foot. " '*Patriots* and tyrants,' " he muttered. He tucked his chin to his chest as he neared the revolving doors and their attendant lenses overhead. A quick spin and he was out on the pavement.

Neither Yueh nor Lane relaxed their postures; they remained squared off, predators gauging vulnerability.

The crowd outside surged and ebbed. People had red ribbons pinned to their jackets. Someone was murmuring in rage. A man wearing a fuzzy hat with earflaps watched the TVs in the front window, his mouth agape, his cheeks glistening with tears. Tim counted his steps from the revolving doors. Four . . . five . . . six . . .

Melissa Yueh's face loomed seventeen times in close-up. Her jaw was set, her eyes shone coal-dark and pissed—the first show of the substance beneath her persona. "You've avoided answering my question again, Mr. Lane."

In the quiet of the street two blocks down, the now-unmarked Chevy van coasted silently to the curb. Tim flipped up the lid on the remote device, rested his thumb on the button. A woman keened softly in the arms of a man.

Lane seemed to gather a sudden, fierce energy. His body tightened and he leaned forward, seventeen images moving in concert, his finger jamming down into the table so hard it bent and whitened. "All right, bitch. Am I sorry they died? No. Not if it brings attention to—"

Tim clicked the button, and Jedediah Lane's head exploded in mosaic.

**19** RAYNER'S CONFERENCE ROOM WAS ALL POSTSWEAT chills and high energy. Robert and Mitchell paced on opposite sides of the conference table while the Stork, kneading out a cramp in his left hand and basking in an almost postcoital glow, sat calmly between Rayner and Ananberg.

Ananberg wore the sleeves of her thin black sweater pushed up to her elbows, her collar tips peeking out with J. Crew perfection. Tim caught her staring at him a few times, her dark, shiny eyes flashing quickly away.

Dumone stood with one hand resting paternally on Tim's shoulder—which Tim allowed and even didn't mind—the other holding a remote with which he slow-advanced the explosion of Lane's head on the overhead TV.

First Lane's eyeballs ejected from their orbits. The skin covering his scalp and face balloon-swelled, then split, his mandible blown off in a single piece. Then his entire head seemed to dissipate at once, to crumble with the slow-motion horror of an avalanche starting. Lane's body remained stiffly in the seat, perfectly headless, tie still set firmly against the collar, one finger vehemently stabbed down into the table.

The camera did a *Blair Witch* swing, catching scrambling techs, militia goons, and Melissa Yueh watching with an expression of unadulterated wonder, a plasma splat of gray matter clinging to her cheek just beneath a mascara-heavy eye.

Dumone froze the screen. Ananberg inhaled sharply, her chest jerking a bit, her lips parting. She caught herself quickly, her usual seen-it-all complacency again taking hold of her features, an expression of icy amusement. Rayner's face was white, save for disks of color at the heights of his cheeks. He propped his elbows on the table, resting his chin on the bridge of his laced fingers, and exhaled loudly.

Robert passed Mitchell, and the two slapped hands. "Motherfucking genius."

Mitchell's face, softer than Robert's, was flushed with excitement. "Brilliant. I'd forgotten—the slightest explosion in the external acoustic meatus can induce massive intracranial pressure. Open a head right up."

"See, that's what I'm talking about. Right there." Robert strode over and grabbed Tim in a forceful embrace, giving him a faceful of rough shoulder fabric laced with nicotine. He shook Tim once, hard, and set him down. Though Robert was a good several inches shorter than Tim, he was undeniably more solid, his thick arms and legs seeming part of a single, immutable block.

Tim took a step back, away. "What's next? A victory lap, then we douse Rayner with the Gatorade cooler?"

His comment was lost in the excitement; Dumone alone took note, fixing Tim with his solemn blue eyes.

Rayner clicked through the channels. News updates all around.

"—perhaps from a rival militia group or an FBI operative—"

The Stork raised his arms like a traveling preacher. "It has begun."

"This will certainly raise public visibility," Rayner said. "And contribute to the execution's deterrence potential."

Robert cracked a pleased smile. "Yeah, I'd say blowing Motherfucker's head off during prime time will sure as shit get the message out."

"It's sufficiently high-profile that now we can back off and do safer, isolated hits," Dumone said. "Everyone will still know it's us."

Robert finally sat, his knee hammering up and down, his hands curling the thick phone book.

The Man on the Street—this incarnation a puffy-jacketed one with a goatee—offered his opinion to an out-of-frame reporter. "I say good riddance, man. A scumsuck like that, sneaks through the law on some"—his next two words, presumably too colorful for the airwaves, were bleeped out— "got the death penalty he deserves. I'm a father of three children, and I don't want some guy like that out there, who we all know killed a bunch of kids." He leaned toward the camera now, in hi-mom posture. "Hey, I say whoever smoked the guy, if you're out there, good job, man." He flashed dueling thumbs-ups before the camera cut away.

"Well," Ananberg said, "now we have our moral sanction."

"Don't be a snob, Jenna," Rayner said. "We don't just want to hear from judges and slick media commentators."

"Yes, how we loathe slick media commentators."

Rayner ignored the barb. "I'll have a full media report ready by the time of our next meeting. Friday evening, shall we say?"

Tim glanced at the painting of Rayner's son, behind which the safe and Kindell's case binder waited. Rayner followed his gaze and winked. "Two cases down. Five to go."

"You boys did well," Dumone said. "You should feel great."

"Right," Tim said.

Robert and Mitchell were waiting by the Toyota truck. As Tim passed, he took note of the tiny clean circles on the otherwise-dirty back license plate, right around the screws, indicating a recent change. Robert caught his arm and gave a squeeze. It seemed as if a good clench could snap Tim's humerus.

"Let's go for an unwinder," Robert said.

The Stork stood for a moment, as if waiting for an invitation to be extended, then climbed into his van and drove away.

Tim stood by his car.

"Come on," Mitchell said. "The post-op drink. A tradition we dare not break."

Robert held up the phone book he'd taken from inside, letting it fall open to the section he'd marked with a thumb. LIQUOR STORES.

Robert stepped aside, and, after a hesitation, Tim slid across the front seat to the middle. The brothers climbed in on either side of him, the doors slamming in unison. Mitchell drove fast and skillfully. Tim sat hunched in the middle, the breadth of two sets of Masterson shoulders leaving him little torso space. Deltoids poked into him unforgivingly on the turns, pounding from Tim's subconscious his relief that Robert and Mitchell were—ostensibly—on his side.

Mitchell stopped at a liquor store off Crenshaw and headed into the store. He emerged with a brown paper bag, about two six-packs wide, which he threw in the back. He pulled off his black Members Only jacket, rolled a pack of Camels in his white T-shirt sleeve, and climbed back in.

"That was a hell of a bang you built," Tim said.

Mitchell kept his eyes on the road. "I know a few things."

He drove the speed limit, threading through downtown. When he turned off Temple, Tim realized where they were going. They arrived at a grand metal gate, the sole break in the ten-foot fence surrounding Monument Hill. Three parallel wires ran atop the fence at one-foot intervals, emitting a low hum. Mitchell rolled down the window, removed an electronic access-control card from the glove box, and held it out the window before the post-mounted pad of the proximity reader. The card emitted a series of blips as it searched for the matching frequency, and then the gate clicked open with a resonant shifting of inner bolts.

Mitchell tapped the access-control card against his thigh. "The keys to the city. A little gift from the Stork."

They left asphalt behind, driving up the well-worn dirt path, the Census Memorial's one-hundred-foot silhouette breaking the purple-black sky above. On the radio Willie Nelson was crooning about all the girls he'd loved before.

When Mitchell put the truck in park, neither he nor Robert made to get out. It was dead quiet up here, just the darkness and the wind whistling through the monument.

"You did a fine job," Robert said slowly. "But we don't like being kept out of the loop like that."

Tim sat crushed between them, keeping his unease from showing, deciding whose throat he'd throw an elbow into first if the situation got ugly, which it looked like it might.

Robert tossed the phone book into Mitchell's lap. "Show our friend your trick." He nodded at Tim. "You'll like this. Come on, Mitch. Let's see it."

A faint scowl etched Mitchell's face. He picked up the phone book and balanced it on the points of his upturned fingers, a magician's show of its three inches of thickness. Then he gripped it along the cut side in both hands, his thumbs a few inches apart. He flexed, and the book buckled. His arms began to shake. Veins stood out on his neck. His eight knuckles went white. A split snaked through the cover, a thin white river on a yellow sea. His lip was curled, a fringe of flesh and mustache, his teeth exposed like a snarling dog's. His breath came harder. The muscles popped up on his forearms, distinct and stone-hard, peaks on mirrored mountain ranges. His entire torso was quaking.

A sound escaped Mitchell—deeper than a cry, more controlled than a grunt—and the book gave with a pleasing whoosh, ripping apart, the rent edges layered with brief ledges of page like compressed sandstone in a cliff wall. He tossed the two chunks of phone book on the dash, red draining from his face, and took the sweat off his forehead with a wipe of his T-shirt. He and Robert glanced at Tim from either side with a certain schoolyard smugness.

Mitchell kneaded one forearm, then the other. Lightly freckled and covered with blond hair, they were nearly as thick as Tim's biceps.

"Whatever blows your dresses up, ladies." Tim's shirt was sweat-pasted to his lower back, but he kept his voice casual and unimpressed. "Now that the arts and crafts are over, what do you say we have that drink and call it a night?"

After a tense pause, Mitchell smiled, and Robert followed his lead. They climbed out, the truck creaking with relief, and stood on the hilltop. Industrial-tire imprints crushed the dirt into patterns. The ground up here was malleable, the dirt auburn red, like finely milled clay. A scattering of sawhorses and pallets broke up the head-high piles of metal sheets. Thick plastic drop cloths snapped in the breeze.

Nyaze Ghartey's concept—a metallic tree, each branch representing a child killed, the crown outstretched protectively like an umbrella—had seemed to Tim pompous and distastefully abstract, but he had to admit now that there was a certain resonance to the sculpture. The framework of the piece was largely complete, though the metal planes had fleshed out only about two-thirds of it. Wood scaffold-

ing covered the structure from top to bottom; the design itself emerged, organic and mysterious, a darker self lurking
within the ordered rectangles. The leaves, metal and
Bernini-thin, seemed mid-flutter on the branches.

Half a quotation had been chiseled into a flat-sided boulder at the front of the monument: AND THE LEAVES OF THE
TREE WERE FOR

To its left a turned-off Sky-Tracker spotlight, the type
that shot a mile-high beam of beckoning light at movie
premieres and cheesy car sales, sat dormant. Tim could
barely make out the small hatch in the trunk of the tree
through which the spotlight would slide and illuminate the
tree from the interior with the proverbial thousand points
of light.

An ambitious task, to outdo the Hollywood sign, but a
task accomplished.

Tim walked over and pulled three Buds from the bag. He
handed one to Mitchell and offered another to Robert, who
shook his head. "Can't," he said, rustling in the bag himself and coming up with a Sharp's.

Robert popped the top and took several deep gulps,
draining half the bottle. He gazed at the tree before them.
"I usually don't like modern crap," he said. "But this, this
is all right."

"It's like Braque," Mitchell said. "All planes and different perspectives. Do you know Braque?"

Robert and Tim shook their heads, and Mitchell
shrugged off the reference self-consciously. Robert circled
slowly, his boots kicking up puffs of dust, drawing close to
his brother's side as if by genetic pull. Mitchell lit two cigarettes and handed one to Robert, and they smoked and
stood side by side, solid and immobile like two inverted
triangles of hammered steel, sucking Camels, Mitchell
with his sleeve-cuffed pack of cigs, Robert with his jacket

collar turned up, both of them humming along to "Georgia on My Mind" beneath bristled mustaches as if no one had bothered to show up and tell them the seventies were over. Mitchell's face, though less severe than Robert's, held a certain acuteness, a sharpness of perception that Tim had not previously seen. The brothers were beside each other, but Mitchell's elbow was in front of Robert's, and he stood square-shouldered while Robert's shoulders tilted slightly toward him in a vague hint of deference.

Robert raised his beer, and the three bottles clinked, a somber toast.

"A glowing tree is nice, but it ain't gonna solve dick," he said. "I'll tell you what would make a good memorial. One guilty and unconvicted fuck swinging from each branch. That's what I'd like. That's the kind of memorial we oughta build for those victims."

"Water the tree with the blood of retribution," Mitchell said.

He and his brother laughed at the formality, the bad poetics.

The twins' standing to either side of Tim made him claustrophobic, not just because of their bulk and proximity but because their sameness was disorienting. Mitchell sat on the dirt. Robert and Tim followed suit.

"It wears you down," Robert said, "seeing good people take it from the wrong end, seeing the motherfuckers reign supreme, no remorse, no hesitation, no . . ."

"—accountability," Mitchell said.

"Yeah. A part of me decided after our sister died that I wouldn't lie down no more, and so now I'm standing up, even though it's not what I would of stood up for before. Lesser of two evils and all that. And I've made my decision, and it's the right one, and I'll tell you what—I won't lose a second's sleep over the pieces of shit we execute. Not a fuckin' second. We gotta stay firm and committed, guys like us. Not give in to cunts like Ananberg." Robert tilted his face back and shot a stream of cigarette smoke at the moon, patches of dirt coloring his denim jacket at the elbows. "I guess I see things clearer now, about what needs to get done. It's like we're stuck in this . . . in this . . ."

"—conundrum—" Mitchell said.

"—where we're fucked if we do and we get fucked if we don't."

"They say the worst cynics are frustrated idealists," Tim said.

Mitchell drained his beer and popped a new one. "You think we're cynics?"

"I don't know what you are."

The wind kicked up, making the scaffolding groan, sending red puffs up off the ground.

"We couldn't wait to get started," Robert said. "It's the waiting that kills you. You find out that your little sister was brutally murdered, and then you're . . ."

"—mired—"

"—in nothingness. Waiting for the investigation, waiting for a suspect to be produced, waiting on forensics, the first court appearance, then the next, then the next. . . ." Robert shook his head. "It's what we hate most of all."

"Now, finally," Mitchell said, "we don't have to wait anymore."

Tim mused on this silently.

"Let us in more next time around," Mitchell said. "We can handle it. We'll win your trust."

The phone-book intimidation tactic hadn't yielded, so they'd moved to Plan B: ingratiation. Tim was no more swayed by it. "We'll see."

Robert leaned forward abruptly. "What, our work wasn't good enough for you?"

"Your work was fine. Excellent, even."

"Then we want in on the kill. You can't deny us that. We *won't* be denied." Mitchell shot Robert a sharp look, but he didn't catch the hint because he was watching Tim closely. "We can help you with your daughter's case," he continued. "With Kindell. Before we vote even, me and Mitch can pay him a little visit. Rattle his cage, bend his elbow, pop a testicle or two. We'll get you whatever answers you want. Who knows—we could even have a hands-on chat with that prick public defender of his."

Tim stared at them in disbelief, trying to order his thoughts. "That's exactly the opposite of how we need to conduct ourselves." If their faces were any indication, the anger in his voice was startling. "This is not a proceed-at-any-cost operation. It's not about rashness and lawlessness. Neither of you have the first idea what the Commission is actually *about*, and you're wondering why I'm reluctant to cut you into the action."

To Tim's surprise neither brother matched his anger. Robert dug at the ground with a stick. "You're right," he said softly. "It's just that your little girl's case, Virginia's case, really"—his cheeks drew up in a half squint, half grimace—"really tore us up. It about broke my fuckin' heart."

Robert's reaction was completely genuine—it had none of the manipulation Tim had sensed in so much of the brothers' previous maneuvering. The expression of empathy surprised him so thoroughly that his anger deflated at once, leaving him with only the sorrow he saw mirrored back at him from both faces. He got busy playing with his bottle cap so his eyes would have something to look at.

"Now and then, no matter what you've seen, a case sails through all the chinks in your armor and strikes home."

Mitchell's throat gave off a rattle when he spoke. "At least our sister lived a few years before getting taken. Not like your little girl."

Robert's face, lit with the distant glow of downtown, was stone-hard with either rage or sclerosed sorrow. "I saw her picture on TV, that clip they ran. The one of her in a pumpkin costume, too big, kept falling down."

"Halloween 2001." Tim's voice was so soft it was barely audible. "My wife tried to stitch the costume. She's not very domestic."

"She was a great kid, Virginia," Robert said with an almost aggressive adamancy. "I could tell, even just from what I saw."

Tim understood for the first time that the brothers weren't simply justifying their desire to kill criminals, but that they'd taken Ginny's death personally, as they took each of the Commission's cases personally. Their sister remained frozen in time, locked in a hellish script, to be rekilled in their minds every time a murderer escaped justice. While this made them flawed participants for a cause that called for objectivity and circumspection, Tim couldn't deny a certain gratitude for their brute emotionality. He grasped at last the note of affection, even admiration, hidden in Dumone's voice when he spoke of them. They mourned with a hurt-animal purity uncomplicated by law or ethic. Maybe they mourned as Tim and Dumone wished they themselves were capable of doing.

Robert's words drew Tim from his thoughts. "She had the look, man," he continued, "the one that the motherfuckers must get after, like she was too pure to stick around this shitty planet too long." He drained his beer and hurled the bottle. It shattered against a pile of stacked metal sheets. "Beth Ann had that look, too."

He tipped his face down into the waiting points of his

thumb and forefinger, and he stayed like that, squeezing his eyes, silent. Mitchell leaned over, hooked his brother's neck with a hand, and pulled him forward until the tops of their heads were touching, just above their foreheads.

Tim watched them, his face numb with dread. "It doesn't get any easier," he said. He had intended it as a question.

Robert pulled his head back. His eyes were red from being rubbed, yet they held not tears, but rage. The dark scaffolding creaked behind him in the wind.

Mitchell leaned back, propped on two elbow-locked arms, his face barely visible in the darkness. "The average sexual assault by an anger-excitation rapist lasts four hours," he said. "Beth Ann wasn't so lucky."

After that they drank in silence.

After Mitchell dropped him at his car, Tim drove back to his apartment cautiously, watching his signals and abiding the speed limit. The radio was abuzz with talk of the execution. From the faces of other drivers, he could tell who was listening to the news and who was discussing it on their cell phones. He even thought he sensed a different mood in the air, as if the city itself had received an adrenaline jolt, absorbed by osmosis from the fallout caused by Lane's death. The night seemed exciting and excited, alive with the animation of risk and high stakes. A proximity to death always brought with it an attendant heightening of the senses.

Joshua was struggling across the lobby with an ornately carved picture frame. He paused when Tim entered, setting it on the floor. Blue TV light flickered in his tiny office, as always.

"Wait, wait!" he shrieked, as if Tim were fleeing. "I have paperwork for you." He leaned the frame against the wall and disappeared into his small office, reappearing with a rental agreement made out to the ever-reliable Tom Altman.

He waited as Tim reviewed it, a finger bearing an immense agate stone coming to rest on the side of his chin. "Cute beard."

"Thanks."

"Did you hear about the guy who got his head blown up on the news?"

"There was something about it on the radio."

"Right-winger." Joshua's hand rose to his mouth, shielding a stage whisper. "One down, fifty million to go."

Upstairs Tim entered his apartment, taking note of the deadness of the air within. It took him about ten minutes with lukewarm sink water and a razor to eradicate his emergent beard.

He opened the window, then sat cross-legged on the floor and thought about what, at age thirty-three, he had in his life. A mattress, a desk, a gun, bullets. A car with fraudulent plates previously owned by a drug runner.

He cleaned his gun again, though it was already clean, oiling, polishing, punching the bore brush through the holes in the cylinder. Each punch of the brush he accompanied with a word describing what he could have done to Kindell in the garage. Murder. Slay. Execute. Sacrifice. Destroy. Slaughter.

The Lane execution had not just righted a judicial wrong, he reminded himself, it had brought him one case closer to Kindell. And to the secret of Ginny's death.

After checking the Nokia, he was surprised by the keenness of his disappointment that he had no messages. Dray had not called since he'd left the notes at the house, which stung like hell. It also meant she'd gathered no further information on the case. When he called, he got the machine. He called back just to hear her voice again, then hung up.

He found himself dialing Bear's number.

"Where the hell you been, Rack?"

"Sorting things out, I guess."

"Well, sort faster. The disappearing act isn't sitting so hot with Dray. Or with me."

"How is she?" Only now did Tim grasp his true motivation for phoning Bear. Tim Rackley, Master of High School Social Dynamics.

"Ask her yourself," Bear said. "And while we're at it, what's your new phone number?"

"I don't have one yet." Tim walked over near the open window. "I'm calling from a pay phone. Still lining out a more permanent place."

"I want to see you."

"Now's not the greatest—"

"Listen, either you can agree to see me, or I'll come track your ass down. And you know I will. What's it gonna be?"

A breeze, contaminated with heat from the alley-backing kitchen below, swept away the dusty smell of the room, if only temporarily. Tim breathed in the amalgam of cool and breath-hot air. The distant touch of a headache cramped him at the temples.

"All right then," Bear said. "Yamashiro, early dinner, tomorrow at five-thirty."

He hung up before waiting for Tim to agree.

Tim lay on the mattress, enveloped in darkness. When he dozed off, he dreamed of Ginny. She was laughing at him, petite fingers covering her child-spaced teeth.

He couldn't figure out why.

**20** YAMASHIRO, A JAPANESE RESTAURANT PERCHED ATOP A hill in East Hollywood, looks down over its steep-sloped front gardens to the distant neon flash of the Boulevard and Sunset. Through the miasma of smog and car exhaust spread low along the Strip, Britney Spears threw a five-foot gaze from a building-side banner ad, all wide grin and vacant eyes, a Dr. T. J. Eckleburg for the aught decade.

About two years back, Tim and Bear had collared a fugitive who'd injured Kose Nagura's wife in a jewelry-store heist, and the restaurant manager had shown his gratefulness in the form of ceaseless imploration for them to dine at his restaurant free of charge. Despite their discomfort at the place's specious high-class ambience and raw-fish fare, they tried to take him up on his offer at least once every few months to avoid insulting him. Besides, the drinks were good, the view from the hilltop bar was the most spectacular in all of L.A., and the building—an exact replica of a grand Kyoto palace—had a certain majestic appeal.

Tim wound his car up the precipitous snaking drive to the restaurant and left it with the valet. As usual, Kose seated him at the best table immediately upon his entering, a four-top at the restaurant's southeast apex, where glass wall meets glass wall, providing a panoramic view of the smoldering billboard- and smog-draped buildings below—a view of the L.A. that the Mastersons deplored. The crass money- and fame-grubbing sprawl of middle-class aspiration for stardom, an asphaltopolis that raised child stars as tall as buildings and rewarded greed and ruthlessness, a town where rapists and child-killers could gorge their appetites in like company.

Tim played with the straw in his water glass, waiting for Bear, rehearsing all the dumb things he knew he was going to say in hope of discovering better wording. A couple to his left was holding hands across the table, casually, as if their easy-found affection were something to be taken for granted, something found everywhere, like frustration, like smog, like aspiring actors. He sensed the deep tug of his need to be with his wife. He reframed his thoughts, deciding what he would impart to Bear, the messenger. A white flag, perhaps.

Bear appeared, a large form in gray polyester pants and a just-mismatched blazer, stretching past one of the sliding shoji walls leading from the inner courtyard. Tim stood, and they embraced, Bear holding him for an extra beat before sliding into his chair.

Tim nodded at Bear's rumpled suit. "You'd better hurry up and get that thing back on the body. The wake's at seven."

"Clever."

"Court duty?"

"Yup. Tannino found out I bet against Italy in the World Cup last year, so he stuck it to me. Two days before I can go out-of-pocket again." Bear's face seemed to move and settle into an expression of weariness. "There's no way for me to say this, so I'm just gonna spit it out." He paused. "If you don't knock off the strong, silent routine, Dray's gonna figure out she's fine without you."

"What does that mean?"

"While you've been MIA, Dray's been going through Ginny's stuff, getting out of the house, seeing friends. She's doing this on her own. You sure you want her to?"

"Of course I don't want her to. But we don't know how to do it together."

"Doesn't seem like you're knocking yourself out trying." Bear picked up the paper-hat-folded napkin, then set it back down. "Are you having an affair?"

Tim fought to find impassivity. "Bear, I understand you're trying to help, but this isn't really—"

"What? My business? Let me tell you what is my business. You may not embarrass your wife. It's your right to embarrass yourself all you want, but Dray's been through enough. You're not gonna drag her through more."

"Bear. I'm not having an affair."

"I talk to Dray every day. And I'm getting a weird vibe from her when your name comes up, like she doesn't trust what you're up to. Plus, if you hadn't Houdinied on her, I hardly think she'd need—" He stopped. Pulled the napkin from the table and smoothed it across his lap, eyes lowered and regretful.

"She'd need . . . ?"

Bear's hands paused. "Mac. She's had some really bad nights. Mac slept over a few times—not like that, just on the couch—to see her through."

"*Mac?*" Tim snapped his chopsticks apart and frictioned off the splinters. Hard. "Why didn't she call you?"

"Because I'm still your partner first and foremost. Mac's one of hers. And that's the wrong damn question. The correct question is, why didn't she call *you?*"

"What'd you tell her?"

"What do you think I told her? That she was being a fucking idiot, that she should have swallowed her pride and called you, like you should have swallowed your pride and called her." Bear took no note of the glances from neighboring tables. He shook his head, disgusted. "You're both stubborn, spiteful people who will die alone."

Tim continued to work the chopsticks back and forth, harder. "We decided we needed to take a little time off. We were tangling up in each other."

"Have you really not seen her in five days?"

Tim felt a sudden heat in his cheeks. He took a sip of water, got a mouthful of lemon. "That doesn't mean I don't love her."

The waiter came up, and Bear ordered quickly for both of them without looking at the menu, naming the spicy shrimp simmered in sake, crab cakes, and seven-spice mussels. He'd been coming here more than once every few months, that was clear. Probably taking the occasional date.

When the waiter left, Bear fixed Tim with an apologetic stare. "Look, I'm just saying you should call her. You need each other. And she needs you—that house went from full to empty in a hurry. Can't really blame her for wanting someone around in the wake of all this, even if it is Mac sleeping on the couch. And while we're at it, when are you coming back to work?"

Tim looked up, surprised. "I'm not coming back, Bear. You know that."

"Tannino's wondering why he's having so much trouble reaching you. He's pulled me into his office twice this week to make clear he hasn't accepted your resignation."

"He doesn't have a choice."

"What are you doing, Rack? What are you up to?"

"Nothing. I'm just dealing with things on my own for a while."

For the first time Tim could remember, he didn't recognize the look in Bear's eyes. "Let me add to the list of things that I will make my business. You can't embarrass me. Not as your partner. And you can't embarrass the service." Bear leaned back, crossed his arms. "I know you're up to something. I don't know what, but I'll figure it out if I want to."

"You're overreacting. There's nothing going on."

"I thought you said you didn't have a phone." Bear's voice was firm, driving. "So what was the bulge in your pocket when you hugged me? It hasn't been *that* long."

Tim had instinctively grabbed his cell phones so as not to leave them unattended in the car with the valets. An unforgivable oversight. "Picked it up this morning. 323-471-1213. Don't give the number to anyone."

"Why all the cloak-and-dagger?"

"There's still a lot of fallout from the shooting, media hounding me, so I'd just as soon stay under for a while."

"Really? I haven't seen anything lately. Everyone's whipped up about the Lane assassination now. You hear about the guy who pulled that off? They're snake eyes on leads—guy must have been an ice-cold professional." He shook his head. "Cranium ventilation. They always can find a new trick."

Tim shrugged. "It's not so bad. One less mutt on the street."

Bear's forehead furrowed into a wrinkled pane.

Tim looked down, played with his straw. An emotion rippled through him that took him a moment to identify. Shame. He realized he was giving off nervous energy, so he dropped the straw, placed his hands on his knees.

Bear pointed at him with a chopstick. "Don't let Ginny's death eat you away. Don't let it corrupt you. There's enough ignorance out there. The one person I don't expect it from is you."

The waiter arrived with their food, and they ate in silence.

A funeral procession passed by while Tim idled at the stoplight at Franklin and Highland. The hearse led, somber and dignified, and a convoy of rain-polished cars followed—Toyotas, Hondas, and the obligatory drove of SUVs. Seized by an impulse, Tim pulled out behind the last car and followed the line of vehicles to the Hollywood Forever Memorial Park. He parked a block and a half away. By the time he'd made his way through the solemn front gate and over the first grassy hill, the ceremony was under way.

He watched from a distance, the mourners arrayed in black and gray, diminutive like figurines. When the sun managed to knife through the smog, Tim donned sunglasses to cut the glare. The presumed widower shovel-turned a scattering of rocks and dirt into the open grave, and, despite the distance, Tim could hear it patter on the unseen casket. The man collapsed to a knee, and two young men stepped forward quickly, chagrined, to help him up. He managed as best he could, a patch of mud weighing down his wind-flickering trouser leg, the sun glimmering off his cheeks.

A murder of crows swept in and blanketed an overlooking sycamore, where they looked on, sleek and inauspicious. Tim waited several minutes for the birds to depart, but they didn't, so finally he turned his back and headed down the too-green slope toward his car.

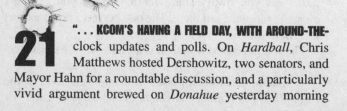

**21** **"... KCOM'S HAVING A FIELD DAY, WITH AROUND-THE-**clock updates and polls. On *Hardball*, Chris Matthews hosted Dershowitz, two senators, and Mayor Hahn for a roundtable discussion, and a particularly vivid argument brewed on *Donahue* yesterday morning during a segment titled, 'The Lane Slaying: Terrorism or Justice?' "

Rayner shuffled through his sheaf of notes while the others sat in varying degrees of attentiveness around the table, waiting for his media recap to conclude. Like mirrored objects, Robert and Mitchell sat on either side of the table, each shoved back in his chair, each with his legs loosely crossed, sneaker resting on opposite knee. Their languid postures suggested boredom; at last an attribute they shared with Ananberg. The Stork listened intently—Tim noted he had a tendency to blink frequently when concentrating—and Dumone, leaning back in his chair, statue-still, hands laced across his stomach, took it all in with a silent, almost magnanimous patience.

Rayner at last reached the final page of his report. "The footage of the execution is making the rounds on the Internet via a chain e-mail with an mpeg attachment—it's the topic of choice in a wide range of chat rooms. A family-values activist appearing on *Oprah* this afternoon expressed concern about the impact the footage has had on children. She drew a comparison to the *Challenger* exploding on live TV or the planes hitting the World Trade Center."

"Except those were *regrettable* events," Robert said.

Mitchell's grin flashed beneath his thick mustache. "It's adult content, all right."

"And now the big news," Dumone said. "I have it on good authority that LAPD recovered an undisclosed amount of sarin nerve gas in the trunk of Lane's car. In a canister prepped for aerosol delivery. A briefcase in the passenger seat contained diagrams of KCOM's air-conditioning system, with the ducts labeled based on ease of accessibility. It seems not unlikely that Lane was planning on leaving a little gift for the government-controlled leftist media on his way back into hiding."

"Why hasn't that information been made public?" Tim asked.

"Because it shows LAPD's ass. Particularly after September 11, intel and enforcement communities aren't rushing to the public to point out their oversights and blind spots. Especially regarding a suspect who's so obvious. Another atrocity was avoided only because of dumb luck."

"And us," Robert added.

Rayner smoothed his mustache with his thumb and forefinger. "The public knows nothing about that, but still the polls are overwhelmingly in our favor."

"We didn't do this for the polls," Tim said, but Rayner didn't appear to hear.

"Three morning talk shows over the past two days featured call-ins regarding variations of the same question: Was Lane's assassination an undesirable event? 'No' scored seventy-six, seventy-two, and sixty-six percent. The proper news shows' pedestrian interviews were fairly well split between tacit approvers and indignant citizens. A significant minority expressed their disgust that such a thing had occurred, regardless of the character of the victim. One commentator referred to it as 'pornographic.'"

"How do you get all this stuff?" Mitchell asked. "I don't see you watching TV twenty-four/seven."

"Media breakdowns on topics relevant to my research are faxed to me twice daily."

Ananberg ran her hands over her thighs, smoothing her skirt. She wore a striped dress shirt with well-starched cuffs, cut like a man's, which oddly made it more feminine, and a sweater arranged in a country-club loop just below her neck. The frames of her glasses peaked out at the top corners. "Grad students," she said. "The ultimate workhorses. And you don't even have to groom them."

"So far my sense of it is, no one knows what to make of

us yet," Rayner said. "So I'd like to raise the obvious consideration at this point, one which I'm sure we've all given some thought to. Do we make our position—though not our identities—public?"

"Absolutely not," Dumone said. "Too much of an operational risk."

"We want more from Lane's death than public euphoria. It may be more effective to take credit and explain how we arrived at the decision."

"I think it's cowardice not to," Ananberg said. "No responsible state—no entity I respect or trust—commits secret executions. It was a public act. I say we leak some sort of communiqué that states how we determined his guilt. 'We citizens who have empowered ourselves thus, made the decision on the following evidence—' "

"We do not submit the defendant to the mob in this country," Dumone said. "Our judges and juries don't grovel for societal support. They make rulings."

Rayner said, "We could release some equivalent to the minutes—"

"Any sophisticated document would be laden with clues for the press and the authorities," Tim said.

"No," the Stork said. "No way we make a statement. Too great a risk."

"It's irresponsible *not* to give the public our rationale," Rayner said. "Without it they're left with nothing but the aftermath of a lynching."

Dumone said, "Lane's death was all about restraint, precision, circumspection. The public will be able to distinguish it as an execution, not a hit."

"Who cares if it's distinguished?" Robert said.

"The difference," Dumone said sharply, "is everything."

Rayner said, "A communiqué would clarify matters *precisely*."

"If you're with us, toot your car horns on your morning commute," Tim said.

"It wouldn't be that vulgar, Mr. Rackley. We're trying to force meaningful dialogue from a recalcitrant public here. How does society feel about criminals who get off through loopholes? Should the system be amended? Was Lane's execution justice?"

"Yes," Robert said.

Tim felt a familiar pull—instinctive resistance in the face of Robert's unequivocality.

"We know it. Anyone who studies the record knows it. That's good enough for me," Mitchell said. "And those who don't get it now *will* after the next execution. We'll soon establish a pattern. We don't need to turn over potentially damning evidence."

"You're going to be in high demand, I'm sure, for talking-head appearances," Dumone said to Rayner. "And, if you'd like, you can always steer conversation in the appropriate direction. Keep dialogue on track—*without* giving anything up. But we're not exposing ourselves at this stage. We can revisit the issue later."

Ananberg leaned back in her chair, thin arms woven across her chest in an inadvertently prudish show of frustration. Rayner tilted his head, his expression one of concession.

Rayner's financial supremacy and facility with armchair social theory ostensibly put him in the driver's seat, but it was ever clearer that Dumone was the on-the-ground chief. When Rayner talked, the others listened; when Dumone spoke, they shut up.

"Can we get to voting?" Robert asked. "I didn't exactly come down here to talk about missives and Oprah Fuckin' Win—"

Dumone fanned a flat hand, a gesture that was at once

soothing and firm, and Robert cut off midsentence. Robert offered his brother a face-saving smirk as Rayner opened the safe and removed another binder from the stack. It hit the table with a slap.

"Mick Dobbins."

"Mickey the Molester?" Robert said. He shot Ananberg a look. "Listen, sugarbritches, Mickey the *Alleged* Molester just don't have the same ring."

Dumone held the binder before him in one hand like a psalm book, letting it fall open. "Groundskeeper at Venice Care for Kids. Indicted on eight counts of lewd acts with a child, one count of murder one. Before the incidents, he was beloved by kids and staff." He passed the detective progress reports to Tim. "IQ seventy-six."

"Does that preclude capital punishment right off the bat?" Tim asked.

Ananberg shook her head. "Two independent psychiatric evaluations failed to classify him as mentally retarded. I guess it doesn't just come down to IQ, it has to do with level of functioning and other stuff."

The remainder of the papers were segmented and passed around the table.

"Seven girls, ages four to five, claimed they were molested by him," Dumone said.

"How?" Tim asked.

"Genital and anal touching. Some digital insertion. One girl claimed to have been sodomized with a pen."

"Intercourse?"

"No." Dumone shuffled through the pages, glancing at the lab results.

"How's this a capital case?" Ananberg asked.

"Peggie Knoll was admitted to the hospital with high fever, shaking chills. Evidently it was a bladder infection—by the time they caught it, it had turned into a kidney infection. She died of"—he flipped open the hospital report—"overwhelming urosepsis."

"Did they do a rape kit?"

"No. Knoll never claimed to have been molested. It wasn't until after her death that the seven girls came forth, said they and Knoll were molested, put Knoll's molest a few days prior to her hospitalization. The DA backtracked—paraded out a few expert witnesses who said if a molest—especially anal-vaginal—occurred in that time frame, it was a proximate cause of the bladder infection."

"How did Dobbins get off?" the Stork asked. He blushed deeply, hiding his face by sliding his glasses farther up his nose. "The trial, I mean."

"The jury found him guilty, but the judge was underwhelmed with the merits and threw the case out for insufficiency of evidence."

"They're overturning juries now," Robert said with disgust.

"There was a decided lack of physical evidence," Dumone said. "Nothing in Knoll's medical records. The search of Dobbins's apartment turned up nothing. The case detective noted a stack of pornography in a bathroom cabinet. Several issues of the magazine *Barely Legal.*"

"I know it well," Ananberg said. Six sets of eyes fastened on her. Mitchell looked distinctly annoyed; Tim alone wore a half smile.

"Pornography don't mean shit," Robert said. "What else? What about the medical reports on the other girls?"

The Stork raised his hand, his eyes, shiny through his glasses, focused on the sheet in front of him. "Medical examinations were inconclusive. No tearing, no scarring, no bruising, no bleeding, no trauma associated with penetration."

"But penetration was just digital," Mitchell said. "That would cause less trauma."

"On a five-year-old girl, something would still be detectable," Ananberg said.

"How long after the alleged molestation were the girls examined?" Tim asked.

The Stork flipped a sheet over. "Two weeks."

"Plenty of healing time."

"Especially if there were just superficial tears or light bruising," Mitchell added.

"No DNA, no nothing?" Ananberg asked. "Anywhere?"

Rayner shook his head. "No."

"So the whole case hung on the girls' testimony? Do you have the interrogation tapes?"

Rayner pulled two tapes from his briefcase. "I got hold of them a few weeks ago." He crossed the room and slid the first one into a VCR hidden in a dark wood cabinet. "The supervising DA and I were in Ivy together." Off the others' puzzled expressions, he added, "My eating club at Princeton."

The tape quality was poor; the recording jerked a bit, and the lighting washed out the interview room to whites and yellows. A young girl sat on a plastic chair, her heels resting at the seat's edge, her knees drawn up to her chin.

The interviewer—presumably a Suspected Child Abuse and Neglect social worker—sat on a low footstool, facing the girl. ". . . and so he touched you?"

The girl hugged her legs, clasping her hands midway up her shins. "Yes."

"Okay, you're doing a good job, Lisa. Did he touch you somewhere you didn't want him to?"

"No."

A frown appeared on the social worker's face, a barely

noticeable furrowing between her eyebrows. Her voice was soft and reassuring. "Are you sure you're not scared to answer, sweetheart?"

Lisa rested her chin on her knees. Her head bounced a few times before Tim realized she was chewing gum. "Not scared."

"Okay. Then I'll ask you again. . . ." Calm, drawn-out sentences. "Did he touch you somewhere on your lower body?"

A tiny voice, almost inaudible. "Yes . . ."

The social worker's face softened with empathy. "Where? Can you show me on these dolls?" Two puppets appeared almost instantly from the social worker's bag, complete with shiny polyester genitalia.

Lisa studied them tentatively before reaching out to take them. She made the male puppet hold hands with the little girl puppet, then looked up at the social worker.

"Okay . . . then what?"

Lisa arranged the puppets in an embrace.

"Okay . . . and after that?"

Lisa chewed her gum thoughtfully for a moment, then put the male puppet's hand on the little girl's chest.

"Very good, Lisa. Very good. And that's how Peggie told you she was touched also?"

Lisa nodded solemnly.

Rayner looked troubled. He exchanged a glance with Ananberg, who shook her head, unimpressed. "Let's watch the rest of the interviews first," he said.

Occasionally fast-forwarding, they made their way through the following six interviews, each of which featured similar questioning techniques by the same social worker.

When the last girl finished tearfully recounting her molestation, Rayner stopped the tape. "It was a damn witch-hunt. No wonder the judge threw out the verdict."

"What are you talking about?" Robert said. "Every one of those girls said they were molested. They even acted it out on the dolls."

"The social worker asked leading questions, Rob," Dumone said. "It's fine for us, trying to pull a confession, but kids are more impressionable. They parrot."

"How were the questions leading?"

"For starters, there weren't any general questions," Ananberg said. "Like 'What happened?' The social worker was prompting, implanting all the information through closed, suggestive questions. So 'Did he touch you below the belt?' turns into 'Where did he touch you below the belt?' And she was conditioning the girls, rewarding them for the answers she wanted to hear—smiling, saying 'Good,' telling them it's okay."

"And frowning when she didn't like what she heard," Rayner added. "If a girl gave the 'wrong' answer, she was subjected to repeated questioning—and the interviewer's tacit disapproval—until she made something up."

Tim glanced through the files at the badly photocopied detective notes. "The girls were in the same circles. Parents knew each other. After the first accusation, there were meetings between the families, conferences at school. Cross-pollination. These recorded interviews happened later. The witnesses weren't exactly working from a clean slate."

"And who knows how many other opportunities there were to have memories implanted and reinforced?" Ananberg added. "Other kids, media . . ." She spun her hand in a double loop, a gestured *et cetera*.

"What about the dolls?" Mitchell said.

"Same criticisms apply," Rayner said. "On top of which, anatomically correct dolls are not recommended to be used with very young children."

"Only with the elderly," Ananberg said.

Robert fixed her with a piercing stare. "This isn't a fucking joke." He gestured to his brother. "Not to us."

"I don't think she meant anything," Dumone said.

"No, he's right." Ananberg ran her hand through her dark brown hair. "I'm sorry. Just trying to defuse the tension in here. It's a, uh, tough topic."

"If you can't handle tough topics, maybe you're in the wrong place."

"Robert. She apologized," Tim said. "Let's keep moving."

Ananberg returned to her usual briskly professional tone. "According to the Ceci and Bruck study published in 1995, questioning young children with anatomically correct dolls is less than reliable."

Mitchell glanced up from the court file. "Who cares about the dolls? According to this, the guy confessed."

"The confession was persuasively called into question by the defense," Rayner said. He strode over to the VCR and switched tapes.

The cold light of a police interrogation room. The camera caught some glare from the backside of a one-way mirror. Mick Dobbins sat hunched in a metal folding chair while two detectives worked him. Despite his solid frame and broad shoulders, his orientation was distinctly youthful. His arms hung loose and heavy between his spread knees, and his left sneaker was untied, his foot turned on its side. One of his overalls straps had come undone; it swayed at his side like a yo-yo waiting to be snapped up.

The detectives had the lights going hot, one of them always staying just out of Dobbins's view, to his side, behind his back. Dobbins kept his head hung but tried to follow the detectives with his eyes, which peered nervously through the sweat-matted tangle of his bangs. His low-set ears protruded from his oddly rectangular head like opposing coffee-mug handles.

"So you like girls?" the detective asked.

"Yeah. Girls. Girls 'n' boys." When Dobbins spoke, his mild retardation was immediately apparent in his low register and plodding cadence.

"You like girls a lot, don't you? Don't you?" The detective raised a foot, placed it squarely on the small patch of metal chair exposed between Dobbins's legs. Dobbins lowered his head more, tucking his chin into the hollow of his shoulder. The detective leaned forward, his face inches from the top of Dobbins's head. "I asked you a question. Tell me about them, tell me about the girls. You like them? You like girls?"

"Y-y-yeah. I like girls."

"Do you like touching them?"

Dobbins wiped his nose with the back of his hand, a rough, frustrated gesture. He muttered to himself. "Chocolate, vanilla, rocky road—"

The detective snapped his fingers inches from Dobbins's face. "Do you like touching them?"

"I hug girls. Girls and boys."

"Do you like touching girls?"

"Yeah."

"Yeah what?"

"I like touching girls. I . . ."

"You *what?*"

Dobbins jerked at the sharpness of the detective's tone. He squeezed his eyes shut. "Strawberry, mocha almond fu—"

"You what, Mick? You what?"

"I, uh, uh, I sometimes pet them when they're upset."

"You pet them, and they get upset?"

Dobbins scratched his head above one ear, then smelled his fingers. "Yeah."

"That what happened with Peggie Knoll? *Is it?*"

Dobbins cowered from the voice. "I think so. Yeah."

After double-checking the file, Rayner paused the video. "That's really the essential segment."

"That's no confession," Tim said.

"Pretty weak," Mitchell agreed. "I'll grant you it wasn't a confession, but I don't think we need a confession here. I think the other evidence holds."

"What other evidence?" Ananberg asked. "Seven impressionable children regurgitating implanted memories? A girl who died of an infection that was never conclusively linked to a molestation that was never proven to have occurred?"

"So let me get this straight," Robert said. "We have seven little girls who testify individually that they've been molested by a retard groundskeeper, we have each of them acting out with puppets the sick shit the freak perpetrated on them, we have them each saying he molested their friend who's now dead from a resulting infection, we have him on tape saying he likes to pet and hug little girls, and you don't think this is an open-and-shut?"

Tim pictured Harrison outside Kindell's, arms crossed. *It's an open-and-shut.*

"No," Tim said. "I don't."

Robert directed his scowl down the table. "Stork?"

The Stork's rounded shoulders rose and fell. "I don't really care."

"If you're gonna sit in this room," Tim said, "you'd better care."

"Fine," the Stork said. "I think he probably did it."

"Franklin?" Rayner asked.

Dumone shrugged. "We're thin on physical evidence, especially with no indication of vaginal or rectal damage on any of the girls and nothing concrete linking the bladder infection and the molest."

"Dobbins has got no criminal history," Ananberg said. "No felonies, no misdemeanors."

"That don't mean shit," Robert said. "A puke can start anytime."

"It just means he's never been caught for anything before." Mitchell exhaled hard through his nose, irritated. "Sounds like you've made up your minds already. Why don't we take a nonbinding preliminary vote to see if we're just wasting our time in continuing our assessment here?"

Ananberg looked to Rayner with an arched eyebrow, and he nodded.

The vote went down four to three, not guilty.

The Stork looked typically indifferent, but Robert and Mitchell were having difficulty keeping their frustration out of their faces.

"We're here to pick up the slack when the courts screw up," Mitchell said. "When we fail to act, there's no other recourse."

"Acting is not always the right decision," Tim said.

Robert's eyes remained locked on the photograph of his deceased sister. "Tell that to the seven little girls who were molested and the dead girl's parents."

"The seven little girls who *said* they were molested," Ananberg said.

"Listen, bitch—"

Dumone rocked forward in his chair. "Rob—"

"You might think you have the answers in here, with your studies and your Freudian bullshit, but you haven't so much as set high heel on the real streets, so don't you fucking tell me you know shit about who's done what."

*"Robert!"*

"Until you spend some time with these pieces of shit, you don't know how they tick." Robert jerked his head toward the TV. "That fucker just *smells* guilty."

Dumone was standing now in a half crouch above his chair, hands on the table, arms elbow-locked, bearing his weight. "Believe it or not, your sense of smell isn't the criterion for our voting. You can argue the merits, argue the cases, or you can hop a Greyhound back to Detroit and stop wasting our time."

The room froze—Rayner's glass halfway to his mouth, Ananberg midturn in her chair.

Dumone's eyes burned with an uncharacteristic fury. "Do you understand me?"

Mitchell's face was drawn. "Listen, Franklin, I don't think—"

Dumone's hand shot up, a crossing guard's signal aimed in Mitchell's direction, and Mitchell stopped cold.

Robert's expression softened, his head ducking slightly under the heat of Dumone's glare. "Shit, I didn't mean it."

"Well, don't pull that crap in here. Do you understand me? *Do you understand me?*"

"Yes." Robert raised his head but could barely meet Dumone's eyes. "Like I said, it was nothing. I was just pissed off."

" 'Pissed off' has no place in our proceedings. Apologize to Ms. Ananberg."

"Look," Ananberg said, "I don't think that's really necessary."

"I do." Dumone kept his glare leveled at Robert.

Robert finally turned to face Ananberg. The emotion had

burned itself out of his face, leaving behind an eerie calm. "I apologize."

She laughed nervously, a single note. "Don't worry about it."

Silence descended over the table.

"Why don't we take a little break before we tackle the next case?" Rayner said.

Tim stood on the half circle of Rayner's back patio, gazing out at the elaborate back gardens. A few motion-sensor lights had kicked on when he'd stepped from the house, shining golden cylinders into the night and illuminating flurries of winged insects.

He heard the screen door rattle open and then close, and he smelled Ananberg's perfume—light and citrusy—when she was still a few steps behind him.

"Got a light?"

Her hand hooked around his side and slid into the front pocket of his jacket. He grabbed her wrist, withdrew her hand, and turned. Their faces were inches apart. "I don't smoke."

She smirked. "Relax, Rackley. Cops aren't my type."

"That's right. Teacher's pet."

She seemed genuinely pleased. "A sense of humor. Who'da thunk it?"

Her hair, fine and dark, looked as though it would be silken. Ananberg was Dray's opposite—petite, brunette, flirtatious—and she evoked in Tim a distinct discomfort. He turned back to the dark sprawl of the gardens. Rows of box shrubs zigzagged before fading into darkness.

Ananberg pulled a cigarette from her pack, stuck it into her mouth, and patted her pockets fruitlessly. "What are you looking at?"

"Just the darkness."

"You like playing Mr. Mysterious, don't you? The brooding routine, the strong, silent thing. I think it gives you distance, comfort."

"You got me all figured out."

"I wouldn't go that far." She set her hands on her hips, studying him. Her curt amusement was gone. "Thanks for sticking up for me in there."

"You don't need sticking up for. I was just speaking my mind."

"Robert can be pretty aggressive."

"Agreed."

"Does that concern you?"

"Absolutely." Tim gave a glance back at the lit windows of the house. Dumone, the Stork, and Robert were waiting at the conference-room table. He scanned the side of the house, spotting Rayner in the kitchen pulling a bottled water from the fridge. Mitchell stepped into view, near his side, and Rayner drew him near, hand resting on his shoulder, whispering something in his ear. Tim glanced back over at Dumone and wondered if he knew that Rayner and Mitchell were swapping secrets two rooms over. Tim had assumed the two disliked each other—the egghead and the redneck enduring each other only as necessary instruments to help attain their respective aims.

"Dumone can keep him in line. Him and Mitchell."

Tim chewed the inside of his cheek. "Your acuity threatens him. And your consistency."

"Does it threaten you?"

"I think it's exactly what we need."

"Maybe so. But it feels petty, somehow. Even to me."

"How so?"

"You see"—her eyes got shy, darted away—"I think it's great that you're seeking an idea of justice that you can hold in your hands. It's courageous, almost. But for me that's like believing in God. I think it would be fun. It would certainly be reassuring. But I stick with my statistics and little dogmatic regurgitations because I know the rules of that game."

A thoughtful noise escaped Tim, but he didn't respond. He worked his cheek, studied the dark shapes of the bushes.

She stood by his side, gazing at the garden as if trying to figure out what he was looking at. "That was something else you pulled off. The Lane hit."

"Team effort."

"Well, you had to front the lion's share of the nerve." She shook her head, and again he smelled her fragrance, thought about her hair. "Robert's right on one count—I'm about as far from the street as you can get. I'm glad I'm on this side of things. Discussing, reviewing, analyzing. I could never do what you do. The risk, the danger, the courage under pressure." She slapped him lightly on the arm. "Are you smiling at me? Why?"

"It's not about courage. Or the thrill."

"Why do you do it, then? Fight wars. Enforce the law. Risk your life."

"We don't talk about it, really."

"But if you did?"

Tim took a moment to consider. "I guess we do it because we're worried no one else is willing to."

She pulled the unlit cigarette from her mouth and slid it back into the pack. "Not all of you." She padded back to the house, head down, dodging snails on the patio.

The wind picked up, bone-cold and wet, and Tim slid his hands into his pockets. His fingertips touched a scrap of paper, which he withdrew, puzzled. A phone number and an address, written in a woman's hand.

He turned, but Ananberg had already disappeared back into the house. After a moment he followed.

All six members of the Commission were seated, awaiting Tim's return. Centered perfectly before Rayner, like an awaiting plate of dinner, was a black binder.

The fourth, Tim thought. Then two more, then Kindell's.

Lost in a blissful contentedness, the Stork was folding blank sheets into paper airplanes and humming to himself—the theme from *The Green Hornet*. Dumone sat cocked back in his chair, a fresh-poured bourbon chilling the V of his crotch.

Rayner leaned over, spreading a hand on the cover. "Buzani Debuffier."

Blank looks all around, except Dumone, who grimaced. "Debuffier's a big, mean, Santero. Goes about six-six on a bad day."

Tim slid into his chair. "Santero?"

"Voodoo priest. They're Cuban mostly, but Debuffier's a Haitian mix."

The Stork's humming reached an annoying pitch.

"Would you shut the hell up?" Robert said.

The Stork stopped, his puffy little hands midfold. He rode his glasses back up the bridge of his nose with a knuckle, blinking apologetically. "Was I doing that out loud?"

Tim reached for Debuffier's booking photo. A displeased man with a shaved head stared back at him, the whites of his eyes pronounced against pitch-dark skin. He wore a flannel, ripped to expose his bare shoulders. His deltoids stood out, ridged and firm, as though he were straining against the cuffs. From the look of his build, he was probably making some pretty good headway. "What's the case?"

Dumone flipped open the binder and paged through the crime-scene report. "Ritual sacrifice of Aimee Kayes, a seventeen-year-old girl. Her body was found headless in an alley, draped in a multicolored cloth, raw salt, honey, and butter smeared on the bleeding neck stump. The top vertebra had been removed. LAPD's ritual-crimes expert found these details to be consistent with Santería sacrificial rites."

"They sacrifice people? Regularly?" the Stork asked.

"Only in James Bond movies," Ananberg said, reaching for the medical examiner's report. "The Santeros mostly kill birds and lambs. Even in Cuba. I did an anthropology study on them in college."

"So what gives?" Robert asked.

"We've got a Froot Loop, that's what gives."

Dumone's chuckle turned into a racking cough. He lowered his fist from his face, then drained the last of his bourbon. "The ritual-crimes expert testified that, based on the specifics of the sacrifice, Debuffier probably believed that the victim was a threatening evil spirit."

"Stomach contents included sunflower leaves and coconut." Ananberg looked up from the pages. "The meal before the slaughter. If she eats, it shows the gods approve of her for sacrifice."

"I'm sure she found that slender consolation," Rayner said.

The Stork waved a hand before his yawning mouth. "I'm sorry. Past my bedtime."

Robert slid a glossy crime-scene photo across the table. "This should wake you up."

"What links Debuffier to the body?" Tim asked. "Aside from the fact that he's a voodoo priest?"

Dumone tossed the eyewitness testimonies at Tim. "Two eyewitnesses. The first, Julie Pacetti, was Kayes's best friend. The two girls were at the movies a few nights before

Kayes's abduction. After the show Pacetti went to the bathroom and Kayes waited for her in the lobby. When Pacetti came out, Kayes claimed Debuffier had just approached her and asked her to go for a ride with him. He'd frightened her, and she'd refused. When the girls went out in the parking lot, Debuffier was waiting in a black El Camino. He saw that Kayes was not alone and took off, but not before Pacetti got a good eyeful."

"A six-foot-six bald Haitian," Mitchell said. "Not exactly inconspicuous."

"The second witness?" Tim asked.

"A USC girl returning from a party saw a man fitting Debuffier's description pull Kayes's body from the bed of a black El Camino and drag it into the alley."

Ananberg whistled. "I'd say that's pretty damning."

"She ran a few blocks, then phoned 911 at"—Dumone checked the report—"three-seventeen A.M. With a physical description of the suspect and the car, the cops got to Debuffier before daybreak. They found him outside his house, scouring the bed of his El Camino with bleach."

"Anything in the house?"

"Altars and tureens and animal hides. There were bloodstains on the basement floor, later determined to be from animals."

"Crazy motherfucker," Robert said.

"Not so crazy he can't resort to premeditated criminality to maintain his blood lust," Rayner said.

"Can I see the witnesses' rap sheets?" Tim said.

Rayner slid them down the table, and Tim reviewed them as the others spoke. Neither witness had any felonies or misdemeanors—nothing a DA could drive a wedge under to get leverage for embellished testimony.

". . . urged no bail, but knowing that Debuffier was broke, the judge just had him surrender his passport and set bail at one mil," Dumone was saying. "The American Religious Protection Association came parading into town, claiming he was being harassed, and posted his bail. Within a day both witnesses were found murdered, stabbed in the jugular—another Santería sacrificial rite. Cops looked into it, got zip. Good clean hits this time around— evidently he'd learned his lesson. Since the witnesses are dead, their statements to police become hearsay, case dismissed. The ARPA reps left town a little more quietly than they came in."

A palpable sense of disgust circled the table.

Rayner put on his best musing face. "It's a sad, sad day when the system itself provides motivation to commit murder."

Tim thought Rayner's assessment evinced a misplacement of accountability, but he elected to dig back into the file rather than comment. An exhaustive review of the remaining documentation didn't turn up any compelling evidence suggesting Debuffier's innocence.

The Commission's vote went seven to zero.

**22** TIM PARKED MORE THAN A MILE AWAY FROM THE GRAVeled drive leading to Kindell's converted garage. The air out here was sharp and fresh, tinged with the scent of burned sap and ash from the long-ago fire that had claimed the accompanying house. Tim stayed off the gravel, his boots quiet on the dirt. He held his .357 low to his side, forefinger resting along the barrel outside the trigger guard. A slanted but still-standing mailbox loomed up out of a crumbled bank of earth. The night felt flat and oddly static, as if it were receding, airless; every sound and movement seemed dulled by its residency within the vastness.

Tim was surprised to see no light up ahead. Maybe Kindell had moved away, scurried off after the trial to inhabit a new dark corner of a new town. If so, he'd taken with him his remembrance of that night—the snatch, the kill, the sawing, the man who had been with him before, planning, eager to partake of Tim's daughter.

The moon shone almost full, an imperfect orb visible through the skeletal branches of the eucalyptus. Tim approached the house silently, freezing when he heard a clattering inside. Someone had tripped, knocking a pan, a lamp to the floor. Tim's first thought was of an intruder, another intruder, but then he heard Kindell cursing to himself. Tim stayed wolf-still, gun lowered, standing equidistant between two eucalyptus trunks.

The garage door swung open with a bang. Kindell stumbled outside, tugging at an unzipped sleeping bag that he'd wrapped around his body like a toga, bobbling a dying flashlight that gave off the faintest yellow-eye glimmer.

Tim stood in plain view less than twenty yards from Kindell, hidden only by the darkness and his own immobility, which matched that of the tree trunks rising around him and the dead weight of the night.

Shivering violently, Kindell shoved open a rusting fuse box and tinkered inside. His other hand, clutching the ends of the sleeping bag at his waist, looked thin and impossibly pale, matching nothing in the night save the bone-whiteness of the moon.

"Damnit, damnit, *damnit.*" Kindell slammed the fuse-box lid, slapped at it, then stood shaking and miserable and unmoving, as if paralyzed by hopelessness. Finally he trudged inside, one end of the sleeping bag trailing him like the train of a gown. Kindell's suffering, however petty, evoked in Tim an immense gratification.

Tim waited until the garage door creaked down, whoomping closed against the concrete, then eased up to the pair of windows. Inside, Kindell was curled into the fetal position on the couch, huddled inside the unfurled sleeping bag. His eyes were closed, and he breathed deeply and evenly, his head rocking slightly on the bunched pillow. His shivering had calmed.

Kindell would never help in identifying his accomplice—this had been made perfectly clear to Dray. If the answers were to be found anywhere, they were in the papers stuffed in Rayner's safe.

Kindell had torn apart Ginny's precious body and now was sleeping contentedly, the truths about her last wretched hours hidden safely inside his skull like personal, horrid keepsakes. Her pleas, the panic smell of her sweat, her last scream. The other face she'd seen beside Kindell's, grinning through wet lips, lascivious in the eyes, not yet anticipating that the turn of events would move from depraved to deadly.

Acid washed through Tim's stomach, seething and curdling.

Numbly, mechanically, Tim set his stance, placed both hands on the pistol, and sighted just above Kindell's ear. His finger slid on the metal and hooked inside the guard, coming to rest against the trigger. He felt the pre-shoot calm descend over him, a precise unmotion. He stood for a moment, watching the delicate rise and fall of Kindell's head through the alignment of the sights.

He floated away, seeing himself from above in his mind's eye. A figure hidden in darkness, gun aimed through a greasy window. Through a confused and solitary childhood, Tim had clung to a desperate belief that there was something that shone in the human spirit that elevated it above meat and bone. With frantic hope and blind knowing, he'd fought his father's code year after strenuous year, and yet here he stood, seized in the grasp of his own want and rage, bent on satiating his own needs at any cost. His father's son.

He lowered the gun and walked away.

Replacing the pistol in the back of his waistband, he sat on the weedy concrete of the charred foundation, facing the freestanding garage. The tremendous responsibility the Commission, a by-all-accounts-illegitimate body of justices, had elected to shoulder struck Tim anew. To deem who was society's scourge, to condemn justly, to be the voice of the people—these were responsibilities that could not be taken too seriously. And they demanded an impeccability of character, for the law was not to be meted out but acted; it was not a promise but a code.

He vowed to uphold that code even when the last binder moved from Rayner's safe to the table, even as he picked through paperwork detailing the dismemberment of his daughter. If he didn't honor it, he was no better than Robert or Mitchell or his father, selling fraudulent burial plots to lonely widows.

Something rustled to his right in the weeds, and his pistol was drawn and aimed as quickly as he turned his head. Dray's form resolved from the dark, clad in black jeans, a black sweatshirt, and a denim jacket. She approached, unbothered by the gun, and sat beside him. Another ghost, another watcher in the night. Sliding her hands into the pouch pocket of her sweatshirt, she flicked her head toward his gun, then the garage. "Second thoughts?"

"Every minute."

"Yeah," she said. "Yeah." She propped her elbows on her

knees, pressed her hands together, and rested her chin on the ledge of her thumbs. She seemed to remember something and quickly put her left hand back in her pocket. The collar of her jean jacket was up; she looked like Debbie Gibson with an attitude problem. "Saw your handiwork on the news. You're creating quite a buzz."

"We aim to please."

"Funny, I never would have thought street justice was your style."

"It isn't. But my old style was found wanting. At least to some people."

"How's the new one fit?"

"A little tight in the shoulders, but I'm hoping I'll adjust."

"You tailor the suit to the man, not vice versa."

He reached over and patted her down casually with one hand. She wasn't hiding a weapon beneath her bulky sweatshirt. "What are you doing here?"

"Just keeping an eye on things. I like to have the creep under my thumb."

The dim flashlight bobbed inside the garage, then a fierce rattling broke the silence.

"What the hell's going on in there?" Tim said.

"I rerouted his mail to a drop box. I got his credit-card numbers, his telephone, gas, and power account numbers, then I canceled everything. It's petty and small, but it makes me feel better."

Tim extended a fist to her, which Dray matched. They knocked knuckles, a modified high five they used only on the range or the softball diamond. Dray leaned into him slightly, touching at the hip, the elbow. He pressed his lips to the top of her head, inhaling the scent of her hair. They sat for a bit in silence.

"You get anything new on the case?"

She shook her head. "I've pretty much run out the leads.

I wanted to see if you'd gotten your hands on that case binder."

"No, it'll be a while, unfortunately."

"We'll have to wait, I guess." Her face crinkled. "It's wrecking me. The waiting. Bracing to find out something even more awful, or maybe to not find out anything at all."

They stared at Kindell's shack for a few moments. Tim bit his lip. "I hear Mac's been hanging out at the house."

The gap opened up again between their hips. Her mouth tensed. "The house was empty and haunted."

"You trying to hurt me, Dray?"

"Is it working?"

"Yes. You didn't answer my question."

"...ieve it or not, everything I'm going through isn't about ___ Mac is staying on the couch because I'm scared of the da___ right now, like a little girl. I know, pathetic, but you're certainly not around to help me with the problem."

"Mac has a thing for you, Dray. Always has."

"Well, I don't have a thing for Mac. He's staying as a friend. No more." She reached over and took Tim's hand, keeping her left hand wedged in her pocket.

A sudden dread gut-checked him. "Take your hand out of your pocket, Dray."

Unwillingly, she withdrew her hand. Her ring finger was bare. A deep-lit pain took hold in Tim's chest and spread out and out, brushfire-fast. He turned away, looking at the house of the man who had consumed his daughter, but Kindell had quieted within and could provide no distraction.

Dray's lips quivered ever so slightly, the pre-quake warnings of anger, of self-loathing, of sorrow—a triple cocktail with which Tim had recently grown familiar. Her face, gloomy and frozen in a half cringe, matched nothing he'd ever known of her. She knuckle-scratched the top of her nose, a gesture she made when distressed or deeply sad. "I feel like you don't want me anymore, Timothy."

"That's *not* true." His voice rose a bit with the inflection, but it was just him and Dray and a deaf man at thirty yards.

"It's too hard for me to wear it right now. I've looked at that ring every day of our marriage, first thing when I wake up, and it always made me grateful." Dray seemed small and vulnerable sitting in the darkness, her arms hooked across her knees the way Ginny used to hold hers when she watched TV. "Right now it just reminds me of your absence."

He plucked up a weed by its roots and tossed it. Its mud-caked cluster of roots hit the foundation a few feet away with a satisfying splat. "I have to see this through. The Commission. Get my hands on that case binder. I can't do that if I'm living at home, in plain sight. It puts me at too much risk. It puts *you* at too much risk. I need to protect Ginny at least in her death, so the men who did this . . ." When he raised his hand to wipe his nose, he saw it was trembling, so he lowered it into his lap and squeezed it, squeezed it hard.

"Timothy." Her tone approached pleading, though for what, he did not know. She started to reach for him but withdrew her hand.

It took another minute or so before he could trust his voice again. "I'm sorry," he said. "I haven't said her name in a while."

"It's okay to cry, you know."

Tim bobbed his head a few times, an intimation of a nod. "Right."

Dray stood up, dusted off her hands. "I don't want to not see you right now," she said. "I don't want to not have you in my life. But I understand why you have to do this for you, for us. I guess we just wait and hold on and hope what we are is strong enough."

He couldn't take his eyes off her hand, her bare finger. The hole that had opened up in his chest continued to dilate, claiming his lungs, his voice.

Something fluttered nearby, settled, and began to chirp.

Dray turned and started the long walk back to the road.

Halfway home, Tim pulled over and sat, hands on the wheel, breathing hard. Though it was February-cold, he had the AC on high. He thought of his waiting apartment, its barrenness and bleak functionality, and realized how ill equipped eight years of marriage had left him for being alone. He pulled Ananberg's address out of his pocket and studied the edge-ripped slip of paper.

Her apartment building in Westwood was security-intensive—controlled access, double-locked glass front door, security cam in the brief stretch of tile that passed for a lobby. Turning from the camera, Tim ran a finger down the directory beside the call box outside and was not surprised to see the numbers listed by last name, not apartment number. He punched the button and waited as the metal speaker harshly projected a buzz.

Ananberg clicked on, sounding wide awake though it was nearly four in the morning. "Yeah?"

"It's Tim. Tim Rackley."

"First and last name. How wonderfully unassuming. I'm in 303."

A loud buzzing issued from the heavy glass door, which Tim yanked open. He took the elevator up. The third-floor carpet was clean but slightly worn. When he knocked lightly on Ananberg's door, he heard soft footsteps, then the sounds of two locks and a chain being undone. The door swung open. Ananberg wore a thigh-length Georgetown T-shirt. One hand held a thick-necked Rhodesian Ridgeback at bay by the collar, the other gripped a little Ruger, the muzzle of which she was using to scratch her leg.

"You should check the peephole. Even if you just buzzed someone up."

"I did."

He knew she was lying, as he hadn't seen the darkness of her eye through the lens. The dog moved forward and nuzzled his nose moistly into Tim's cupped hand.

"Impressive. Boston usually hates people."

"Boston?"

"I inherited him from an ex-boyfriend. Harvard asshole."

She turned and headed back into the oversize studio. Past the kitchenette, diminutive dining table, and TV-facing couch, two bureaus cordoned off the sleeping area, which was no more than a full-size bed wedged beneath the room's single large window. She snapped her fingers, and Boston trotted to a fluffy disk of a dog bed and lay down. The pistol she slid into the right bureau's top drawer.

She stepped closer to the bed, leaving them a few steps' space. They eyed each other across a frayed throw rug. Crossing her arms, she lifted her T-shirt off over her head. Her body, thin and wonderfully shaped, was unexploited by weights or vigorous training. Modest, firm breasts rose above the in-curve of her stomach. Her gaze held the sapient matter-of-factness of examining nurses and prostitutes. It was frank and distressingly genuine, a sad, doleful ritual in a sad, doleful apartment.

Tim's eyes strayed uncomfortably to the single place mat on the dining table, the T-shirt puddled by the box of Kleenex on the floor. He understood more concretely that she'd been touched by death and loss, as had they all.

"I'm afraid you misunderstood me. I can't . . ." His hand

described an arc of some sort but failed to extract better words. "I'm married."

"Then why are you here, Rackley?" She pulled a cigarette out of a pack on her nightstand and lit it.

"I need a favor."

"I offered to give it to you, or hadn't you noticed?" She winked at him, and he returned her smile. She stubbed out her just-lit cigarette in a candle on the bureau, fell back on the bed, and pulled a blanket across her body neither shyly nor modestly.

"I'd like you to get me the public defender's notes from the Kindell file. As a good-faith gesture. I know you have access to it. It's too hard to wait without . . . *something*."

"I can't break policy. Bring it up at a meeting, we'll take a vote."

"We both know Rayner will never let that fly."

Her eyes never broke from his; for a moment it seemed they were looking straight into each other. He knew that his suffering lay exposed and vulnerable, and there was little he could do to shield it from her gaze. He cleared his throat softly. "Please."

"I'll see what I can do, but I'm making no promises." Reaching over, she clicked the bedside light down a notch. "Come here."

He walked over and sat on the edge of the bed. She hooked an arm around his waist and tugged him until his back was propped against the curved wooden headboard. She poked him until he shifted slightly left, then raised his arm and adjusted it out of her way. Content, she burrowed into his side, her head at the base of his chest.

"Comfortable?" he asked.

She strung a delicate arm across his stomach, and he was taken by how thin it was at the wrist. "You love her, huh?"

"Deeply."

"I've never loved anyone. Not like that. My shrink says it's the result of an early loss. My mom, you know. I was fifteen, just entering sexuality. It's all linked, death and sex. Fear of intimacy, blah, blah, blah. That's probably why I like being with Rayner. He takes care of me and doesn't make me feel too much."

"How was she killed? Your mother?"

"A motel-room murder/rape. There were lots of head-lines and prurient speculation. Sort of glamorous, come to think of it. I came home from school, and my dad was sit-ting there in the kitchen, waiting for me, the smell of for-malin coming off his clothes from the ME's. To this day, I smell formalin. . . ." She shuddered.

Tim stroked her hair, which was even finer and softer than he'd imagined.

"He looked utterly broken, my dad. Just . . . *defeated*."

"What happened with the case?"

"They caught the guy a few weeks later. The jury was, for the most part, white trash, unemployed, and utterly in-competent. They ruled 'not guilty.' The evidence was so overwhelming that the *Post* speculated openly about bribery. But maybe it wasn't. Maybe it was just plain inanity, like most things are." She shook her head. "De-fense attorneys with deep pockets and jury consultants. Not technically a loophole in the law, more like sanctioned corruption." She made a noise of disgust deep in her throat. "They say it's better for one hundred guilty men to go free than for one innocent man to be put to death. How long does that sententious bullshit bear weight? After the one hundred guilty men commit one hundred more murders? A thousand?"

"No," Tim said. "It holds weight when the one innocent man is you."

She grinned faintly. "I know that. I *know* it—I just don't

always feel it." Her face felt warm and comforting against his chest. He kept listening, kept stroking her hair. "My dad sold real estate, but he was on a mortar crew in Korea, and some of his old platoonmates had become cops. One night a few of them and my dad rounded the guy up, took him for a drive to a warehouse in Anacostia. I'm fuzzy on details, but I know that when they found the body, they had to print it to make the ID because there wasn't much left in the way of dentals."

Tim remembered how Rayner had claimed that her mother's killer had died in a gang beating, and he wondered if he knew the real story. That depended on how deep the intimacy ran between Rayner and Ananberg.

"I remember when my dad came home that night and told me what he'd done. He sat at the edge of my bed and woke me. He smelled of grass and his knuckles were split and he was shaking. He told me. And I felt nothing. I still feel nothing." Her voice was quieter now, muffled against Tim's chest. "Maybe I'm just not wired that way or I'm missing that gene, the conscience gene. Maybe when I get to the gates of heaven or whatever you Christians believe in, they'll turn me away."

She shook off a shiver, then turned her face up to him. She pressed her lips together, working up the courage to ask something. Her voice shook a little when she finally did. "Will you stay with me until I fall asleep?"

He nodded, and her face softened with relief. She settled back into him. Soon enough her breathing grew regular, and he sat with the warmth of her face against his chest and stroked her hair. After twenty minutes he slid carefully out from under her and slipped out so silently Boston didn't even raise his head.

**23** TIM PULLED UP TO DUMONE'S APARTMENT A LITTLE BE-
fore 7:00 A.M. A graceless stucco complex that
exemplified bad seventies architecture, the
building was less than a block off the 10 at Western. Next
door, the *ampm* threw off fumes of gasoline and shitty coffee. The just-risen sun gave out a pale straw light to which
Tim felt unfamiliarly attuned. He still had not slept.

His surprise at Dumone's early-morning cell-phone
summons was surpassed only by the fact that Dumone had
given him his home address rather than picking a public
spot to meet. Had Tim not felt a strong intuitive trust for
Dumone, he would have speculated about an ambush.

Tim walked down the concrete walk that threaded along
the building. A whistle called out, and there was Dumone,
waiting for him behind a dusty screen door. They shook
hands, Dumone's mouth twitching in response to the formality of the greeting, and he stepped aside and allowed
Tim to enter.

It was a ground-floor, single-bedroom job that smelled
of stale carpet. A budget laminate bookcase and desk
housed awards, plaques, and a few guns encased in glass.
Dumone swept his arm grandly around the interior. "Get
you something? Pellegrino? Mimosa?"

Tim laughed. "Thanks, I'm fine."

Dumone gestured for Tim to sit on the couch, then sank
into a dusty brown La-Z-Boy. His eyes seemed unusually
shadowed, his skin stretched tight across his temples.

Tim raised his hands, let them fall back into his lap. "So?"

"I didn't really call you here for a reason. Just wanted to see you." Dumone raised a handkerchief and coughed into it, and again Tim noticed faint specks of blood on the cloth.

"You okay? Want me to get you some water?"

Dumone waved him off. "Fine, fine. I'm used to it." The handkerchief settled in his lap, clutched in a knuckle-thick hand. "Early on, when I was first married, I worked construction some weekends. The job didn't pay so hot, the wife and I had just gotten hitched. Extra dough, you know? They had me swinging a sledgehammer, knocking down plaster in these old houses in Charlestown. The ceilings—" He coughed again, one finger twirling in the air, indicating the ceiling, holding the strain of the story. "Asbestos. Of course, we didn't know then." He shook his head. "Not good. I was invincible anyway, dodging bullets by day." He smiled, and again his eyes gathered that gleam that said he was astute enough to find amusement in all matters.

"We were all invincible once. And smarter."

"Yes," Dumone said. "Yes." A wistfulness touched his features. "I'm sorry that I haven't known you longer, Tim. Rob and Mitch, hell, those two are like sons to me. The kind of sons you worry about a little—you smooth down their hair and send them out into the world hoping to God they'll do okay. And they have," he added quickly. "They've done real fine. But you. I hardly know you well enough, but I'd guess you'd be the kind of son you'd want to pass things on to, if you had anything worth passing on."

"That's quite a compliment," Tim said.

"Yes. Yes, it is."

"I've enjoyed meeting you, too. Our . . . friendship . . ." "Friendship" seemed an odd word for whatever they shared. "I'm glad you're in there steering the ship during our meetings."

Dumone nodded, a thoughtful frown on his face. "I suppose someone has to."

They sat not much longer, enduring the awkward silence. "Well," Dumone said. "Thanks for stopping by."

**24** THE NEXTEL CHIRPED ANNOYINGLY, PULLING TIM FROM the sweaty daytime sleep into which he had finally drifted. He rolled over on his mattress and grabbed the phone.

Robert's Marlboro voice came too loud through the receiver. "Motherfucker hasn't left the house since we got here last night. Spends all his time tinkering around in that basement downstairs, where they found all that voodoo shit."

Tim rubbed his eyes hard, knowing it would leave them red and bloodshot but not caring. "Uh-huh."

"His house is over by the garment district downtown. How far away are you?"

"About a half hour," Tim lied.

"All right. Well, the Stork got us tapped in to his phone lines from a junction box up the street. Debuffier's mother just called to remind his ass not to forget their lunch. Noon at El Comao. Know where that is?"

"Cuban joint on Pico near the Federal Building?"

"That's the one. So he'll be peeling out of here in about twenty minutes. I thought you'd want to swing by, take a sneak-and-peek through the house with us. Mitch is gonna bring some explosive sheet along in case we decide to set a charge now."

"I made clear you were doing surveillance *only*," Tim said.

"I know, I know, but we're all getting the sense that Mother-fucker stays bedded down. We just thought it wouldn't hurt to have some explosives on hand, in case the . . ."

Mitchell's voice in the background: "—optimal—"

"—opportunity arose. It might be our only window for a while."

"No way. You just started surveillance yesterday. All we're doing today is taking a look through the interior to get the lay."

"All right, fine. We'll just take a gander, then. Mother-fucker's at 14132 Lanyard Street. Oh, and Rackley? How are you gonna know where to find us?"

"I'll find you," Tim said.

"We're blended into this block like a panther in the jungle, my friend. We're—"

"Let me guess. Service van with tinted rear windows."

A long silence.

"I'll see you soon." Tim hung up, slid his gun into his waistband, grabbed the Nextel but not the Nokia, and headed for the door. He paused with his hand on the knob. Backtracking, he retrieved a pair of black leather gloves from the bag beside his mattress. With lead stitched into the lengths of the fingers and positioned strategically across the bands of the knuckles, the gloves could put horse-kick power behind a simple punch. Tim threw them into his pocket and headed downstairs to his car. Once he got to within a mile of Debuffier's house, he pulled over and idled at the curb.

Both sides of the street were lined with garment sellers' stalls, elongated rooms jammed into the same structure like piano keys. Many of the booths had roll-up, storage-style doors, opening the entire storefronts to the sidewalks. The district had a Third World feel to it—drab functionality and cheap, raw product offset by bright colors and excess. A young boy burrowed into a chest-high heap of Dodgers shirts. Enormous spools of fabric were propped against walls, doorways, tables. A mound of moccasins spilled out onto the curb. The air smelled of candy and burnt churros.

Wheelbarrows, parked trucks, and exhaust crammed the street. A guy with comb-mark-stiff hair strutted past, wearing a sweatshirt with a peeling Versace emblem, his pinky intertwined with that of a girl holding a purse proclaiming Guci—marked down one *c*.

Bastard offspring of the city of varnish.

The guy threw Tim the stink-eye, probably figuring he was checking out his girlfriend, so Tim looked away to defuse matters. A young man with a bushy beard came by, T-shirts draped over his arm. He caught Tim looking and held up a sample. The shirt featured Jedediah Lane's head midexplosion, under a bloodred caption that read TERROR-ISM BLOWS. Tim studied the photo as if it contained some inscrutable secret or the power to pardon. For an instant he wasn't sure whether the caption referred to Lane himself or Lane's assassin. At the vendor's approach, Tim shook his head, and the man moved on.

With laughing Mexican colors and a robust husband-wife team working the register, the stall beside Tim's car drew his attention. It exclusively featured wedding-cake ornaments. Tim sat staring at the plastic brides and grooms of all shapes and ethnicities, feeling his temperature starting to rise, wondering how a marriage between two people who loved each other madly could feel as though it were slipping away.

With relief he saw that he'd passed the requisite ten minutes to put him at Debuffier's at the specified time, and he drove off. He parked several blocks away and strolled around the corner. Chipped-stucco houses rose humbly behind cheap metal fences. Two kids with basketball players' numbers shaved into the backs of their heads zipped past on elongated skateboards, catching air off a buckle in the sidewalk left over from the last earthquake. Rusted cars languished along the curb on both sides of the street, and—to Robert's credit—there were a handful of service vans, which made sense given the block's apparent demographics. The decals and signs were varied and colorful. Armando's Glass Works. Freddy's Industrial Cleaning. The Martinez Bros Carpet Care. Several of the eponymous entrepreneurs were spending their Saturday sitting on browning lawns, petting Rottweilers and drinking Michelob from the can. The unusually brisk wind carried the sweet-rot smell of lukewarm beer and old wood.

On the north side of the street, Debuffier's house loomed larger than its neighbors, a sprawling wooden abomination of no discernible architectural style. The porch's arched entrance should have lent a warmth to the house, but the wood was fragmented, the splintered ends jutting out to add sloppy denticulation to the mouthlike hole. The roof, even more perplexing, was a cacophony of styles—here pitched, there hip-and-valley. Sitting importantly back from the street behind a lawn long since gone to dirt, the house itself was not so much large as complex—a collision, most likely, of the labors of rival builders over virtually unrelated phases of building.

Most of the parked vans' side windows were tinted. Tim crossed to the north side of the street, opening up a better angle from which to glance back into the van interiors through the windshields, but the majority of the vans were partitioned. Freddy's Industrial Cleaning looked most suspect. From how low it was sitting on the shocks, it was housing either heavy equipment or a few full-grown men. The Caucasian name didn't help either.

Tim walked over, pretending to fumble in his pockets for the keys. He paused at the driver's door, waiting. The clicking of the doors' automatic locks told him he'd bet right. He slid into the seat, facing forward, and pretended to adjust the radio despite the fact that the neighboring yards were all empty. The van smelled of sweat and stale coffee, and the dash was high; Tim wondered if the Stork had trouble seeing over it when he drove.

He moved his lips only slightly when he spoke. "Not bad, boys."

A crumpled VanMan Rental Agency receipt was wedged in the cup holder, beside a Big Gulp. Tim could just make out the name on the top line, written in the Stork's shaky hand: *Daniel Dunn.*

Danny Dunn, Tim thought. An appropriate alias.

Robert's voice, peeved and cracked from dehydration, lofted over his shoulder. "How the hell did you find us?"

"Just sniffed you out." Tim removed his lead gloves from his back pocket and slid them on. "Have you switched the car out?"

"Yessiree," the Stork said. "I brought the van first thing this morning."

"Where's the car you sat in last night?"

Robert's gruff voice again. "I peeled out and returned it, then bused back. Relax—we're all clear."

"Good."

"Debuffier left early for lunch, so let's get on it." A set of keys tapped Tim on the shoulder, and he took them and started the van. "His house is on a double lot, so it backs on the street one over. Pull around the block and park there—much quieter."

"There's a gap in the back fence begging to be utilized," the Stork said.

"Where's Mitchell?"

"Over there. He'll meet us at the back door in five."

Tim eased around the block. "Good vehicle," he said. "Silent. Ordinary. Forgettable."

"I'm glad you're pleased with my selection, Mr. Rackley." The Stork sounded incredibly proud of himself, almost gleeful. "I even took back the first van they rented me because it gave off a distinctive rattle."

"Kind of like you," Robert said.

Tim parked a few feet away from the triangular gap in the fence. The street was dead quiet, so he got out and pulled open the rear doors. Already wearing latex gloves, the Stork and Robert burst from the back, inhaling deeply and fanning their shirts. Robert ducked through the fence gap immediately. The Stork shouldered a black bag by the strap, staggering under its weight. Tim took the bag from him, slammed the rear doors, and ushered him through the fence.

Mitchell was crouching at the rear door, Robert at his side. Mitchell's eyes lit on the Nextel's bulge in Tim's pocket, and he stood up violently. "Turn off the cell phone. *Now.*"

Tim and the Stork froze. Tim reached down and turned off the phone. "You have electric blasting caps on you?"

"That's right."

If Mitchell had electric blasting caps, Tim's cell phone should have been nowhere in the vicinity. When induced, Nextels, like most mobiles, kick out an RF signal just prior to ringing, responding to the network and identifying themselves as operational. The induced current, sufficient to ignite an electric blasting cap, can set off a boom ball before the phone even chirps. Tim understood now why

Robert hadn't suggested they maintain phone contact during the entry.

Tim's eyes went to the explosive sheet at Mitchell's feet, a twenty-pound roll of place-mat-thick PETN, pentaery-thritetetranitrate being a bitch to pronounce but easy to rip or cut, a stick of gum to C4's Bubblicious. It peeked out from Mitchell's det bag, olive drab, the shade of death.

"Can't you follow instructions?" Tim tried to keep anger from his voice. "I made *extremely* clear you were to do nothing but surveil."

"And we haven't. I happened to have the bag with me—"

"We'll deal with this later." Tim nodded to the door. "What's the situation here?"

Mitchell returned to his anthropologist's crouch by the knob. "It's a tough one. Outswinging with a latch protector, so we can't work the credit-card slide."

The Stork set his hands on his hips, then gestured Mitchell aside with an impatient flick of his hand. "*Move.*"

Adjusting his glasses, he leaned forward for a closer look at the lock. He brought his face to within inches of it, tilting his head like a predator inhaling scent. He spoke softly, with a singsong cadence, a girl talking to her favorite doll. "Restricted-keyway tumbler lock with reinforced strikes. Aren't you a pretty one? Yes, you are."

Tim, Robert, and Mitchell's exchange of amused looks was cut short when the Stork reared back, his eyes still intently focused on the lock but his hand extended as if beckoning a waiter. His plump fingers snapped. "Bag."

Tim swung the bag down to his feet. The Stork's hand rustled within and removed a can of spray lubricant. He inserted a thin extension tube into the nozzle and directed the spray toward the cylinder. "We'll just lubricate you up, won't we? That'll make things easier for us."

Next he reached for a pick gun. The tool, with its pull-handle trigger that set a thin protruding tip in continuous motion, resembled an electric hand drill or an elaborate sexual device. Fisting the unit, the Stork slid the tip into the lubed lock and initiated it, working a complicated angle through a precise series of clutchings and readjustments. He set his ear to the door, presumably to listen to the pins jumping above the shear line, his other hand gripping the knob. His mouth was shifted to the right, clamped down on his lower lip. He seemed oblivious to the fact that he was in the company of others.

"There you go, darling. Open up for me."

There was a shift in the noise of the pins, a click indicating a sudden symmetry or resonance, and the Stork's other hand moved lightning-fast, twisting the knob, which gave up a half turn.

He looked at the others with a satisfied and slightly worn-out grin. Tim half expected him to light up a cigarette. The Stork's smile faded quickly as he leaned forward, setting his shoulder against the door.

"Wait," Tim said. "What if there's an ala—?"

The Stork shoved the door open.

The insistent beeping caused Tim's mouth to go dry, but the Stork calmly walked over to a keypad on the wall and punched in a code. The alarm ceased.

They entered, pistols drawn, and listened for any signs of movement in the large chamber of the house. Mitchell and Robert had matching Colt .45s, single-action semiautos that require cocking before the first round can be shot. They fire with only three pounds of trigger pressure instead of the fifteen a double-action demands. The big-bore guns were powerful, hair-trigger, and illegal, not unlike both brothers.

"How did you lift the code?" Tim whispered.

"I didn't. Every alarm company's got a reset code." The Stork pointed to the emblem at the base of the keypad. "This one's an IronForce—30201."

"As simple as that?"

"Yessiree."

They stepped through a small room containing a broken washing machine and into the kitchen. Food-caked plates and soggy boxes. Mustard yellow linoleum peeling up at the edges. Endless empty rum bottles and a thin layer of crumbs covering the countertops.

A faint tinny echo sounded somewhere in the house, slightly animated, almost vocal. Tim's hand shot up, flat, fingers slightly spread, a point man's patrol warning. The others stood perfectly still. A minute of silence passed, then another. "Did you hear that?"

"No, nothing," the Stork said.

"Probably the pipes knockin'."

"Let's get moving," Tim said, his voice still lowered. "Stork—get back outside. A two-tap horn alert if he happens to come back early."

"He did *leave* early."

"That's why you're gonna keep an eye out for us." Tim waited for the Stork to scurry outside. "Safe the house and meet back here in two minutes. I'll take the upstairs."

"Look," Robert said, not bothering to whisper, "we've been on the house all night, all morning. There's no one else—"

"Do it," Tim said. He disappeared through the doorway toward the front of the house, moving through several rooms stuffed with oddities—boxes of auto calendars, overturned tables, stacks of bricks. A pile of bright fabric curled around the base of the stairs; Debuffier had probably bought it on garment row. Tim searched the upstairs rooms, which reeked of backed-up plumbing and incense. All the mirrors had been covered, draped in swatches of colorful cloth. Debuffier either fancied himself a vampire or feared his own reflection; from his booking photo, Tim would've put money on the latter. Each room was empty and uninhabited; the master bedroom was probably downstairs. Tim took care not to leave footprints where dust had collected more heavily on the floor.

Robert and Mitchell were waiting for Tim in the kitchen. Tim's watch showed 12:43. "Clear?"

"Except for the basement door," Mitchell said. "Solid steel set in a steel frame. Locked."

"We'll get the Stork on it in a minute." Tim snugged the .357 against the small of his back. "Let's take a slower turn through the ground floor. Focus on details so we can draw up a full blueprint of the place later."

Another sound, a metallic moan, this one undeniable. Tim felt his stomach constrict, his mouth cotton. He inched in the direction from which the sound had come, through the other doorway, the twins just behind him.

"What was that?" Robert asked.

Mitchell adjusted the strap of his det bag, which was slung over his shoulder. "Sounds like a furnace straining." His tone was unconvincing.

Tim turned the corner into a back hall that dead-ended in a bathroom and came face-to-face with the enormous steel rise of the basement door. Its placement within the drywall indicated that it had been newly installed. Tim tapped it lightly with a knuckle—solid and thick as hell. Leaning forward, he placed his ear to the cold steel but got back nothing except the quiet hum of the water heater. The hall was dark—pink, flowery curtains had been pulled shut over the single window overlooking the side yard.

"Robert, run out and get the Stork. Tell him I want through that door into the basement."

12:49. If Debuffier had left early, he'd have been gone an hour now. His transit time to the restaurant was at least ten minutes, so he'd likely be home within ten or fifteen minutes, depending on how much he disliked spending time with his mother. As Tim waited tensely, Mitchell sized up the door with a breacher's imprecise precision, spread fingers pressing into the steel as if it would give.

Struggling under the weight of his bag, the Stork returned with Robert. He thunked down the bag, gave one glance at the large bolt of the door lock, and proclaimed awfully, "That's a Medeco G3. I'm not tangling with her."

Another sound, paradoxically guttural and high-pitched, issued faintly through the door. Tim noted from the sheen of sweat across Mitchell's forehead that the sound was having the same unnerving effect on him.

Half-moons of sweat had darkened Robert's T-shirt under the sleeves. "Probably just some mumbo-jumbo crap. A tied-up lamb or some shit." His thumb flicked nervously back and forth across his forefinger, as if trying to make a cigarette materialize.

"I could blast the door," Mitchell offered.

"No way," Tim said.

Mitchell had one of the blasting caps out of his pocket and was working it in his hand. "I want to know what's down there. That's where they uncovered all the weird shit on the house search."

The Stork's mouth shaped into his crescent of a smile. "I could let Donna have a look around."

Robert's and Mitchell's brows furrowed with humorous synchronicity. "Donna?"

"Bust her out," Tim said. "Whatever she is."

"*Whoever* she is." The Stork removed a shoebox-size unit with a protruding black-plastic-coated rod and a blank liquid-crystal TV screen the size of a Post-it. The rod, a flexible fiber-optic minicam, had a fish-eye lens embedded in the tip. He clicked a switch, and the screen reflected back their three drawn faces in a washed-out blue light.

"Big deal," Robert said. "It's a Peeper—we've all used 'em. It'll never fit under the door. Gap's not big enough."

"That's not Donna." The Stork extracted a tiny Pelican case from the bag and laid it lovingly open. Inside was an incredibly slender rod, almost a black wire, that ended with a wafer-thin rectangular head. "*This* is Donna."

He removed the Peeper's protruding rod and screwed Donna in its place, pausing to knead a knot from one arthritic hand. The head slipped under the door effortlessly, and they caught an up-close glimpse of a dead mouse bunched on the splintering wood of the top stair. The screen blinked out, then back on. "Come on, baby." He looked up at them apologetically. "She's a little finicky." His hands were shaking, and he flexed and unflexed them, grimacing. He tried to clutch the thin rod and exhaled hard in frustration.

"We got it from here," Tim said. "Leave her with us, go post out back. Remember, two-tap the horn."

"But—"

"*Now*, Stork. We're unprotected in here."

With a sad parting look at Donna, the Stork hoisted his bag and retreated. His footfall was so silent that when he turned the corner, it was as if he'd vanished.

Robert and Mitchell crowding around him, Tim worked the wire, trying his best to angle the unseen lens. They took in the basement in vertiginous flights as the lens swept back and forth. The screen blinked off again.

"Goddamnit, Donna," Tim said, "work for me." As soon

as he realized, with needling embarrassment, that he'd personified and pleaded with a minicam, the screen bloomed anew, and he found himself thinking that maybe the Stork had something. His prognostication of a bleary future—himself and the Stork double-dating twin upright vacuums bedecked with wigs—was quickly interrupted by the steady basement view his firmer grip on the wire granted.

A stretch of stairs, maybe ten, leading down into a cold concrete box of a room. Urns and drums were scattered about, as well as dribbles of red and white powders. From atop a mound of melted wax protruded a chorus of still-lit candles, reflected back in a mirror leaning against the wall. In the middle of the room sat a refrigerator/freezer, the freezer compartment above. Feathers were strewn across the floor, lending it a fuzzy, organic texture like a tight-stretched hide. A single wobbly and scarred table held a few more candles, two headless roosters, and an incongruous pencil sharpener. It was hard to picture Debuffier sitting down here puzzling over the Sunday crossword.

Robert exhaled tensely. They all started when the sound—now even more clearly a moan—rose again into faint audibility. The jerk of Tim's hands brought the inside of the door into view, along with the thick steel bolt thrown through hasps drilled into studs on either side. No kicking down that door.

Relinquishing Donna to Mitchell, Tim stood, frustrated. He fingered aside the clingy pink curtain and peered into the side yard. Partially in view, the Stork was flattened against the far fence in a position of cover halfway to the van. Hiding.

Tim snapped back from the window. "Let's go, let's go." He yanked Donna out from under the door, tucking the entire unit under his arm like a football. The det bag already looped over his shoulder, Mitchell followed Robert down the hall. Their best evac path was through the kitchen and out the back door.

Leading the twins, Tim entered the kitchen just as Debuffier's shadow fell across the laundry room through the window of the back door. With a violent flare of his hand, Tim gestured a retreat, but the key had already hit the lock. Robert and Mitchell ducked into a closet, and Tim rolled beneath the kitchen table just as Debuffier yanked the door open and stepped inside.

An empty rum bottle, knocked by Tim's shoulder, tilted, but he snatched it, stretched over himself in an awkward, twisting supine position. A grumbling filled the kitchen as Debuffier fussed over the alarm, presumably to see why it didn't go off. Then he crossed the kitchen, his enormous legs drawing into upside-down view, size-seventeen black loafers halting mere feet from Tim's head. A stack of mail hit the table with a slap. Debuffier wore no socks; the dark strips of his ankles were just visible between his shoes and the frayed bottoms of his jeans. Tim's breath pushed a flurry of crumbs into a two-inch roll beneath the table.

Debuffier's hand swung down into view, holding—of all things—a carton of pencils. Then he trudged out of sight, down the dimly lit back hall. Tim heard the enormous basement door swing open, then closed. The dead bolt slid home, then Debuffier's footsteps down the stairs came rumbling silently through the kitchen floor into Tim's cheek.

Tim rolled out just as Robert and Mitchell were emerging from the closet.

"Let's di-di-mau," Robert hissed.

Before Tim had time to turn, the sound came up through the floorboards as if suddenly enhanced, liberated, an echoing, distinctly human groan. The three men froze in the kitchen.

Tim wanted to say, "We go"—the words were almost out of his mouth when they evanesced, and Robert and Mitchell fell into silent line behind him, heading into the house interior.

Tim had Donna unwound and ready by the time they reached the door, and he slid her through the gap. Debuffier had draped black sheer cloth over the mirror and tied a white handkerchief over his head. Wearing overalls with no undershirt, he stood with his back to the door, stooped slightly, his enormous shoulders rippling with some unseen motion. Whirring. Pause. Whirring. Pause.

Tim barely had time to realize that he was sharpening pencils when a tinny human voice echoed in response, it seemed, to the whirring. "*God no. God, God no.*"

All three men stiffened, but there was no one else in sight in the small screen. Tim swung the lens, taking in the entire basement, but it was empty, save the tureens and bricks and feathers now kicked up and swirling. They remained on all fours above the small TV screen, blind men searching for a dropped penny.

Debuffier turned, his face powdered in white streaks. Testing the point of a pencil with the pad of one huge finger, he crossed to the refrigerator and swung open the top door of the freezer. A woman's head, framed perfectly by the box of the freezer, gaped out at the room, her mouth stretched wide and screaming. Alive. Sweat-darkened wisps of hair lay pasted down across her forehead. What appeared to be open sores dotted her face. Her head had been fit through a hole cut into the partition between fridge and freezer.

Debuffier slammed the top door shut, muffling the piercing screams, and opened the refrigerator door. The woman's body was curled into the lower unit, shivering and naked, also covered in small circular wounds. From her clawing feet to the abbreviated stretch of her neck, she seemed to hang suspended in the deadening white glow of the refrigerator light, the formaldehyde float of a primordial creature on a scientist's shelf.

Debuffier bent over, reaching for the soft flesh above her collarbone with the pointed end of the pencil. He shifted his massive weight, blocking their view of the woman, then the screaming ratcheted up a level, the sound numbed, like the woman's head, in the tomblike box of darkness, disassociated from the body, the inflicted torment, the world.

Robert stood up, trembling, in full-body drench. He drew his gun and aimed at the lock. Before Tim could respond, Mitchell grabbed Robert's wrist and said in a harsh whisper, "No. We don't get through that lock with a bullet."

As Robert came increasingly unwound, Mitchell seemed to grow more collected; nearly two decades' experience defusing live bombs served him well in the face of an active horror.

Sweat streaked in great droplets down Robert's temples. "We do not walk away."

"No," Tim said. "We don't." He turned and snapped his fingers, his voice a loud-whispered rush of urgency. "Ten-second hold, boys. Focus. New game plan, new priorities. I call 911. We blast through the door. We neutralize De-buffier, nonlethally if we can. We secure the victim. Then, if we have the luxury, we consider our own position."

Mitchell dug through the det bag, his razor knife out, a blasting cap having magically appeared, held between his teeth so his hands were free. He pulled the explosive sheet out and unrolled it a few turns. Working with rapid efficiency, he sliced out a disk of PETN, leaving behind a cookie-cutter hole.

Tim jogged into the kitchen before turning on his cell

phone, so as not to trip Mitchell's blasting caps. Stretching his T-shirt across the receiver, he spoke in a scratchy voice. "I have a medical emergency at 14132 Lanyard Street. In the basement. Repeat: in the basement. Please send an ambulance immediately." He snapped the phone shut, turned it off, and headed back down the hall.

The screaming reached an unbelievably high pitch, drawn thin and fine like a silver wire. Unshaken, Mitchell dug a can of spray-on glue from the bag, misted the back of the disk, and slapped it on the door over the lock.

*"God oh God stop please stop."*

Robert was moving from foot to foot in an odd kind of hot-coal dance, as if alleviating the burn from the screams, his face colored with rage and excitement. "Move it move it move it move it move it."

Mitchell ripped off a strip of explosive sheet and dropped the blasting cap from his mouth onto it. As Tim stretched the protruding wires down the hall, Mitchell finished priming the sheet, sandwiching it around the blasting cap and sticking it to the door. Driven by the screams, Robert and Mitchell followed Tim around the corner, Mitchell clutching a nine-volt in the vise of his fist. Tim handed off the wire ends to him.

Robert was breathing too hard, his nostrils flaring. "Do it. Do it. Do it."

Tim had to dispense with his whisper now, to be heard over the woman's screams. "Now, listen. We need to do this right. I'll be the first through the—"

*"Please. Please. Oh God please."*

Robert seized the wires from Mitchell and touched them to the battery. Tim had time only for an instinctual reaction, opening his mouth so his lungs could vent and flex air, preventing the possibility of rupture in the face of the overpressure. The house seemed to jump with the explosion, drywall dust clouding the air, and already Robert was up and running for the stairs, weapon drawn.

"Shit!" Ears ringing from the sharp-edged ping of metal rent, Tim stood and followed Robert in a sprint. Robert had already thrown the door open and disappeared through the haze of dust down the stairs, no backup, no strategic entry. Tim heard the blast of three erratic shots, and he shouldered hard against the now-jagged door frame at the top of the stairs, his elbows locked, his .357 downpointed, Mitchell closing fast from behind.

Robert swept down the stairs as if floating, his gun raised. Debuffier had swung the refrigerator door all the way open so it was bent back against its hinges, revealing the stretch of curled and terrified flesh within; he crouched behind it, using it as a shield. A chunk of drywall from the blast had landed on the second-to-last step, enough to send Robert into a stumble. Debuffier sprang up, nimble and catlike, and rushed Robert, a blur of size and lean, dark muscle. Robert's mass blocked Tim's angle on a shot, so Tim continued his charge down the steps. Debuffier reached Robert before he'd regained his balance and swatted the pistol from his grip. Debuffier seized him, his massive hands nearly encompassing Robert's rib cage, and hurled him up the stairs at Tim.

Robert's shoulder connected hard with Tim's thighs, sending him into a cartwheeling fall down the final three steps. Tim's .357 clattered off the side of the stairs, striking the concrete with a clang, and a numbness rang through his shoulder and hip that would later mean pain. He kept in his roll, trying to come up on his feet but landing jarringly on his knees, still hunched in a somersault crouch. The thick stock of Debuffier's leg broke his vertical field like a pillar, and Tim swung hard and sharp for the knee, angling for a break but instead connecting with the dense muscle of the thigh. His lead-weighted fist landed with the solid pop of a dinner plate dropped flat on a bed of water, and Debuffier howled. A fist rose like a too-large sun, connecting with Tim's crown. Tim felt the skin of his head pinch against the bone, saw a brilliant burst of light, heard Mitchell's boots thundering down the stairs behind him, then he was up in the air, Debuffier's hands crushing him at the shoulders, his feet dangling, a marionette under the appraising and pitiless eye of an Italian puppeteer. Debuffier's breath wafted coconut and sour milk across Tim's face.

Tim drove his head forward into Debuffier's chin, heard a pleasing crack, and the hands relaxed, for just an instant. Tim felt himself lowered a few inches, his feet finding the ground again, and, as Debuffier's hand reared back to deliver a paralyzing blow to the head, Tim rotated in, Green Beret style, a downstriking punch to the groin, quick and hard like a bear river-plunging for fish. The lead band across the back of his glove seemed to draw his fist down faster, harder, lending it a crushing momentum, and the line of his knuckles connected with the hard ridge of Debuffier's pubic bone.

There was a single instant of perfect balance and stillness, then the world flooded back into motion—Robert yelling, a shrill banshee wail echoing within the metal box of the mostly closed freezer, the shattering yield of Debuffier's bone as a skin-muffled crunch announced the instant and comprehensive fragmentation of his pelvis.

Debuffier's animal bellow of pain found resonance in the concrete walls and came back from the four corners of the room compounded. The freezer door was mid-swing, the woman's petrified expression flashing into view. His face an in-twisted vortex of pain, Debuffier half stood, one knee brushing the floor but not bearing his weight, his eyelids stretched so wide that the top curvature of his eyeballs was visible. His hands hung loose and open around his hips, frozen, as if contemplating how best to grasp a balloon filled with broken glass.

Mitchell thundered down the last few steps, but Robert had already found his pistol and was standing in full Weaver, head cocked, one eye closed.

Debuffier raised his hand. "No," he said.

The bullet took off his index finger at the knuckle before sucking his head in around the hole opened up at the bridge of his nose. His body smacked concrete, a widening pool spreading beneath his head with oil-slick deliberateness.

A tureen lay on its side, draining soapy water.

Robert stood over him, feet spread, and discharged two more bullets into the pulpy mess of his head.

"God*damn*it, Robert." Tim limped over to the refrigerator and swung open the freezer door. The woman's face stared back, weak with terror, broken bits of lead visible in several of her sores. He saw where Debuffier had drilled holes in the sides of the freezer to provide ventilation. A weight belt had been fastened around her neck, tight beneath the chin, making her unable to duck out of the hole. One of her eyes had been punctured—it oozed a cloudy liquid that caked her lower lid.

She was weeping. "Oh, no. There are more of you. Oh, my God, I can't."

"We're here to help you." Tim reached for the weight belt, but she shrieked and turned for his hand, gnashing wearily. Mitchell and Robert were at Tim's back, radiating horror and breathless silence.

"I'm not going to hurt you. I'm a U.S. de—" Tim stopped, struck by the illegitimacy of his presence. "I'm going to get you out and help you."

Her face seemed to melt, wrinkling at the forehead. She cried in soft barks with her voice alone, not producing any tears. Tim reached slowly for the weight belt and, when she made no movement toward his hand, uncinched it.

Robert and Mitchell had the lower door open. When they touched her, she shrieked again, but they guided her quickly down and out and laid her on the floor. The smell of pus, panic sweat, and day-old meat rose from her body. Lying limp on the concrete, arms jerking, legs quivering, she began to keen—deep, split-open moans.

Robert took three staggering steps toward the corner and leaned against the wall. He was crying, not loudly or with force, but matter-of-factly. Tears forged tracks through the drywall dust that had collected on his cheeks.

Someone had probably reported the explosion or gunshots; police units were likely en route already, in addition to ambulances.

Mitchell was holding the woman's head tenderly in both hands, trying to smooth her stiff hair. He spoke to her with an eerie calm. "We killed him. We killed the motherfucker who did this to you."

She began to convulse violently, limbs thrashing on the concrete, and Mitchell cradled her head so it wouldn't bang against the floor. Just as quickly as it had gone into motion, her body went limp, save her right leg, which continued to twitch, one broken toenail scraping concrete. Mitchell was up in a crouch over her, ear at her mouth, fingers checking for a neck pulse. He applied a sternal rub, digging his knuckles into her breastbone, and when he got no response, he began chest compressions.

The woman's head rocked slightly with Mitchell's movement, her good eye slick and white, a porcelain egg. Tim stayed nearby, on his knees, ready to take over, though he knew, from some until-now-unrealized sense he must have acquired on blasted fields and in evac helicopters, that she was beyond reviving.

A few paces away, Robert was muttering to himself, fists clenching in quick, furious pulses. Streaks of sweat stood out on his shirt.

Mitchell stopped, arms bulging to stretch his sleeves. He stood and laced his fingers, bringing his hands to his belt. The more furious the activity, the calmer and more focused he grew. "She's done. I'll have the van waiting by the back fence." He turned and headed up the stairs.

Robert ran over to the woman. "No. Take over, Rackley. *Take over.*"

Tim dutifully worked on her, but her mouth was cold and vacant against his, her body board–stiff, yielding upward around the union of his hands like cardboard pressed into carpet. Her lips had gone blue. He checked her carotid pulse again and got back only the dense coldness of marble.

Robert's face was moist, a blend of sweat and smeared tears, and a high shade of red that looked as if it stung.

Tim got up, retrieved his pistol, and tapped Robert gently on the forearm. "Let's clear out."

Robert wiped his mouth. "I'm not leaving her."

Tim placed a hand on Robert's shoulder, but Robert knocked it off. The wail of a distant siren reached them.

"There's nothing more we can do here," Tim said. "We go now. Robert. Robert. *Robert.*" Robert's head finally snapped around. He blinked hard and wiped the sweat off his forehead. Tim squatted and fixed him with a calm, steady gaze. "I'm not asking anymore. Move."

Robert rose dumbly, a child following instructions, and made his way up the stairs.

The woman's head was tilted back on the hard concrete, her jaw stretched open. Tim gently pressed her mouth closed before stepping over Debuffier's humped body and moving upstairs. Mitchell had wisely cleared the equipment from around the twisted metal door. As Tim stepped out into the backyard, he heard vehicles screeching up to the front curb. Just past the gap in the fence, the van was waiting, door slid open, and he stepped up and in.

The twins sat in the rear, backs against the walls, Robert's face flushed and combat-shocked, Mitchell's shirt stained where he'd held the woman's head. Tim yanked the door shut behind him, and they pulled out from the curb.

"You ever jump into the fray like that again," Tim said, "I'll shoot you myself."

Robert didn't show a flicker of response.

The Stork, sheet-white and sitting on a phone book to see over the high dash, glanced back over his shoulder. "I'm sorry, I didn't . . . couldn't go in. I was too scared." Grimacing, he clutched his heart, bunching his shirt. "I got the car and waited for a sign, for someone to come out." He fumbled in his pockets, pulled out a blue pill, and popped it.

"You did fine," Tim said. "You followed orders."

Robert clenched his sweaty bangs, his hair protruding in tufts between his fingers. "We could have gotten there earlier."

"No," Mitchell said.

"We could have . . . could have cut surveillance shorter. Just gone right in last night. She was there. She was in there the whole time."

Tim looked over at Robert, but Robert wouldn't meet his eyes—he was looking everywhere, nowhere.

"Don't play ifs," Mitchell said. "That's a no-win game. It's throwing yourself against a rock."

A series of cracks in the road made the van thrum with metallic urgency.

Robert bowed his head forward, then smacked it back against the wall of the van, so hard it dented the metal out in a crater. His voice was still strained, his throat wobbly and constricted. "Christ oh Christ. She looked so much like Beth Ann."

He leaned over and threw up into his fist.

**25** **AS TIM PULLED THROUGH RAYNER'S FRONT GATE BEHIND** the van, he was not surprised to see Ananberg's Lexus with its Georgetown license-plate frame. The gate whirred, rotating closed behind them, folding them protectively into the large rise of the Tudor stage set. Robert stumbled out first, trudging for the house, and the Stork followed, his face drawn and bloodless. Mitchell seemed almost to glide behind them, steady and light on his feet. Tim parked and brought up the rear, a sheepdog herding toward the stone front step, but before they could arrive, Rayner opened the door, his eyes swollen and bloodshot, Ananberg up on tiptoe behind him.

Rayner seemed not even to notice the walking-dead appearance of the crew advancing on him. He started to speak but had to clear his throat and start over. "Franklin's at the VA hospital. He's had a stroke."

They sat spread out evenly across the chairs and sofas of the study, as if needing a buffer from proximity. Tim and Rayner had played unelected spokesmen, swapping information with flat, toneless, just-the-facts-please-ma'am sentences.

Robert hurried to get down a few bolstering bourbons.

He drank without hesitation, pausing only to suck ice. A different type of post-op drink. The Stork drank milk through a straw—Tim guessed his palate abnormalities made drinking from a glass difficult for him. The Stork had settled down significantly now that the immediate threat had passed; his odd detachment seemed to make him impervious to trauma.

Ananberg kept glancing at the still-moist stain on the front of Mitchell's shirt.

Robert looked exceedingly weary. He shook his head, his eyes glazed with grief. "I can't believe the old man had a stroke."

Tim thought of his morning meeting with Dumone, the quiet apartment filled with the smell of stale carpet.

Rayner sat leaning forward in his charcoal glen-plaid suit, gold cuff links peeking out from the sleeves. The thin white band of his mustache looked fake. "I got the news and called over about an hour ago. The nurse wouldn't put him on to talk. I guess he wasn't in full control of his faculties and speech. No visitors tonight. I'm getting him transferred to the VIP floor at Cedars first thing tomorrow. We can have more control there."

"Of his mouth?" the Stork asked.

"Of his care." Rayner's annoyed gaze lingered on the Stork. "Franklin has an older sister, but he asked she not be contacted. He doesn't want her flying out, fussing over him."

"Unmarried," Ananberg said, by way of explanation.

The ensuing silence was broken only by ice clinking against glass and the slurp of milk through the Stork's straw.

"I think we could all use some time. What do you say we take the rest of the weekend off, meet Sunday night?" Rayner said.

Robert's eyes were focused on absolutely nothing, as if they were peering down an endless well. An alcohol blush had bloomed on his face; now that he'd started drinking, Tim wondered if he'd be able to stop.

Mitchell sat with his hands folded in his lap, the points of his thumbs touching. His arms he held tight to his sides, giving him a compact, focused bearing. His eyes had narrowed, almost to a squint, as though he were running net-explosive-weight calculations in his head. He was supremely calm, almost relaxed.

Tim looked uneasily from one brother to the other, his anger and disgust growing. "Take some time off? This isn't a church committee—we have matters to discuss."

Rayner cleared his throat, clasped his hands piously. "Let's not start pointing fingers here. I know the execution went badly—"

"No," Tim said. "The execution did not go badly. It *aspired* to go badly."

"I have to agree with Tim's assessment," Ananberg said. "This was a mess."

"You weren't there," Robert said.

"That's exactly irrelevant. This blows up, we all go to jail."

"Look. Things were complicated. We didn't mean for it to go down that way, it just happened."

"Well," Ananberg said, "who happened it?"

All eyes settled on Robert, except Mitchell's, which tracked the pendulum of the grandfather clock. Robert tilted his glass at Tim. "Rack fucked up, too."

"Amen to that," Tim said. "I should have set firm ROEs. We have strict procedures in place here. We need strict procedures in the field. There are gonna be some new rules."

"Like what?" Mitchell asked.

"Not now," Rayner said. "We're in no shape to talk about anything."

"When we come back, we're discussing this," Tim said. "At length."

Rayner stood and flared his hands down the fabric over his thighs, smoothing wrinkles. "Monday at eight."

When Rayner passed him, Tim was surprised to see genuine grief in the downturn of his mouth.

The TV was murmuring in Joshua's office, so Tim decided to forgo the elevator and sneak up the back stairs. His apartment waited. Mattress. Desk. Dresser. He pulled the child-size desk chair to the window and sat with his feet up, breathing exhaust through the screen, listening to someone yelling in the Japanese restaurant across the alley. It was remarkable how much angrier anger seemed when conveyed in an Eastern tongue.

He checked his Nokia voice mail—two messages. The first was Dray. Her voice, recognizable to him in so many indescribable subtleties, moved right through him. She was doing her best to soften her tone, make it more feminine, which meant she was regretful and wishing to convey affection.

"Tim, it's me." A long, crackling pause. "There are, uh, some forms here that need joint parental signatures. To cancel Ginny's medical insurance. Dissolve what's left of her college fund. Crap like that. If you could . . . If you could stop by sometime, that'd be great. I'll be around tomorrow. Or I could leave them on the kitchen table, if you want, and you could do it when I'm at work. But I'd rather that . . . that . . ." A sigh. "I'd really like to see you, Timothy."

Bear's startlingly gruff voice broke Tim's momentary lapse into happiness.

"Rack. Bear. How about a fucking phone call?"

He got Dray's machine, so he left a message, then called Bear. Bear said he'd like to see Dray, too, so Tim agreed to meet him at the house tomorrow at noon.

He got into bed, since he had little else to do. Because of the brightness of the downtown street and the inadequate city-issue blinds, darkness didn't really happen in his apartment. Night was a slightly altered attitude toward the hours, no more. It lacked lethargy.

As a preemptive strike against the images he'd found beneath the coroner's sheet, Tim tried to imagine Ginny in a peaceful pose, but everything came back trite and inauthentic. In life she'd never reclined peacefully in dandelion fields; there was little reason for her to do so now. His mind returned again and again to Debuffier's bullet-split face, to the death they'd dealt him and the lives he'd be unable to take in the future. There was a cheapness to the killing; it lacked righteousness. It was like gaining a fortune through inheritance.

Lane was dead and Debuffier was dead and Ginny couldn't have cared less.

After a while Tim found the emptiness of the room bad company. When he turned on the news, Melissa Yueh's face peered out, gleeful and tainted with a red, almost sexual excitement. "The city is heating up again after another execution of a suspected criminal, Buzani Debuffier. Debuffier was shot and killed immediately after apparently committing a violent torture/murder."

"Violent torture/murder" seemed redundant to Tim, but then he wasn't selling ratings. Footage rolled of guys in Scientific Investigation Division windbreakers poking through the debris at Debuffier's. ". . . LAPD won't disclose if they believe the case is related to the Lane assassination, but inside sources indicate that bits of rare explosive wire were found inside devices at both scenes—"

Feeling his stress ratchet up another notch, Tim flipped the channel. *Leave It to Beaver* flickered out at him in black and white. June scrunched Beaver in a hug, and the Beav closed his eyes. The scene was cloying to the point of repugnance, but Tim left it on.

He fell asleep to it.

**26** TIM SLEPT LATE AND SHOWERED LONG. THE KHAKIS AND button-up shirt he'd hung in the bathroom to steam out the wrinkles actually smoothed out decently.

He dressed in the living room, near the comforting murmur of the television. After a commercial featuring a bronzed and exuberant woman astride an elaborate exercise machine, Rayner appeared on a plush talk-show couch looking particularly unaggrieved—perhaps his sorrow over Dumone's stroke had been feigned after all. Or perhaps he couldn't help but perk up when he saw himself reflected back in the lens of a camera. He was, of course, commenting on Debuffier's death, waxing poetic about vengeance and duty and this travesty we call justice.

The pervasive theme of the show was that Debuffier had gotten what he'd had coming to him. With a few exceptions, the audience was energetic and sanctimonious, and the host, a Geraldo rip-off in an ill-advised maroon suit, claimed that the "counteroffensive against murderers" was inciting Americans to take back the streets. When a caller proudly related that his cousin in Texas, inspired by the Lane hit, had "shot a burglar dead" the day before yesterday, the news received whoops and cheers.

Rayner cleared his throat uncomfortably. "Well, it seems to me—and I've discussed this with several sources close to the investigation—that the person or persons behind these executions aren't seeking to promote wholesale vigilantism. They've chosen these cases quite specifically—cases in which the justice system appears to have failed. I'd guess their motivation is to open up discussion about these shortcomings in the law."

Tim watched Rayner's betrayal with the horrified anticipation of a first-day-on-the-floor med student at a thoracotomy. Rayner's need to issue a communiqué had been thwarted, so he'd chosen to tackle the issues as a commentator rather than leaving the Great Unwashed to think independently about the Commission's efforts. His tedious media analyses had been nothing more than preparation for future orchestration. Before long he'd be feeding information to handpicked journalists to spin coverage. Maybe he'd done so already.

The TV host's arms spread wide, bent at the elbows, microphone dangling like a baton. "Or they're just kicking ass and taking names."

Rayner's eyes were unaffected by the tight smile that flashed on his face. "Perhaps. But I think these executions—however misguided—are part of a *dialogue*. They're indicative of a growing sentiment in Americans today. We're simply fed up with the law. We don't believe that the law owns justice anymore, that the law will work for us."

A hefty man in a Cleveland Browns sweatshirt called out, "Yeah! Screw the courts!"

Off Rayner's expression of pained forbearance, Tim

clicked the remote. One channel over, John Walsh from *America's Most Wanted* was holding forth on *Crossfire*. Tom Green solicited passersby to target-shoot at crime fliers of the FBI's 10 Most Wanted. Howard Stern implored viewers to wager guesses about the respective lengths of Lane's and Debuffier's penises.

Tim felt sick by the time he turned off the TV.

He used his socks to dust off a pair of oxfords, which he laced loosely in anticipation of blisters. He deliberated over belts. Only when he pulled cologne from his dopp kit did he realize he'd been dressing up to see Dray.

He stopped by Cedars-Sinai on his way to Dray. The Beverly Hills–adjacent medical center rose glittering and imperious between Beverly and Third, a reassuring architectural display of order and competence. Tim got tangled up on Gracie Allen Drive before finding Lot #1 off George Burns Road. Trusty Tom Altman, aided by a smiling Arizona license, had little trouble talking his way past reception. After passing a woman wearing a mink over a hospital gown and an octogenarian with a Yiddish accent singing "Anything Goes" and raising his bathrobe for each glimpse of stocking, Tim found Dumone's room on the VIP floor.

He tapped the slightly ajar door with his knuckles before entering. A disgruntled expression on his pale, crumpled face, Dumone sat shored up by a clutch of pillows. Blanketing the nightstand to his left were flowers and gift baskets.

Tim couldn't resist a smile, and Dumone joined him, his grin pulling up only the right side of his face. "This place is all marble and plants and pillow fluffers. I feel like a pit bull at a poodle show."

Tim crossed, and they regarded each other warmly for a moment. "You look like hell."

"Don't I know it. Look at this crap Rayner sent over." Dumone's hand rooted around one of the gift baskets and emerged with a foil-wrapped bag of coffee. "Guatemalan Fantasy. Sounds like a blue movie."

The droop of his face slurred his words, just slightly. To his side a monitor blinked at intervals. His left arm lay limply in his lap, hand coiled. An IV ran into his good arm, and an oxygen tube fed his nose.

The wardrobe stood open just enough to reveal Dumone's hung shirt and slacks, his Remington dangling in a shoulder holster.

"They let you keep your revolver?" Tim asked.

"Once I explained who I was, showed 'em my conceal-and-carry. I told them my weapon goes nowhere without me. They agreed sweetly, then took all the bullets, the bastards. They're used to negotiating with old-school producers. A simple cop like me doesn't stand a chance."

He jerked forward, seized by a violent coughing fit, hand held up to stave off any impulse Tim might have to help. Finally he quieted, his breath rasping. He took a moment before speaking again. "Rob and Mitch wanted to come by, but I put the hold on them. Wanted to talk to you first, get the lay."

"Are you feeling—?"

Dumone cleared his throat loudly, cutting him off. "Threw a clot. Had it on the radar, was just a matter of time. Let's talk shop. I'm not much good at the other."

He listened quietly and attentively, nodding from time to time, his mouth set slightly to the side. When Tim finished filling him in, Dumone pulled in a deep, halting breath and exhaled shakily. "What a shit storm. You gotta get things back on track."

"First and foremost I have to get the ROEs more clearly defined."

Dumone nodded, the oxygen tube rustling against his chest. "It's *all* about the rules. They're the only thing that separate us from vigilantes and Third World thugs. How we go about our actions is the entirety of who we are. Without perfection we're a lynch mob."

"Robert and Mitchell are hungry for more operational control, but after this I've got no choice but to pull them back. Robert entirely."

"How about Mitch?"

"He's more poised under pressure than Robert, but he's also straining at the bit. He brought explosives to a surveillance job, for Christ's sake. And Rayner's being oddly indulgent of them."

Dumone's forehead wrinkled. "I don't know why that would be—there's no love lost there from either side, last I checked."

"Well, Rayner's content to—"

"You're in charge. You. Not Rayner. Rayner bribes us with a room in a nice house, but that does not put him in the driver's seat. My vote goes with you. If you have to roll heads, roll heads. Tell Rayner to get his mug off the news. Have Rob ride the bench after that bullshit. Use Mitch if you need him. Run the show according to your judgment, and work things slowly back to a good balance." He coughed jerkily, squinting through the pain. "Rob and Mitch give you jaw, send 'em to me."

"Thanks." Tim nodded and rose. "Enjoy your coffee."

"You kidding me? If I can't stir it into hot water, I don't trust it."

Tim rested a hand on Dumone's shoulder, and Dumone gripped him at the wrist. It was a brief gesture but an intimate one.

"You're at a crossroads, Deputy." Dumone winked. "Lay down the law."

Bear's rig was already hogging the curb when Tim pulled up. He parked across the street. The murmur of voices from the backyard reached him halfway up the front walk, so he circled, lifted the latch on the side gate, and stepped through.

Fowler, Gutierez, Dray, and about four other deputies milled around the Costco picnic table, surrounding Tim's paint-splattered boom box, which was throwing out Faith Hill from back when she still twanged. They were all fisting beers, and their heads turned in unison toward Tim. Mac, sleeves double-cuffed to show off muscular forearms, was leaning over the grill, dousing a clumsily arrayed mound of charcoal with too much lighter fluid. Bear sat sideways on the deck chair with the snapped straps, waiting for Tim by himself, exuding loyal outrage. He was wearing a jacket, despite the fact that it was the first sunny afternoon in two weeks, and a baseball cap with an embossed gold star.

Tim's hands moved before his mouth could, gesturing out through the gate. "I should go. I didn't realize you were having a party." He prayed that the hurt indignation in his voice wasn't as apparent to them as to his own ears. He felt foolish in his nice clothes.

"Oh, come on, Rack. There's no reason to be like that. Come in. Have a burger." Mac wore a we're-all-friends-here frat-boy smile. He'd propped a large, flat cardboard box against the side of the grill, as if tempting the gods of conflagration. Next to it lay a basketball.

Dray approached fast, talking low so only Tim would hear her. "I'm so sorry. Mac took the liberty of inviting everyone back from the station. I didn't know you were coming."

He felt the impulse to peck her on the lips in greeting. Her aborted lean told him she'd resisted the pull of the same habit.

"He seems awfully at home here," Tim said.

A shadow flicker of remorse crossed her eyes. "He knows this is our home."

"Does he?" Tim looked away. "I'll just sign the forms, then get out of here and leave you to your thing."

"It's not my thing."

Mac threw a lit match on top of the charcoal briquettes, then studied them with disappointment. He added more lighter fluid.

"Where's the paperwork?" Tim asked.

He followed her inside, nodding to the others. Bear stood and followed them inside, walking through the circle of deputies just to make them move out of his way.

"Could you grab another jar of pickles?" Mac called after them.

Dray grimaced and slid the door shut behind them. They turned and watched Mac leaning over the charcoal briquettes, examining them. A burst of orange flame leapt up, and he reared back, face flushed, then shot a handsome smile over at them to cover his embarrassment.

Dray headed into the kitchen, rubbing her bare ring finger uncomfortably. "The forms are in here."

Tim turned to Bear. "Why don't you give us a few minutes?"

"Oh, sure, great. I'll be outside with Wile E. Coyote." Bear closed the sliding door behind him a little harder than necessary, in case Tim had missed the point.

When Tim entered the kitchen, the forms were laid out neatly on the table. He sat and signed where they were marked. Dray was at the sink, straining against the pickle-

jar lid, elbow pointing out. She gave the lid a good glare before subjecting it to hot water from the tap. "No update? On Ginny's case? Kindell?"

"Nothing yet. I'm working on it."

"I see you made the news again. You and your posse."

"I don't want to discuss that. Not unless we're alone."

"This time with a victim in the middle of it. Signs of a confrontation. Narrowly avoiding police. Aren't you worried it'll get out of hand?"

"It did get out of hand."

Dray gave the jar a half turn under the faucet. Steam rose from the sink. "Why don't you get out before it does again?"

"Because I made a commitment to this. I need to see it through."

"They say men think logically, women emotionally. The way I see it, neither are very good at either." She turned to face him. "Tim, you have to realize you're off track here. Whatever it is you think you're involved with, what you *are* involved with is crap."

"We hit a snare, but we're working it out."

"Tell that to Milosevic and his pig-faced cronies when you're sitting next to them at The Hague. I'm sure they'll empathize."

"Point taken, Dray. I'm very aware of where we don't want to end up."

"Bear's dialed into the fact that you're up to something dicey. Don't think he'll let you get in too deep before he pulls you out."

"He'll get tired of that routine," Tim said. "Just like you're getting tired of it."

She turned back to the sink. "You're still wearing our wedding band." She threw off the question casually, but he could hear the hopefulness hiding in her voice.

He shifted uncomfortably, something prying at the cage of his ribs. That he was unable to put the ring aside as she was made him feel deeply vulnerable. "I can't get it off over my knuckle."

The lid still didn't give, so she started banging it against the counter, angrily. Tim crossed and tried to take it from her, though she didn't relinquish it immediately, not from stubbornness, Tim guessed, but because she wanted to keep banging something. She finally let go and stood with her head down and her arms loose at her sides.

Tim turned the lid, and it gave with a pop. He offered the jar back to her. The Great Deliverer of the Pickles.

She set the jar on the counter. "When Ginny died, we started talking different languages, you and I. And what if we never find our way back? What a fucked-up love story this makes. Happy couple, trauma, separation. I don't know about you, Timmy, but I give it a thumbs-down for predictability."

"Don't call me Timmy."

She was already walking out. She appeared in the back-yard a minute later. Mac said something to her that Tim couldn't make out through the window.

Dray said, "Get your own fucking pickles."

Mac made a shrug at the guys and went back to the burgers. Tim would have left out the front door if Bear weren't waiting for him out back, like a passive-aggressive dog.

When he stepped outside, the cardboard box was open on the patio, parts strewn about. Mac was now up on Tim's ladder, struggling under the weight of a basketball back-board. With a shoulder he pinned it against the wood paneling where the wall peaked to meet the chimney. He smiled when he saw Tim, two fat nails protruding from his mouth like iron cigarettes. His eyebrows were slightly singed. "Bet you never thought of this, huh? The patio makes a perfect little court."

Tim stared at the pristine strip of wood at the chimney's edge; he'd painted it with a three-fourths angular liner brush so he wouldn't stain the bricks.

Mac pounded the nail through the backboard, and the wood panel beneath split. Tim felt his teeth grind so hard his skull vibrated. Dray was sitting backward on the picnic table, feet on the bench, her head lowered into her hands, her face hidden by the drape of her bangs. Beside her, Bear watched the proceedings with the horrified absorption of a rubbernecker at a particularly grisly car wreck.

Another volley of bangs, and then Mac called out, "Is it straight?"

Fowler and Gutierez paused from dribbling on the patio to flash him thumbs-ups. "Good enough."

The backboard was at a four o'clock tilt.

Tim walked over and stood before Bear and Dray, one foot up on the cooler.

Dray gestured limply to Mac but couldn't muster words.

"I'm on my way," Tim said.

"I'm following," Bear said.

"You can't leave me stuck here."

"He's your guest, Dray," Tim said.

The other deputies were at the rear fence line, smoking and speaking in lowered voices.

Dray's face was drawn and weary, and the dark pockets beneath her eyes looked like bruises. Tim remembered when they first met, at a fire-department fund-raiser. She'd been wearing a yellow dress dotted with tiny blue flowers. The straps crossed in the back, showing off a diamond patch of skin just below her nape. She'd walked past him, pursued by a fire chief—older guy, as all her exes were—and she'd sent a breeze of jasmine and lotion his way that had on him the kind of effect usually reserved for shitty romantic comedies and Pepe Le Pew. Later that evening he'd caught her out in the parking lot getting a sweater from her car, and they'd spoken for about forty-five minutes in the intimate space between vehicles. He'd kissed her, and she'd gone home with him, and for months afterward firefighters from Station 41 had fixed Tim with cold, aggressive glares every time their paths crossed, a reprisal he gladly endured.

Only in hindsight had he realized how noteworthy Dray's feminine getup had been that night; she'd not worn the dress since, nor anything yellow, nor especially anything with little blue flowers. Now she looked tired and world-weary and unspecifically pissed off, like a stoic dust-bowl mother with a child hanging from her neck and three more behind her, around her, waiting to be fed.

"I lied to you, Dray," Tim said. "I'm not wearing my wedding band because I can't get it off over my knuckle. I'm still wearing it because I can't not."

Her lips parted slightly. Her chest rose beneath her tank top and stopped with a held breath. Her eyes were brilliant green in the sunlight and as large as he'd ever seen them.

Mac's voice rose, disrupting them. ". . . so we called the Milpitas guys the Mil-*penis* guys," he was saying, recounting his week at EOB SWAT training, his fifth time through the program and in all likelihood the fifth time he'd fail. "Good little rivalry. I shot a two sixty-two on the test."

"In your fucking dreams you shot a two sixty-two," someone said.

Mac's finger made the sign of the cross on his barrel chest. "It was pretty funny. They had this bull dyke on their squad—"

Dray was on her feet. "Why'd you use that word?"

Mac stopped, glanced at Gutierez and Fowler for support. "I don't know. Because she was, I guess."

"Why? Short haircut, good build? Working hard on the job?" Her arms were crossed, and Tim knew from her expression that she was all about the fight right now and not the content, and so they'd be at it for hours. "I field that shit all day, and you can bet your ass she does, too."

Bear signaled Tim with a jerk of his head, and Tim followed him out through the side gate. Bear pointed to his truck, and they both climbed in and sat for a moment. They could still make out Dray's voice, the fricatives and raised syllables.

"On the warpath, ain't she?" Bear said.

"It's a thickheaded way for her to beat up on herself."

Bear fingered one of the schisms in the heat-cracked dash, then wiped his moist palms on his slacks. He was giving off discomfort like a scent, fiddling with the hockey puck of a watch strapped to his wrist. Tim waited, knowing Bear didn't like to be pushed when it came to words.

"Look, Tim. This is a tough thing to ask you. It's about the killings. This vigilante stuff."

Tim felt an icy band of sweat spring up on his forehead, just at the hairline.

"I know you quit and all, but . . . we'd like your help apprehending the guy."

Tim made sure he breathed a few times before he answered. "Why's the service involved?"

"There's some talk the guy could be a fugitive—his fuck-all attitude, probably. Like he's got nothing to lose. Mayor Hahn's going ballistic on this one. He tapped Robbery-Homicide, Chief Bratton is leaning on us to pull together a fugitive list from their profile, we already have FBI up our asses—Tannino says fuck 'em all, if we're doing the work anyway, we might as well try to get the collar ourselves, carve us a bigger piece of the pie at budget time."

"Makes sense."

Bear's hand rustled in his jacket. "Just give this a listen for me, would you?"

"I'm not really—"

The microcassette recorder peeked out from Bear's fist like a trapped canary. He flipped it and punched the side button with a thumb. Tim heard his own barely disguised voice issue forth. "I have a medical emergency at 14132 Lanyard Street. In the basement. Repeat: in the basement. Please send an ambulance immediately."

Bear clicked it off. He stared at Tim expectantly. Tim got busy studying the front lawn through the window.

"Personally, I don't buy the fugitive angle." Bear's tone was driving, knowing. "I'm thinking the guy's former military or PD. He's got the radio formality, repeating key information."

Tim recalled being impressed with himself at the time of the call for refraining from spelling out the street name using a phonetic alphabet. Somewhere beneath his guilt and fast-hardening shame shone his admiration for the meticulousness it took to be a competent criminal. A single lapse in a high-heat moment—the location repeat—had narrowed the ground Tim was standing on considerably. A helpful tip from a friend and partner, granted from a position of plausible deniability.

"This jackass"—Bear shook the recorder—"is usurping the law, stealing it from the same people who are gonna track him down. That's liable to piss people off—understandably so, if you ask me. If I was this guy, I'd be pretty concerned. I'd make sure I knew exactly what I was into."

Tim waved his hand, palmed some sweat off his forehead, then looked at his watch. "Shit. I'm late for a . . . meeting." In his split-second hesitation yawned another void he'd later fill with worries. Bear's eyes seemed cold—another of Tim's concerns, trickling in, seeking the emptiness.

"What meeting? You don't have a job."

"Exactly. It's an interview. Private security gig." Tim pushed open the door and stepped out onto the curb.

"That's good." Bear's face held a not-so-subtle warning. "A lot of people need looking after these days."

**27** **"WE'RE JUST FINISHING UP THE MEDIA RECAP, MR. RACK-**ley," Rayner said when Tim entered the conference room. Rayner stood at the head of the table, a thick manila folder laid open before him on the granite surface, press clippings protruding messily.

"If you *ever* pull a move like you pulled this morning on TV without our collective and express approval, I'll—"

"You're not in charge here," Rayner said. "Why should I have to listen to you?"

"Mutual assured destruction. That's why." Tim stared at Rayner until Rayner looked away, then slid into his chair. "Your comments were unsubtle and reckless. Don't do that again, or anything like it. If something shows up in the press, I'll know if it smells like you. Before we act, we agree on matters here. That's an inviolable rule."

The others were present, but without Dumone there seemed an imbalance. Some element of gravitas had been lost. Before, they'd been a commission; now they were just six pissed-off people in a room.

They all kept their picture frames turned in like mirrors; the Stork alone positioned his facing away from him. To Tim's right, Dumone's wife peered out from her still-present frame, gazing at the empty black chair before her. Not for the first time, Tim thought about what cheap props the photos were. Facile, like a gimmick for one of Rayner's chat shows.

Ananberg observed Tim silently from the seat beside him. She looked spent, strung out on an adrenaline hangover. They were all beaten up—Robert in particular. He still hadn't raised his head. It had been a hellacious twenty-four hours, between the Debuffier execution and Dumone's stroke. Only the Stork and Rayner, shielded by their inherent yet opposite superficialities, remained imperviously alert.

Rayner took a sip of water. "I'd like to finish the media recap now." A shuffling of papers. "On CNBC last night—"

"The instant we became aware that Debuffier had a live victim in hand, the sole objective should have been rescuing her and saving her life." Tim spoke with Dumone's resolve and authority, and, as when Dumone spoke, the others were silent. "The only valid reason to kill Debuffier would have been as a necessary tactic to extract the victim, *which it was not*. I had injured him nonfatally—"

Robert spoke slowly and vehemently. "I shot Debuffier because it was the quickest way to get to the victim." He finally pulled his head up, revealing his face.

"No. You shot him because you wanted to play hero."

"We voted he should be executed," Mitchell said. "He was executed."

"*There was no longer a need to execute him*. He was committing a crime that could have put him away. We could have secured him and turned matters over to the proper authorities."

"Then we would have had to stay with him and gotten caught," Robert said.

"We do not kill people to avoid getting caught," Tim

said. "If covering your own ass is your primary objective, you don't belong here."

"Come on," Mitchell said. "The guy had a torture victim captive in his basement, for Christ's sake. What are the odds that we'll stumble into a situation like that again?"

"These are not predictable situations. We never know what we're going to stumble into."

"Then you should be grateful *I* thought to come prepared, since you sure as hell weren't. You were busy riding my ass for bringing my det bag. Without it we wouldn't have gotten through that door."

A laugh escaped Tim. "You hold that to be a well-planned, well-executed mission? You think you can take control operationally? With *that?*" He turned to Rayner—who wore a worried, atypically passive expression—and Ananberg, looking for support.

"We met our mission objective," Mitchell said.

"The outcome isn't the only thing that matters," Ananberg said.

"No? Isn't that our argument? The ends justify the means?"

Robert was gazing at the table, fingers drumming the granite; Mitchell had become the mouthpiece.

"The means *are* the ends," Tim said. "Justice, order, law, strategy, control. If we lose sight of that when we operate, the whole thing comes unwound. Results do not override rules."

"Look, what happened, happened—there's no need to go pulling pins on a sweat grenade now. Robbie got a little fired up and jumped the gun on our basement entry—"

"He was unpredictable, dangerous, and off his game." Despite the heat the argument was generating, Tim had yet to raise his voice, a restraint Dray abhorred in him.

"People fuck up sometimes." Robert seemed unsettled

and highly agitated. "No matter what happens, an operation can spin out of control. We've all had that happen."

"Calm down, Robert," Mitchell said sharply—the first severe note Tim had heard either twin use with the other.

"The guy was poking holes in her." Robert's voice, unusually high, shook from the memory.

"We can't act emotionally during a live operation," Tim said. "An untimed entry like that gets us killed five times out of ten. We lose our angle, our element of surprise, tactics, strategy—everything."

Mitchell leaned forward, his jacket bunching tight at the biceps. "I understand."

Tim turned his stare to Robert. "He doesn't."

Robert rose to a half crouch above his chair. "What's your fucking problem, Rackley? We killed the prick. Instead of riding my ass for going in two seconds early, why don't you think about what we did accomplish? Think of the puke off the streets, put down, never again eyeing a sister, a mother, a girl at a bus stop."

Even across the table, Tim picked up a hint of alcohol on his breath. "The point of this, of us, is not merely to kill. Do you understand that?" Tim waited impatiently, glaring back at Robert. "If not, get out."

Tim found himself thinking about what angle he'd take on a jab if Robert came across the table at him. Mitchell rested a hand on Robert's shoulder and pulled him gently back down into his chair. The Stork's head was bent; he rubbed his thumbnail with the pad of his forefinger, an annoying, repetitive gesture that called to mind autism.

Robert's voice was so low it was barely audible. "Of course I get it."

Tim fixed him with a stare. "Why the face?"

"What?"

"You shot him in the face. That's a highly personal kill shot."

"Your blowing up Lane's head I would hardly label dispassionate," Rayner said.

"Lane's head shot was strategic to ensure the safety of those around him. This was specifically not. You're supposed to aim at critical mass. If the gun kicks high, you still get the neck. A chest shot has more stopping power, too, especially with a big guy."

Rayner's eyebrows were raised, frozen in an expression of distaste or respect.

"So I shot Motherfucker in the face. What are you saying?" Robert was flushed, the muscles of his neck pulled taut.

"You're not starting to enjoy this, are you?"

Robert stood up again, but Mitchell yanked him back down. He stayed in his chair, eyeing Tim, but Tim turned to face Mitchell. "And what's this about a rare explosive wire linking the explosives?"

"It's media horseshit. I use standard wires. There's no way they could link them."

"Well, someone in forensics knows the two executions are linked and leaked that fact, with a slight skew, to the media. How do they know? And so quickly? It had to be the explosive."

Mitchell grew finicky under Tim's glare.

"That wasn't a commercial blasting cap, was it, Mitchell?"

"I don't use anything commercial, not for a key component. Don't trust it. I make all my own stuff."

"Great. So could forensic analysis determine that the initiation portion of your homemade blasting cap was similar to the earpiece device? This is LAPD bomb squad we're talking about, not some Detroit Scooby-Doo with a magnifying glass."

"Maybe." Mitchell looked away. "Probably."

"Who gives a shit anyway?" Robert said. "It doesn't affect anything."

"I give a shit, because if it happens and *we* didn't plan it, that's bad news. There's a reason we voted against a communiqué"—an angry eye toward Rayner—"not that we'd want to claim this mess anyway. The bomb squad matching the two explosives is going to bring the heat, and we don't have room for missteps."

Tim leaned back in his chair, weathering the Mastersons' aggressive stares. "Let me make something else clear, since you two seem so eager to run and gun: You don't have what it takes to lead this kind of operation."

Robert and Mitchell coughed out identical snickers. "Mitch blasted the door," Robert said. "I was the number-one man through."

"And I was the one who jumped in and saved your ass when you missed three shots, tripped down the stairs, and got tossed like a Nerf ball by Debuffier."

The muscles of Robert's face had tightened, compressing his cheeks into sinewy ovals.

"I run the show operationally," Tim said. "My rules. Those were the conditions. And since it's clear none of you have given any thought to defining our operational rules, how's this: You have none. I'm the sole operator on a kill mission. You will not be on-site when a hit goes down. That's just how it is."

"Let's talk about this," Rayner said. "You're not solely in charge here."

"I'm not negotiating these terms. They stand, or I walk."

Rayner's lips tightened, his nostrils flaring with indignation—the spoiled prince used to getting his way. "If you walk, you'll never get to review Kindell's case. You'll never know what happened to Virginia."

Ananberg looked over at him, shocked. "For Christ's sake, William."

Tim felt his face grow hot. "If you think for a minute that I'd stay here and participate in a venture of this severity to get my hands on a file—even a file that could help solve my daughter's death—then you've underestimated me. I will *not* be blackmailed."

But Rayner was already backpedaling into his polished-gentleman persona. He hadn't dropped his guard before, but the picture beneath it was as nasty as Tim had imagined. "I didn't mean to imply anything of the sort, Mr. Rackley, and I apologize for my phrasing. What I mean is, we all have aims we're seeking to forward here, and let's keep our eyes on the ball." He cast a wary glance at the Mastersons. "Now, how *would* you like to handle matters operationally so you're comfortable?"

Tim took a moment, letting the pins and needles leave his face. He met Mitchell's eyes. "I still may need you. And you." He nodded at the Stork, as if the Stork gave a damn. "For surveillance, logistics, backup. But I handle target neutralization alone."

Mitchell's hands flared wide and settled in his lap. "Fine."

Ananberg's eyes tracked over one chair. "Robert?"

Robert ran a knuckle across his nose, studying the table. Finally he nodded, glaring at Tim. "Affirmative, *sir*."

"Excellent." Rayner clapped his hands and held them together, like a delighted Dickensian orphan at Christmas. "Now, let's get back to the media recap."

"Fuck the media recap," Robert growled.

The Stork clasped his hands and raised them. "Here, here."

Rayner looked like the teacher's yes boy who'd just had his test tubes stomped by the class bully. "But the sociological impact is certainly relevant to—"

"Bill," Ananberg said. "Get the next case binder."

Rayner huffily pulled his son's crestfallen image off the wall and punched buttons on the safe, issuing a steady stream of words under his breath.

"Wait," Mitchell said. "Are we voting without Franklin?"

"Of course," Rayner said. "The binders don't leave this room."

Robert said, "Then conference him in."

"He could be overheard talking in his room," Ananberg said. "And we don't know if those phone lines are secure."

"He gets exhausted pretty quickly," Rayner said. "I'm not sure if he has the focus or stamina right now to pay these deliberations the meticulous attention they demand."

"I say we wait for him to recover," Tim said.

Rayner faced them, his hands trembling slightly. "I spoke to his doctor at length today. His prognosis. . . . I'm not sure that waiting for his recovery is the wisest idea."

Robert blanched. "Oh."

Mitchell got busy scratching his forehead.

Shock turned to sadness before Tim could get a handle on it. It took him a moment to regain his composure, then he nodded at Rayner to move ahead.

Rayner grabbed a binder and tossed it on the table. "Terrill Bowrick of the Warren Shooters."

On October 30, 2002, three seniors at Earl Warren High had gotten into a sixth-period altercation with the starting lineup of the school basketball team. They'd retreated to their vehicles and returned with ordnance. While Terrill Bowrick stood guard at the door, his two co-perpetrators had entered the school gymnasium, where they'd fired ninety-seven rounds in less than two minutes, killing eleven students and wounding eight.

The coach's five-year-old daughter, Lizzy Bowman, who'd been watching practice from the bleachers, had caught a stray bullet through her left eye. Greeting Angelenos on their doorsteps Halloween morning was a front-page photo of her father on both knees, clutching her limp body—a reverse *Pietà* for the new millennium. Tim remembered vividly how the coach's jersey had borne a blood imprint of his daughter's face, a crimson half mask. Tim had set down the paper, dropped Ginny off at school, then sat in his car in the parking lot for five minutes before walking to his daughter's classroom so he could see her again through the window before leaving her.

The two gunmen, lean stepbrothers bound by a perverse codependence, had claimed there had been no premeditation. Their father was a pawnbroker—they'd been transporting the weapons between two of his stores, just happened to have dueling SKSs and four mags in the trunk when they'd lost their cool. Second-degree murder at worst, their defense lawyer claimed, maybe even a push for temporary insanity. A foolish argument, but good enough to get past your average foolish jury.

The prosecutor, unable to play the brothers off against each other and faced with wrathful media and a community hell-bent on vengeance, had realized he could roll Bowrick with a grant of immunity. Bowrick, a second-time senior who'd just stumbled across the threshold of his eighteenth birthday and thus was sweating heavy, could testify that they'd planned the shooting in the preceding weeks, thus establishing premed and giving the prosecution an express train to murder in the first. The stepbrothers, also not Oppenheimers in the classroom, were legal adults as well.

The prosecutor slid the immunity grant past the media by pointing out that Bowrick was the least culpable co-conspirator and that his participation had been the least egregious. He slid it past his division chief by making clear that Bowrick, a twig of a kid with a lame arm and a limp, could play to jury sympathy and that all the evidence to prove up the premed was circumstantial. By providing independent corroboration, Bowrick could shore up the case.

After Bowrick testified, the brothers were convicted and fast-tracked for capital punishment. Bowrick walked with a plea to a lesser charge—accessory after the fact—and was granted a deal for probation and a thousand hours of community service, no time served.

"So that's what a school shooting buys you these days."

Mitchell joined in Tim's disgust. "About the same sentence you'd get for spray-painting graffiti on your neighbor's shiny new Volvo."

"Let's bear in mind that he was only an aider and abetter," Robert said. His eyes, glassy and loose-focused, betrayed the slightest identification with Bowrick, the outsider.

"Maybe he didn't fire the weapon because he couldn't hold it properly with an atrophied arm," Tim said.

"And regardless, Robert," Rayner said, "an aider and abetter is subject to the same sentence as those who actually perpetrate the crime."

"Less the gun enhancements," Robert said.

"No one needs the gun enhancements. It was a capital-punishment case."

Robert tilted his head, a gesture of concession. "Right," he said. "That's right."

"The case precedent is pretty clear on this one," Ananberg said, "particularly for accomplices of this type. Aiders and abetters have gotten dinged on special circumstances for everything from lying-in-wait allegations to multiple-murder allegations."

Bowrick's booking photo sat faceup to Tim's right, the border nudging his knuckles. Despite Bowrick's attempt to approximate good posture, the flare of his dishwater-blond bangs barely notched the five-foot-eight line painted on the wall behind him. A jagged half-coin pendant dangled from a thin gold necklace. Sullenness pervaded his features. He didn't have the confidence to give off surly; his was the pasty-white face of hope beaten down to unhappy submission. He was sullen like a kicked dog, like the kid picked last, like a deflowered girl after her lover's too-hasty departure.

Ananberg backed them up, and Rayner led them through the case from the beginning. They started by scouring the evidence reports—admissible and inadmissible. Their evaluative capabilities had drastically improved as they'd grown more familiar with Ananberg's procedure, leading to sharper focus, more incisive arguments, and a wider exploration of potentialities. The deliberations were all the more impressive given the divisiveness at the meeting's outset.

When the final document had made its way around the table, Tim slid it into the binder and glanced up at the others. "Let's vote."

Guilty. Unanimous. Ananberg, who'd cast her vote last, crossed her hands on the table, her expression oddly content.

"There is one major complication," Rayner said. "After he went state's evidence, Bowrick went into hiding." He spread his hands, Jesus calming the seas. "The good news is, he didn't go into witness protection. Not formally. But he was getting death threats, his property vandalized. After someone tried to burn down his apartment, he switched his name and moved away. Only his probation officer knows where he is."

"I'll find him," Tim said quietly.

"If he's still under the thumb of his PO, he's still laying his head somewhere in L.A.," Robert said.

Mitchell's fingers strummed on the table. Stopped. He looked at Rayner. "Can you pry where he's staying from the PO?"

"Too messy," Tim said before Rayner could respond. "Too many trails leading back to us."

"We know he's logging community-service hours," Robert said. "Why don't we run a check on what programs are up where, give a glance?"

"I said I'll find him," Tim said. "Without stoking any fires. I'll take care of it quietly. You all sit tight and keep silent."

Rayner was standing at the safe, his back to the others. Before Tim could move to rise, Rayner turned and let another black binder drop on the table. Tim's eyes went past him to the last black binder in the safe. Kindell's.

He wondered if Ananberg had even attempted to get him the public defender's notes from Kindell's binder.

Rayner followed Tim's gaze behind him to the open safe. He smiled curtly, reached back, and closed it. Tim continued to find Rayner's petty power plays galling, despite their transparency.

"What do you say we tackle one more case now while our brains are warmed up?"

Tim checked his watch. 11:57.

"I got nowhere to go," Robert said.

Ananberg's laugh, sharp and short, rang off the wood-

314 • GREGG HURWITZ

paneled walls. "I don't think any of us has anywhere to go. Tim, do you have to get home?"

"I don't have a home, remember?"

Robert's mustache shifted and rose. "That's right. None of us do, do we, Mitch?"

"No home, no family, no records. We're ghosts."

The Stork emitted a wheezy little laugh. "No taxes either."

"Ghosts." Mitchell grinned. "We are ghosts, aren't we? We just come out of our graves now and then to take care of business."

Tim nodded at the binder. "What's the case?"

Rayner folded his hands atop the binder and gave a magician's pause. "Rhythm Jones."

"Ah," Mitchell said. "Rhythm."

It would be difficult to live in L.A. County and not have at least a passing awareness of the Rhythm Jones–Dollie Andrews case. An ex-rapper of modest acclaim, Jones was a small-time dealer with a propensity for turning out girls. His first name derived from the fact that he was always bouncing, as if to a private beat. According to street lore, his mother had named him in the crib. As an adult he threw off a sloppily endearing vibe, all fat smile and bopping head. Usually he wore a Dodgers jersey, hanging open to reveal the RHYTHM tattoo stenciled in Gothic across his chest.

For a few chance weekends in his twenties, he'd spun vinyl with the East Side DJ set, but he'd quickly found himself back in his hometown, South Central. Three years and two hundred pounds later, he was the go-to man for shitty rock and petite white girls who'd hook for a twenty or a spoonful of liquid nirvana. He was a notoriously vicious sex addict; his charges had been known to hobble into emergency rooms, towels crammed down both sides of their pants to stanch the bleeding.

He'd been indicted on two counts of possession for sale and one count of pimping and pandering, but due to a combination of dumb luck and cowed witnesses, he'd never been convicted.

Until Dollie Andrews.

Andrews was an off-the-bus Ohioan who'd taken the archetypal Hollywood header, from waitressing actress to back-alley blow-jobber. But she'd finally gotten her dream: After her body had been found smeared into Jones's ratty couch, punctured with seventy-seven knife wounds, her modeling eight-by-tens had been released to a ravenous press, and her short-cropped towhead curls and the just-right width of her hips had etched her persona posthumously into the zeitgeist.

Jones had been found sleeping off a PCP high one room over; he claimed complete amnesia regarding the past two days. None of Andrews's blood had been found on his body, his clothes, or under his nails, though a crime-scene technician had discovered traces in the pipes beneath the shower drain. The weapon, bearing a clean set of ten-point prints, had been recovered from a trash can outside. Motive? The prosecutor had argued sexual rejection. One of Andrews's colleagues had captured her on camcorder wholesomely proclaiming she'd never give it up for black meat. In certain boxcars composing the train wreck of public opinion, this was known to pass for virtue.

To Jones's immense disadvantage was the egregious ineptitude of his lawyer, an acne-faced kid just out of school whom the overburdened public defender had thrown to the wolves on the nothing-to-gain case. Given the circumstances under which the body had been found, several witnesses who claimed Jones had been stalking Andrews for weeks, and the unanimous testimony of two medical examiners that the stabber had been a forceful, right-handed male around five feet ten, Jones had been convicted by a jury after less than twenty minutes of deliberation.

The verdict had brought out the Leonard Jeffrieses and the Jesse Jacksons, who had proclaimed that, as a non-professional-athlete black male accused of killing a white woman, Jones wasn't being given a fair shake. The resultant political pressures had accelerated Jones's Writ for Ineffective Assistance of Counsel, which was granted.

Verdict overturned.

Meanwhile, some jackass in long-term record storage had misfiled the evidence and exhibits, which left the prosecutor with no forensic reports, no photos of the body to flash at the jury during the second trial, nothing more than the testimony of four white cops.

Verdict, not guilty.

The case files were discovered the following Monday, mistakenly filed under "Rhythm."

Jones slipped out of sight, lost somewhere in the faceless obscurity of L.A. slums, protected from the heat of further inquiry by the generous parasol of double jeopardy.

As Rayner finished reviewing the specifics of the case, Tim's eyes were drawn to the picture of Ginny, propped on the table before him. He glanced again at the other photos in sight—Ananberg's mother, Dumone's wife, and the Stork's mother, an imperious-looking, heavyset woman with an expression of disgruntled impatience common to pugs and Eastern European immigrants. This was their purgatory, Tim realized, to oversee deliberations about L.A.'s most vile crimes and criminals, to play silent chorus to a seedy drama. This was how Tim had chosen to honor his daughter.

". . . reasonable doubt," Mitchell was saying. "It's not no doubt. There's never *no doubt*."

But Ananberg held strong. "If someone were planning to frame him, it would be the perfect way. He's a known drug abuser with countless enemies. Get him when he's high as a kite, hack up a body in his living room, and voilà."

"Sure," Robert said. "Forensic stab patterns are a breeze to fake. Especially seventy-seven punctures."

Rayner's head snapped up from the court transcript. "Oh, come on. We all know facts can be tailored. The public defender failed to produce a single expert witness for the defense."

Robert's hands were both spread on the table, white from the pressure. "Maybe there wasn't one who could represent the defense's version of the facts in . . . in—"

"—good faith," Mitchell said.

"Please," Ananberg said. "Expert witnesses are like whores, but more expensive."

Rayner's head jerked a bit at the simile.

Tim watched Robert closely. Robert's fuse, for obvious reasons, was considerably shortened by murderers of women. Tim reflected on the firmness of his own conviction about Bowrick's guilt and realized he held the same defensive rage for killers of children. Anger guarding trauma, ever vigilant. And—for purposes of the Commission—ever polluting.

"The verdict was overturned only because the evidence was misfiled and could not be presented." The Stork flipped through the forensic report with one hand, and with his other he rubbed his thumb across the pads of his fingers, swift and ticlike. "It's fairly conclusive."

"This case was thrown out the first time around due to incompetent counsel," Ananberg said. "By definition that means no respectable defense was mounted. There could

have been considerations available that were never ex-
plored. Plus, the evidence is hardly damning—they found
no blood whatsoever on his person. Seventy-seven stab
wounds and no trace of blood on him? He was wacked-out
on angel dust—I doubt he had the clarity of mind to burn
his clothing and exfoliate with a loofa."

Mitchell spoke very slowly, as if monitoring himself.
"We have a body in his living room, a weapon bearing his
fingerprints, and traces of the victim's blood in his shower
drain."

"It is remarkably compelling physical evidence," Tim
said.

Ananberg regarded him, surprised, as if he were breaking some heretofore unspoken alliance.

"What the fuck do you want?" Robert said. "Live
footage of the murder? If that evidence hadn't been lost,
this guy would've already been fried." His voice was rising, his face starting to color. "He was caught dick deep *at
the crime scene*, which happened to be his house. You're
overthinking this one, Ananberg."

"He's a pretty street-smart guy. And it's such a stupid
crime scene. . . ." Ananberg shook her head. "The evidence
doesn't seem damning to me. It seems convenient."

They moved through the formal procedure swiftly, as it
was obvious there would not be a unanimous decision. The
vote went four to two; Rayner sided with Ananberg against
the others.

"For fuck's sake," Robert said. "You're letting the prick
off the hook because of a bunch of stupid liberal bullshit."

"This has nothing to do with politics," Tim said.

Robert threw up his hands, bouncing forward in his
chair so its arms knocked the table. The framed picture of
his sister fell facefirst to the marble with a clap; Rayner's

water slopped over the side of the glass. "The guy's a fuck-ing sleazebag."

"Which, last I checked, is not a capital offense." Anan-berg placed her hands palms down on the table, a vision of resolution. "I'm just not convinced he did it."

Robert ran a hand through his bristling red-blond hair, leaving a flared Mohawk path like a dog's raised hackles. He cocked back in his chair. His voice, low and muttering, held a startling element of malice. "If he didn't, a nig like that's guilty of something else."

Tim leaned forward, chair creaking, willing his voice not to betray the full measure of his rage. "Is that what you believe?"

Robert looked away, his jaw clenched.

"Of course not," Mitchell said.

"I wasn't talking to you. I was talking to your brother."

When Robert turned back, Tim noticed that his eyes were strikingly bloodshot, pink veins radiating out from his pupils, leaving wakes in the white-sea haze of his sclera. "I didn't mean it. It's just after this thing, with Debuffier . . . I mean, the guy fucking kept her in a *refrigerator*." He grabbed the fallen frame in front of him and smashed it down against the table once, twice, three times. His face dissolved, and he raised a hand to his eyes. Broken glass was spread across the table. His hand, cut from the glass, left a bloody smudge above one eyebrow. Mitchell reached over and kneaded the thick muscles of Robert's neck.

"Dumone is like a father to me," Robert said. His lips were trembling. Tim waited for him to break, but he re-mained stubbornly on the edge between composure and grief.

"You need some time off from this," Rayner said. "To get your perspective back."

"No, no. Back to work. I need work." When Robert looked up, his eyes were scared. "Don't you do that to me."

"You're a liability to our aims," Tim said. "You're sitting it out for a while."

Robert remained bent over the table, shoulders drawn forward and around so his trapezius muscles pulled high and hard around his neck. His head was raised, tilted up from his hunch like a pointing dog's, his eyes bright. "You've been trying to cut me and Mitch out from day one. You of *all* people should understand our needing to be involved. To do more. Don't tell us to sit back and let others handle it. You're giving us the same bullshit answers your dad threw back at you when you went to him for help."

Rayner jumped in angrily. "That's *enough*, Robert."

Off Tim's expression, Robert looked away uncomfortably, maybe even a touch ashamed. "Yeah, that's right, you forget. We know about when you went to him for help, and he turned you out. We were listening."

Tim felt his pulse beating at his temples. He sifted through the anger, searching out a sharper vexation. "I was told you'd been listening to me since the day of Ginny's funeral."

Mitchell strummed his short-cut nails on the table. "Dumone already apol—"

"I went to see my father three days before that." Tim faced the Stork, who was only now perking up to pay attention. "So how were you listening to me at my father's?"

"Yes, well, I'm afraid I was mistaken when I told you that before. I ended up doing it a few days earlier. Broke in when you were at work and your wife went to the grocery store."

Tim studied him closely, then Robert. He decided to believe them for the time being. "Listen," he said, "we already have a guilty vote in on Bowrick. I'm handling it alone, as I pointed out earlier. Robert, you take some time off—and I mean *off*—and catch your breath. And be advised, when you come back, I'm not tolerating another word of your racist bullshit. Is that clear? *Is* it?" He waited for Robert to nod, a barely discernible tilt of his head.

"Then we'll move to Kindell," Rayner said. "And I've already embarked on the tedious process of selecting a second set of cases for our next phase."

"One step at a time. Right now I need you all to leave."

Rayner's mustache twitched in a half smile. "It's my house."

"I need to sit alone with Bowrick's file. Would you rather I ran copies and took them home?" Tim stared from face to face until the others rose and shuffled out of the room.

Ananberg lingered behind. She shut the door and faced Tim, sliding her arms so they were folded across her chest. "This is coming unglued."

Tim nodded. "I'm going to slow things down, see what I can get on Bowrick, see how Dumone fares. I can handle this operation largely on my own. If I need to use Mitchell, I'll stick him on surveillance and keep him well clear of any situation that might go hot."

"Robert and Mitchell won't settle for being your spy and errand boys for long. They're obsessed. They're all about black-and-white logic, no mitigating circumstances."

"We need to keep phasing them out operationally so they're permanently on the sidelines before we embark on the next phase of cases."

"And if things don't move the way we want them to?"

"We invoke the kill clause and dissolve the Commission."

"Can you make this work without Dumone?"

Tim looked up at her. "I don't know. That's why I'm

handling Bowrick myself. I can make sure it's done right, then move on to Kindell."

"You must be eager to get to Kindell."

"Like you wouldn't believe."

Ananberg removed a thrice-folded document from her purse and slid it down the length of the table. It stopped when it hit Tim's knuckles.

The public defender's notes.

"Rayner had me run a copy of this at the office. I accidentally made two. Put it in your pocket, do *not* look at it until you get home, and don't ask me for anything else."

Tim resisted the overwhelming urge to flip through the pages. As much as it pained him, he wedged the public defender's notes into his back pocket. When he looked up, Ananberg was gone.

The sudden silence rankled him, and he tried to soothe his unease. He couldn't risk Rayner's walking in here and finding him examining the purloined documents, and he couldn't leave abruptly after saying he was going to stay to study Bowrick's file. He had to play it cool—he owed Ananberg that much.

He dimmed the lights overhead, then propped Bowrick's photo up against Ginny's frame. He stared at Bowrick's discontented face for a long time before flipping open the binder.

**28** THE NOTES FROM KINDELL'S CASE BURNING A HOLE IN HIS jeans, Tim left without finding Rayner to announce his departure. As he pulled out of the driveway, the house loomed behind him, dark and falsely antiquated. It wasn't until the wrought-iron gate swung closed behind his car that he realized he'd imbued the building itself with an ineffable quality of emotion, something like sadness and menace mixed together.

He drove a few blocks, then parked and flipped through the public defender's notes on Kindell. His excitement quickly gave way to disappointment. A summation of the lawyer's pretrial talks with Kindell, the typed notes were poorly organized and incomplete.

Some of them were chilling.

*The victim was the client's "type."*

Client claims to have taken an hour and a half with the body after death.

Tim's stomach lurched, and he had to roll down the window and breathe in the crisp air before mustering the courage to continue.

A single sentence on the fifth page slapped him into shock. In an attempt to jar himself back to lucidity, he found himself reading it over and over, trying to attach meaning to the words so they'd make sense again.

*Client claims he carried out all aspects of the crime alone.*

And then the sentence beneath: *Had spoken to no one regarding Virginia Rackley or the crime until the handling unit arrived at his residence.*

Through an all-enveloping numbness, he finished scanning the report, turning up no new information.

Kindell would have had no reason to deceive his public defender, nor his public defender to lie in his confidential record-keeping. Unless the case binder revealed additional facts—perhaps buried in the public defender's investigator reports—then Tim had been off the mark all along. Gutierez, Harrison, Delaney, his father—they'd been right.

Tim's conviction about an accomplice had grown into an addiction that had shielded him from the full brunt of

Ginny's death. If Kindell had in fact been Ginny's only murderer, then Tim's options were concrete, as finite as the sagging walls of Kindell's shack. There was little left for him to do but confront Kindell however he decided and face the reality of his child's death.

Dray had gone to sleep—the answering machine picked up on a half ring—and he left her the news, coding it in case Mac happened to be around.

Held in the trance of a sudden exhaustion, he drove home and fell into a blissful, dreamless block of sleep. He lay on the mattress for a few minutes upon awakening, watching the motes swirl and drift in the slant of morning light from the window, his mind returning obsessively to the last black binder awaiting him in Rayner's safe.

If it didn't miraculously yield compelling evidence for an accomplice, he realized with some satisfaction, then he'd deal with Kindell soon enough.

He just had to get to Bowrick first.

He showered, dressed, and headed out for a cup of coffee. He sat in a corner booth at a dive of a breakfast joint one block down, flipping through the *L.A. Times*. The Debuffier execution had grabbed the headline again, but the story contained little about the actual investigation. Man on the Street reared his ugly head again, claiming, "You don't need the law to tell you right from wrong. The law told that voodoo bastard he was in the right, but he wasn't. Now he's dead, and the law says that's wrong. I say it's justice." Tim noted with some alarm how clearly Man on the Street was articulating his own supposed position.

Another article announced that a moral-watchdog group was protesting a vigilante game Taketa FunSystems had put into development called Death Knoll. The player had a choice of automatic weapons with which to outfit his video-screen counterpart before setting him out on the streets. It featured tomato-burst head shots and limb-severing explosions. A rapist got you five points, a murderer ten.

A back-page story about two immigrants shot in robberies took the edge off some of Tim's hypocritical indignation.

He returned to his apartment and sat in his single chair, feet on the windowsill, phone in his lap. For reference he'd smuggled out three pages of notes he'd taken from Bowrick's file. For inspiration he logged on to the Internet and found the *L.A. Times* photograph of the coach clutching his dead daughter outside Warren High School. For a long time he looked at the man's face, twisted with anguish and a sort of shocked disbelief. Tim was struck, now, with the heightened empathy that fear fulfilled provides.

And he was struck also with the alarming needlessness of it all.

He rubbed his hands, studied his three pages of notes, and formulated a strategy. Bowrick had skillfully arranged his own relocation to duck threats and possible attempts on his life; he was going to be hidden smart and well. Normally Tim's tracking resources were virtually unlimited. Each government agency, from the Treasury Department, to Immigration, to Customs, controlled an acronymous computer database or eight—EPIC, TECS, NADDIS, MIRAC, OASIS, NCIC—but they were all inaccessible now. To obtain information about Bowrick, Tim couldn't call his rabbis at other agencies, his CIs, or his contacts inside companies. He couldn't talk to anyone in person, nose around any locations, or leverage any snitches. He'd have to street-smart his way through, like a criminal, which he supposed he was.

He started with Bowrick's last-known, reached the apartment manager, and pretended to be a bill collector. A long shot, but Tim knew to start with the ground-ballers. No forwarding information. But he did get the date Bowrick moved out: January 15.

Posing as a postal inspector investigating mail fraud, he called the gas, power, water, and cable companies and presented a gruff voice and a false badge number. He was amazed—as always—at how easy it was to elicit confidential information. Unfortunately, all Bowrick's listings were for addresses prior to January 15; he had been smart and registered everything under his new name, whatever that was. Telephone was usually the most current listing, but the address Pac Bell had was for his last-known, and the number had long been disconnected.

Giving Ted Maybeck's name and badge number—he figured Ted owed him one for throwing the infamous high five—Tim tried to talk his way through the DMV bureaucracy but got nowhere. DMV staff was either incompetent or tough; those displaying the latter trait were also well schooled on privacy policies. According to the case binder, Bowrick had no car of his own—his mother used to drop him off at school, which, Tim recalled, had made him the object of derision among other seniors. In fact, the majority of the student character testimonies had been scathing—all except for that of one girl, an Erika Heinrich, who'd pointed out the vicious bullying that Bowrick and the now-deceased gunmen had received at the hands of the basketball team.

Dead ends all around. Tim had fallen into the pursuit as if he were working up a warrant, and the sudden halt brought him quickly to frustration. He slid open the window and leaned into the slight breeze. He hadn't realized how stifling the room had grown with the rising sun and his own body heat. He closed his eyes and thought about the police report, waiting for a piece of information to rise out of place and trip his thoughts. None did.

Tim thought of the slump of Bowrick's shoulders, his caged-rat unappeal. He tried to imagine having a child capable of such destruction. Could even a parent love someone so cruel and odious? Could anyone?

Tim sensed a shift in instinct, a puzzle piece sliding and dropping into place. The jagged half-coin pendant that he'd seen in Bowrick's booking photo—a lover's necklace. Each party wore one piece of the same coin. Erika Heinrich's character testimony suddenly stood out all the more. The one sympathetic account. The girlfriend.

Tim logged on and entered *Erika Heinrich* into Yahoo People Search and got two hits—a seventeen-year-old in Los Angeles and a seventy-two-year-old in Fredericksburg, Texas. The grandmother? One of Tim's former saw gunners in the Rangers was from Fredericksburg, so Tim knew it was a predominantly German community—maybe that explained the *k* in the first name.

He located the more eligible Erika's phone number on the screen and dialed. When a woman answered, he tried his best salesman voice, and it came out surprisingly well. "Is this Erika Heinrich?"

A voice edged with irritation. "This is her mother, Kirsten. Why, what'd she do now?"

"I'm sorry, we must have the names crossed in our database. I'm calling from Contact Telecommunications to let you know you're eligible for—"

"Not interested."

"Well, if you have family out of state, our rates are *extremely* competitive. Two cents a minute state-to-state, and just ten cents a minute to Europe."

A weighted pause, broken only by mouth breathing. "Two cents a minute long-distance? What's the catch?"

"No catch. Can I ask who you're with now?"

"MCI."

"And for local?"

"Verizon."

"Well, we beat both MCI and Verizon by nearly *four hundred percent*. There's simply a once-a-month twenty-dollar charge for—"

"Twenty-dollar charge? See, I knew you guys were all full of shit." She hung up.

Tim had no phone book in his apartment, Joshua was out, and the corner telephone booth's had been ripped from its cord. Two blocks down he located another booth, this one with the book intact. He flipped through and found the nearest Kinko's, then picked another a bit farther away from his apartment. He called and got their number for incoming faxes, a service they provided for people without fax machines willing to abide the buck-a-page fee.

Back upstairs he called MCI and got a male customer-service rep. He hung up and called back twice before he got a woman. He softened his voice, trying his best approximation of pitiful. "Yes, hello. I'm hoping you can help me with a . . . with a somewhat embarrassing personal problem. I've just . . . um, been separated from my wife, our divorce papers went through last week, and, uh . . ."

"I'm sorry, sir. How exactly can *I* help you?"

"Well, I'm still responsible for paying my wife's . . ." He let out a sad little laugh. "My ex-wife's bills. Her lawyer just sent along her telephone bill, and it seemed . . . well, it seemed unreasonably high. I don't mean to imply my wife is dishonest—she's not—but I'm worried her lawyer is monkeying around a bit with the numbers. You know how lawyers can be."

"I was divorced once myself. You don't have to tell me."

"It is . . . it is hard, isn't it?"

"Well, sir, it'll get easier."

"That's what people keep telling me. Anyway, I was wondering if you could fax me the telephone bill for review, just so I can make sure these numbers are accurate. If they are, of course, I'll happily reimburse my wife, it's just that—"

"If some lawyer's giving you the markup, you want to know."

"Precisely. My wife's name is Kirsten Heinrich, and she's at 310-656-8464."

The sound of fingers flying across a computer keyboard. "Well, as much as I'd like to help you, I'm not permitted to turn over her records to unauthorized . . ." More typing. "Sir, this account is listed under *Stefan* Heinrich."

"Yes, of course. That's me."

"Well, technically it's still your account, so until she changes the name, I *am* authorized to grant you access to billing information. Which fax number would you like me to send your last statement to?"

"It's actually my local Kinko's—I lost my fax machine along with my new Saturn—and the number is 310-629-1477. If you could send the last several bills, that would be most helpful."

With Verizon, Tim claimed to be Stefan Heinrich from the outset and asked for the last three months of bills to be faxed over so he could review what he believed were some false charges.

He ate lunch alone at Fatburger, giving the faxes an hour to trickle through the various bureaucratic chains of command, then drove over to Kinko's and picked up the stack. Back at his apartment, he hunched over the pages with a yellow highlighter, looking for triggers, his tongue poking his cheek out in a point.

Bowrick's move had occurred less than two months ago, and Tim prayed he and Erika had, in fact, been a couple and that they were still in touch. He'd seen men forsake their cars with their telltale Vehicle Identification Numbers, their pets with registered pedigrees, even their own children to go into hiding, but they could always be counted on to contact their girlfriends. Drawn back to the bang, like a dog to his vomit. With a loner like Bowrick, the chances were even better.

The first two bills gave Tim nothing, and he felt a dread settle over him in anticipation of having to call every number in the entire stack, but then he noticed a recurring regional number matched with a recurring time. Roughly 11:30 P.M. every Monday, Wednesday, and Friday. He looked closer and saw that there were also calls made to the same number, less regularly, around 7:30 A.M.

Clever, clever Bowrick.

Bowrick knew that if someone was determined to find him—a reasonable possibility, given that he was partially responsible for one of the most publicized mass killings in Los Angeles history—that his pursuer could trace calls originating from people closest to him. So instead of having calls ring through to his apartment, he'd set contact times where he could be reached out-of-pocket.

Tim called the number and let it ring and ring, since he guessed it was a pay phone. After the seventeenth ring, a man picked up. He spoke with a strong Indian accent. "Stop calling, please. This is a pay phone. You're driving my customers away."

"I'm sorry, sir, but my girlfriend was supposed to pick up. I'm sort of worried she's not there, so I want to cruise over and look for her. Would you mind telling me where you're located?"

"You will buy something and not just poke around?"

"Yes, of course."

"Corner of Lincoln and Palms."

Tim knew already, but had to ask to clear the Politically

Correct censor he was surprised to find lurking in his head. "And your store is a . . . ?"

"7-Eleven."

He hung up, checked his watch: 8:11 P.M. He was surprised to find he'd been going for nearly thirteen hours. The time had passed in a blur, unbraked by thoughts of wife and daughter, ethics and accountability. Just satisfying work, a blend of instinct and focus.

He had a little over three hours until Bowrick's possible scheduled Monday-night phone call but decided to drive over to stake out the territory. The 7-Eleven sat on a busy cross street, so it was easy for Tim to remain inconspicuous. He parked on the far side of Lincoln at a meter, where he had a clear angle to the store entrance. The meters weren't in operation after six o'clock, so he didn't have to worry about traffic officers.

He entered the 7-Eleven and bought a Big Gulp of Mountain Dew and a tin of Skoal. Caffeine and nicotine—two bad habits forged on stakeouts. Debuffier peered out from a grainy photo on a tabloid front page by the register, beside another shot of his oversize body bag. The headline shrieked ANGEL OF GOD TAKING OUT THE TRASH. The pay phone was in the back, between a single bank of outdated video games. A pock-faced kid was getting jiggy on the Centipede ball.

Tim settled back into his car and waited, keeping an eye on the twin glass doors that strobed in and out of view between passing trucks and cars. So his concentration wouldn't be compromised, he kept the Nextel off; the Nokia he'd left at home. He worked his way through half his dip, spitting into an empty Coke can. A hypnotic state of dulled focus, similar to that elicited by distance running and vacation photos, overtook him. His ass grew numb.

His reflection in the rearview showed that the black eye
Dray had given him two weeks ago was in no rush to va-
cate his face, though it had considerately faded to a wide
bluish smudge.

Eleven-thirty came and went with no sign of Bowrick.
Tim waited until 1:15 A.M., just to be stubborn. He finally
pulled out from his spot, his lower back throbbing, his
gums sore from Skoal, vowing to wear a weight belt and
chew sunflower seeds the next day.

At home he set his alarm clock for 5:30 so he could get
back across town in case Bowrick had slid his call time to
Tuesday morning. He slept, woke, and returned to his post,
stopping only to buy a Polaroid camera and a weight belt,
which he notched around his waist for added back support.
The meters went live at 7:00 A.M., and within fifteen minutes he had to loop around the block to avoid being cited
by a traffic officer.

He sat spitting sunflower-seed shells into yesterday's
Big Gulp cup until 10:15 A.M. He had Bowrick's occasional 7:30 A.M. call figured as a prework check-in with the
girlfriend, so it was likely Bowrick would be tied up on a
job for the next few hours. Tim left, ate a quick sandwich,
and sat stakeout from 11:30 to 2:30, in case Bowrick decided to make a lunchtime stop. Tim returned again at 4:30
and sat a long postworkday shift, through the 11:30 P.M.
target time until 1:00 in the morning.

Exhausted and dejected, he headed for home. Gripped
by insomnia, he sat up, studying the marked phone statements. Erika Heinrich's most recent bill listed calls only
through the first of the month—what if it was outdated?
The call pattern could have shifted in the past three weeks.
Tomorrow was Wednesday—one of Bowrick's regular call
days, so Tim vowed to give it another twenty-four hours.

When Tim finally turned on his Nokia, he had only two

messages from the past two days. The first was a couple minutes of monotone rambling from Dray, expressing her disappointment that the public defender's notes hadn't turned up any new leads. All day, he was alarmed to realize, he'd tucked his thoughts of Ginny beneath some defense mechanism in his mind, hidden from sight. The emotional sting returned even harsher, like a fresh wound slapped, shattering the respite he'd found in its hiatus.

In the next message, Dray let him know that Marshal Tannino had called again—apparently for the second time this week—concerned about Tim and wanting to check in on him. Ananberg had called the Nextel last night around 3:00 A.M. Her message simply said, "Tim. Jenna."

He was pleased that the rest of the Commission hadn't bothered him, as he'd requested. Having Robert and Mitchell out of the way for the time being was a relief. He replayed Dray's first message twice, looking for places where her voice cracked around the edges, indicating want or longing.

He sat at his small desk, studying his wallet-worn photo of Ginny, feeling his thoughts percolate, blur, disregard their boundaries. Later he tried to sleep but failed. He was on his belly, watching the alarm clock when it clicked to 5:30 and emitted its galling buzz.

He sat the stakeout straight through the day, leaving only to piss twice and grab a burrito from a stand up the street. His head, displeased at its lack of stimuli, swam in hangover haze. The air felt more exhaust than oxygen, and the sea breathed no hint that it was hitting sand ten blocks away.

At the stoplight ahead, a vendor of dubious naturalization was selling tiny U.S. flags for ten bucks a pop. America—land of ironic opportunity.

Afternoon eased into dusk, dusk to night. When 11:15

rolled around, Tim loosened his weight belt one notch, letting the cramping tighten his lower back and push him to alertness. Twenty minutes later he was still sitting upright, eyes trained on the store entrance. At 11:45 he started cursing. Midnight came, and he turned over the engine and threw the car into gear.

He was just pulling out when Bowrick rounded the corner.

# 29

**BOWRICK SPENT A GOOD FORTY MINUTES ON THE** 7-Eleven phone before emerging, spitting once on the sidewalk and walking back up Palms. Tim had pulled the car over on Palms in anticipation of Bowrick's heading back in the direction from which he'd arrived. He'd assumed Bowrick would show up on foot due to his history without a car; his new residence couldn't be far away.

Bowrick walked with a distinctive slouch, shoulders humped, hips tucked slightly like a spanked dog's, favoring his right leg. His black-and-white flannel hung open, fringing his thighs like a skirt. Tim waited for him to turn the corner onto Penmar before following on foot. Two blocks down, Bowrick lifted the latch on a waist-high fence and slipped into a ragged front yard with an oval of dirt that used to be a lawn. The house itself, a prefab with tract-home simplicity, sat slightly crooked on the lot, its Ty-D-Bol turquoise clapboards water-warped and misaligned. By the time Tim strolled past, Bowrick had disappeared through the front door.

Tim retrieved his car, parking a few houses up from

Bowrick's, and sat pretending to study a map. After about five minutes a tricked-out Escalade pulled up and honked despite the late hour. Bowrick emerged holding a small duffel bag and hopped into the car. As it passed Tim, he caught a glimpse of the driver—a Hispanic kid in a wife-beater tank top with orange fire tattoos on his shoulders and neck.

Probably off to do a late-night drop.

Tim waited until the sound of the engine faded, then grabbed the camera from his backseat and approached the house. He searched the front yard for dog shit and, not noticing any, hopped the fence. Six strides, then he flattened himself against the side wall and pulled on latex gloves. The neighboring houses were a good thirty feet away, not because the yards were ample but because Bowrick's house was so small it couldn't fill even its modest plot. Tim edged over and peered through the window. The house, basically a single large room, recalled Tim's apartment in its bare functionality. A desk, a flimsy bureau, twin bed, sheets thrown back. Tim made his way to the rear and peeked through the bathroom window to ensure that the house was empty. The back door housed a mean Schlage and two dead bolts, so Tim returned to the bathroom window, popped the screen, and wormed his way through, coming down with his hands on the fortunately closed toilet seat.

No toothbrush in the toothbrush holder. No toothpaste.

Tim slipped into the main room. Two folded shirts and a pair of socks waited on the bed, as if Bowrick had set them there to be packed, then decided against them.

Bowrick was clearly gone for an overnight, probably longer.

Tim pulled the chair out from the desk, placed it in the middle of the room, and stood on it. It took eight Polaroid shots to provide panoramic documentation of the interior. Tim set the hazy white photos on the bed to resolve, crossed to the desk, and began rifling through the drawers. Bills and a checkbook belonging to David Smith. Five twenties hidden under a paper tray in the top drawer said Bowrick wasn't gone for good.

A tacky shrine had been set up on an overturned crate in the corner. Fake gold cross, a miniature oil painting of Jesus wearing the crown of thorns, a few burned-down candles. Its presence in Bowrick's house served only to reinforce Tim's distrust of men who turned their moral compass over to a God who tolerated Joe Mengele and Serb death squads. He cut short his condemnatory thoughts, recognizing he'd come to the case with prejudice. He refocused on taking in information before filtering it.

Tim searched the closets, drawers, mattress, cupboards beneath the sink. Two hard hats—one cracked—and Carhartt overalls were mounded on the closet floor. The carpet curled up from the wall seams, and he pulled it back farther to see if it hid a gun safe embedded in the floor. No weapons in the house. Largest blade was a steak knife on the brief run of counter tile that passed for a kitchen. Two doors, two windows—great kill zone.

He meticulously replaced everything to its original position. He smoothed his footprints out of the carpet, left the second desk drawer halfway open as it had been, adjusted the bottom right corner of the comforter so it drooped to touch the ground just so.

The Polaroids had dried on the bed, and he checked the room against them. He'd replaced the sole Bic pen too close to the edge of the desk. The top sheet needed to be folded over just under the pillows. A *Car and Driver* magazine on the bureau required a quarter rotation to the right.

He retouched and reskewed until everything in the room perfectly matched the photographs again.

Then he slid out the bathroom window, replaced the screen, and eased back out onto the sidewalk. He contemplated calling the Stork, but the man's distinctive looks made for dangerous stakeout material. He called Mitchell from the car, but Mitchell kept his cell phone turned off even when unnecessary, as was the habit of any smart EOD bomb tech. He reached Robert with his next call and had him hand the phone off to his brother, which he did angrily.

"I've just left Bowrick's place."

"Holy shit, you found him alrea—"

"Listen to me. He lives at 2116 Penmar, but I believe he headed out for a few nights. I've been on it for the past three days, and I need to sleep. I want you to head down here and keep an eye on the house—very low-profile. Just you. Alone. Do not get spotted. And don't bring weapons. Do you understand me? No pistol, no nothing. Just sit on the house and alert me if he returns. I'll be back at nine hundred tomorrow to take over for you. Can you do that?"

"Of course."

"I'll keep the Nextel on."

Tim felt slightly euphoric, as he always did on the trail. To celebrate he debated allowing himself the indulgence of returning Dray's call, the thought calling forth a crisp picture of his daughter's room waiting still furnished across the hall. With the image came the bristling of imbedded thorns, a sudden crashing return from the salve of numbness. Now that he was off task, his thoughts became his enemies again; it was as if, finding nothing else on which to teethe, they turned cannibalistic. His mind nosed around his vulnerabilities, moving deliberately from Ginny to Dray to Robert to all other things that had recently spun from his grasp. When he emerged from his thoughts, he was a few blocks from his building. He anticipated stepping into the apartment's empty embrace and how different it would feel from his house, which would smell of wood and lingering barbecue and ketchup-stained paper plates in the trash can. Thoughts of the myriad compelling security and safety concerns managed to put a pretty good damper on his yearning for a spontaneous visit.

He took a pull off the bottle of water left over from lunch, but it didn't help dissolve the sourness at the back of his throat. It remained, firm-rooted and dry—most likely the aftertaste of death and murder, both of which he'd been steeped in for the past month. Maybe he needed something stronger to wash it away.

A neon martini glass beckoned from a dark-tinted window, and he jerked the Beemer left into a parking lot and coasted up to the white valet stand.

The thrumming bass from the car pulling out and the all-black attire of the couple whisking in indicated that Tim had accidentally arrived at a club rather than a bar. He disliked hip in most of its variations, but it was too late now, and besides, a drink was a drink.

As he got out of his car, a kid with slicked-back hair presented a ripped stub from an effluvium of bad cologne, then slid behind the wheel and screeched around the corner. Tim looked at the five blank spaces in front of the club and turned a befuddled glance at the remaining valet. "Is there some reason you can't leave the car right here?"

The valet coughed out a snicker. "Uh, *yeah*. It's a '97."

A bouncer manned a maroon rope in front of the door. He was fit, half white, half Asian, and handsome as fuck. Tim disliked him instantly, blindly.

Tim approached and flicked his hand at the dark door, from which issued cigarette smoke and a tune heavy on beat and metallics. The bouncer kept his head tilted back as if in a constant state of boredom or appraisal. "Get in line please, pal."

Tim looked around at the empty entrance. "What line?"

"Over there." The bouncer pointed to a red roll-up carpet—some night promoter's brainchild—that stretched to the right of the rope. Tim exhaled hard and stepped over onto the carpet. He made for the rope, but the bouncer didn't move.

"You want me to wait here?"

"Yes."

"Even though there's no one in line?"

"Yes."

"Is this *Candid Camera* or something?"

"Man, you are *clueless.*" Something vibrated on the bouncer's waist, and he took a long look at a row of colorful, belt-adhered pagers. He squeezed the banana yellow one and glanced at the backlit screen. "How'd you get your black eye?"

"Freak badminton accident."

The guy's head rolled to its usual back-tilted perch on his wide neck. "You gonna start trouble at my club?"

"If you keep me out here, I might."

The guy's laugh smelled like gum. "I like your style, pal." He unclipped the rope and stepped aside, but not far enough that Tim didn't have to lean to get past him.

Tim entered and spotted a stool at the bar. As he headed over, a guy in clay-colored jeans with endless pockets eyed him derisively. "Nice shirt, pops."

Behind the bar a translucent rise of shelves glowed phosphorescent blue. Tim ordered a twelve-dollar vodka on the rocks from an attractive redheaded bartender wearing a rubber vest with a zipper teased down to reveal cleavage.

A couple of girls were grooving up on a light box out on

the dance floor. The crowd swelled and ebbed around them, wafting Tim's way the smell of designer cologne and clean sweat. A couple lay sideways in a booth, licking each other's faces, e-ravenous for sensation. The surge of sex and exuberance charged the air, approaching-storm strong, and in the middle sat Tim, immobile and square, watching the proceedings like a chaperon at a mixer. He found his glass empty and gestured to the bartender for a fresh one.

A girl beside him leaned curve-backed, elbows propped on the bar, facing the noise. He accidentally caught her eye and nodded. She smiled and walked off. Two guys in rumpled shirts sidled up in her place, their faces ruddy and moist from the dance floor, and ordered shots of tequila.

". . . my old boss Harry, you could smell the burnout on him. He was your classic dump truck, barely followed up any leads for his clients. When I started in the public defender's office, he had a guy in custody for a murder two, said his alibi was this bartender he was hitting on all night, a hot girl with red hair somewhere off Traction. Didn't know where. Harry stopped by a few places, found shit, they convicted his client the next week. Fifteen to life. A few months later we come in here—God knows why, Harry's brother-in-law invested in the joint or something—and guess what?"

The guy pointed behind the bar at the redhead in the zippered vest. "There she is. And she remembers the client. Only problem is, our boy got shanked in the yard at Corcoran two days before." He exhaled hard. "There's only justice for the rich. If you have a house to put up for ten percent of bail, can get your ass out of custody and working on your own case, your alibi, you're all set. If you're broke and you can't remember, if your PD can't find the hot redhead bartender somewhere off Traction . . . well, then." He threw back another shot. "I come in here now, when I'm close to burnout. It reinvigorates me, inspires me to cover every damn angle." The bartender served another round of shots, and he slid a once-folded twenty toward her. "She's my muse."

His friend said, "It's a stupid fucking job we do."

This declaration was followed by a clink of glasses, thrown-back shots, sour-faced head shakes. The talker caught Tim watching and leaned over to offer a sweaty hand.

"Name's Richard. Why don't you join us for a shot?" His slur was just noticeable above the pumping music.

"No thanks."

"No offense, but I don't see any better options around for you." Richard turned to his friend. "Oh, well, Nick, guess our friend here doesn't want to join us. Guess he's busy being his own man."

"I'm not big on public defenders." Alcohol had loosened Tim's tongue—he remembered anew why he rarely drank.

"Don't see why not. We get paid shit, we burn out young, and we represent mostly reprehensible pricks. That's a pretty appealing package, no?"

"Yeah, well, I've been on the other end of the equation you're bitching about. Seen people walk free who shouldn't have."

"Lemme guess. You're a cop. Shoot first and ask questions later." Richard snapped off a drunken salute. "Well, Officer, I'll tell you, for however many cases you've seen go down wrong, Nick and I here have got you beat. I got a kid today—"

"I'm not interested."

"I got a kid today—"

"Take your hand off me, please."

Richard stepped back while Nick got busy securing their next round. "When this kid was sixteen, he broke into his cousin's house to steal a VCR." He held up a finger. "One strike. Goes to a high school football game, talks some shit after, tells a teacher's kid he's gonna beat the crap out of him if he catches him talking to his girlfriend again. Strike two. Threat of immediate assault with intent to commit GBI. That's grievous bodily injury—"

"I know what GBI is."

"Now, the third strike, the *third* strike, my friend, can be *any* felony. This kid goes into Longs Drugs and steals a toilet-paper holder—a goddamn toilet-paper holder. That's 666, petty theft with a prior. It's a wobbler, but they file it as a felony. Guess what? Strike three. Twenty-five to life. No negotiation, no judicial discretion, nothing. It's fascism."

"His dad used to beat him. He didn't *really* mean to shoot up his school."

Richard sighed. "Not so simple. Not so specious. But you do have to look at the *individual*. Then the angles and distances between him and his surroundings become measurable. What those angles compose is what constitutes perspective. And perspective is *exactly* what you need to pass judgment on an individual's actions." Though his words were running together drunkenly, Richard was still articulate as hell. A practiced drinker.

"How about passing judgment on an *individual?*"

"Leave that to God. Or Allah, or karma, or the Great Pumpkin. At the end of the day, it doesn't matter if someone is *evil*. It matters what they've done and how we deal with it."

"But we have to carry out our judgment on individuals."

"Of course. So what determines the strictness of punishment? Irredeemability? Lack of contrition? Unfitness to participate in society? No one so much as examined these factors for my client today. This kid is screwed. He's gonna have to punk for some gangbanger for the rest of his life

over a thirty-seven-cent fucking toilet-paper holder."
Richard's voice wavered, either from rage or grief, and his
face contorted once, sharply, presaging a sob that never
came. Instead he grinned. "That's the reason for our little
party tonight, my friend." He raised a shot glass. "Cele-
brating the system."

His buddy put a hand on his shoulder and steered him
down onto the barstool.

"It goes both ways," Tim said.

Richard looked up, his eyes red-rimmed and drooping.
"Yeah, yeah, it does."

"I've seen guys walk through loopholes I'd never even
dreamed of. Chain of custody. Speedy trial motions.
Search and seizure. It's not justice. It's bullshit."

"It *is* bullshit. But why can't we have good procedure
and justice? So the court spanks the cop for"—his hands
fluttered, seeking a phrase—"illegal search and seizure or
whatever, and *next time around* the cop does his job right,
with respect for civil liberties. The trial goes clean. Guy
gets convicted, receives a fair sentence. Then it's right all
the way around—we have our cake and eat it, too."

Nick slumped forward, his forehead thumping against
the bar. Tim thought it had to be a joke, but Nick remained
there. Richard didn't notice. He leaned in, his breath carrying a sickening combination of breath mints and tequila.
"Lemme let you in on a little secret. PDs don't like their
clients, generally. We don't want to see them go free. We
*want* them to get convicted." He held up a wobbly finger.
"However. More important than that, we want tough guy
cops like you and hard-on DAs to respect the Constitution,
the Penal Code, the Bill of Rights. And everyone chips
away at them, these rights, slowly over time. Detectives,
prosecutors, even judges. But not us. We're fucking
zealots. Zealots for the Constitution."

"Jews for Jesus," Nick muttered from his facedown slump on the bar.

"And we protect . . . we protect that thing, that stupid, distant, abstract fucking piece of parchment, despite the scum we represent, despite the crimes they may have committed or may commit after we get them off because some dumb-ass cop doesn't fulfill the oral announcement of intent to search after the knock and notice and puts us in the fuckdamned position of having to point it out and let some mouth-breathing reprobate walk out the fucking door, in all likelihood to do whatever he's done again."

Richard tried to stand but fell back onto the stool. Nick was making raspberry noises against the bar.

"We fight fascism in the petty details." Richard pivoted to face the bar, letting his hands slide up, covering his face. "And it's awful. And we lose sight of the prize, the aim, sometimes, because we just wallow in this . . . in this . . ." A jerking inhalation led to a sob, but when he lowered his hands, he was smiling again. "We need a shot. Another shot."

"Trying to break the Breathalyzer record and win a Kewpie doll?"

"What, are you gonna arrest me, Officer? Drunk and disenfranchised?"

"If I do, I'll be sure to Mirandize you."

"Funny, that's funny." Richard laughed hard. "You're okay. I like you. You don't talk much, but you're okay. I mean, for a cop." He leaned heavily on the bar, his shirtsleeve soaking up spilled alcohol. "Lemme let you in on a little secret. I'm leaving my office. Going across the street to federal—believe it or not, federal sentencing is even more draconian. I'm gonna go throw myself against that wall for a change."

"Why do you do it?" Tim asked. "If you hate it so much?"

Nick raised his head, and his face looked startlingly sober. "Because we're worried no one else will."

Richard drummed the bar with his forefingers. "And it makes us pretty unpopular. Didn't used to be that way, not with Darrow and Rogers. The greats. Now a PD's just a knee-jerk apologist. A pushover. A softie. Dukakis. We're Dukakises. Dukaki."

"And Mondale," Nick said. "We're Mondale, too."

"And guys like me feel like guys like you are running the show these days," Tim said.

"Are you kidding me?" Richard spun around on the barstool, twirling a full rotation before stopping himself. His head jerked back with a hiccup. He looked distinctly nauseous. "Have you been watching the news? This vigilante business—it's meeting with general societal approval."

"The people who have been executed are hardly—"

Richard bellowed out a bad imitation of a game-show buzzer, tilting from the stool onto his feet. "Wrong answer."

"Right. Just have faith in the system. The system you just described to me from your angle and I described to you from mine. Why should we hold on to that faith? Why shouldn't someone try something better? Take matters into their own hands?"

Richard clutched Tim's arm, and for the first time his voice was soft and cracked, not giddy or deadened with tired irony. "Because it represents such *hopelessness*."

He leaned over and vomited on his shoes.

A girl two stools over looked down at her splattered capris and screamed. The smell rose from the puddle, rank and heated. Richard grinned, his chin stained with puke, and raised his arms, Rocky style.

The bartender was cursing a blue streak, and a gym-enhanced security bozo was closing fast, barking into a radio. The bouncer from outside plowed through the crowd and grabbed Richard.

"All right, asshole, I told you before, you get hammered in my club again, you're fucking finished." He threw a full nelson on Richard, bending his head forward and making his arms stick up like a scarecrow's. The other guy seized Nick's shoulder and jerked him back off the bar.

"Take it easy," Tim said. The bouncer slammed Richard against the bar. Tim's hand shot out and grabbed the bouncer's thick neck, thumb digging into his sternal notch. The bouncer gagged out a sound and froze. "It wasn't a suggestion," Tim said.

He waited for the bouncer to release Richard. The other guy let go of Nick and stepped wide, eyes on Tim, looking for an angle. Several people were watching, but for the most part loud music covered the sound of the commotion. The dance floor remained a swirl of oblivious motion.

Tim removed his hands, holding them up in a calming gesture. The bouncer took a quick step back, coughing.

Tim said, "I don't much like to fight, and I'm sure you could kick my ass anyway, so what do you say we just do this the easy way. These guys are going to pay their tab—" he nodded at Nick, who fumbled a few bills out of his pocket and onto the counter, "I'll walk my acquaintance out of here, and you'll never hear from us again. Sound good?"

The bouncer glowered at him.

"Okay." Tim shouldered Richard and half dragged him to the door, Nick scurrying close behind. They stepped outside, and the cool air hit them like a chest-high wave.

"That asshole," Richard slurred, rubbing his elbow. "Why didn't you badge him?" He fumbled in his pocket for his valet ticket, but Tim dragged him to the curb and hailed a passing cab. He deposited Richard inside and stepped back to let Nick slide in.

Richard opened his mouth to say something, but Tim rapped the window with his knuckles, and the cabbie pulled away. Tim headed back to the valet stand and handed off his ticket. The bouncer was back at his post by the rope, rubbing the raised red mark on his neck. "You all right?" Tim asked.

"You'd better get the fuck out of here. Fast."

They stood in tense silence, waiting for Tim's car to be pulled around.

**30** TIM SAT ATOP THE PLAYGROUND SLIDE AT WARREN ELEmentary, a few blocks from his old house, his feet pointed downward on the aluminum slant, clutching a bottle of vodka loosely in his lap. The small, unadorned merry-go-round sat still and silent, a flipped spider with bunched metal legs. Swings rattled in the night breeze; a tetherball bounced against its post. The air smelled of tanbark and asphalt.

He'd been here last on a lazy Sunday when Ginny had interrupted his edging the back lawn to make him walk her over, hand in hand, so she could again study the monkey bars that she was too afraid to swing across. They'd stood there silently, father and daughter, while she circled the bars, examining them from all angles, like a horse she was planning to mount. When he'd asked if she wanted to try, she shook her head, as always, and they'd walked back home, hand in hand.

Tim was shivering, though he wasn't the least bit cold. He found himself walking, studying the ground at his feet. He found himself on his porch, ringing his doorbell.

Some commotion, then Mac answered. It took Mac a moment to recognize him and take his hand off the butt of the Beretta stuffed into the waistband of his sweats. Behind him, even through the thickening haze of his grief and anger, Tim could see the blanket and bed pillow on the couch from which he'd been roused.

"I want to see Ginny's room," Tim said.

Mac's body swayed, as if he'd taken a step, but he hadn't. "Look, Rack, I don't know if this is such a—"

Tim spoke low and calm. "You see that pistol in your hand?"

Mac nodded.

"You'd better step aside or I'm gonna take it from you and ram it down your fucking throat." His voice wavered hard.

Mac's mouth pulsed in a half swallow, half gulp before smoothing back into a handsome inscrutability. "Okay."

Tim pushed open the door, and Mac stepped back. Dray was coming down the hall, knotting her bathrobe, her mouth slightly agape. "What are you—?"

He lowered his head when he passed her and shoved into Ginny's room, locking the door behind him.

He heard the sound of Dray and Mac talking down the hall, but he was too drunk to shape the sounds into words. He took in the room blurrily, the mound of stuffed animals in the corner, the pleated shade crowning the pink porcelain lamp on the diminutive desk, the inane glow of the Pocahontas night-light. Only when he curled up on Ginny's bed did he realize he still held the vodka bottle. The last thing he remembered before dozing off was setting it gently on the floor so it wouldn't spill.

When he awakened, it took him a few moments to remember where he was. He'd curled into the fetal position to fit on the small bed. He scooted up against the headboard, rubbed his eye, and felt the pinch of crust against his lid. Dray was sitting across the room, back to the wall, facing him. The faint gray light of early morning, split by the slats of the venetian blinds, fell across her face.

He glanced at the now-unlocked door, then at her. She had an unbent bobby pin in her mouth, angled down over her plump lower lip.

"I'm sorry," he said, placing his feet on the floor. "I'll leave."

"Don't," she said. "Yet."

Her stare made him uncomfortable, so he studied the yellow and pink flowers of the wallpaper.

"You were crying last night," Dray said.

He clasped his hands, pressed the knuckles to his mouth. "I'm sorry."

"Don't you *dare* apologize for that." She leaned her head back until it thumped softly against the wall. "Maybe you should have done more of it."

He blinked hard, kept his eyes closed. "I don't know what to do to diminish the hurt. There's got to be something, some outlet for the victims. If not, if we don't get anything from the courts, from the laws, what are we supposed to do?"

"Mourn, stupid." She propped her chin on the union of her fists. "And, Tim?" She waited for him to look up. "We're not the victim. We're related to the victim."

He sat with that one for a few minutes. Then he said quietly, "That is a damn powerful insight."

Dray took a deep breath, as if preparing for an underwater plunge. "You and I, we have a tough time starting conversations, not having them." She lowered her arms until they stuck straight out, her elbows resting on her kneecaps. "I went to the grocery store today for the first time. Shopping not for three, not even for two. I skipped the candy aisle because Ginny, you know, and I bought less stuff, just for me, and I got to the checkout counter, and it was thirty-something dollars. So cheap I almost started crying." Her voice cracked, a seam of vulnerability. "I don't want to shop for one."

He felt something break inside him and spill relief. "Andrea, I—" He sat up sharply. "Wait a minute. You didn't go to the grocery store the day I went in to work, the day of the Martía Domez shooting?"

"I couldn't get off the couch that day. What's going on?"

"The Stork said that's when he broke in and bugged my watch. I left it at home."

"No way. I was here all day." She let a sigh puff out her cheeks. "They must have had their eye on you longer than they're letting on. You knew they were manipulating you from the get-go—"

"I'll have to talk to Dumone. I know I can trust him."

"How do you know that?"

"I just do. I know it in my bones."

"Well, maybe the Stork and Rayner wanted a transmitter on you a week early, and they didn't let on."

"Maybe." His mind seethed with troubling thoughts. He vowed to get some answers from Dumone or in the next meeting at Rayner's, to learn the precise parameters of the Commission's stalking of him. His unease had been ratcheted up another notch—if his trust had indeed been violated, he'd be forced to implode the Commission.

Dray remained backed against the wall, watching him with moist eyes. Her neck bore the mark of her nails from earlier scratching. "Come here," he said.

She rose with a groan, knees cracking, and crossed to Ginny's bed. She lay down, her face on his chest, a wisp of hair falling to frame the outer edge of her eye. He put his spread hand over the back of her head and cradled it to him. She nuzzled into him like an animal, like a baby. They breathed together, then breathed some more.

He pulled her hair back out of her face, and their eyes met, held. Her hand tightened on his chest.

"I feel like we just found each other again," he said.

His phone, wedged in the front pocket of his jeans, vibrated against them both. Dray backed up off him, her knees and elbows pressing into the mattress, her chin resting on his stomach.

He flipped the phone open. "Yeah."

Mitchell's voice came with the staccato fire of cop argot. "The subject's at the ten-twenty."

"Okay." Tim turned off the phone and regarded Dray, savoring a final trace of comfort and, beyond that, feeling the stone edge of need bulldozing through him.

She raised her eyebrows. He nodded. She pushed herself off him and stood, straightening her shirt.

He wanted desperately to put his mouth on hers, but he feared if he started, he wouldn't stop. He *had* to be across town, and he hated himself for it.

On his way past her, they pulled together in a spontaneous embrace, caught sideways, her hands clasped around his waist, his arm down over her back, her face pressed to the side of his neck, chin resting on his shoulder.

It was all he could do not to turn his head and kiss her.

**31** **TIM SPOTTED MITCHELL BEHIND THE WHEEL OF A PARKED**
pizza-delivery car halfway up the block from
Bowrick's. A lit Domino's sign was adhered to
the roof, but the doors weren't painted with the logo, a minor but noticeable lapse. Tim pulled open the passenger
door and slid in. The interior smelled of cheap vinyl and
stale breath.

In the change in Mitchell's face, Tim saw the toll the Debuffier incident had taken on him. His eyes and cheeks had
darkened somehow, as if stopped-up thoughts had bled into
them and grown stagnant. A vein had broken in his left eye,
a dead snake zigzagging out from his pupil.

"He was dropped off by a gold Escalade, new plates at
0557, looked like he'd tied a few on last night. He stayed
inside until 0624, then emerged in worker's coveralls with
a hard hat under one arm. Caught the bus two blocks north
at the corner."

"Bus number?"

"He took the 2 to the 10. I tried to call you, couldn't get
through, so I followed him through the connection, then
downtown."

"Where'd he go?"

"You'll love this. The memorial. The new one going up
downtown, for the people killed in the Census bombing.
They have Bowrick and a few other community-service
monkeys sandblasting metal for the sculptor. Some genius
figured they could reform criminals and get the thing built
at the same time. Irony or something. He can't operate the
sandblaster much with his lame arm, but they have him

gofering around. Him and a bunch of convicts. They even break for prayer sessions. It's like some fucked-up penance cult. As if sandblasting metal gets you off the hook for shooting up a school."

In the backseat, gloves and black balaclavas peeked out from Mitchell's olive-drab duffel. Tim grabbed a hood, rolled it, and slid it into his back pocket. He pulled two flex-cuffs from the rubber-banded bundle as well.

Curved in dueling loops like mouse ears, flex-cuffs worked like heavy-duty garbage-bag ties. Once they were cinched around an arrestee's wrists, there was no easy release; they could only be notched tighter. The hard plastic strips were so unforgiving that detention-enforcement officers sometimes had to use pruning shears to cut them off. They were standard issue for ART raids, and Tim always liked having a few handy to restrain the unforeseeable.

"Did he have a lunch with him? A brown paper bag or a lunch box or something?"

"No."

"All right. So lunch is probably provided, but he might be back between twelve and one—if not, I'd guess between four and six. I'm gonna slip inside, be there waiting for him. If he's not alone when he returns, give me a double tap on the horn. You are not to leave this post. Where's Robert?"

"Not here."

"I do not want him on-site. Clear?"

Mitchell used two fingers of each hand to smooth his mustache. "Clear. I'm gonna split and switch out the car. I don't want to be sitting here in this thing much longer."

Tim nodded and got out. He strode down the cracked sidewalk, letting his elbow dip to touch the handle of his .357, which felt reassuringly solid beneath his T-shirt. He passed two beautiful Mexican girls jumping rope, an old-timer walking a pit bull, a low rider with tinted windows.

He circled the block and ducked through two backyards so he could approach Bowrick's house from the rear.

He wriggled through the bathroom window again and sat at the desk. Bowrick's checkbook lay out, and Tim flipped through it. Bowrick made semimonthly paycheck deposits, each around five hundred bucks. A series of check entries caught Tim's eye—two hundred dollars a week, every week, to the Lizzy Bowman fund. The name fluttered through Tim's memory awhile before striking a cord. The coach's daughter shot during Bowrick's assault on Warren High.

The kid was making his amends, working victim memorials, donating cash.

The parents of the twelve kids who ate lead from an SKS would probably be touched.

Tim pulled the chair around to the shadowed west wall, held his gun in his lap, and sat with his thoughts, which he found bad company. Lunchtime came and went with no sign of Bowrick. The shadows shifted in the room as afternoon came on, and Tim scooted the chair over to keep it in the dimness, staying on the hinge side of the door.

Bowrick did not show up at five, or six, or eight.

Tim found his mind drifting to Richard, the beaten-down PD who could see through the cracks and fissures of the system to the unbroken foundation beneath. The insurge of Tim's own grief last night had scalpeled open a part of him, and the freshness of his sorrow, he found, had dulled his anger, his conviction. If there was anything objective towering out of the morass of his grief, he'd lost sight of it. To steel himself he thought of the child-killer he awaited. He thought of eleven dead students and one dead little girl. He thought of the closed casket at Ginny's funeral, and why it had been.

But matching his emotion step for step was the steady advance of another, more rational force. The cracked bedrock beneath the Commission. Lane's and Bowrick's pursuit— like Tim's—of an idiosyncratic ideal they thought of as justice. The ways in which they'd all failed. Were failing.

A little after nine Tim heard a key scratch its way into the front lock. He pulled his balaclava from his rear pocket and rolled it over his head. It covered everything but the crescent of his mouth, the spots of his eyes. The smell of dirt, sweat, and cigarette smoke preceded Bowrick into the room. He slammed the door and crossed to his closet, not noticing Tim in the darkness. Bowrick tossed his hard hat into the closet and pulled off his shirt. His back was marred with pocks, crescents of shiny, tight-pinched flesh.

He was just lowering his arms when he noticed that the chair was not in its place by the desk. His eyes closed in a long blink. He turned calmly, expectantly, saw Tim sitting in the darkness. His shirt was balled at the end of his fist like a mop.

He took note of the .357 aimed at his head. His hands rose, fell to his thighs. "Go on then," he said. "Shoot me."

His upper lip held the scraggly strands of a mustache forced before its time. Up close he was so slight as to suggest preadolescence. His appearance impressed upon Tim that the legal definition of adulthood was stunningly arbitrary, as preposterous as bar mitzvah manhood; some males are boys at twenty-two, some are men at sixteen. It was all in the gathering of focus, the shouldering of responsibility, the potential for menace. Tim had not counted on Bowrick's seeming so much younger than himself, but why this was a sudden, essential criterion escaped him. In Bowrick's frailty Tim sensed for maybe the first time the space between culpability and punishment.

Tears eased down his cheeks, but Bowrick was otherwise completely unaltered—no jerky breathing, no reddening of the face, just the silent flow of tears, like thin faucet streams. His mouth set in a suggestion of a smile, of sadness and expectation, of weary relief.

Tim's grip remained perfectly firm on the gun, but his trigger finger did not recoil.

"What are you? Dad of a kid who got shot? Uncle? Priest?" Bowrick's bangs, greasy, long and thinned in tendrils, dangled over his eyes. "Fuck, man, if I was you, I'd shoot me. Go for it." He tossed his shirt aside, his lame arm pulling back to his stomach like a snail retracting. His chest bore a bad Pink Floyd tattoo—the face from *The Wall*.

Tim sorted through his legal arguments, his abstractions about justice, his ethical conclusions, but couldn't find a mainstay. He searched for anger next, couldn't locate it.

"Well, go on, then." Bowrick's voice stayed tough, but the tears kept coming.

"Why so eager?" Tim asked.

"You don't know what it's like, fucking waiting for it. Always waiting for it."

"My violin's in the car."

"Hey, fucker, you asked." He rolled his head back. Took a deep breath. "It ain't so clean like you think. I don't know if one of the guys who got shot is your kid brother or something, but those guys were mean as shit. Ran that school like it was their own party, coach looked the other way 'cause he didn't want to lose Sections."

"So you help two thugs shoot his daughter in the eye. Sounds like justice to me."

Bowrick laughed, high-pitched, his voice breaking, tears still running. "There ain't no way back from something like I did, but I tried to set my shit straight. Tried to get my accounts balanced before I meet the Big Guy." He nodded at Tim's gun, wiped one cheek hard. "Let's find out if I did."

Tim firmed his lips, lined the sights, but his trigger finger still disobeyed him. All five feet eight inches of Bowrick winced and trembled. Tim slid the gun back into his waistband and rose to leave.

Both doors splintered in simultaneously. Balaclava hoods lowered, Robert and Mitchell burst into the room, guns leveled, Mini Mag-Lites strapped to their right forearms, shooting thin beams of light parallel with the barrels of their .45s.

"Everything okay?" one of them said. He nodded at Tim reassuringly as the other stutter-stepped toward Bowrick, gun-facing him.

Tim's rage flared hard. "What the hell are you doing in here?"

"You took a while. We thought something might be wrong." Tim recognized the coarser voice as Robert's, which meant Mitchell was the one closing hard on Bowrick. An abrupt aggression role reversal that was mind-baffling but gut-logical. That Mitchell had appeared was an inexcusable breach of conduct; that Robert was present was worse. Tim's mind went immediately to the lies surrounding the digital transmitter's appearance in his watch. Maybe the Commission had always played by its own rules behind his back.

"Nothing's wrong."

"Good," Mitchell said. "Then let's do him and split."

Bowrick had back-stepped to the desk, his head ducked in anticipation of the shot. His thin arms crossed his chest, hands outspread over the balls of his shoulders.

"No," Tim said.

Mitchell regarded him in disbelief, his eyes two white-shining orbs beneath the black fabric of the hood. "What?" The gun inched over, aimed now somewhere between Bowrick and Tim. "We're doing this whether you like it or not."

Before he could think, Tim's hand was down and through the draw. He center-sighted on Mitchell's head and saw Mitchell's sights staring him back in the face. Robert swung his gun at Tim, then back at Bowrick, agitated in the unfamiliar role of mediator. "Let's calm the fuck down here. Let's calm down."

Bowrick's eyes were closed, his head still recoiled. Tim eased slowly over until he stood between Mitchell and Bowrick, squinting against the light of the Mini-Mag. When he leaned back, he felt the heat of Bowrick's fear emanating from less than a foot behind him. He kept his eyes on the muscles of Mitchell's forearm, reading them. His finger lay on the side of the gun parallel to the barrel, just outside the trigger guard, ready to flick and squeeze at the slightest prompting.

"Move. I'm not fucking around here. *Fucking move!*" Mitchell pulled his gun sharply right and fired, the bark matched by a flash of flame at the barrel. The bullet bit out a chunk of closet frame. Bowrick muttered something low and fearful behind Tim. Robert was yelling, but right now it was just Tim's eyes and Mitchell's eyes peering out from the depths of dark wool, locked on each other.

Tim stayed perfectly still, gun trained on Mitchell's head. "If you make one more movement with your gun hand except to lower your weapon, I will shoot you." He spoke softly, but he knew Mitchell heard every word, even over Robert's yelling. "Believe me, you don't want to exchange bullets with me at close range."

They faced each other over their respective barrels.

Finally Mitchell rode the hammer forward and half spun his gun so it sat sideways in his hand, uncocked. He slid it into a hip holster and thundered out the rear of the house, boots pounding on the floor. Tim looked at Robert and jerked his head toward the door. Robert took a deep breath, then holstered his weapon and jogged out after his brother.

Tim half turned to keep an eye on Bowrick, then slid his own gun back into his waistband. Bowrick slid down to the floor, milk-pale and trembling, his eyes and nostrils red at the rims. His teeth were chattering.

"You're gonna want to leave. Right now. Don't wait for them to come back." Tim's footsteps broke the near silence. The rear door hung crooked on its frame, and Tim pushed past it and into the shitty backyard.

He was almost to the fence line when he heard Bowrick retching. He stopped, exhaled deeply.

A minute and a half later, Bowrick emerged, stuffing crumpled bills into his pocket, wiping his nose on his sleeve. He started when he saw Tim waiting, still wearing the hood; he turned to run but stopped when Tim made no motion.

"Oh. It's you. I just . . . I just called a buddy, gonna pick me up in five minutes." Bowrick's eyes darted nervously to the yard's perimeter, which Tim had been scanning assiduously. "Will you wait with me till he shows?"

Tim nodded.

**32** TIM HAD BARELY EXITED INTO MOORPARK WHEN HE NOticed the flashing lights behind him. He eased over to the curb. It was a sheriff's car, not CHP, but on the off chance he didn't know the deputy, he turned on the dome light and kept both hands in sight on the wheel.

The deputy angled the spotlight into his rearview, so he squinted as the dark form approached. He waited for the knuckle tap, then rolled down his window. Dray leaned over, resting both hands on the sill, smirking. "License and registration." She took note of his expression. "What's wrong?"

"I need to talk to you."

"I figured. I pulled you over before you raced home and got into it with Mac."

"Are you solo?"

"Yeah. Why don't you follow me. Let's get off the road."

Tim followed her car. Eventually they pulled off onto a dirt road that crested the top of a little canyon, then rolled a few meters, gravel crunching under the wheels. Tim got out and joined Dray, sitting on the hood of her car. He'd forgotten how well she wore her uniform. Down below, a wedge of eucalyptus and a freestanding garage took shape in the darkness. Through a dimly lit window, Tim could see Kindell's figure stooping and rising, as if moving items from the floor to a counter, and he was simultaneously surprised and not surprised that they had wound up here.

"He had a water pipe burst in there last night." Dray's lips pressed together until they whitened. "Don't know how that could've happened. Unfortunate thing is, the place isn't code, so he's got no one to complain to." She clicked her teeth and turned to him. "What's going on? You look like hell."

"I couldn't go through with an execution. Today. At the last minute I just couldn't . . ."

Dray laced her fingers and rested her cheek on the points of her knuckles, regarding him. "Who was it?"

"Terrill Bowrick."

She whistled, let the sound fade slow. "You guys don't screw around. Straight to the scum A-list."

"Mitchell gun-faced me when I pulled the plug on the operation."

"What'd you do?"

"Stared him down. He left furious, but he left."

"Why couldn't you go through with it?"

"When I confronted Bowrick, I saw his remorse. I saw *him*, not just a person who committed a crime I couldn't understand." Though the night was cool, he felt the tingle of sweat across his back. "And he looked a lot like me."

Dray made a noise deep in her throat. "When I shot that kid, the first thought I had the minute I cleared leather, just as I was aiming and being aimed at—it wasn't about life or death or justice. The only thought I had was that he was the handsomest kid I'd ever seen. And I shot him. And he's dead. And that's that. Procedure, rules, a deadly-force clause that I trusted in—those are the only things that let me quit prying at myself from time to time."

She gestured to Kindell's distant shadow in the window, bending and hauling. "I've come slowly to see you did the right thing. By not shooting Kindell that night. I can't say I don't relish the sight of him suffering, but I've put some miles between me and Ginny's death, and the picture re-solved a bit. Like this . . ." She waited, head cocked like a dog zeroing in on a sound too distant for human ears. "The law isn't individual. Its aim isn't to redress loss—it's sepa-rate from loss, really. It's not there to protect individuals but itself." She nodded, as if pleased with how the senti-ment had formed itself into words. "The law's selfish, and that's just how it's gotta be."

"Why all this clarity now?"

"You don't ask why clarity comes, you just hope it does."

Tim nodded, then nodded again. "Clarity came tonight when I saw Bowrick in my sights. I don't know where I've been the past two weeks."

Dray let her breath out through clenched teeth. "I fuck up fast and hard, but you're always cool. Always level. So much so, if you're left alone, you can talk yourself into anything. I mean, what were you hoping the Commission would give you?"

He thought hard, but the answer stayed dumb. "Justice. My justice."

"Like against a fascist census? Like voodoo protection from evil spirits? Like against school bullies?"

"Point taken. Hypocrisy realized."

"Everyone thinks they can own justice, but you can't. It's not a commodity. There is no 'my' justice. There's just 'Justice' with a capital *J*."

"Is breaking into Kindell's house and busting his water pipe 'Justice' with a capital *J*?"

"Hell no. It's just vandalism." Her eyes, pristine green, hid a glimmer. "I said I had clarity. I didn't say I had maturity." She let out a soft laugh, then her face hardened the way only hers could—mouth drawing taut and chiseling out her cheekbones, squaring her jaw. "Don't think I'm sitting here in judgment of you because I've managed to string together a few thoughts in the past twenty-four hours. I'm not."

They sat for a few moments with the night breeze and the eucalyptus branches scraping overhead. "I can't do it anymore," Tim said. "The Commission."

"Because it's getting out of control?"

"No. Because it's wrong."

The sound of Kindell tripping and splashing echoed in the canyon, then faded into cricket-broken silence.

"They've been double-playing me from the beginning. I'm getting out, and I'm taking Kindell's files with me."

"What if they won't give them to you?"

"I'm getting out anyway."

"Then we'll never know what happened to Ginny."

"We'll find some other way if we have to."

Tim slid the unregistered .357 from his hip holster, released the wheel, and spun it so the bullets fell one after another into his palm. He handed Dray the bullets, then the gun.

He got into his car. When his beams flashed past Dray, she was still sitting on the hood, staring out at the dark of the canyon.

Rayner's front door was open, sending out a shaft of light into the night. As Tim pulled nearer, he saw that the driveway gate had been pried from its tracks and shoved open, its end post describing an arc in the concrete. Tim left the Beemer across the street, hit a jog, and slipped through the gate.

Groaning issued from inside. Tim approached the front door fast, painfully aware of his lack of weapon. At the base of the foyer stairs, Rayner lay on his back, propped up on one elbow, his shoulders and head resting against the newel post.

Tim saw blood on his face, his chest.

Tim stepped onto the porch, and Rayner jerked back, startled, until he recognized him. A path of blood led from the conference room, terminating at Rayner's resting place—he'd dragged himself across the foyer. A phone perched in an alcove at the base of the stairs remained well out of his reach.

Tim stopped before the doorway and made an interrogative gesture.

Rayner's voice came jerky and weak. His upper lip was split, right through his white mustache, and his bathrobe was torn on the right side. "They're gone now."

He raised a blood-soaked bathrobe sleeve, a pajama cuff

protruding, and pointed with a weak, tremulous hand toward the far side of the foyer.

Tim leaned forward and saw Ananberg's body sprawled facedown near the door to the library. The excruciating angle of her limbs—one arm bent backward at the elbow, her right leg caught beneath her so her hips rose in an awkward tilt—made clear she was lying as she'd fallen. Her cream chemise was spotted with blood.

Tim entered cautiously and used his elbow to shut the door so he wouldn't smudge whatever prints may have been left on the door handle. He inhaled deeply, caught a whiff of explosive residue. His thoughts were stampeding, a swirl of furious movement.

He crossed to Ananberg and checked her pulse, though he already knew. A fall of sleek hair blocked her eyes. Tim wanted her to brush it away with the heel of her hand, rise sleepy-eyed, and crack wise about his startled expression, his shirt, a flaw in his logic. But she just lay there, inert and cold. He pulled her hair out of her face for her, ran his fingertips gently down her porcelain cheek. "Damnit, Jenna," he said.

He glanced through the open door of the conference room. Despite his limited view, he saw that the picture of Rayner's son had been thrown on the floor. One of the paper shredders was jiggling and giving off a repetitive whine, stuck on something.

Rayner's voice rasped at him. "Call 911."

Tim had already flipped open his cell phone. As he demanded an ambulance to the address, he peeled back Rayner's bathrobe. Tattered fabric fluttered around the gaping wound in his side. One of his ribs was visible, a white sheen in the rich, dark glitter.

When Rayner spoke, Tim could see that his front teeth were both chipped, and he knew it was from having a pistol rammed into his mouth. "They dragged us out of bed . . . tried to get me to open the safe. I wouldn't." He raised a hand, let it fall. "Jenna tried to fight . . . after I got shot. . . . Robert lost his cool . . . snapped her neck with a twist of his hand, just like that. . . . Jenna, Jesus . . . poor, proud Jenna . . ." He tugged at the burnt edge of his robe, his fingers tense and pinching. He was dying, and they both knew it.

Tim's head buzzed with disbelief. "They're ruthless."

"Without Franklin around to reign them in anymore . . ."

"What did they take?"

"The not-guilty case files. Thomas Black Bear . . . Mick Dobbins . . . Rhythm Jones. And they took Terrill Bowrick's." His voice was warbling now, growing weaker.

Even through his heightened concern, Tim felt a stab of relief that Kindell's binder had been left behind.

"I tried to stop them. . . . If they kill indiscriminately. . . . it will ruin what we are . . . my doctrine . . ."

"Were there any other files in there? The ones you were reviewing for the second phase?"

"No." Rayner double-blinked and looked back at Tim unsteadily. "Nothing."

The four stolen binders contained weeks, maybe even months, of man-hours. They had the complete details of the police investigations. Locations, addresses, relationships, habits. Endless trails for locating the accused.

Essential intel for planning a series of hits.

"I'm calling the authorities, getting them on the trail."

"Absolutely not. You . . . can't. An investigation . . . the media. . . . It'll destroy my message. . . . my name . . . my legacy. . . ."

Rayner's arrogance and pride still drove his every thought, even here, even on the cusp of death. His mouth was slightly ajar, enough so Tim could see the protrusions of his chipped front teeth. His gums were rimmed with blood. Tim had no good answer for why his store of disdain was greater for Rayner than even for Mitchell or Robert—for anyone, in fact, save himself. The reek of shamelessness, perhaps. His father's scent.

"Robert and Mitchell aren't interested in naming names. . . ." With great effort Rayner tilted his head forward off the post to look at Tim directly. "If we leave them be, they'll leave us be. . . ."

"There are innocent people at risk of being killed."

"We don't know that." Rayner's eyes were a jumbled mix of desperation and stifled panic. When he spoke again, the wound in his upper lip spread, a seam between two flaps of skin. "The kill clause . . . Mr. Rackley . . . or did you forget? The Commission is . . . dissolved."

"The kill clause also states we have to tie up loose ends. You don't consider this a loose end?"

The whirring of the paper shredder continued in the background with maddening regularity.

"I'm a professor of social psychology . . . a prominent advocate. . . . Don't undo my life's work. Don't ruin what I've tried to"—he lurched forward, racked with pain—"accomplish here because of those two . . . maniacs. They're not our business. . . . What they do now isn't part of what we were. . . . The press will pollute everything. . . ." His eyes tearing, Rayner pressed a hand to his side in a futile attempt to stanch his bleeding. He looked desperate and utterly crestfallen. "Please don't drag . . . my name through the mud. . . ."

"Robert and Mitchell are going to kill people *we* ruled not guilty. We're part of this. We set it in motion. We own responsibility for whichever way it spins."

Rayner's face was going white. He made a sound of disagreement, a sharp exhale turned to a fricative against his teeth.

"I'm protecting those people," Tim said. "That's more important than your reputation."

Rayner rolled his head back and laughed, a soft, crackling chuckle that chilled Tim. "You say this to a dying man. You're an idiot . . . Mr. Rackley. You'll never know what happened to your daughter. . . . You don't have the faintest idea. . . ."

Tim stood abruptly, his heart hammering. "You know what happened to Ginny?"

"Of course. I know everything. . . ." He was wheezing, expelling words in great exhales. "There *was* an accomplice. . . . I know who. . . . I found out. . . ."

The puddle of blood grew beneath Rayner, spreading along the seam at the base of the bottom step. His taunting was concise and vicious—Tim felt the words like a stiletto prying in a wound.

"Go ahead . . . leak my name to the cops, the press . . . but . . . you'll never know. . . ." Rayner's eyes steeled with a smug intractability, and Tim felt a quick rush of affinity for whichever Masterson had tried to smash through his expression with a gun barrel.

Tim's voice came low and harsh, and it held a note of menace that surprised even him. *"Tell me who else killed my daughter."*

Rayner grimaced, his teeth shining through the split upper lip. His spitefulness vanished, replaced with terror at death's final approach. His hand inched out, trembling, and gripped the cuff of Tim's pants.

Tim stood over him, glaring down, arms crossed, watching him die.

Rayner's body seemed to retract slightly, as if curling

into itself, though it hardly moved. He looked up at Tim, floating in a sudden calm. "I loved my boy, Mr. Rackley," he said, and then he died.

Tim stepped away, his pants pulling free of Rayner's fingers. He had little time before the ambulances arrived, and he'd be damned if he was going to leave without Kindell's case binder. Especially in light of what Rayner had told him.

Following the trail of Rayner's blood, he entered the conference room, the whine of the paper shredder growing louder, and walked past the blast-blown victim photos on the immense table. Aside from some black scorching near the baffle, the safe was perfectly intact. The door hung slightly open, its lugs still extended in the locked position. Tim leaned closer, noting the frag scars, like little scratches, also near the baffle. He sniffed the air, twice, deep, waiting for the smell to navigate through his memory; it unlocked a box that had been closed since Somalia in '93. Fifty-grains-per-foot det cord.

Mitchell had probably slid about two feet of detonation cord inside the baffle and stuck a blasting cap in the protruding end. The explosion would have overpressurized the air pocket inside the safe, flexing the door outward to the point that the locking lugs unseated themselves and the door popped. The metal baffle would have acted as a buffer, protecting the case binders beneath.

That the door had snapped back to its original shape with no permanent damage was testament to Mitchell's precision and skill. Robert and Mitchell had opted for an explosive breach, which was louder and riskier than picking the safe. Tim hoped that meant they didn't have the Stork on board, the only one who could have accomplished the latter.

Tim nudged the door open with a knuckle. Only two binders remained—Lane's and Debuffier's.

Kindell's was missing.

Behind him the paper shredder continued its laments. Tim's eyes closed with the horror of the realization. He ran over to the shredder, banging into a high-backed chair and knocking it over. A single page had crumpled up in the machine, jamming the blades. Tim ripped it free, and the bottom half shot through, dissipating into tiny squares.

Roger Kindell's booking photo, torn just below the eyes.

Robert and Mitchell had shredded Kindell's file, and the secrets it held. The ultimate act of aggression, the final step in the power play, a declaration of war.

The Mastersons were now operational.

Tim stared at the half photograph, feeling his frustration grow to rage. The agony of all he had lost rattled through him, leaving him winded. He finally lowered the top half of Kindell's head into the whirring blades.

He stopped on his way out only to retrieve Ginny's framed picture from the table.

**33** BEAR'S VOICE WAS RAGGED WITH SLEEP, GRUFFER EVEN than usual. "What?"

Tim threaded the needle between a Camaro and a semi on a two-lane slide to the freeway carpool lane, drawing a cacophony of bleating horns. Even in February the L.A. morning came on hard and relentless; the sun matched the explicitness of the town itself, all too eager to skip foreplay and be revealed.

"You heard me. Those are the names and addresses. Do you have them?"

"Yeah, yeah, I got 'em. What is the extent of your involvement in this?"

"Call local PD, get cars to Mick Dobbins *now*. Put out a BOLO on Terrill Bowrick *now*, As I said, I don't have a current address for Black Bear—"

"Thomas Black Bear's doing a nickel in Donovan for grand larceny."

"Then don't worry about him. I have no current for Rhythm Jones either, so put out another BOLO. He's in grave and immediate danger. And get to William Rayner's before the bodies chill."

"How are you caught up in this?"

Tim was anxious for Bear to stop talking, call dispatch, and put out the Be on the Lookouts. "Yamashiro at five-thirty. I'll bring all the answers."

"Fuck Yamashiro. You want me to get on the horn, I need some answers now."

"You don't want those answers now. You want to get those subjects in protective custody without being compromised by the knowledge that we know you already have anyway. I'll clear the air when I see you."

"You'll do more than that." Bear hung up.

Tim tried Robert's and Mitchell's Nextels next, but their respective voice mails picked up without a ring. He left no messages.

In the widening range of dire potentialities, Tim saw his foolishness clarified, amplified, and he took a moment to bask in an unadulterated self-contempt before pulling himself back to utility.

That the Mastersons had shredded Kindell's case binder instead of taking it indicated they weren't interested in pursuing him. Kindell alone among the suspects they'd leave be, to torment Tim with his continued existence. For the hits they'd start with Bowrick and Dobbins, since both had known addresses, and then they'd get on Rhythm's trail. Black Bear, they'd soon learn, was safe from them in prison.

Tim's objective was clear: Before and above all else, he had to ensure the safety of the targets.

Bowrick was gone already; Tim had watched him climb into the tricked-out Escalade and disappear into the rush of traffic on Lincoln.

At a stoplight he called information to get Dobbins's address. An apartment in a shitty part of Culver City, south of Sony Pictures. He got snagged in the morning commute, so it took nearly a half hour to get to Dobbins's place, a cracked stucco job from the fifties.

No crime tape, no forensic van from SID, no signs of any police presence or violent activity. Dobbins's apartment, 9D, was in the rear.

Tim rang the doorbell. No answer.

Dread tightening his jaw, he peered through the window into the shabby interior, expecting to see the retarded janitor's body sprawled on the shabby carpet amid an ellipse of blood spatter. Instead he saw a framed Tony Dorsett poster, a brown La-Z-Boy, and an obese and slightly bored cat licking itself. He had his pick set in hand when an ancient woman lost in a toothpaste-blue bathrobe and a constellation of curlers inched around the corner and shook a drugstore bag in his direction. A plastic canister of Metamucil fell out and lost itself in a patch of long-dead juniper.

"What are you doing?"

"Hello, ma'am. I'm a friend of Mick's. I was just dropping by to—"

"Mickey doesn't have any friends." She crouched, one varicosed leg protruding from the slit of her bathrobe, half covered in a thick compression stocking.

"Let me get that for you."

She snatched the canister back from him as if recovering stolen goods. "The police came by and hauled him off. He didn't do anything. Not before, not this time. He's a good boy. It almost broke his heart, the last time. That business with the kids, all *meshugaas*. The way he was treated, it was *beyond belief*. He loves children, that one. *Loves* them. He's a good boy."

"How long ago did the police come?"

"You just missed them."

He tempered his relief, weighing the possibility that Robert and Mitchell had impersonated police officers to kidnap Dobbins. "And they had uniforms?"

"Of course. Two cars full of them, the cops—flashing lights, the whole to-do. Blocking up the driveway. I was fit to be tied. *Fit to be tied*."

Nosy Old Woman—the investigator's best friend.

"Thank you, ma'am. I'm going to see if I can't help out our Mickey."

"Someone should be so good as to look out for him." She placed a mottled hand on her plush bathrobe, in Pledge of Allegiance position. "Besides me."

Tim headed back to his car, formulating his next step. With Black Bear, Bowrick, and Dobbins temporarily accounted for, Tim had just one more target to cover. Rhythm Jones, he remembered from the case review, didn't have a current address. To find him before the Mastersons, he'd need access to the same clues they had. Rayner had been paranoid about confining and limiting Commission materials, but he was also a master strategist. Tim would have bet he kept copies of the case binders stashed away somewhere—another of his nifty insurance policies.

The question was, where?

▮ Dumone rustled in his hospital bed and looked up at Tim. Though the lights were off and the curtains drawn, Tim could see that his eyes were sunken, deeply shadowed, his skin sallow. Dumone had difficulty raising his head. "What's wrong?" His voice was barely discernible.

Tim shut the door behind him, crossed, and sat bedside. Chest leads bumped out the fabric of Dumone's gown, and multiple wires snaked from his sleeve. The continuous monitor cast a gentle green glow across his pillow's edge. Moved by a sudden impulse, Tim took his limp left hand.

"Don't do that," Dumone said.

Tim let go, feeling a flush of embarrassment, but Dumone reached across with his right hand, grasped Tim's wrist, and held it in an approximation of warmth. "Can't feel anything in that hand."

"You've had a setback."

"Another stroke last night," Dumone slurred. "I just rolled in from the ICU and boy are my wheels tired." He tried to pull himself to a more upright position but couldn't, and he shook his head when Tim moved to help. "Give it to me. The bad news. You look worse than I probably do."

"Robert and Mitchell have gone off the deep end. They killed Rayner and Ananberg, stole the case binders."

Dumone exhaled deeply, his body settling into the sheets. "Mary mother of Jesus." He closed his eyes. "Details."

Tim brought him up to speed in a low voice devoid of emotion. Dumone kept his eyes closed throughout. At one point Tim caught himself watching for the rise of his chest to make sure he was still breathing.

He finished, and they sat together a few moments, the

occasional blip of the monitor the only thing breaking the silence. When Dumone opened his eyes, they were moist. "Rob and Mitch," he said gently. "Christ, boys." He squeezed Tim's wrist, squeezed it hard. "You know you'll have to stop them."

"Yes."

"Even if it means you use deadly force."

"Yes." Tim took a deep breath, held it until he felt the burn. "Did Rayner ever tell you who Kindell's accomplice was?"

"No. Not a word." Dumone's upper lip trembled on one side. "He couldn't give you that before he died, the manipulative bastard."

"The Stork lied about when he installed the digital transmitter in my watch. Do you know when they started listening in on me?"

"I didn't oversee all surveillance—we each took different candidates. We'd been at it, the search, for the better part of a year, so we couldn't all keep track of everyone. You started out on Rayner's list. Rob and Mitch handled the fieldwork, as usual, with the Stork thrown in if they needed gadgets. So I don't know. I got involved once Rayner got serious about you, right around your daughter's funeral. What's up?"

An image came to Tim—standing out on Rayner's back patio with Ananberg, watching Rayner whispering to Mitchell in the kitchen. "Maybe they were involved."

"Involved in Virginia's death?" Dumone shook his head, jowls swaying. "I don't care how far out of their tree they are, they wouldn't murder a little girl. They're not sexual predators, not sickos. Zealots, maybe. Vicious, yes. More than I guessed. But they hate—and I mean *hate*—scum like Kindell. What would they have to gain by murdering Ginny?"

"I don't know. Another high-profile Commission execution down the line."

"Come on, Tim. It's not like they could have anticipated how Kindell's trial would go. In all likelihood he'd have been locked up. And they wouldn't help kill a girl just so they could kill a patsy for killing her. It makes no sense. And you know damn well that however fucked up they might be—Rob and Mitch and Rayner—they wouldn't do that. Plus, there's *no* way Ananberg would stand for it."

Ananberg certainly wouldn't have. But she—like the Stork—might not have been in on the plan.

"Why wouldn't Rayner have just told me who the accomplice was, then?" Tim asked. "He's covering something up, something that would damage his reputation."

"Rayner's always been an information tyrant—how he gets it, how he guards it, how he leaks it—that's his power reservoir. What makes you think he'd relinquish control of that, even in death? He's a megalomaniac. There's still his reputation to guard, his cause to go down in the annals. If you abide the kill clause, then Rob and Mitch get written off as a couple of loose cannons who acted on their own, and he goes down as the compassionate professor who did his damnedest to influence public policy and protect victims."

Tim remembered Robert's mortification about the dead woman in Debuffier's freezer, Rayner's queasiness when graphic crime-scene photos circled the table, the hurt vehemence with which Mitchell had discussed Ginny's death at Monument Hill, and he knew that Dumone's instinct was correct. They wouldn't have participated with Kindell in Ginny's murder or molestation.

"You're right. But Rayner knew what happened to Ginny that night—he wasn't bluffing. And since the twins shredded Kindell's folder, the secret may have died with him."

Dumone's hand tightened around Tim's wrist, as if in anticipation of what Tim was about to ask.

"I'm dead-ended here, on all fronts," Tim said. "With Ginny. With Robert and Mitchell. If I'm gonna stop them, I need to know if Rayner kept copies of the case binders anywhere."

Dumone's breathing grew shallow and raspy. If Tim pursued the Mastersons and sought protection for the targets as they both knew he must, both Tim and Dumone would be implicated, prosecuted, probably imprisoned. Dumone's telling Tim the location of the case binders would essentially be turning over hard evidence on himself.

Dumone gripped the bridge of his nose with his thumb and forefinger, pressing the baggy flesh around his eyes. "He kept one extra set at his office. Go get them. Blow this thing open. Stop Rob and Mitch however you can. Find out who else killed your daughter. I have no more answers for you. I have nothing." He removed his hand and studied Tim through reddened eyes. "If there's one thing I regret in this life, it's dragging you into this thing, son. I hope someday you'll find clear to forgive me."

"We all own our decisions. Don't put that on yourself."

"Of course. I'm being condescending. Maybe that's what happens when you're knocking on death's door." He coughed hard, and his face crumpled in pain.

"Want me to call a nurse?"

Dumone searched Tim's face. "Leave me a bullet."

Tim opened his mouth, but no sound came out.

"There's nothing more for me to do here but waste away. And we both know that doesn't suit me well."

The blip of the monitor. The greenish glow across the pillow. Cold coming off the floor tiles.

Tim reached down and removed a full speedloader from

his belt pouch. He slid out a single bullet and deposited it in Dumone's waiting hand.

"Thank you for not making me do the bullshit."

"We've never done the bullshit."

"Set this right, Tim. Get your answers."

Tim nodded and rose. At the door he turned. Dumone lay quietly, watching him. He raised his right hand and tapped his forehead in a salute.

Before leaving, Tim returned the gesture.

Tim drove into Westwood, winding past the row of dilapidated mansions with chipped fraternity signs and shirtless youths spraying party refuse from porches. It took him the better part of an hour to find a parking spot, even within one of the many campus lots. A quarter got you about seven minutes on the meter, a ploy worthy of his father. A change machine was graciously provided on every floor. Before he left, he'd deposited about nine bucks into the unit.

The UCLA campus was alive with students of all shapes, sizes, and ethnic backgrounds. A gargantuan woman in a muumuu and red pigtails was making out with a slight Persian man about half her size beneath a tattered poster advertising the Korean Independence Movement Day bash.

Diversity in action.

Tim entered the John Wooden Center and called information. An adenoidal voice informed him that Dr. Rayner's office was on the first floor of Franz Hall.

A plaque announcing WILLIAM RAYNER was adhered to the last door on the corridor—the other professors, Tim noted, had respectfully availed themselves of a few lowercase letters. The translucent window panel was dark; no shadows moved in the adjunct professor's office. A glimpse at the seam of light at the jamb showed that the last secretary out hadn't bothered to key the dead bolt.

Tim pretended to peruse the grade postings, which were affixed beneath a photocopied *Vanity Fair* profile of the dearly deceased, until the hall was clear. Tom Altman, man of many resources, accommodatingly supplied a laminated driver's license that made the shitty, state-issued latch bolt play hide-and-seek.

Tim closed and locked the door behind him, passed an assistant's desk, and entered the larger room in the back. Sturdy oak desk, metal filing cabinets, shelves of books— most of them Rayner's own. A spin through the file draw- ers revealed them to hold mainly classroom materials. The computer's screen saver, a photograph of Rayner's boy, bounced repetitively around the screen like a physics- defying missile in an Atari game.

Tim nearly broke a sterling letter opener prying the lock from the desk's enormous bottom drawer. A tall stack of canary yellow files filled it to the rim. Tim raised the first and thickest file, and his own name stared back at him from the tab.

His pulse quickening, he opened it.

A stack of surveillance photographs. Tim heading into the Federal Building. Tim and Dray at a window table at Chuy's, each gripping an oversize burrito. Tim's father at the Santa Anita track, leaning over the home-stretch rail, a spray of betting slips protruding from a tense fist. Tim walking Ginny into Warren Elementary on her first day, the WELCOME, YOUNG SCHOLARS sign flapping overhead. In September. Six months ago.

As he flipped through them, a sense of outrage burst through the numbness, heating his face, pinching him at the temples. Robert and Mitchell had stalked him for months, with notepads and cameras, capturing him and his intimates at work, at school, brushing their teeth.

The next ten files also bore his name. He scattered them across the desktop, turning pages. Medical records. Elementary-school grades. Drug testing going back to age nineteen. Bullet-riddled Transtar targets. Endless assessment tests from each stage of his career—army enlistment, Rangers qualifying, the Marshals Service application.

Snippets jumped out at him from the paperwork montage:

*20/20 vision.*
*No Axis 1 or Axis II disorders.*
*1.5-mile run qual time—9:23.*
*Bench press—310 lbs. for two reps.*
*Disturbed sleep post Croatia tour, some reported anxiety.*
*Toilet trained at 2 years, 1 month.*
*Seclusive, but high level of sociability.*
*Assertive, dominant, takes the initiative, confident.*
*Childhood family atmosphere—unstable and unpredictable.*
*Deserted by mother, age 3.*
*Facial expressions indicate control and reserve, but not absence of feelings.*
*No history of drug or alcohol abuse.*
*Unimpaired impulse control, unimpaired decision making.*
*Antisocial practices—extremely low.*
*No adolescent conduct problems. Despite father.*

His eyes caught on a thick sheaf of questions titled "The Minnesota Multiphasic Personality Inventory." He vaguely recalled filling out the five-hundred-question assessment during one application process or another.

*Item 9. If I were an artist, I would like to draw flowers.*
The "false" bubble darkened by a #2 pencil.

*Item 49. It would be better if almost all laws were thrown away.* False.

*Item 56. I sometimes wish I could be as happy as others seem to be.* True.

*Item 146. I cry easily.* False.

And then the sheets of interpretation, written in Rayner's hand:

*0 for 15 on the Lie Scale—extremely reliable reporter.*

*F Scale moderate—consistent and reliable, but reflects aptitude for nonconventional thinking.*

*High score on Responsibility Scale indicates subject possesses high standards, a strong sense of fairness and justice, self-confidence, dependability, trustworthiness.*

*Strong (even rigid) adherence to values.*

*Good little soldier—a phrase Robert had used with Tim during the intel dump outside the KCOM building.*

*Low depression, hysteria, psychopathic deviates.*

*Low hypomania.*

*Conscientious to the point of being moralistic, but flexible, creative, independent thinker.*

*Healthy balance of acquiescing and disagreeing response styles.*

*Paranoia—moderate.*

*Father wound leaves subject susceptible to intense bonding with father figure. Important Dumone remains unpolluted, must have pure interaction with subject.*

Tim looked at the spread before him on the desk, a montage of the most intimate pieces of his life, a construction of the most private parts of his brain. His father's rap sheet. *I sometimes tease animals.* His reason for military discharge underlined in red—*to spend more time with family.*

Rayner—Mussolini of the Information Age—had managed to compile a remarkable range of confidential information, enough to lay Tim as bare as a split frog on a dissecting slab. A hot burst of intense, little-boy shame faded back into anger and a sense of deep and profound violation.

Tim thought about Robert's immense skill in bringing back information about the floor-to-roof inner workings of the KCOM building. Robert and Mitchell had applied that skill to Tim, bringing Rayner back every inch of him.

With a trembling hand, Tim lifted the last file from the drawer. It contained a sheaf of paper listing literally hundreds of other potential recruitment candidates. A few names Tim recognized from the Company, the feds, the SEALs. On the twentieth page, he ran across a spate of his former colleagues.

> *George "Bear" Jowalski—too old, slowing down operationally.*
> *Jim Denley—just moved from Brooklyn, unfamiliar with Los Angeles.*
> *Ted Maybeck—anxiety disorder potential.*

Glancing back at the drawer, Tim saw that its bottom contents were, at last, revealed. Seven black binders.

His stomach clenched when he saw the white label on the last spine. ROGER KINDELL.

He pulled out the binder, alarmed by its lightness, and opened it.

Empty.

He stared for a moment at the blank binder interior, as if

the enormity of his disappointment might force documents to materialize.

Rayner must have anticipated Tim's coming after the Kindell file at some point. He certainly had amassed enough personality data on Tim to make precise projections of his future behavior. Since Rayner believed that the Kindell file was the key item he'd need to keep out of Tim's hands to assure Tim's continued cooperation, he would have placed it in a location even more secure than a locked drawer in a locked office.

The thin plastic film of the cover's inside flap bumped slightly up. Tim dug in the pocket, his fingertips touching metal. A safety-deposit key, #201—of course, no bank name imprinted on the brass. He pocketed it.

Clearing his head, he refocused on his objective. Not how he'd been maneuvered. Not the ways Rayner, Robert, and Mitchell had pried into his personal life. Not Kindell.

Protecting the targets. Particularly the one likely next in line.

With a sweep of his forearm, he cleared the desk of papers bearing his name. He slid Rhythm Jones's binder before him, pleased to note its heft. He spent about an hour and a half hunched over the desk, flipping through Rhythm's file and biting his bottom lip à la Bill Clinton in empathy mode.

Almost every character appearing in the court transcript and eyewitness testimonies linked to Rhythm was a transient or a nothing-to-lose punk who'd be tough to leverage. Druggies, pimps, low-rent dealers. It made for tough tracking. The best angle Tim could come up with was a Jones cousin, Delroy, who'd made good, graduating high school and heading off to USC on a track scholarship. Rhythm's defense attorney, in a rare moment of adequacy, had dragged the kid in as a character witness. The prosecution had tried to discredit Delroy by outing him as a lookout on a convenience-store stickup when he was twelve, a juvy transgression the DA had managed to get unsealed.

Tim slipped out of Rayner's office, assorted binders and files rising from the cradle of his hands, secured by his chin. Hurrying to his car, he ignored the parking ticket adhered to the windshield and dumped the paperwork in the trunk.

He drove over to USC, pulled aside one of the many free-roving security guards, drowned him in law-enforcement patois, and asked him to be a team player and call HQ to get a dorm-room number. The guard complied all too willingly. After relaying the information, he shook his square head, drowsy eyes dulled with either stupidity or the friction wear of walking a foot beat in South Central, and muttered, "Black kids," with equal parts lassitude and disdain.

Delroy's dorm-room door was opened by a cute, dark-skinned girl clutching a fat science textbook and wearing Delroy's track jersey like a dress. She didn't ask to see Tim's badge when he identified himself. He took note of the uneasiness that flickered across her face, her rigidly polite tone, and added impersonating an asshole white cop to the list of reasons he disgusted himself today.

Yes, this was Delroy's dorm room. No, he wasn't here. He'd gone door-to-dooring in the West Side, collecting donations for an adult-literacy program he volunteered for in South Central. He'd gone alone. He had no cell phone, and he'd left his pager behind. She didn't know where he'd started or what section of the city he was covering, but she did know he'd be back to run the football coliseum stairs at around 6:00 P.M., as he did every preseason night. Tim told her not to answer any questions about Delroy to anyone else and always to ask to see a badge before opening the door, and she'd regarded him with barely restrained annoyance until he'd left.

Outside, he called the adult-literacy program's offices, but they were closed Thursdays through Sundays, which Tim thought might have made a good joke were he in a better mood.

At Doug Kay's salvage yard, Tim traded out the BMW for a '90 Acura with a dented side and clean plates. Kay received the Beemer keys with a pleased little smile, handed Tim an Integra key on a bent paper clip, and scurried off, losing himself among cubes of metal before Tim could change his mind.

Tim spent the next two hours stopping in at hardware stores, costume shops, and pharmacies, assembling what veteran deputies and crotchety old-schoolers call a war bag. Then he went home for his gun.

When he pulled up, he saw Dray sitting at the kitchen table sipping coffee and reading the paper as she always did afternoons when she got home from the graveyard shift. He got out of the car and stood on the walk regarding her, his house, for a moment of relative calm. Mac was nowhere in sight. Ginny could have been at school.

Dray looked up, saw him standing outside momentarily intoxicated by the spell of what once was, and she was up and at the front door, ushering him in to the kitchen table as he cleared his head, self-exorcising the Ghost of Christmas Past and returning to reality like an autodefenestrated body slapping sidewalk.

"What the hell happened? Bear's called three times. He's onto you, I think."

"Yes. And in an hour and a half, he's going to know everything." Tim shot a nervous glance down the hall. "Where's Mac?"

Dray gestured at the window. At the far side of the

backyard, Mac was sitting up on the picnic table, feet on the bench, facing away from the house. Three empty bottles of Rolling Rock were lined beside him; he was working on a fourth. "He's busy sulking—got cut from SWAT today."

"Shocking."

"What went down?"

He relayed the events of the past fifteen hours, and she listened in silence, though her face spoke prolifically. He finished, and they sat together a moment.

When she studied him, he braced himself against the heat of judgment in her stare, but it was absent. Maybe she was too tired to give it. Maybe he was too tired to pick it up. Or maybe her concern had mellowed her anger into a sort of weary contemplation.

"Why the hell would they kill Rayner and Ananberg?" she said. "They didn't have to. They could've gotten those files without killing them." She pressed the skin at her temples. "Those men, who would kill just like that. Unnecessarily. For barely a motive. Those men have been watching us for months? Surveilling us with our *daughter?*"

His throat was so dry it hurt when he spoke. "Yes."

"Jesus, they put their time in to get you." Her hands balled into fists, and she thunked the table so hard her coffee cup jumped and hit the floor tile a good four feet away. In her face he saw the expression mothers of fugitives wore when he came to haul their sons away. It was a funereal expression—extrapolated loss, sorrow compounded with inevitability. She pressed the flat of her fist square against her forehead, hiding her eyes. "If you do what's right, if you come clean to protect those targets, you're going to wind up in prison," she said.

"Probably."

When she lowered her hand, four strokes of white remained on her skin where her fingers had been. "Do you feel like a hypocrite?"

He tried to gauge her anger by reading her eyes. "Yes. But I'd rather try to be right than consistent." The reason he felt as if he hadn't slept in days, he realized, was that he hadn't. He slid his hand into the empty pocket of his hip holster; he'd put the holster back on during the drive over.

Dray smiled the kind of smile that said nothing was funny. "Fowler worked on a ranch growing up, in Montana. There was a job, he said, on the slaughterhouse killing floor—a guy had to stun the cows with a prod, then cut their throats." She leaned forward on the table. "They had to rotate the job every Monday. Not because it was tough to live with. Because the men started liking it too much. They wanted their turn."

"You're saying Robert and Mitchell got a taste of something they liked?"

"I'm saying release comes in a lot of flavors, and most of them are addictive."

They studied the puddle of coffee on the linoleum.

Tim cleared his throat. "I need my gun."

"Your gun," she said, as if she were unfamiliar with the word. She rose and headed down the hall to the bedroom. Tim heard the chuck of the gun safe unlocking, and then she returned and set his .357 on the table between them as if she were up for a nice, casual game of Russian roulette.

He placed the safety-deposit key from Kindell's case binder on the table and slid it over to Dray. "I'm not going to have time to pursue this right now. And even if I did find which box this key fit, I couldn't get at the contents without a subpoena."

She picked up the key and clenched it in a fist. "It's just legwork. I'll figure out which bank, go in at lunchtime in the uniform when the managers are on break, flash badge, intimidate a junior banker into opening up." She nodded once, gravely. "You do what you have to do."

Tim felt the need to convince, to justify. "If Robert and Mitchell get on this spree," he said, "who knows when it'll end. I can't sit in a jail cell and let it go down."

"You can't play Lone Ranger–hero either. Not in good conscience."

"I won't. I'll keep disseminating information through Bear so the service and local PD will have as much as I do. Given my responsibility for this mess, I don't mind being the one on the line, in the crosshairs."

"Bear can handle it. The marshals, LAPD—they can track these guys down."

"Not like I can."

"True," she said. "True." She let out a sigh, angling it up so it puffed out her bangs. She glanced at the pistol, then at him, then away. "You have no authority behind you, Tim. No sanction of the U.S. Marshals, no weight of the Commission. It's just you now." She looked up from the coffee-cup fragments, her face holding equal parts concern and daring. "Can you be your own judge and jury?"

He took his gun from the table and holstered it on his way out.

**34** TIM GOT TO YAMASHIRO A FULL HOUR EARLY AND SUR-veilled it as best he could, in case Bear was planning to spring a trap. Rather than taking the winding, no-options road up the hill to the restaurant, Tim squeezed his car into an out-of-sight meter between two

preposterously large SUVs down on Hollywood Boulevard. He checked the area in a closing spiral, finally walking up the steep drive and drawing strange looks from the
valets who had no doubt never seen anyone arrive at the
hilltop restaurant by foot.

As always he was greeted warmly by Kose Nagura and
whisked to his and Bear's usual table overlooking the hillside Japanese gardens and the Strip below. After the waiter
came by and deposited two lemonades, Tim withdrew a
tiny brown bottle, released a thin stream into Bear's drink,
and gave it a swirl with a chopstick.

Bear arrived at five-thirty on the button, sliding into the
seat opposite Tim and gripping the small tabletop at both
sides like a giant serving platter. "You'd better give me
some answers pronto here, bud, because I'm not liking
what's adding up."

"You have the targets under protection?"

Bear spoke slowly, as if this alone held back his growing
anger and unease. "We got Dobbins in protective custody.
Rhythm and Bowrick we can't seem to find. You want to
tell me what the fuck's going on?"

"You see Rayner's?"

"Came straight from there. As ugly as you promised.
You want to tell me what the fuck is going on?"

The waiter dropped off a complimentary dish of pickled
vegetables, and Bear shooed him off without removing his
eyes from Tim.

*"Do you want to tell me what the fuck is going on?"*

A sea of heads took a tennis-match swivel, then went
back to talking and dipping toward tweezer-thin lacquered
chopsticks. Great drops of perspiration stood out on Bear's
forehead. His face looked weighty, intensely vulnerable.
Tim felt like Travis come to shoot Old Yeller.

He took a sip from his glass, braced himself, and began,

interrupted only by Bear's terse dismissals of the oversolicitous waiter. When he finished, Bear cleared his throat, then cleared it again.

Tim said, "Have some lemonade."

Bear complied. He mopped his brow with a napkin, and it came away dark with sweat. He munched a few bits of pickled vegetable, made a face, and spat them out.

Tim slid a sheet of paper toward him with carefully prepared notes. "These are all the leads I can think of, which are admittedly not many. Get after them. And find Bowrick. And Rhythm."

"News flash, Rack, but the U.S. Marshals and LAPD have different priorities in the face of all this than running down a guy like Rhythm Jones to tell him his life might be threatened. Guess what? When you push drugs and turn out girls, you're generally aware people are gunning for you. We'll visit Dumone ASAP and suss out Rayner's office. And we'll send a car by Kindell's, but I'm with you—if the Mastersons shredded his file, they ain't interested, and keeping him alive with the secret to Ginny's death rattling in his misshapen head fucks with you worse and is therefore preferable to them." He folded Tim's list into his pocket. "As for the targets, we've contacted those we can contact, but we're gonna focus on finding Eddie Davis and the Mastersons, not them."

"There's no difference."

"You gonna teach me strategy, lawman?"

"There's a team gunning for Rhythm Jones."

"Not the whole team, Rack. They're missing you." His righteousness was undercut by a piece of spinach clinging to his incisor. Tim gestured and Bear buffed it off with his napkin.

"You've known since you heard that taped 911 call what I've been doing, Bear."

Bear looked away, letting out a jerking sigh. "You've been as much a father to me as anyone's ever been—"

"You're older than me, Bear."

*"I'm talking right now, and you're listening."* Bear's anger was working its way into his face, coloring the rims of his eyes, turning his face an unhealthy white. "You were an officer of the federal courts. A law-enforcement agent of the attorney general. This is going to wreck Marshal Tannino. He loves you like family." Bear's voice was disdainful but also morose, even sorrowful. He gave off a hurt betrayal, that of an unjustly smacked dog. Tim felt his self-loathing anew in Bear's expression, and the anger, once present, bled through him until its bearing was unclear.

At the table beside them, two Hollywood agents, dressed like affluent Mormons, talked indecipherable industry babble over sashimi.

"About half a million criminal cases go through the L.A. court systems a year," Bear continued, his voice rising at a healthy clip. "Half a million. And you found what? Six you didn't like? So you're willing to shitcan the system because here and there something don't work its way through like it should? Jedediah Lane was acquitted by a jury. It was your job to protect people like him. Congratulations. You've just added your name to the proud tradition of mob violence. Revenge killings. Street justice. Lynchings." He was shaking hard enough that he spilled some of his lemonade over his knuckles when he took a sip. "You don't deserve to call yourself a former deputy."

"You're right."

"You swore you'd never be like him," Bear said. "Your father. If there was one fucking thing I knew in the world, it was that people could rise above the shit they were brewed in. I knew that because of you. I *thought* I knew that because of you."

Tim's face numbed, and he felt a sheen of moisture gloss his eyes. "I wanted to take something back. After Ginny. Do you understand that?"

"I don't agree with it. I do *not* fucking agree."

"That's not what I asked. Do you understand?"

Bear swallowed hard, his Adam's apple jerking up, then down like a piston. "Of course I understand. But that has nothing to do with what you've done. I also wanted to take something back after Ginny. I also loved her. She was my niece, practically. I wanted to shoot a trucker who was manhandling a woman in a bar where I stopped that night, the night she was killed. Guess what? I didn't. Just that simple. I fucking didn't. There is no right way to take something back like that. You just stare at it and you learn it's empty, you're empty, and that's the hard fucking painful fact of the goddamn catharsis—which is a word I'm sure you thought I didn't know—that you don't get anything *back*. Life ain't a Spiegel catalog. You just go on with that part of you missing, period, the end."

Tim started to say something, but Bear raised one hand violently. "I'm just getting started. If every father killed three men to get at who killed his daughter, where would we be? These killings of yours. Lane. Debuffier. Were they unlawful? Yes. Was there malice? Yes. Willful? Yes. Deliberate and with premeditation? Yes, yes. You're eye-to-eye with two murder ones. And don't think I'm not gonna bring you in. Right here, right now." His left cheek twitched up in a squint, physical discomfort's overture. He belched quietly into a raised fist.

"You can bring me in, Bear. Just not now."

"You don't think?"

"I need to finish the job. The Mastersons are out of control, on a rampage. I'm uniquely positioned to deal with them—I know their MO, their habits and patterns. You

need me in the field, feeding you information. I can coop-
erate—through you—with the service, with LAPD. Let's
deal. Once we reign in this . . ."—Tim took a moment to
search for the phrase—"lethal force I've helped to unleash,
I'll come back and face the music."

"Oh, sure. After all this, Tannino'll happily turn you out
on the streets to keep up with your vigilante activities.
You're a civilian now, Rack. What are you thinking?"

Though Tim already knew what Bear's answer would be,
he kept laying groundwork for later. "My cooperation, intel, ass on the line, and eventual surrender. That's what you
get. I don't care if Tannino wants the deal—you don't have
to work it out now. It's what I'm offering. It's the basis on
which I'll be working."

"No. Why should the marshal trust you now? Why
should I trust you now?"

"I'm finding my way back—to society and to what's
right. You can trust that."

"Forgive me for needing more."

"We've cut deals with mutts before."

"Can you imagine the shit Tannino would catch if things
get worse and it comes out we had you and turned you
loose? Or that we didn't come after you full steam? No
way. No deal." Bear leaned forward, his right arm across
his stomach, clutching. The cramping was just getting
started. "Give me your weapon."

"I can't do that."

"We'll have a showdown. Do you want that here, at
Kose's place?"

"I'll come in. You'll get me. You have my word. But I'm
finishing this thing."

His arm tightening across his stomach, Bear lurched forward, his elbow thunking the table, knocking over his

glass. He studied the spreading stain for a moment, then looked up at Tim, realization giving way to fury. He cross-drew with his left hand, a single, economical gesture that ended with the barrel pointed at Tim's head. "You piece of shit," Bear gasped. "You fucking mutt."

A woman shrieked across the room, but surprisingly, no-body moved. Tim scooted back in his chair and dropped his napkin on the floor. "It's just hydrogen peroxide. Don't worry—it'll break down into oxygen gas and water in your stomach."

Bear's face was awash with sweat, his voice a coarse groan squeezed through the tightening vise of his gut. His torso was spilled across the table, but his face and the muzzle were up and pointed. "So help me God, I'll shoot you before I let you leave here."

Tim kept his eyes on Bear's. He rose slowly, Bear's front sight inching up to track him, then turned and walked out of the restaurant.

**35** FRIDAY-AFTERNOON RUSH HOUR IN L.A.—A PREVIEW OF purgatory. Tim found himself mired in it en route to USC. He'd stopped by the house of Erika Heinrich, Bowrick's girlfriend, and peeked through the windows but found no one home. The only girl's room was on the west corner of the house, facing the street.

It was a well-baited trap—Bowrick would show eventually.

The more Tim lurched and braked along the 110, the more he missed his Beemer.

His Nokia vibrated, and, grateful for the reminder, he pulled it from his pocket and threw it out the window. It hit the concrete and turned to a drove of bouncing pieces.

Tim had given Bear the Nokia number, and he wasn't about to take any chances on a cell-phone trace. From here on out he'd use the Nextel, since the number was known only by the Stork, who was likely hiding under his bed about now, and Robert and Mitchell, who, as SWAT guys out of Detroit, would have no clue about cutting-edge electronic-surveillance technology.

Tim had turned over Robert's and Mitchell's Nextel numbers to Bear in case the service wanted to put the ESU geeks on them, but even if they elected to pursue this route, it would take them days to set up.

Tim called Robert and Mitchell again, but they'd both—either wisely or luckily—turned off their phones; voice mail picked up right away. Tim strained to come up with a timely and low-rent version of phone trap-and-trace that he could take advantage of despite his limited access to resources. To his advantage was his latitude of movement outside the law—he could move quicker and dirtier than Bear and the deputy marshals—but he had trouble seeing how he could get it done without a direct line to network technology and a team to move block to block with hand-held tracking units. He decided to keep trying Robert's and Mitchell's phones to ascertain whether they were still being used; if they weren't turned on, they couldn't be tracked.

From what Tim had seen, Mitchell kept his phone off out of habit; Robert was the best bet for telephone contact. It occurred to Tim that the Mastersons might be keeping their cell phones turned off because they were tinkering with electronic explosives, preparing them. It also struck him that wherever they lived, it was far enough away from

Rayner's Hancock Park house that they'd needed a phone book to find a liquor store in the area.

By the time Tim exited the freeway and made his way to Memorial Coliseum, it was close to 6:45, and he was concerned he might have missed Delroy Jones's practice altogether. He entered the embrace of the stadium, momentarily disoriented by the thickness of dusk against the immense stretches of drab concrete. He spotted a single form in a red-and-yellow nylon sweatsuit, pounding its way up the great steep columns of stadium steps. Up one column, across the top, down the next. Then the same thing all over again.

Tim retrieved a Gatorade bottle from his war bag, then sat at the top of the steps watching Delroy sweat his way up to him. He took a huge swig, relaxing as Delroy reached the top, eyed him with a streetwise scowl, and jogged across the bleacher in front of him. Tim's appearance screamed cop—it had even before he'd joined the service.

"Delroy Jones?"

Delroy did not slow. "Who wants to know?"

As Delroy hammered down the next set of steps, Tim rose calmly, walked ten feet to his right, and awaited his return. Delroy was breathing harder when he reached the top again. Tim noticed he winced slightly on his left steps, as if weathering a pulled hamstring.

"How'd you like your coach to hear about you playing lookout on a stickup?"

Never breaking stride, Delroy made a clicking noise of dismissal. "I was twelve years old, five-oh. You're gonna have to do better than that."

Across the bleachers, down the stairs. Tim walked ten more feet, set the Gatorade at his feet, and sat. Delroy was panting hard as he approached the top again.

Tim took a shot. "How about this. Present tense. I know

your cuz Rhythm has pressured you to open up the college market. A lotta rich kids here, a lotta recreation. I also know you said no, but we have pics of you two together, and we can get those in the hands of your coach. Your scholarship's coming up for renewal in, what? Four months?"

Delroy ignored him, got halfway across the bleacher, then stopped, still facing away, his shoulders heaving as he caught his breath. He walked back, ran a hand across his forehead, and flicked a spray of sweat down on the concrete. The two men glared at each other, pit bulls squaring off over a rib eye.

"Who the fuck are you?"

"I'm trying to protect your cousin."

"And I'm a Caucasian orthodontist. Nice to meet you."

Tim offered the Gatorade bottle, which Delroy ignored. "Rhythm Jones. Where can I find him?"

"He don't go by Rhythm no more. Goes by G-Smooth."

"It must be tough explaining the 'Rhythm' tattoo across his chest then, huh?" Tim sucked his teeth once, twice, a tic intended to annoy. "Now, listen Delroy, *you're* gonna have to do better than that. Don't throw me false names and bullshit leads. There's a contract on your cousin, and the hit is closing in. You're going to help me because you want to save your cousin's life, and you're going to help me because if you don't, I will grip right and squeeze hard. I'll have your rap sheet all over the *Daily Trojan*. I'll distribute photos of you and Rhythm to everyone in the athletic department, everyone in the financial-aid office. Your face next to Rhythm's infamous mug, it'll make all the white assholes who run this campus pucker. Now, what's it gonna be?"

Delroy's eyes flicked back and forth nervously. "Look, five-oh, I'm trying to train here, mindin' my own bidness.

Why don't you back off? I ain't a shot-caller. Shit, everyone interruptin' me, aksin'—" He caught himself, but Tim was already on his feet.

"Did someone else press you?"

Tim's reaction brought out an anxious twitch in Delroy's face. "Shit, man. I thought it was just a bling-bling thing, get resolved. You think those motherfuckers are gonna cap him?"

"I know they are. Did you give up an address?"

Delroy took an uneasy breath, then stepped back and pulled up his sweatshirt, as if showing off a waistband gun. Wide purple bruises had flowered across his ribs on the left side—boot marks, most likely. "Motherfuckers didn't leave me much of a choice."

Tim gunned the Acura through the streets of South Central. He turned right at the waffle and fried-chicken shack, as directed, and slowed to a crawl, counting addresses under his breath. Rhythm's stash house was blocked from view by a stucco wall, the only one on the block. Tim left the car up the street and circled back, pulling on his lead gloves. The wooden gate was unhooked, the latch resting just outside the catch. He knuckled it open.

Front door ajar. An arm in view, flat on the floor from elbow to wrist. Tim unholstered his .357, closed the gate behind him to block the view from the street, and entered the house. He moved along the right wall, gun extended, elbows locked, his shoulder brushing a wall-mounted phone by the front door. The arm belonged to an obese body he assumed was Rhythm's. It lay in the prone position, humped over a considerable belly, the head largely blown off. Residual powder burns, speckling, star-shaped entrance wound—it had been up close and personal.

It must have given Robert and Mitchell gratification to

ice a sexual predator like the one who killed Beth Ann. It must have whetted their appetite.

Farther in, a white corpse lay, also facedown, with no visible signs of violence. Tim tilted the already-stiffening body with a toe and took note of the two gunshot wounds in the chest, both high on the breastplate. Another body lay just out of view in the hall, two shots to the back—one between the shoulder blades, the other in the kidney. A scrawny black kid, no older than twenty, no taller than five-five.

Tim did a protective sweep of the rest of the house. A folding table with a scale and a couple keys of either cocaine or Southeast Asian heroin in the back room. A security camera on a tripod knocked over in the far corner. A cheesy smoked-glass mirror with a gaudy gold frame. Three heavy-duty security bars made the back door impervious to kick-ins.

A fourth corpse lay sprawled across the kitchen linoleum, Caucasian, chest opened up by a larger-caliber round. Joint body—lots of tats, strong lats triangulating a strong torso. An AK-47 lay beside him, the strap still hooked around his neck. Door muscle, from the looks of him. One of his hands held a bleating telephone, his forearm wrapped in coiled black cord.

Standing over the body, Tim closed one eye and peered through the bullet hole in the window, sighting on a burnt and deserted apartment building about 125 yards away, across the house's surprisingly expansive back lawn and an empty lot. An impressive shot. As a SWAT precision marksman, Robert probably worked with a McMillan .308 caliber, police model.

Tim returned to the living room and examined the fallen security camera. The tape was missing—no surprise. Tim followed the snake of the electrical cord to a wall outlet behind a minirefrigerator. When Tim opened the refrigerator door, a puff of humid, rotting air sighed out at him. Room temp. Save for a fringe of mold on the plastic shelf, the fridge was empty. Tim pulled the unit out from the wall and swapped the plug for that of a lamp he retrieved from across the room. He clicked the switch. Nothing. A dead outlet.

Dummy security camera.

Tim scanned the room, his eyes resting on the wall-mounted mirror. He walked over and pressed the tip of his front pistol sight against the glass. There was no break between the sight and its reflection. He tugged at the mirror, but it didn't give, so he shattered the glass, gunstock leading his gloved hand.

Inside the small cave cut into the drywall and lathing, a handheld video lens stared out at him curiously. He slid the tape from the unit before returning it to the jagged mouth of the mirror. On his way out, he crouched over Rhythm's body, examining what was left of his famous face.

He would have liked to have felt sorrow.

He drove for fifteen minutes before finding a Circuit City. He went for a TV/VCR combo because they were displayed in the back corner. He rewound the tape about an hour, then fast-forwarded the grainy black-and-white video. The angle covered most of the living room and the front door; the sound was surprisingly good.

Rhythm was bopping around the room, belly jiggling, talking into his cell phone and gesticulating madly with his hand. The doorman whom Tim had found supine in the kitchen was standing perfectly still at the door, arms crossed, one hand clasping the other wrist, AK slung over one shoulder. The other Caucasian emerged from the back room toting two keys, the scrawny black teenager at his side. The kid slapped five with Rhythm and disappeared into the bathroom near the rear door. When white boy held out a brick in offering, Rhythm stuck a fat hand into the bag and ran a powdered fingertip across his gums.

The shrill ring of the telephone interrupted an incipient conversation beatifying Biggie Smalls. The doorman grabbed the wall-mounted phone by the front door. "Yeah?"

The phone continued to ring. He held the receiver away from his head and glanced at it, then trudged into the kitchen.

"That damn phone broke already?" proclaimed Rhythm. He was half dancing now, bending deep at the knees, lost in shtick. "I just bought the motherfucker."

Tim noted shadows moving beneath the front door, approaching from the knob side.

The doorman disappeared from view. The mike barely picked up the fragile sound of tinkling glass. The sniper bullet.

Then the front door flew open, the handle punching into the opposing drywall and sticking. Mitchell stormed in, heavy off the kick, both hands tight on his .45.

Rhythm stopped bouncing. White boy's hands, still clutching the bags of coke, shot up and out wide. Without hesitation, Mitchell double-tapped him, and he moved back in a half stagger, half slide, bouncing off the bathroom door and falling facedown like a plank. The bags of coke he'd dropped at first impact slapped the floor with chalky poofs.

His too-wide face rearranged in an expression of blind rage, Rhythm lunged forward at Mitchell, his old-school Nikes slipping on the spilled cocaine just as Mitchell swung the sights. Rhythm's legs went out from under him, and he fell forward, three hundred–plus pounds of flesh colliding with dingy floorboards.

Mitchell was across the room in a flash, sliding on a lead knee, his other leg bent and trailing, elbows flared, both hands locked on the .45, which seemed to coast through the air until it stopped against Rhythm's forehead.

Rhythm grunted once, loud, and quivered, beached-whale immobile. His eyes rolled up, wide and fearful, crescents of white cupping the bottoms of his irises.

"Rhythm," Mitchell growled down at him, "meet the blues."

His arms jerked with recoil, and Rhythm's head pulsed once and threw spatter. Mitchell was up, moving backward to the door, gun covering the room.

The bathroom door, jarred from white boy's collision, continued to creak open. Mitchell's head and pistol locked on something, probably the scrawny black kid inside. A second later the kid slowly emerged, pants unbuttoned, arms held up, showing off his empty palms.

The kid tamped down his evident terror. "I didn't see nothin'. I'm gonna turn around, and I'm gonna walk away. Real slow."

He turned and walked out of the camera's view, down the far hall. Mitchell watched him go. The .45 dipped, then snapped back up and fired twice.

"Good for you, bud," Mitchell said.

A faint screech announced a vehicle pulling up to the curb. Mitchell grabbed the dummy security tape, backed up, and disappeared out the front door. His entire appearance had taken less than two minutes.

The rev of the unseen vehicle rose and died.

Tim hit "stop" on the VCR and popped the tape. When he turned, a young salesclerk, maybe seventeen, was at the end of the aisle, her eyes on the now-blank screen. She opened her mouth, but no sound came out. Her hands gripped and pulled at each other, pressed against her stomach.

She and Tim faced each other for an excruciating moment.

"I'm sorry," Tim said.

He left her standing there, her mouth working on nothing.

■ The back door, featuring a panoply of graffitied street tags, had been kicked in so often it sat crooked in the frame. When Tim shoved it, it swung open, leaving the doorknob and a surrounding patch of wood stuck to the jamb.

The apartment building smelled of urine and ash. Part of the interior had been burned out, but the structure still held. Where the flames had burned hottest near the entrance, a semicylindrical gap reached up all four stories to the roof. A heap of human feces awaited Tim on the stairs to the second floor. Each floor had three rooms to the rear, facing the stash house. Keeping his flashlight pointed at the floor, Tim moved through them, searching out the best angle on Rhythm's kitchen window over a hundred yards away. A wrecking-ball crane in the deserted lot broke the center rooms' views to Rhythm's window, so Robert would have been forced to chose right or left. The fourth floor provided too elevated an angle, giving very little vantage into Rhythm's kitchen, so Tim returned to the third floor and gave it a closer perusal.

He knew he wouldn't be so lucky as to find a shell, since .308s were manual action—one had to jack the bolt to kick out the shell after firing. Robert had fired only a single shot, Tim assumed—no need to fuss with the bolt at all. And even if Robert had reloaded, he was too much of a professional to have left anything behind, especially a .30-caliber shell with a nice thumb spread across the brass.

Nothing caught Tim's eye in the two end rooms on the

third floor. He thought about how quickly Robert had showed up at Rhythm's in the getaway vehicle less than two minutes. The second floor would have put him that much closer to his vehicle downstairs. Tim headed down another flight and crouched in the doorway of the room on the right to get a better angle with his flashlight. The pan of dust near the window, darkened with stray ash, was scuffed up in two points.

A bipod.

He eased over to the window, sat where Robert had sat, and breathed awhile. He thought about what he knew.

If given a choice, Robert took the sniper position offset right from a frontal view.

He preferred the tactical advantage of the elevated position.

He used a bipod. Sitting stance versus prone.

Mitchell liked a knob-side approach on a kick-in.

They weren't leaving behind witnesses.

Tim closed his eyes, thought about the shot, the dash downstairs, the quick drive to the house to pick up Mitchell. He turned the Masterson strategy over in his mind, working at it like a tough knot.

Robert and Mitchell knew they didn't stand a chance on a dynamic entry with the AK-47-toting doorman there and waiting. All windows to the front of the stash house were blocked by the stucco wall. The only sniper angle was on the kitchen window.

How do you move the muscle to the kitchen?

The doorman had picked up the front telephone, his usual telephone, and found it broken. He'd had to move to the kitchen to get the second-nearest phone, which had brought him into the crosshairs.

Not just a lucky break.

Tim ...ught of Mitchell's entry, how he'd moved into the ro... confidently, aggressively. Not even a split-second hitch ... get a read on the space.

R...ert and Mitchell had broken in earlier, disabled the fro... phone, and gotten the lay of the pad. The stash h...se's back door was triple-barred, so they'd picked the front-door lock.

Tim felt a tingle of sweat springing up on the back of his neck when he thought about what that meant.

He walked downstairs, around the block, through the front gate of the stash house. The door remained slightly ajar, as he'd left it. He squatted and eyeballed the door-knob lock—a Medeco double cylinder, six tumblers waiting inside to ruin your day. There was no way Robert and Mitchell could get through a lock like that without help from a pro.

Tim ran a gloved fingertip over the keyway, and it came away shiny with spray lubricant.

# 36

**"THE DEAL'S ON." TIM LEANED AGAINST THE PAY-PHONE** interior. He'd contacted Bear through the operations desk. "I'm still offering my cooperation. I don't need yours."

"Good, because you're not getting it." Bear's voice sounded cracked and dehydrated. "Excuse my irritation, ...ut I just finished *vomiting*."

"You can be furious with me later—and you'll be right But for now grab a pen and listen." Tim talked quickly, ...ing him to the mess awaiting him at Rhythm's stash ... and to the Stork's involvement. The Stork would be better hidden than a Nazi in an Argentine forest; he wanted the service on it full bore.

When he finished, Bear said, "Listen. I'll deal with you, like this, but you gotta understand something. Tannino ain't gonna play ball on this one. He wants you, and the boys are tracking hard. I'm Tannino's deputy. When he says fetch, I fetch."

"I get it," Tim said. "Play it both ways."

The faint beat of a one-note chuckle. "No other way I can help you."

"So help me."

A long pause. "Not much in the way of evidence at Rayner's house. His office had a bunch of surveillance shit on you—as you know—but not much else. Creepy to look at it. Speaking of, I didn't know you had anxiety attacks after Croatia."

"They weren't att—" Tim took a deep breath. "C'mon, Bear. What else?"

"Kindell was safe and sound. He didn't want to come in—doesn't trust police custody, imagine that—and we couldn't really justify it anyway, as he's not looking like a target. And the big news—Dumone suck-started his revolver this afternoon in his hospital room."

Though he'd braced himself for the news, it still took Tim a moment to speak again. "Is Tannino taking the case public?"

A long pause. "Tomorrow night."

"How much of it? Am I gonna make the news?"

"*That* I will not answer." Tim heard Bear hawk up some phlegm and spit. "I got work to do."

"Fine. Do me one more favor."

"I think we're well over the limit already."

"Ananberg had a Rhodesian Ridgeback. Damn fine dog. He's probably trapped in her apartment right now, starving and full of piss. If the investigators find him, they'll dump him at the pound. Go pick him up. You need the company anyway."

Bear grunted and hung up.

Tim tried Robert's and Mitchell's Nextels again—immediate voice mail—then called the Stork and got a message saying the number had been disconnected. The Stork was too technologically savvy even to have the old Nextel in service; he'd shit-canned it already and moved on to a new phone.

The freeway was surprisingly empty at 11:30 P.M. Wisps of fog collected around Tim's headlights. He exited and parked nearly four blocks from Erika Heinrich's on the off chance someone else—deputy or hit man—was sitting on the house. It took him half an hour, but he cleared the two surrounding blocks, checking out parked cars, roofs, and bushes.

Erika's bedroom window was not only uncurtained, it was open.

Kids.

Tim crept to the sill, just beneath one of the outswung shutters, and eased up for a look. Erika lay prone on a bright yellow comforter, flipping through a glossy magazine, legs bent up behind her, sandal dangling from a cocked toe. Alone.

Bowrick was a smart kid—he'd disappeared convincingly once before. Maybe he had a second safe house. If so, Tim hoped it was as well hidden as his first.

Watching Erika on her bed flipping pages and humming to herself, Tim vowed to find Bowrick before Mitchell or Robert could put a hole in his head that matched the one they'd left in Rhythm's. It wasn't that he had felt a softening of his disdain for Bowrick—though he had—but because he could not watch a seventeen-year-old girl in the

safety of her own bedroom and not want the world to ad-
here to its obligations to her. Admirable piousness from a
former deputy–cum–Peeping Tom.

If he talked to her, she'd convey his appearance to
Bowrick, who would steer clear of her house. Tim wanted
to see Bowrick, to convince him to leave the state or go into
police custody. He didn't want to scare him farther afield in
the city, where the Mastersons might flush him out.

On the drive home, Tim listened to the radio to see
whether there was any breaking news about the Commission or himself. There was not. The service would guard
their information, deploying it when strategic. The command post in the Federal Building would probably go full
steam through the night, with everyone from Tannino to the
assistant U.S. Attorney to Analytical Support Unit reps lost
in a haze of coffee fumes and speculation.

His building was deathly silent. Off the lobby Joshua
started humming to himself with vibrato and shuffling
through some papers in his ersatz office. Tim paused about
ten feet from the door, eyeing the keys on their pegboard
hooks behind Joshua's desk. Most of the apartments had
been rented, but Tim took note of the few remaining keys:
401, 402, 213, 109.

Joshua looked up and waved, a simple raise of his hand
that Tim returned. He wondered if Bear had told the truth
about the press conference or if Tannino was going to leak
the news early.

"Any good true-crime stories on TV?"

Joshua shrugged. "They're regurgitating the same pap
about Jedediah Lane."

On the elevator ride up, Tim mused on the gloom that
moved through buildings such as this. People either running from something or on their way down in the world.
And Joshua was the gatekeeper; he exhibited not only sad-

ness but the morose authoritativeness derived from extensive exposure to sadness. Like a mortician. Like a cop.

Once upstairs Tim took apart his doorknob and spread the parts on a towel before him. Sitting back on his heels, he dialed yet again and pressed the Nextel to his cheek as he worked.

He got a ring.

"So," Mitchell said.

"So," Tim said.

A long pause, broken only by the faint sound of Mitchell's breathing and the rustle of his mustache against the receiver.

"You've been keeping busy," Tim said.

"We have a plan for this city. Always have. And we're not letting the Rayners and Ananbergs stand in the way anymore."

"Clearly." Tim waited but got no response. "You and Robert cut quite a wake." Mentioning the Stork would dull a possible tactical advantage. "I saw Rhythm. Or what's left of him."

The beat of silence gave away Mitchell's surprise. "You wouldn't be coming after us, would you, Rackley? We were gonna cut you a break, leave you be. Part of us figures we owe you."

"I also saw the three other guys you killed—"

"Crack dealers and gunrunners."

"—including the kid you shot in the back."

"Oh, come on. Can you really tell me a kid hanging out in a crack house with Rhythm Jones would ever have been anything but a burden to society?"

"Probably not. But, you see, you can't punish someone *before* they commit a crime. The Constitution's quite specific about that."

"Don't wrap yourself in the flag. We've seen what you've done, you fucking hypocrite."

"I've wised up."

"Yeah? To what?"

"Punishment is not justice. Vengeance is not a way to grieve. And whatever justice is, it isn't ours to administer."

"Maybe not. But I'll tell you this—something crossed over in me when I saw that girl in Debuffier's basement. When I held her in my arms, watched her die. Well, we're done with it. We're done with school shooters and child molesters and terrorists. There are more people behind bars in this country than who live in the entire state of Hawaii. We're losing the war, my friend, in case you haven't noticed, and Robbie and I are gonna launch a counterassault. We're gonna put the plan into overdrive. And we don't need votes or case history or any of that bullshit."

"That was never the deal."

"Never the deal? You're the one who broke up our party. *You* defaulted on your responsibility, your obligation to the Commission. We voted on Bowrick. We found him guilty. The kill clause, Rack, or don't you remember? It goes into effect the instant a member of the Commission breaks any protocol. Who broke the rules first? Who broke protocol by not executing Bowrick as we'd ruled?"

"I did."

"You bet your ass you did. So now anything goes. Our agenda moves forward with you dead or alive."

A jiggle of the screwdriver, and Tim removed the latch bolt from the doorknob assembly. "Anything goes? Including shredding Kindell's file?"

A chuckle. "Yup. We offered to help you with that motherfucker. We could have found out who was in on it with him and cleaned them both up. You could have been on board with us. But, no, you were too good for us. So it only makes sense you wouldn't want any part of that case binder now. Hell, you don't want to dirty your hands with that, Your Honor."

Mitchell shifted the phone, and Tim strained to make out any background noise but could not. The ensuing silence had the air of a standoff.

"You never answered my question," Mitchell said.

Tim fitted the last puzzle piece of the altered doorknob in place. "Yes, I'm coming after you. Here's another answer: Yes, I'm going to find you."

Tim snapped the phone shut and set it down. He reinserted the knob without its latch bolt back into the front door. Though it looked perfectly ordinary, it was now just a freestanding core of metal, unattached to the jamb. He wedged a wooden doorstop tight beneath the gap, driving the end gently with a hammer so the solid-core door had no give or sway within the frame. Countermeasures against a battering ram.

He'd thought about picking up a motion sensor, but it would have been nearly impossible to hide in the bareness of the hallway. He made a note to look for a small IR unit he could angle beneath the door gap. He'd lay the beam diagonally to the knob side of the door, the side from which Mitchell preferred to pivot on a kick-in.

His window screen popped out easily. His fire escape looked down directly on the wide alley where backup cars would most likely be positioned to catch him in the event of a raid. He climbed silently down one level and stood staring into the apartment below his. Unlike Tim's unit, it had a distinct bedroom and living room; the latter and a bathroom faced the escape. Putting his face to the living-room window, he noticed that the inside latch had a built-in lock. The bathroom pane was opaque, so he couldn't see the inside mechanism, but the window didn't budge under pressure.

The second-floor living room was equally secure, but the bathroom window had been inched open to let the room air. Tim slid it the rest of the way. No screen. He leaped up, grabbing the bars of the fire-escape landing above, and eased himself through the window. The toilet provided a nice step down to the cheap linoleum.

He eased the bathroom door open and stood, regarding the two bodies sleeping side by side in the master bed. His footsteps to the bedroom door were completely silent. He didn't exhale until he reached the living room. The front doorknob was the same as his had been before he'd altered it—standard Schlage single-cylinder lock. He thumbed the embedded button until it popped out, then opened the door and stepped into the hall. The hall ran north-south—both end windows looked out onto busy streets. The stairwell was located at the north end.

Tim moved to 213, down three doors on the far side of the hall. He picked the lock quickly, not concerned about sound since he knew the apartment wasn't rented. The empty room, like Dumone's apartment, smelled of stale carpet. An amoeba stain in the far corner, the size of a garbage-can lid, might have been blood.

Tim walked to the window. The abbreviated fire-escape ladder ended six feet above an alley too narrow to accommodate a car. Ten yards north, another lane between buildings darted west.

Tim left, keeping the front door unlocked, and took the stairs down. He walked to the corner phone booth, flipping a quarter on the way. It came up heads four times in a row. He slotted it and called Mason Hansen. Tim had worked with him closely on several cases when Hansen had been a security specialist in the subpoena group for Sprint Wireless, and he'd kept in touch ever since Hansen had made the move to Nextel last October.

"Hello?" Hansen sounded worried, his voice thin and sleep-cracked.

"Is this line secure?"

"Jesus, Rack, call me at work tomorrow."

"Is this line secure?"

"Yes. Christ, it's my home number, I hope so. Are you back on the job already? I thought you took leave after the shooting." Hansen whispered something to his stirring wife, and then Tim heard him walking into the other room.

"Are you on a cordless?"

"Yes, I—"

"Pick up a landline."

"What the hell is going on?"

"Just do it."

Various clickings. "All right. Now tell me what's going on."

"If I gave you a phone number, could you go back and pinpoint what localized cell sites it's been tapping in to the network through?"

"Do you have a warrant?"

"Yes, I have a warrant. That's why I'm calling you at home at three in the morning."

"Back off the sarcasm. This seems sketchy."

"Not for now. For now you're just answering questions."

"Well, the answer to your question is no. Do you have any idea how much data that would be? We'd have to keep records of the location of every cell phone at every moment in the entire nation."

"If you can't get it done retroactively, then how about in the future? If I gave you a number, could you pinpoint the cell-phone location then?"

"Not unless you flash me a paper with a judge's signature and we do the whole deal. Handheld units, mobile teams in the field—you know the routine."

"I don't have access to those kinds of resources. Not on this one."

"What are you working?"

"I can't talk about it." Tim allowed himself a deep exhale. "I've been trying two numbers all day: 310-505-4233 and -4234. I just got through to the first, so I know the phone is on, right now, sending locating bursts to ID itself to the network. You're saying that does us no good?"

"I'm saying that does us no good unless you deploy a full-force *authorized* investigation. That's not a favor I can pull out of a hat, even if I was willing to."

Tim tried to dissipate his frustration and had a hard time of it. "Can you identify the cell site an incoming call came in through?"

"We don't have the technology in place for that. Incoming calls are free on Nextel, so the system records on them are less precise. But we *can* put a tracer on outgoing calls, since those are logged by Billing. See what cell sites they're pinging. We use it sometimes to track fraud charges. But it's not actively regulated—we don't have the manpower. Once we start it up, it spits out an update every six hours, and I can't throw a wrench into that program without express clearance from above."

"I can't keep on top of the guy by myself. Especially on a six-hour delay. That's why I called him now. Late at night I figure he's bedded down at his primary location."

"Well, starting tomorrow, I can give you his first-and-last."

First call in the morning, last call at night. Usually made from the bedroom or close to it. Guys on the run don't take the time to install landlines.

"Can you do anything more to-the-minute?"

"Not unless you give me more. Why didn't you call me earlier? We could have gotten on the outgoing calls."

"I didn't get how the technology worked. Plus, I wanted to ascertain that at least one of the cell phones was active."

"What, before you bothered me?" Hansen laughed. "Call me tomorrow, you bastard. At the office."

The walk from the corner seemed longer than a block.

Tim rode the elevator up and used a pen through the gap beneath the door to push the stop back. Once inside he took a quick spin through the TV channels. KCOM ran a report regarding the ongoing Lane and Debuffier investigations but made no mention of recent developments.

Tim called his own old Nokia number and accessed his messages. Dray, worried. Two hang-ups—probably Bear or Marshal Tannino.

He reached Dray at home. She sounded tense and a bit breathless. "You're all right?" Her voice cracked, just slightly, but he heard it.

"Yes," he said. "Robert and Mitchell know now. You have to be careful. Keep an eye out for trouble."

"I always do."

"I don't think they'd come after you—it's not their MO—but you shouldn't take any chances."

"Agreed. You on the trail tomorrow?"

"First thing."

"Check in and watch your ass."

"I will."

They hung up.

Tim sat and considered how to attack the case in the morning. The Stork was the weakest link—he was the one most likely to sell out to save his own ass, if Tim could find him and apply pressure. Tim thought of the receipt he'd noticed crumpled into the cup holder of the van the Stork had rented. *Daniel Dunn.* VanMan Rental Agency.

A solid lead, unless the Stork had planted the slip of paper there for Tim to find. Purposeful misdirection seemed unlikely, as Tim had found the receipt just prior to the Debuffier hit, when the Commission was less openly contentious.

He'd get on it first thing in the morning.

Exhaustion hit him all at once, as if it had been saving itself for an ambush. He hadn't slept in nearly forty-five hours, and the brief alcohol-clouded slumber he'd gotten then, curled on Ginny's bed, had been less than refreshing.

He lay on his mattress, examining the cottage-cheese ceiling. It reminded him of fresh-burned flesh. His thoughts pulled him back to Ginny on the coroner's table, to the sight he'd beheld when he'd drawn back the hospital-blue sheet, to the sound the sheet had made being peeled.

There were more pleasant images he could have fallen asleep to, but then, he didn't have a choice.

**37** HE WAS UP AT FIRST LIGHT, AN OLD RANGERS HABIT that reemerged in high-stress times. On the KCOM morning news, a less attractive and less ethnic reporter than Yueh carried the story of a double homicide in Hancock Park. William Rayner, of course, was mentioned by name, Ananberg described as a "young female teaching assistant." Authorities were, predictably, "baffled"—Tanninospeak for get-your-cameras-out-of-my-boys'-faces-and-let-them-do-their-jobs.

After showering, Tim flipped through the phone book and found the sole listing for VanMan Rental Agency. It was over in El Segundo, a few miles from the airport.

He located it in an industrial stretch, held tight in the corner of a moderately busy intersection. The parking lot extended over a half acre, the office itself standing at the front near the sidewalk, small and functional, like a bait shack. Through the high chain-link fence, Tim saw row after row of vans of all types.

Sitting in the car, he lost the hip holster, double-wrapping rubber bands around the grip of his .357 and slipping it in his waistband. Then he retrieved a jacket from the backseat. He pulled a few flex-cuffs from his war bag and coiled them in his pocket.

When he slid open the glass door and stepped up into the office, he felt the floorboards give slightly under his weight. A portly man in a yellow oxford shirt sat examining his schedule, one chubby finger tracing over the free Bank of America calendar pinned up on the cheap paneling behind the high front counter. He turned at the sound of the sliding door, his cheeks rosy, his bare scalp thinly veiled by a comb-over that had probably lost its conviction about the same time as the Carter administration.

"Stan the Van Man at your service." He rose and offered Tim a soft and slightly sweaty hand.

"Big shop you have here," Tim said. "You've got, what, fifty vans?"

"Sixty-three up and running, four in the shop." He beamed with pride.

Probably the owner, probably not the full-time front counterman. Good.

Tim searched the small office interior. A sun-faded Disney tourist poster curling out from its tacks on the wall showed a small girl astride Mickey's shoulders in front of Sleeping Beauty's castle, just as Bear had carried Ginny last July through the very same stretch of park. Several wood-framed photos on the rear desk showed off a cheerful, pudgy family; even the dachshund could have stood to pay Jenny Craig a visit. One shot showed the Van Man family gathered before a decorated Christmas tree wearing green-and-red sweaters. Everyone looked excessively pleasant.

A bribe would probably not go over well.

A messy Rolodex sat at the counter's edge, the category cards sticking up in white plastic. AIRPORT. BUSINESS-TO-BUSINESS. INDUSTRIAL. TOUR GROUPS. TRAVEL AGENTS.

"I'm a travel agent—Tom Altman," Tim said. "We've spoken a few times . . . ?"

"Oh, you probably spoke to my guy, Angelo. I'm only here Saturdays, holding down the fort."

"That's right, Angelo rings a bell. Well, listen, I booked a van for a family to head down to Disneyland—"

"Disneyland. Our most common destination. Nothing like seeing a family get off the plane from North Dakota or Ohio, load up in one of my babies, and head on down to Mousetown." His grin, genuine and untroubled, made Tim envious.

"Must be gratifying."

"Mine drag me down there at least twice a year. You have kids yourself?" His smile lost a few watts at Tim's expression.

Tim's throat clicked on a dry swallow. "No." He forced a grin. "The old lady's been pushing lately, if you know what I mean."

"Believe me, friend, I know that tune." He winked and elbow-pointed at the framed pictures behind him. "I know it five times over."

Tim joined Stan's hearty laugh as best he could.

"So, Tom Altman, what can I help you with?"

"Well, I was driving by, saw your sign, and remembered I had a client I hooked up with your racket here who never ended up paying me my booking fee. It's not a huge amount of money, but it's been happening to me more and more lately. I was wondering if you wouldn't mind telling me the total amount of the rental so I could send him a bill?"

"That shouldn't be a problem." Stan slid an immense book that looked like a jail ledger over in front of him. "Name and date?"

Tim couldn't remember if the Stork had also driven the van to the Commission meeting the night before the Debuffier execution. "Daniel Dunn. February 21."

"Let's see. . . ." Stan's tongue poked out of his mouth slightly as he scanned down the enormous page. "Don't see it."

"Try the twenty-second."

"Here we are. He rented out one of my Econoline E-350s. He had it back before eight. That's $62.41 for the day." He smiled, again with pride. "Here at VanMan, we log every cent, every inch."

"You charge mileage? We take a slightly higher booking fee for charges over a hundred bucks."

"No mileage charge unless they exceed seventy miles a day. And let's see. Odometer was at 45,213 when Dunn picked it up. . . ." His tongue emerged again, along with a calculator he pulled from an overstuffed breast pocket. He poked at the keys with the end of a well-chewed pencil. "Fifty-seven miles. Sorry, friend."

"I remember he rented another van first, but he brought it back because it gave off a rattle."

"It sometimes happens," Stan said, a bit defensively. "Rattles are tough."

"Well, maybe he put on more mileage with that van, pushed the total over a hundred."

"I doubt it if he traded it in."

"Would you mind checking for me?"

Stan's stare took on a bit of suspicion.

"I'm sorry, things are just kind of tough right now in the travel-agency business, what with the Internet and everything. I can use every cent I can pick up right now." Tim figured a guy who kept his records in a jail ledger probably hated computers.

Stan gave a little nod. His puffy finger scanned down the page, then back up. "Here it is. Six miles." He gave an exaggerated frown. "Sorry."

"That's all right. You helped me clear up some paperwork anyway."

They shook hands again. "Thanks for the business," Stan said.

"Sure thing."

Tim sat in his car for a moment, figuring. The Stork had arrived with the van at Debuffier's the morning of the hit. The Stork had probably picked up the van, then returned home to load up his black bag of tech gear. He probably hadn't taken the bag with him to pick up the van; it was conspicuous as hell, particularly since the Stork could barely lift it himself. He would have parked his own car far away from the rental office so no one could ID it later, and Tim couldn't imagine him leaving his beloved and priceless trinkets unattended in his trunk in this part of town while filling out bullshit paperwork.

*I even took back the first van they rented me because it gave off a distinctive rattle.*

An obsessive perfectionist like the Stork would have turned the van around at the first sound. Why had it taken him three miles to hear the rattle?

Because he was going somewhere else, completing a shorter round-trip. Like driving home to pick up his black bag.

Then he'd returned to VanMan and switched rentals before heading to Debuffier's.

Six miles.

Three miles each way to the Stork's house.

Three miles from VanMan Rental Agency.

Tim started driving in a widening spiral, looking for everything and nothing, recalling what he knew about the Stork. A pharmacy $R_x$ sign in a strip mall caught his eye, and he pulled into the lot, passing the usual suspects—Blockbuster, Starbucks, Baja Fresh.

He pictured the Stork's round face, his sunburned scalp and flat nose. *Not that it's any of your business, but it's called Stickler's syndrome.*

The Stork took plenty of prescription meds, but, in Tim's experience, patient-confidentiality issues, DEA security, and his own lack of contacts in the field made tracing drug records next to impossible. Plus, the Stork was wise enough to be exceedingly careful about how he acquired his drugs. It was doubtful he'd be so foolish as to use a nearby pharmacy, if he used a pharmacy at all.

Tim closed his eyes.

The Stork's house was likely within a three-mile radius of where Tim sat.

*A connective-tissue disorder that affects the tissue surrounding the bones, heart, eyes, and ears.*

Somewhere an optometrist had to have a file containing the Stork's lens prescription, but again the Stork would know not to leave telling records anywhere near his house. Plus, his glasses looked as if they hadn't been updated since the sixties.

Tim reversed his thoughts, considering the banal, the seemingly harmless. What are activities people do near their home? Which of these leave records?

Grocery shopping. Post office. Library.

Weak. Difficult. Maybe.

Tim opened his eyes again, gripping the wheel in frustration. Across the lot the yellow-and-blue sign caught his eye. He felt a quick surge as something in his mind crossed over, connected.

*Now and then I'll rent black-and-white movies when I can't sleep.*

He got out, his step quickening as he approached Blockbuster. The stenciling on the door said they were open until midnight, but the classic-movie section was anemic at best. Even Tim, hater of old movies, had seen most of the twenty or so black-and-white videos leaning on the shelves.

The acne-crusted kid at the counter was wearing his visor backward and sucking a Blow Pop.

"What's the best place to rent old black-and-white movies around here?"

"I don't know, man. What do you want to watch those for? We just got the new *Lord of the Rings*." The Blow Pop had stained the kid's mouth green.

"Is there a manager here?"

"Yeah, man. I'm it."

"Would you mind suggesting another video-rental store around here?"

The kid shrugged. A passing customer with an abundance of facial piercings leaned on the counter, chewing her lip. "You an old-movie nut? Go check out Cinsational Videos. With a 'cin' like in 'cinema,' get it?"

The manager removed his Blow Pop and brayed laughter. "Sounds like a porn shop."

"It's the only place around here for that stuff. They don't got it, you gotta head up to the West Side, like to Cinefile or Vidiots or somewhere."

Tim thanked her and asked for directions, which she explained with dramatic gestures and clanking jewelry.

Six blocks over, two down, on the left. Tim parked up

the street. A quiet area, mostly apartments. The store, a stand-alone square building, was set back from the street behind four slanted parking spaces and a streetlamp. Glass front door, windows cluttered with posters—a lot of Cary Grant and Humphrey Bogart. The hanging sign was flipped to OPEN. Someone had Magic Marker–ed in the times; on Mondays through Saturdays, the store didn't close until 1:00 A.M. The late hours matched the Stork's inadvertent description and would likely necessitate a security camera inside.

The front door knocked hanging chimes when Tim entered. A kid with movie-star looks sat on a stool, engrossed in a video playing on a nineteen-inch TV on the counter in front of him. No customers.

Tim glanced above the counter and found the security camera—cheap Sony model from the eighties, run on VHS tapes. It hung from a ceiling bracket, angled across the counter at the front door. *Glass* front door. And visible through it were the two center parking spaces, most likely where someone would park late at night.

"Someone called me earlier in the week, said something about a problem with your security camera. I wanted to take a look."

"On a Saturday?" The toothpick the kid had been working in his mouth bobbed with his words, his eyes never leaving the screen. Clint Eastwood gritted his teeth, scowled, and shot through Eli Wallach's noose.

Tim took note of the narrow door behind the stool—probably a small office. Above the knob was what looked to be an autolocking double-cylinder, requiring a key on both sides.

"Yeah, well, my crew's been slammed lately. I wanted to see what the problem was so they'll know to bring any necessary parts next week."

"Necessary parts? Like what? I installed the thing myself. It's working fine."

Tim's rising irritation was directed as much at himself as at the kid. With a younger worker, he should have played the authoritative angle, impersonating a police officer or a deputy marshal. But now that he was committed, he couldn't exactly back up and start over.

"Well, the owner called me last week and asked me to come by. I might as well make sure everything's okay."

The kid shifted on the stool, his eyes leaving the screen for the first time. He looked obstinate and mistrustful. "My dad never told me about anyone coming by. He would've."

Tim raised his hands as if to say What the hell and turned to leave. When he reached the door, he threw the lock and flipped the sign so it read CLOSED.

The kid had gone back to his movie, but he sensed Tim's presence and looked up. He caught sight of the front-door sign, and his hand darted beneath the counter and came up with a dinky .22. Tim closed fast, his left hand sweeping out, catching the gun at the barrel and angling it away from both of them. His right hand pinned back his jacket, revealing the .357 tucked in his waistband.

They were frozen together, motionless, Tim's gun revealed but not drawn, the other weapon pointed between NEW RELEASES and FRANK CAPRA.

Tim braced for the gunshot, but none came.

The kid was breathing hard, a spill of blond hair down across his right eye.

"Don't do anything," Tim said, his voice dead calm. "I'm as nervous as you are."

After another moment he twisted the .22, slowly, and the kid released it. Tim slid out the cartridge, cleared the bullet from the chamber, and handed the gun back to him.

"Step back from the counter, please. Thank you." Tim let his jacket fall back over his gun and walked around to the other side. He patted the kid down gently, using his knuckles. "What's your name?"

"Sam."

"All right, Sam. I'm not going to hurt you, and I'm not going to rob you. I just need to get my hands on your security tapes from the past few weeks. Could you please open that office door? Thank you."

Between a tiny desk and a large, lined wastepaper basket sat a cabinet with a row of security VHS tapes, marked by date. Above the cabinet a *Sunset Boulevard* one-sheet, probably hiding a safe, fluttered with the breeze from the AC vent.

"Why are there two tapes for each date?"

Sam was trembling a bit. "They only fit eight hours on each, so we split them, day and night. We recycle them every month or so."

"All right, Sam. I'm going to borrow the night tapes. Is that okay?" He waited for Sam to nod.

"Shit, man, if that's all you want, you can keep them. Just get out of here."

"Okay. In a second. Will you help me put them into this bag? This one here? Thank you."

They silently loaded the tapes into a plastic wastepaper bag, then Tim stepped back, fisting it like a cartoon robber. He pulled the toothpick from the kid's mouth, turned him around, and cinched a flex-cuff around his wrists.

Pulling out his Nextel, Tim dialed 911. "Yes, hello, I've accidentally locked myself in the back room of Cinsational Videos in El Segundo, and I'm trapped. Can you please send help?"

He stepped out into the store proper, shut the door behind him, then jammed the toothpick into the keyhole and snapped it off. He pulled the tape from the security camera overhead. On his way past the counter, he paused, the movie credits catching his eye. He counted out four hundreds and laid them on the floor behind the counter, then unhooked the VCR and tucked it under one arm.

He hurried nonchalantly to his car and drove away, Cinsational's CLOSED sign peering out after him.

Back in his apartment, Tim watched tape after tape on fast forward, a process more tedious than time-consuming. The tapes were color and surprisingly good quality, providing a clear angle encompassing the counter and front door.

He lucked out on the fifth tape, February 4 at 12:53 A.M. Nearly forty minutes passed without a single customer, then a car pulled up and took one of the front spaces, its headlights shining into the store interior. When the driver pushed through the front door, Tim recognized his distinctive conformation. The Stork poked around off camera, reappearing when he shambled up to the counter with three videos. He paid cash and left, climbing into his car.

When the car backed up, Tim saw it clearly, bathed in the streetlamp's glow—a black PT Cruiser. With its forties-style narrow hood, rounded fenders, and sloping liftgate, it seemed a perfect, slightly embarrassing match for the Stork's aesthetic.

Tim froze the frame, leaning close to the screen. The license plate was lost in one headlight's reflection off the glass door. Rewinding, he slowed the tape just as the Stork pulled up. Again the plate was illegible, bleached out in the headlights' gleam. When the Stork turned off the car, the grill fell immediately into shadow, backlit by the streetlamp. Tim let the tape play, watching for the enhanced spill of light from the door when the Stork entered; it illuminated the dark grill for a split second, still not enough for Tim to read the license number. He inched the tape forward and back but couldn't make the plate resolve.

He reached Dray at the sheriff's station. "Tim?" He could hear her shifting the phone, and then she spoke in a hushed voice. "Bear's bringing the heat. There were deputy marshals all through the house last night, searching through our stuff."

"What'd you tell them?"

"I told them we're no longer in touch. That I hadn't seen you since Thursday morning. Mac never saw you when you came back here after Rayner's."

Dray upheld fire-forged allegiances above all else, a trait Tim was forced to attribute to her four brothers or at least to her growing up with them. She was your strongest ally, once you had her.

"And Bear believed you?"

"Of course not."

"Any progress on the safety-deposit key?"

"No. I've been flatfooting my ass to different bank branches every spare moment I have, but nothing so far. I'll match it up, just a matter of when."

"Listen, Dray, I don't want to involve you further in this, but—"

"What do you need?" Her voice said, Shut up and tell me.

"Chrysler PT Cruiser, black, registered somewhere in El Segundo. Give me a ten-mile radius around city limits. There can't be that many of them—I think they just started making it in 2001. Pull up license photos, cross-check them against a picture of Edward Davis, former FBI sound agent, Caucasian, Quantico, New Agent Class Two of '66. Strange-looking guy—you'll know him when you see him." He heard her pen scratching on paper. "Also run the alias Daniel Dunn, see if anything rings the cherries."

"Check."

"You have any good intel?"

"Bear's being pretty tight-lipped around me, but he's also checking in every few hours, I think just to hear my voice. It must remind him of saner times."

"Or to press you for info."

"He did mention Tannino's leaning toward a press conference this evening, though he wouldn't say what they're releasing. My guess is they'll put out a shout to Bowrick, who they still haven't located. If he's not dead already. Oh—and they had to release that retarded guy. The janitor, accused of molesting those kids."

"What? When?"

"Just a few hours ago. It's tough to keep protective custody on someone against their will—you know that. He was agitated as hell the whole time. You can probably understand why."

Tim felt his heartbeat pounding at his temples. "I gotta go."

"I'll get on the car for you. I'll need some time to get it done quietly."

"Thank you." He moved to hang up, but then an image caught him—Ananberg back at Rayner's after the break-in, dead eyes hidden beneath her sleek hair. He brought the telephone back up to his face. "Dray, I really . . . thank you."

"I'm a deputy in Moorpark. What the hell else am I gonna do?"

Something in the Acura's dash started to rattle at ninety miles per hour. As Tim screeched off the freeway exit, it occurred to him that he might be heading into a cleverly devised setup. Dray would never betray him—that he knew—but if Bear wanted to disseminate misinformation to Tim, she was a plausible route. And Dobbins a plausible lure.

Not Bear's style, but it was a possibility Tim couldn't ignore.

When he reached the vicinity of Mick Dobbins's apartment, he was torn between urgency and caution. He did a quick drive through the surrounding blocks, closing on the building, but in the end his foot approach left him ambush-vulnerable.

No answer when he rang Dobbins's bell. No one visible through the window.

He turned at a slight movement beside him, expecting to see Bear and a legion of deputy marshals, but instead it was the same old woman from before, wrapped in the same fluoride-blue bathrobe, her hair still contorted in curlers. She drew back in a posture of exaggerated caution, one liver-spotted hand clenching her bathrobe closed at the throat.

"Look who's poking around here again. Mr. Twenty Questions."

"Where's Mickey?" Tim asked.

"There you go again." Her eyes flashed heavenward, her hands shaking twice, an exasperated plea for divine intervention. "What do you want with him? Everyone pulling and shoving at him—it's enough already. Leave him in peace."

"I'm a friend of Mickey's, remember? I got the police to release him. Did someone else take him?"

"No one else has been nosing around"—she squinted at him—"except you. Mickey probably went down to the park. It's after-school time. He likes to watch the children play. He misses them, because those schmucks took it away from him, his work at the school, those kids he adored so."

Tim fought to maintain a façade of patience. "Which way is the park?"

She pointed an unsteady finger. "Just up the street."

When Tim flashed past her, she let out a little shriek. He hit a dead sprint, sighting the park ahead, a half block rimmed with sycamores. Fluorescent Frisbees drifted over the abbreviated field, mothers chatted beside strollers, infants kicked up sand in a play box. Tim pulled up in the picnic area, trying to condense the whirlwind of motion, scanning the area for Dobbins. A mother sat with a notepad across her knees, her gold pen flashing in the sunlight. Children kicked and screamed from swings. Colorful clothing. The smell of baby powder. Cell phones chirping.

Across the park Dobbins sat on the edge of a wide brick planter, watching a group of kids play tag, his face heavy with sadness.

As Tim started to cut through the crowd, Dobbins rose and began to head in his direction. He walked with a deliberate gait, his beak nose pointed down, watching his shoes.

A movement from his left side, a thick plug of a man parting the crowd, solid and purposeful, seeming to glide through the bustle. Black jacket, low baseball cap, head ducked, hands in pockets. Mitchell.

Tim ran, cried out, his voice lost with the shouts of gleeful children.

Despite all else that had gone down, he was shocked that Mitchell would attempt a shooting in an area crowded with kids. The thought barely had time to register when Mitchell's hand flashed up from his pocket, gripping a plastic flex-cuff. One tough plastic strip was curved around to make a dinner-plate-size circle, the notched end already snared through the catch. Just waiting to be tightened.

Mitchell swept behind Dobbins, who continued walking toward Tim, studying the ground at his feet, oblivious. Tim yelled, shoving a father out of the way. Dobbins's head was just rising to check out the commotion ahead when the loop of the flex-cuff dropped over his head like a snare.

Even over the low rumble of the crowd, Tim heard the shrill zippering sound of the plastic pulling through the catch, and then Dobbins sucked in a creaking gasp, hands at his throat, and fell to his knees. A little girl screamed, and there was a flurry within the already-moving crowd, people running away, kids dashing to parents.

Mitchell was several strides from Dobbins now, but he turned as Tim approached, now fifteen yards away. Their eyes locked. Mitchell's expression of utter tranquillity never gave way, not even as he drew, a quick, reflexive lift of his .45 that rivaled Tim's own. Tim's weapon was clear of his waistband but pointed directly down at the ground; he didn't dare raise it with children and parents streaming through his line of sight, crying and shouting.

Splitting the distance between them, Dobbins lay on the ground, now flat on his back, expelling great, abbreviated choking sounds. His body was remarkably still, save for one foot that ticked back and forth, pendulum-steady, the untied laces brushing asphalt. Over Mitchell's shoulder Tim saw a tan Cadillac coast into view on the street behind the park, Robert at the wheel.

Tim stared down the bore of Mitchell's gun, a hypnotic black dot that sucked in all his thoughts, leaving him with only a nonspecific buzz in his head. Mitchell's right eye was closed, his left focused on Tim's face over the lined sights. Children flashed between them.

Mitchell lowered his gun and took two jogging backward steps, then turned and sprinted to the car. Tim raced after him but got only a few steps past Dobbins before his conscience leash-jerked him back.

He slid to Dobbins, the asphalt scraping his knees even through his jeans. Dobbins's neck sported deep scratch marks above the tight band of the flex-cuff; Tim could see the corresponding flesh stuck beneath the nails of his scrabbling fingers.

A cluster of people had gathered, watching warily from a few feet. Children were crying and being pulled away. The mother Tim had observed earlier looked shell-shocked, her weighty purse slung over one shoulder, her notepad flat against her thigh. Three people were on cell phones, anxiously providing the park's address and a queasy description of the emergency.

The mother stepped forward, pulling an overburdened key chain from her purse and letting it dangle. "I have a knife."

Tim grabbed the key chain and snapped off the pocketknife—an elegant sterling-silver trinket from Tiffany. The blade was thin, which would help, but not serrated, so sawing against the thick plastic would be tough going.

Tim moved Dobbins's hands away, but they shot back to his bloody throat, obscuring Tim's view. He pinned one of Dobbins's arms beneath a knee and slapped the other away until a man stepped from the crowd and held it down.

Dobbins's face was tomato red. A vein bulged on his forehead, and the skin around his neck was sucked in tight, leaving hollows.

Tim slid the blade under the embedded band, cutting through a thin layer of Dobbins's skin in the process. He tried to turn the knife to get the cutting edge up against the flex-cuff, but there was not enough give; Mitchell had yanked it incredibly tight, smashing down the top half of Dobbins's Adam's apple.

Beneath him Dobbins jerked and expelled a ticking gurgle.

Tim turned the knife, fingering through the blood to find Dobbins's larynx. He walked his fingers down until he felt the soft give of the cricothyroid membrane, then cut a lengthwise slit through Dobbins's flesh. A burst of air shot out through the hole, accompanied by a spray of blood.

"Your pen. Give me your gold pen." Tim snapped his fingers, his hand out to the mother. Anticipating him, she unscrewed the pen barrel and shook it so the rollerpoint ink cartridge fell. She handed him the hollow tube of the top half of the pen, and he turned it and inserted the tapered end into the bloody gap. It slid in smoothly.

The sound of sirens, still distant.

Tim sucked once to clear the tube and spit a mouthful of blood on the pavement, fighting off images of hepatitis and HIV, and then Dobbins's body lurched forward as he drew air through the pen barrel directly into his throat. His sloped eyes gave off no anger, just a panicked disorientation.

"Come here," Tim said. The woman came forward and crouched. "Hold this. Hold this." She took the pen barrel from Tim's blood-moist fingers, tentatively at first. He firmed her hands with his own, then rose.

The crowd parted, leaving him a few feet on either side. A crimson spray decorated the front of his shirt; his hands were stained to the knuckles. He jogged out of the park, back down the sidewalk to his car, spitting a bit of blood every few steps.

Driving away, he passed an ambulance and two cop cars just turning onto the block.

# 38

**TIM CHANGED OUT OF HIS SHIRT AND TOOK A PRO-**
longed shower, scrubbing his hands and under
his nails, letting the bathroom fill with steam.
Turning the dial almost all the way to "hot," he stood beneath the stream, shoulders slumped, head hung, letting the
water strike him at the crown and run down over his face. It
felt blissful and clean and painful.

Once dressed, he went to the corner booth and called
Hansen at the Nextel office to check what cell site had been
routing Robert's and Mitchell's outgoing calls.

"Your boys are smarter than you think. Not a single call.
I'd say either they dumped the phones or they're using another phone for outgoing."

Before he could express his doubt that Robert and
Mitchell were sufficiently technologically sophisticated to
take those countermeasures, a thought struck him: The
Stork *was*. Having a second phone exclusively for outgoing calls was a brilliant idea—one that none of Tim's fugitives had ever come up with.

"Well, I just had a little run-in that may provoke a phone
call," Tim said. "Will you mind keeping on it, just in case
they slip up?"

Tim thanked him and walked up the street to the store
from which he'd rented his Nokia. The diminutive store
owner didn't so much as comment on the last phone he'd
rented Tim, now scattered in pieces at the side of the 110.
Tim selected the same model, and the owner wordlessly
started the paperwork for the identical financial arrange-

ment they'd agreed upon previously. Money doesn't just talk; it silences.

Tim would keep the Nextel, too, because that was the number Robert and Mitchell knew and the only means they had of getting in touch with him. His elaborate game of musical phones would have made a mutt like Gary Heidel proud.

Tim charged his phones side by side near the outlet and sat Indian style on the floor staring at exactly nothing.

He recalled Mitchell's expression of confusion on the playground—he'd truly been surprised Tim had come after him. Depending on whether their surveillance on Dobbins had overlapped with the police's picking him up last night, they might not even be aware that the authorities had been alerted.

If Tannino went ahead with the press conference, they'd know soon enough.

Within a few hours Robert Masterson, Mitchell Masterson, Eddie Davis, and Tim Rackley would be names known coast to coast. Tannino would likely keep Dumone's, Ananberg's, and Rayner's deaths separate, at least for the time being. Tim turned on the television to see if any word had leaked, but aside from a nothing-new update about Rayner's murder and Melissa Yueh's announcement that KCOM would be airing a special report at seven o'clock, there was zilch.

Yueh collected her papers, tapping them once neatly on her anchor desk to line the edges. "In other news, Mick Dobbins, the formerly accused child molester, was attacked today in a Culver City park by an unidentified man who cinched a hard plastic garbage-bag tie over his head. He nearly asphyxiated, but another man performed an emergency tracheotomy, then fled the scene. Eyewitnesses helped the police compile this sketch of the assailant."

A composite flashed up on the screen that looked more like Yosemite Sam than Mitchell Masterson.

"Police would not reveal whether this attempted murder is linked to the Lane and Debuffier executions, but they did indicate they were considering the possibility."

A shot of the park showed Culver City PD pushing bystanders back from a circle of asphalt marked with crime-scene tape. To the side the back of Bear's wide frame was readily apparent. He'd sweated through his sport coat at the armpits. The impromptu huddle around him included Maybeck, Denley, Thomas, and Freed.

Colleagues turned adversaries.

"Local authorities are looking for both men. Dobbins was taken to Brotman Medical Center, where he is reported in stable condition."

Tim turned off the TV and sat at his desk. He'd have to give Dray at least twenty-four hours on the car. The safety-deposit key could take hours, could take weeks.

His thoughts, once turned to his wife, didn't readily depart. Dray, who kept her nails short and unpainted. Dray, who always held other people's babies awkwardly away from her body, like leaking trash bags. Dray, two-ring shooter on a Transtar target with a Beretta at fifty yards.

He folded his hands in his lap and sat in the relative silence because that was what'd he'd heard that people seeking peace did. He closed his eyes, but spotlit in the dark was Kindell's bent hacksaw, worn to the nubs, still sticky with Ginny's blood. He wondered what other items waited in the surrounding blackness.

He set the VCR to record the seven o'clock press conference, in case he wasn't back in an hour. He left down the fire escape, for practice, and so he could keep the doorstop wedged in place while he was gone.

Erika Heinrich's bedroom light was on. Tim parked four blocks away and duplicated his previous cautious approach to the house. Her sash window was open, the blurry whites and blues of a television screen poorly reflected in the upper pane. Tim squatted beneath the window just as the KCOM news jingle wound up.

Marshal Tannino's televised voice carried outside in bits and pieces. ". . . these three men . . . renegade law-enforcement officers . . . wanted for questioning in connection with the Jedediah Lane and Buzani Debuffier killings . . . repeat: No charges have been brought. . . ."

Tim rose to a crouch, bringing his eyes level with the sill. Terrill Bowrick sat beside Erika on her bed, both of them staring at the small TV on her dresser. Bowrick's adolescent slump rounded his back, his hands dangling between his thighs. He looked even younger than Tim remembered, his face pale except where dotted with acne, his neck and arms thin like a girl's. He looked incredibly weary, as if he hadn't slept in days.

In contrast the televised Tannino looked stiff in his best suit—a navy blue number—and his Regis Philbin tie. His hair, lit with dozens of camera flashes, seemed exceedingly blow-dried. He gestured to an easel, on which sat enlarged photographs of Robert, Mitchell, and the Stork. "Any sighting of these three men should be reported to . . ."

No picture of Tim. No mention of Tim.

They probably wanted to nab the Medal of Valor winner quietly, spare the L.A. law-enforcement community another public debacle.

Bowrick's mouth, fringed with a meager mustache, was thin and bent down in a slightly open frown that suggested tears would not be long in coming. His face had whitened extraordinary degree. Erika was rubbing him between the shoulders in a repetitive, soothing motion. Their faces both held an exhausted calm, as if fright and worry had worn away all vitality.

The door to the adjoining bathroom was ajar. Pink tile. Lights off. Empty. A chair was backed to the bedroom door, wedged under the knob. Mommy didn't know about the special houseguest.

". . . suspected of targeting alleged murderers and child molesters, suspects who were released by the criminal-court system."

A flurry of waving hands and pens. An explosion of questions, one winning out.

"Was the Mick Dobbins assault today related?"

"We believe so, yes."

"How are the Vigilante Three choosing their victims?"

Tannino grimaced at the nickname. "We have no information about that at this time."

"We have it from a reliable source that UCLA Professor William Rayner's death and that of his teaching assistant could be connected to these events. What is the nature of their involvement?"

"I'm not going to comment on that."

"Can you substantiate rumors that Franklin Dumone, the prominent Boston police sergeant who shot himself today at Cedars, was involved?"

"No. Next question."

"Why is the U.S. Marshals Service involved?"

"This case dovetails with and is an extension of the Lane assassination, the investigation of which fell under federal jurisdiction."

"So why isn't the FBI in charge of the investigation?"

"We're working closely with the FBI." Tannino lied well. In private he referred to the FBI as the Fucking Bunch of Idiots.

"Any guess as to who the next intended victim will be?"

Bowrick's mouth didn't move at all, but he creaked, "Oh, God."

Tannino glanced away, just for a second, but it was a poker tell. "That's all the information we can disclose at this point."

Erika's hand stopped making its circles on Bowrick's back.

Tim leaped up, grabbed the protruding frame above the window, and slid down into the bedroom, landing on his feet. Bowrick and Erika reacted violently, lunging off the bed, dragging the comforter and sheets to the far side in the process. They stood side by side, cowering, their backs to the closet door.

The house smelled of bratwurst, and Tim thought, How's that for stereotypes?

Erika fell to her knees, trembling, embracing Bowrick around his waist. He had one hand up, forearm angled as if shielding light from his eyes.

"Don't shoot him, oh, God, don't . . ." She broke down.

"Some men are coming to kill you," Tim said. "Hide better."

A moment of stark disbelief. Bowrick lowered his hand.

Tim leaned back through the window and swung the sturdy, German jalousies shut, blocking the view from the street. When he turned again to face the kids, tears were sparkling on both their cheeks.

"Let 'em get me," Bowrick said. "I don't care anymore."

"Is that true?"

He sniffled, wiped his nose with his sleeve. "No."

Erika found her voice. "Who *are* you?"

Tim gestured to the window, now shuttered. "This is stupid. Your coming to this location is stupid. There are trails to lead them here."

"What am I supposed to do?" Saliva formed a bubble sheet in the corner of Bowrick's mouth.

"Not this."

"I got nowhere to go."

"Go to the cops."

"The cops fucking hate me."

"Keep your voice down."

"They won't do shit for me, and if they do, it'll be worse being in custody than being out here. Trust me—I know."

Frustration tightened Tim's chest. "You figured it out before."

"They found me before."

"No, *I* found you before."

Bowrick's hand came up, four fingers angled at Tim, like a wooden puppet pointing. Erika was still on her knees, her cheek mashed against Bowrick's side, watching.

"You saved my life."

"I didn't save your life. I decided not to take it."

A voice carried down the call. "Erika! Dinner's on the table."

Erika stared at Tim, a lot of white showing in her eyes. Tim looked at her and said softly, "I'm in the bathroom. I'll be there in a minute."

"I'm in the bathroom!" she called out. "I'll be there in a minute."

"Well, move it! I didn't spend all this time cooking to eat a cold meal."

Erika's eyes jerked down at the floor—a hint of embarrassment, even here, in all this.

Tim tilted his head at Bowrick. "You know how to hide. Just do it better."

"I can't." Bowrick's lips started quivering, severely, and

the tears came now, full force, fording his lips. "I don't got nowhere to go."

"You don't have another safe house?"

"No, man. A buddy of mine helped me set that up. He's in Donovan right now, went down for grand auto. I got . . . I got no one."

"Save it for the talk shows. For now get lost. And well."

Bowrick's teeth clicked as he studied the floor. His voice came in a small whine. "They're really gonna do it, aren't they? Hunt me down and kill me?"

"Yes."

His lower lip sucked in, wavering behind the line of his front teeth. Erika's arms tightened around his thigh.

Tim said, "Go to the police."

"I'm *never* going to the police. Never again."

"Call your probation officer."

"He'll make me come in."

"Go to Mexico."

"I can't . . . I can't be apart from Erika like that."

"This is *not* my problem, kid. Do you understand me?"

"Help him. Would you help him?" Erika sobbed out the words.

Tim stared at her, stared at him.

Footsteps coming down the hall, rapidly, sped with anger. "Erika Brunnhilde Heinrich, you get your rear to the dinner table *right now*."

Tim clenched his teeth until he felt his jaw swell at the corners. "Come with me," he said. He pushed open the shutters and stepped out into the night.

He was across the front lawn when Bowrick caught up to him, jerking slightly with his limp, breathing hard. "Where we going?"

"Don't talk."

A pair of headlights illuminated the street, and Tim

grabbed Bowrick by the shirt and yanked him against the side of the neighboring house. The car passed. Green Saturn. Family.

Tim kept close to the house fronts in case the need arose to take cover, Bowrick doing his best to keep up. They reached Tim's car and climbed in.

"What kind of car is this?" Tim asked as he pulled out.

"Acura."

"Wrong. The first answer is, 'What car?' The second, if you're pressed hard and need specifics, is, 'A green '98 Saturn.' Like the one that just passed us. Think you can remember that?"

"I won't tell nothing about this. I swear to God."

"You're a snitch, Bowrick. Answer my question."

He looked out into the night, and Tim saw his sullen expression reflected back off the window. "Yes, I can remember that."

They made it a few blocks without anyone talking. Bowrick played with his hair in front, grabbing it in a fist and tugging gently. "They raped her," he said.

The wheels hammered over a divot in the road.

"Four of 'em. On the bus after an away game. The others cheered."

Tim watched the road, the unending flashes of road reflectors.

"She wanted to testify at the trial, but I didn't want to put her through it. My mousefuck of a public defender wouldn't have given a shit anyway, and, hey, fuck, I never needed it since I made out pretty good with my immunity grant. It don't change what I did, but I . . . I just wanted to say it."

Tim turned on the radio. A beat-pumping dance number rattled the speakers. He turned it off. He stared straight ahead at the road. "I didn't know," he said.

Bowrick dug at something between his teeth with a nail. "Of course you didn't."

They'd driven about four blocks in silence when Bowrick laughed. Tim shot him an inquisitive glance, and he smiled—the first time Tim had seen him smile.

"God, I love that chick." Bowrick shook his head, still smirking. "Her middle name is *Brunnhilde*."

Tim pulled into the parking lot of a Ralph's grocery store, parked, and got out. Bowrick stayed in the car. Tim circled and tapped on the window. "Come."

"Why?"

"Because I don't trust you in the car."

Bowrick unbuckled his seat belt and let it snap back on the recoil. Tim led the way into the store, moving aisle to aisle ahead of Bowrick, collecting Visine, Comet, Sudafed, three prepackaged wedges of poppy-seed cake, a six-pack of Mountain Dew, Vicks Formula 44M, and a jar of vitamin-C tablets.

Bowrick followed him, making noises to demonstrate his bafflement. "Just got a sudden urge to do a little grocery shopping?"

Back outside, Tim pulled around behind the store, near the dark loading dock. Digging through the trunk, he found the first-aid kit he'd transferred from the Beemer. He freed the empty syringe from beneath its leather strap, grabbed a needle in a sanitized paper sheath, and returned to the driver's seat.

He removed the plunger and squeezed a stream of Visine into the empty shot barrel, then sprinkled in some Comet. Placing a vitamin-C pill on the dash, he smashed it with the butt of his gun and swept the resultant powder into the barrel as well. The liquid fizzed, giving off a slight crackling noise. Replacing the plunger, Tim cleared the air from the syringe.

He turned to Bowrick, who was watching him with growing unease, facing sideways in the passenger seat so his back was pressed up against the door.

"Give me your arm."

"Are you fucking crazy?"

"Give me your arm."

"No way, man. You're fucking high."

"Believe it or not, kid, you're not my only concern right now. So give me your arm or get out of the car, because I have more important things to take care of."

Bowrick studied him for a while, sweat glistening in the strands of hair on his upper lip. "This gonna kill me?"

"Yes. I've orchestrated the entire chain of events over the past three days because this is the easiest way I could think to kill you."

Bowrick held out an arm, clenched his fist. Tim slid the needle into the pale blue throb at the base of his biceps, careful to penetrate only the epidermis. Ignoring the stink of Bowrick's fear sweat, he eased the plunger down, and the skin at the needle's tip immediately wilted and colored.

"Ouch," Bowrick said.

When Tim removed the needle, tiny black-tinged bubbles welled up from the flesh puncture. He said, "It'll scab up in a few hours, scab up good."

He started the engine and drove away.

"What the fuck was that?"

Tim shoved one of the poppy-seed cakes at him, with a can of Mountain Dew. "Eat this."

"What the fuck . . . ?"

"Shut up. Eat it. Hurry."

Bowrick started shoving the cake into his mouth, swallowing large mouthfuls with gulps of Mountain Dew.

"Now this piece. *Go*. Eat it."

Crumbs clung to Bowrick's face.

"Drink this. Get it down." Tim pressed another can of soda into Bowrick's side until he took it. Bowrick popped the top and forced down a few gulps. Tim opened the Sudafed box in his lap and fumbled out four thirty-milligram tablets. "And these. Take them." He thrust the cough-syrup container at Bowrick. "Wash it down with this."

Bowrick complied, grimacing. "Why are you doing all this shit to me?"

When he realized he wasn't going to get an answer, he threw his hands up and smacked them against his thighs. His knee was starting to shake up and down, a nervous tic brought on by the caffeine and the pseudoephedrine. After a while he started poking at the bruise, watching it spread and darken. Tim drove fast, enjoying the silence.

They headed back toward downtown. To their left, way up in the hills, Tim saw the darkened silhouette of the memorial tree, barely visible through the scaffolding.

He pulled into the parking lot of a large, two-story complex. Harsh hospital lighting bled through the closed blinds. His knee hammering up and down now, Bowrick strained to make out the cracked wooden sign out front. L.A. COUNTY RECOVERY CENTER.

"What the hell?" Bowrick said as they got out. "What the fuck is going on?"

Tim grabbed his arm and yanked him toward the building. Bowrick stumbled along, breathing hard. Tim shoved through the front door, dragging Bowrick behind him. The admitting nurse sprang to her feet, her black chair rolling back across white tile and hitting a garbage can five feet back. The lobby was otherwise empty.

"I caught my goddamn brother here with *this*." Tim yanked Bowrick's arm toward the nurse, revealing the nasty bruise on the soft underside. "He's supposed to be clean—been off for more than six months." He glared at Bowrick threateningly. Through the sweaty tangle of his bangs, Bowrick looked genuinely repentant. "He was *supposed* to have been off for more than six months."

"Sir, please calm down."

Tim took a deep breath, held it, then exhaled. Releasing Bowrick's arm, he leaned over the counter and spoke softly, conspiratorially. "I'm sorry. It's been a very hard year. Look, this has already caused my family and Paul here a great deal of embarrassment. Is this clinic, you know, discreet?"

"We have complete patient confidentiality. One hundred percent."

"I don't want my family name on any paperwork."

"It doesn't have to be. But first things first—"

"Do you have inpatient care? He's been talking crazy, talking suicide, me and our mom can't keep an eye on him twenty-four/seven."

"It depends whether his medical evaluation indicates that he needs to be admitted." She looked at Bowrick, pale, sweaty, panting. "Which I would say seems likely. We have a forty-eight-hour confidential hold"—checking her watch—"which takes us to Monday at midnight. Then he'd have to be reassessed, and we'll discuss more permanent arrangements." She stepped out from behind the desk and took Bowrick gently by the arm. He followed her in a sort of daze.

"Let me show you to an exam room. I'll page our public-health nurse. She'll be with you shortly, and then we can determine if he's eligible for residential housing."

"He's eighteen. Can I leave him here?"

"It would be better if you could stay with him."

"I think I've had enough of him right now."

"That's your choice, sir. If you wouldn't mind waiting at least until the public-health nurse arrives—it should be less than ten minutes. I have to watch the front desk."

"Fine," Tim said. "That's fine."

She closed the door behind her, and then Tim crossed to Bowrick, pressing two fingers to his neck to find his carotid pulse. Way elevated heart rate.

"You have nausea and the sweats," Tim said. "You scratch your arms a lot. You're having insomnia. Nervousness, anxiety, and irritability you seem to have covered pretty well already. You've been having a lot of suicidal thoughts lately. Rub your eyes so they're red. Good—keep rubbing. The poppy seeds and the dextromethorphan from the Vicks should ding your opiate drug tests for at least the next two days. See if you can make yourself puke later tonight, to make sure they keep you on. When you're assigned a room, write the number on a slip of paper and tape it behind the hinged lid of the garbage can outside the lobby. Call your probation officer the second you leave. If you don't, I'll come looking for you. And believe me, I'll find you."

Bowrick looked up, one hand laid across his racing heart. He was still breathing hard; saliva had gummed at the corners of his mouth. Some icing was smeared on his lower lip. "Why didn't you tell me the plan?"

"I wanted you to look alarmed, resistant, and pissed off."

"You're smart. You're fuckin' smart."

"The sad truth is, most of what I know that's clever, I've learned from the mutts."

"The mutts, huh?"

"That's what we call them."

"*Them.*" Bowrick flashed a faint grin.

Tim withdrew from the room. He was just closing the door when Bowrick called out. Tim stuck his head back in. "How long should I stay here?"

Tim thought about this long and hard. "Give me forty-eight hours."

**39** TIM'S ATTEMPT AT SLEEP WAS JUST THAT. HE DRIFTED off with a mind full of dead Ginny and woke from a vision of himself standing knee-deep in bodies with his hands stained red past the wrists, which he thought pretty uninventive.

Four A.M. found him sitting on his chair with his feet on the windowsill, watching steam drift up from a busted pipe in the alley below. The Nextel rang.

He walked over slowly, picking it up on the third ring.

Robert this time—the voice rough like unpolished metal. "Think you're pretty smart, don't you?"

"Depends on the day."

"If you are, you'll heed a word of advice: Get the fuck out of Dodge. You're on our list."

"And you're on mine." In the background Tim could make out wisps of a television news report. He turned on the TV, hit mute, and clicked through the channels until the newscaster's lips matched the faint words he was picking up through the phone: KCOM.

The photos of the Stork and the Mastersons flashed off the screen, replaced by a singing guy in a bird suit advertising a chicken joint. Still no mention of Tim, no photo.

"I can't believe you'd be so fucking irresponsible to force a confrontation on a playground," Robert said. "We had guns drawn, with kids around. Someone could have gotten hurt."

"Someone did get hurt."

"Not hurt enough." The snap of a Zippo punctuated his point, followed by the sound of smoke blowing across the receiver. "The press now, our faces—*shit*. Why'd you have to go and do that? You fucked us all." Something in Robert's voice gave way, revealing his sense of betrayal and a measure of desperation. "And Dumone—" His voice cracked, and the words shut off like water from a fast-turned spigot.

Tim was unsure how to respond, so he didn't. He wasn't eager to prolong the call—he wanted to get off and call Hansen.

"I don't hear your name on these reports," Robert said. "What'd you cut a deal?"

"No. I'm going down, too. On a slight delay."

"This won't stop us."

"I didn't figure."

"You just turned this into an endgame. We got shit to lose now." Robert's laugh sounded part cough, though it wasn't. "If you or any other piece-of-shit L.A. law-enforcement flunkies get in our way, you're gonna eat lead. This is our one true deed. We get nothing from it. No cash, no fame. It's public-service work. We're gonna . . ."

"—restore—" Mitchell's voice came faintly in the background.

"—a bit of sanity to this world. We're gonna get this done, then we're gonna regroup and do it all over again, do it until someone stops us. And if we go out, shit, at least we take a bunch of pukes with us."

"Option B," Tim said. "We turn ourselves in together. We work out something, something fair and just."

"You don't get it, do you, you double-crossing fuck? No one's turning themselves in. You'd better be grateful there *were* kids on that playground today, or Mitch would have capped your ass and we'd be laughing at the expression on your dying face right about now."

Click.

Tim was already walking to the door, stuffing the Nextel and Nokia into his front pockets. He half jogged to the corner phone booth.

Hansen sounded duly irritated. "This better not be Rackley."

"I just got a call. I need you to go in and check if it came from either of the numbers I gave you."

"First of all, this is a favor *I'm* doing *you*, so don't order me around. Second, I can't do that. I'm in at six o'clock, and I'll see what we have then."

"Please, this is—"

"Call me at six or fuck off."

The next two hours passed with excruciating slowness. Just in case the lead panned out, Tim loaded up his gear and sat waiting in his car, the Nokia in his lap, number already input and waiting on the phone's tiny screen.

The dashboard clock switched from 5:59 to 6:00 A.M., and Tim clicked "send."

"What do you have for me?"

Hansen spoke in a slightly lowered voice. "There's only one person who can retrieve this intel from Nextel, and you're talking to him, so I'm not turning over shit unless you give me your word it goes no further than this call."

Tim bit his lip—no dealing with Bear until he could corroborate the location independently. "You have my word."

"One outgoing phone call. 4:07 A.M. Tripped a cell site at Dickens and Kester. The cell sites are especially close there, so you're working with about a one-block radius."

"Thank you," Tim said. "Thank you."

"I have a wife and two kids, Rack. If you're involving me in something shady, you're gonna hear about it."

The morning light broke through a scattering of cumulus clouds, throwing broad shafts of grainy light that seemed to dissipate on their way down. Morning dew misted the asphalt, the freeway resembling a still, black river. The occasional puddle threw a calming patter against the car's undercarriage.

Tim parked three blocks over and approached Dickens through two adjoining backyards, high-stepping between rows of rhododendron. Studio City, a mishmash of strip malls and residential blocks, basked in an early-morning tranquillity. No barking dogs, no slamming doors, just the chopping of sprinklers across well-trimmed lawns and the soft whir of traffic on Ventura one long block away. Tim scanned the nearby rooflines and picked out the cell site, six abbreviated metal tubes perched atop a phone pole.

Robert would not have called Tim to make idle threats in the middle of an operation; in all likelihood the 4:07 A.M. call had come from wherever he and Mitchell were bedded down for the night. Or, Choice B—it had been bait for an ambush.

Tim came out between two houses and their shared driveway, sticking low to the ground in a rotar-ducking crouch. From behind the safety of a gargantuan garbage can, he surveyed the block. Perfect stillness. He eased out onto the sidewalk and moved down the street, taking it in.

Ford Explorer in the first driveway, hood cool. GTE phone junction box at the corner. A blue gardening truck parked curbside, the hump of a lawn mower poking up the tarp. Tim pulled up the tarp to make sure. A stack of newspapers outside the door of the second house across the street. Fresh mud in the tire tread of an Isuzu. One mailbox flag up. A house with wooden slat blinds, all closed. Tim drew nearer, peeked in a side window, and saw a little boy sleeping in a race-car bed.

Tim made his way around the corner, up the west side of the block. Six houses down, the residential street spilled onto Ventura Boulevard, where a guy in a store apron was lugging some cardboard boxes to a Dumpster. A Honda Civic coasted by, two blondes in gym clothes bobbing to muffled music. Up ahead the stoplight changed to red. Someone yakked away in the corner phone booth, wearing a sweat suit, hood pulled over his head like a boxer. More garbage cans at the curb. Two newspapers on the doorstep of house three. A Pacific Bell van at the curb across the street, empty, windshield misted with condensation.

Tim eased forward, alive with heightened perception. An alarm clock buzzed one house up and was quickly turned off. Something from his thoughts edged up, out of place, and he fanned through the images he'd freeze-framed in his head to see if he could identify what was troubling him. Fresh mud in the tread. Gardening tarp. GTE junction box. Newspapers on the doorstep. Boy asleep. Nothing rang a dissonant note.

Up the street the chubby guy in the phone booth shifted, and the sun glinted off something square at his waist. Tim strained to make it out. The man's face was still shadowed by the sweatshirt hood.

Pac Bell van. Dumpster. Slat blinds. Mailbox flag. GTE junction box.

In the phone booth, the guy's hand rose, touching his shadowed face with a knuckle, as if he were starting to cross himself. The thing at his belt glinted again. A cell phone.

Tim felt his stomach clench twice, hard. Why the hell

was a guy with a cell phone making a call from a phone booth? The hand to the face—not the start of a prayer but a gesture of habit, the Stork sliding his glasses up the insignificant slope of his nose. Tim's mind whirred, a slide show of images.

Store apron. GTE junction box. Alarm clock. GTE junction box. Pac Bell van. GTE. Pac Bell. A shift and a click as the tumblers aligned in Tim's mind. A Pac Bell van had no business servicing a GTE region. Tim slowed, slowed, stopped. He half turned, bringing the back door of the Pac Bell van into sight, now about fifteen yards behind him. For an empty van it was sitting too low on its shocks.

Tim wasn't sure what happened first, his dive or the rear doors of the van kicking open, but he was fully extended to his left, angling for the gap between two cars at the curb when the first dull crack of a bullet sounded. He hit hard on his shoulder, his face grinding asphalt as his momentum carried him into a graceless roll. The cars to both sides of Tim rocked on their tires, their windows shattering in rapid succession, two distinct paths of holes and veined glass leading to the gap and Tim's body. Car alarms beeped and whined all up the block.

Tim popped up in a shooter's stance on the sidewalk, .357 drawn, using the trunk of the rear car as a shield. He fired twice, his bullets punching holes in one of the van's outswung rear metal doors.

The van screeched out from the curb, laying down five feet of rubber, one rear door secured, the other swinging on its hinges. Tim glanced down to Ventura—the Stork had disappeared from his stakeout post in the phone booth— then stepped into the street. He fired once more as the van rounded the corner, the bullet sparking off the wheel well of the right rear tire.

The sound of the van's engine faded, leaving Tim with

bleating car alarms and the raw, cool pain of road stain on his face. Locks were being turned, doors opened.

Tim jogged back up the block, favoring a tender knee. As he made his way through the adjoining backyards to his car, he called Bear, speaking quickly and concisely to convey all relevant information about the ambush. Bear confirmed the specifics in a voice strained with impatience and anger, then hung up to get on it.

On his way to the 101, Tim passed three cop cars with screaming sirens, and he turned slightly in his seat to hide whatever damage might be visible on his face.

It wasn't until he'd merged onto the freeway that he realized he'd been shot.

**40** HE BLED THROUGH HIS T-SHIRT HIGH ON THE RIGHT sleeve. At a stoplight he peeled it back, revealing two slits in the ball of his shoulder. They were small enough that he figured them to have been caused by fragments rather than direct hits, maybe from a bullet breaking apart when it skipped off the asphalt. He walked his fingers across his back but could feel no exit wounds. Though his right hand could still clench—a good sign—he steered with his left to avoid any unnecessary strain. A dull throbbing took hold of the shoulder, more an ache than a sharp pain. It was manageable.

He parked several blocks from his apartment building and sifted through his war bag in the trunk. He found the appropriate medical supplies and threw them into a plastic grocery bag the car's previous owner had left wadded up in the far corner of the trunk.

He didn't have a clean T-shirt or any way to hide the bloody sleeve, so he walked swiftly, head lowered, keeping to the edge of the sidewalk. Crossing the lobby, he heard Joshua's voice ring out, but he kept walking. Footsteps approached as he waited for the elevator. Grimacing, he slung the bag over his shoulder, letting the two layers of plastic cover the wound. Though the resultant pain wasn't excruciating, he had to concentrate not to grit his teeth. He turned just barely, keeping the abraded flesh of his right profile out of view.

Joshua was standing at a polite distance, arms folded, hands flattened and pressed against his biceps. "So what do you think of all this business in the news?"

"I haven't been watching."

"The Vigilante Three?"

"I heard something about it on the radio."

Joshua's expression changed, and he took a step to the side for a better vantage. "Jesus, your face. What happened?"

"I fell off my bike."

"Motorcycle?"

"Yeah—it's fine. Happens all too often. I just gotta clean it out."

"Let me take a look."

"No. That's all right. It's not pretty."

"You people always think fags are fragile. You forget we've seen it all. The eighties were not a kind decade for us."

The elevator arrived, and Tim stepped on, pivoting to keep his shoulder out of view.

"Last offer," Joshua said. "I can give you a ride to the emergency room."

"No, really. I'm fine." Tim punched the fourth-floor button, and the doors started to slide shut. "Thanks, though."

Once in his apartment, he wedged the doorstop back into place to secure the front door and gingerly pulled off his T-shirt. A look in the bathroom mirror confirmed there were no exit wounds; the frags were embedded in the dense ball of muscle composing his anterior deltoid. He popped four Advil, then rotated his arm at the shoulder to ensure that it had full range of motion. It did.

He drew a wet rag across the area to clarify the wounds' edges, then gritted his teeth and sank the tweezer prongs into the first laceration. They went in a good inch before clicking metal. He withdrew the copper sliver easily. It took some rooting in the second wound before he located the fragment. Because it was irregular, the frag came out slow and rough, tearing flesh on the way. He had to stop twice and wipe his forehead to keep sweat from running into his eyes.

He held the squirt top of a bottle of distilled water inches from his shoulder and squeezed hard, sending a probing jet into the wound to flush any smaller particles.

Repeating the process for the second laceration was predictably more painful.

After irrigation with hydrogen peroxide, the wounds looked like two tiny pink mouths. Feeling Terminator-tough, he regarded his work with a measure of satisfaction before bandaging it.

His face was another matter. The flesh all around his right eye was scraped up, leaving what looked like a bloody pirate patch. Tim had to scour out the dirt and bits of gravel with a washcloth.

After putting on a fresh shirt, he used his new outgoing phone to check his old Nokia voice mail. Dray had left a message saying she was still working the leads, no luck yet. The message's time stamp reminded him that Bowrick had just thirty-six hours left before the recovery center required a reassessment or put him back out on the street.

Lying back on his bed, he exhaled deeply and let his muscles relax.

The Stork, clearly aware of cell-phone-tracking technology, had probably orchestrated the call from Studio City. With his help, Robert and Mitchell had walked Tim into a well-orchestrated trap. It had not occurred to him what a strong team the three made, even without him—the Mastersons providing operational muscle and strategy while the Stork played technological puppet master.

He vowed not to underestimate them again.

He popped four more Advil and fell into a deep, sound sleep—no nightmares, no images of Ginny, no thoughts of Dray, just a blank white corridor of unthought. He woke abruptly after nightfall, sweaty and still veiled in a dream haze. The room was dark, the alley below surprisingly peaceful. The needling question as to what had awakened him sharply from so deep a slumber helped clear his head. His shoulder pulsed impatiently, eager to heal.

He sat up in bed, his legs hanging off the mattress in front of him. He felt constrained in his clothes, which had sleep-shifted around him. His watch showed 9:13 P.M. He stood and went to the window. At the end of the alley, a dark car waited, visible through the steam of the broken pipe. The passenger door opened, but no dome light went on.

Bad news.

Tim turned back, facing the door across his dark apartment.

The slightest scuffling sound in the hall. The pinpoint scratch of dog nails against floor.

Tim thought, How?

His eyes tracked down to the doorstop wedged hard beneath the door, then up to the decoy knob that he'd detached completely from the surrounding jamb. With excruciating slowness, he reached behind him, slid the window open.

A shattering impact shook the apartment. The entire doorknob, propelled by an unseen battering ram, flew from the frame, striking the floor once and smashing into the wall beside Tim. The door itself, pinned by the doorstop, bent in but did not swing open.

From the flurry of shouting, Tim could somehow discern distinct voices—Bear and Maybeck, Denley and Miller. He leapt through the window onto the fire escape as the door splintered and gave way behind him. Immediately the alley below lit with headlights—the car he'd spotted before and another at the south end. As he flew down the ladder, they screeched forward, closing on the fire escape from either side.

The hammering of boots through his apartment above seemed to vibrate the entire building. The deputies were yelling "Clear" as he hit the third landing, and then he could make out Bear's deep rumble of a voice hurling profanities. Ignoring his throbbing shoulder, Tim slid down the ladder to the second landing. Two spotlights angled up from the cars in the alley blanketed him, moving with him. Raising an arm to shield his eyes, he ran to the outfacing bathroom window, the flimsy landing shaking with his steps. It was still screenless, still inched open.

He threw it open and, using the landing overhead, swung himself in. He hit the toilet hard. When he shoved out through the bathroom door, two bodies jerked upright in bed, startled faces and flying paperbacks bathed in the light of dueling reading lamps. He was through the living room in a flash and out into the hall.

Flashing blue and red reflected in the windows at either end of the corridor—LAPD backup. The door to Room 213 was unlocked, as he'd left it. He sprinted through the apartment, out the living-room window onto the fire escape. The alley on this side of the building was too narrow to accommodate a car, but sure enough a vehicle was waiting thirty yards down on the main street. Good work, Thomas and Freed.

He slid down the ladder and hung from the bottom rung, his shoulder screaming, his feet dangling a few inches from the ground. He dropped and hit the ground running. Down the alley two car doors opened and closed, and for a brief moment he and Thomas and Freed were sprinting directly at each other. In the lead, Thomas stopped, raising his shotgun. Freed pulled up at his side as Tim froze, hands half spread, staring down the bore from about thirty yards. Water dripped from a leaky pipe to Tim's left. Freed's head rotated slightly, just enough for his eyes to fall on Thomas, questioning, then Tim sprang forward, running toward them again. Thomas shouted, thighs flexing, shotgun firming at his shoulder but not firing.

Tim banked hard down the alley ten yards north of the fire escape and hurtled forward over boxes and fences with a nearly out-of-control momentum, the noise of his pursuers following him. After two forced turns, he came out on Third, only a half block from his building, practically skidding to halt himself. He flagged a cab and ducked into the backseat. An opera singer wailed from both speakers, her voice piercing and wobbly.

"Go. That way."

The cab driver pulled out sharply. "I can't flip a U here, pal."

Tim slid low in the seat as the cab passed the front of his building. Two cop cars were parked at the entrance, flanking the Beast, which idled at the curb. Bear's broad frame was immediately evident among the other Arrest Response Team deputies, cut from the headlights' glow like a dark statue. Joshua stood facing him, wearing a plush bathrobe, shaking his head. They did not look his way as the cab passed.

"Get to a freeway," Tim said. "The 101. Hurry up."

The cabbie waved a meaty hand dismissively, his other busy keeping time with the aria, sweeping back and forth as though spreading butter on toast.

One block away, a block and a half. Tim felt no abatement of his unease. When they turned the corner onto Alameda, he experienced the suffocating sensation of moving into an ambush, his second in less than twenty-four hours. The city seemed to pull in and around him—random, disparate movement suddenly given direction and meaning, a car here, a bystander's turned head, the glint of binocs from a passing apartment building—and Tim thought again, How? How are they still on me?

Behind the wheel of a dark Ford sedan parked curbside, a face glowed with the light of a GPS screen. Coke-bottle glasses, pasty skin—the archetypal electronic-surveillance geek. Tim's eyes tracked up a telephone pole, spotting a cluster of cell-site tubes.

Beaten at his own game. Somewhere, through his quickening alarm, a phrase rose into consciousness: the Revenge of the Nerds.

Several blocks away, the whine of sirens became audible, closing in.

Tim dug in his pockets, pulling out the Nextel and the Nokia. The Nokia was certainly clean—he'd just gotten it, and no one had the number. The Nextel's top button glowed green, showing a good connection to network.

The cab was surrounded by trucks and cars and two

other taxis. The cabbie accelerated to make a green light, and they started up the ramp to the freeway, the other lanes and traffic peeling off. Tim leaned out the window and took his best shot, tossing the Nextel through the open back window of the taxi beside them as it drifted away, its lane veering right.

The cell phone struck the sill and bounced in, landing in the lap of a surprised matron wearing an excess of makeup. Oblivious, Tim's cabbie turned up the radio and kept humming, kept conducting. Tim twisted in his seat, looking out the rear window. A wall of vehicles with blaring sirens swept right, hard, just before the exit, following the other taxi and closing in hard. Down on the patchwork streets below, he made out the flashing lights of two vehicle checkpoints he'd narrowly missed.

It wasn't until they'd passed two exits without any sign of a tail that he relaxed.

He had his weapon, loaded with six bullets, his Nokia phone, the clothes on his back, and a little over thirty dollars in cash. The rest of his stuff was in the trunk of the Acura, which he'd go back for tomorrow, if the area was clear. He'd signed the lease on his apartment as Tom Altman, so that meant his bank account was either frozen or soon would be. He had the cabdriver drop him off at an ATM and succeeded in pulling out six hundred dollars— the maximum withdrawal.

He walked up the block and made a call from a phone booth. Not surprisingly, Mason Hansen was in the office.

"Working late?"

A long pause. "Rack, listen, I . . . Look, they told me what was going on. I had to . . ."

"They pulled my phone number from the records of the cell phone you sourced for me, didn't they? And you confirmed it for them." A cop car drove by, and Tim turned away, hiding in the phone booth like a down-at-heel Superman. "You knew mine was the number dialed at 4:07 A.M."

"Your colleagues came in with warrants. What was I supposed to do?" His voice picked up anger. "And you didn't exactly come clean with me either. You're in deep shit."

"You can stop your trace. I won't be on long enough."

In the background Tim heard the faint chirp of another line—probably Bear calling in. He was about to hang up, but Hansen's voice caught him.

"Uh, Rack?" A nervous pause. "You're not gonna come after me, are you?"

The note of anxiety in Hansen's voice shot straight through Tim, leaving him wobbled. "Of course I'm not going to hurt you. What do you think I am?"

No answer. Tim hung up.

His palms had gone slick with sweat, a reaction his body reserved not for fear or strain or even sadness, but for shame.

**41** SINCE HE FIGURED BEAR WOULD HAVE DEPUTIES ALL over Dray's for the night, Tim cabbed back and checked into a shitty motel downtown, a few miles from his old apartment building. He'd be able to scout the Acura first thing in the morning and maybe reclaim it.

The bedspread smelled like shaving cream. He called her from the Nokia, knowing they couldn't be set up to trace it. "Andrea."

A sharp intake of air. "Bear said you'd been shot. They found blood, bandages in the bathroom when they flushed you out."

"Superficial. It's nothing."

She heaved a sigh that kept going and going. "Say it again," she said. "I thought I might not . . . Say my name again."

He hadn't heard relief like that in Dray's voice since he'd phoned her from base after a deployment to Uzbekistan went a week over. "Andrea Rackley."

"Thank you. Okay. Deep breath." She followed her own instructions. "Now, you want the bad news or the bad news?"

"Start with the bad news."

"I got nothing and more nothing. 'Danny Dunn' didn't put out. And I'm oh for twenty-three on black PT Cruisers in the area. None of the licenses checked out. Not a one."

Tim felt his last flicker of hope gutter.

"That and the damn safety-deposit key took me all day today. Good thing I don't have to work for a living. I'm hitting a few more banks first thing tomorrow, so we'll see."

Tim tried to keep the disappointment from his voice. "When you talked to Bear, did he mention why my name isn't out to the media?"

"The service isn't salivating at the prospect of the press. And the district office isn't eager to follow LAPD's nose-dive in public esteem. I'd guess they're determined to keep it in the family until they nail your ass. Let the out-of-towners take the heat for now. Plus, it's not as though you're a live threat to kill innocents. You're just after them." She snickered. "The Vigilante Three."

"Let the animals kill each other."

"Something like that. Or maybe they know you stand a

better chance than they do at tracking down your team before things get even more out of hand."

"Then why are they kicking down my door?"

"Tannino's got his ass to cover. And the service's. A lot
of due diligence getting thrown around."

"He must regret ever laying eyes on me."

"I don't know. Bear claims Tannino's upset that he
couldn't protect you more on the Heidel-Mendez shooting.
He knows it was a good shooting, and he knows you got
hung out. He admires the way you went, Bear says, that
you threw in your badge like an old-schooler. Gary Cooper
all the way. But he thinks that's what pushed you over the
edge, especially after Ginny. He feels partially responsible,
the dago softy."

Tannino's decency, in the midst of all this, moved him.
But if the full-force ART entry on Tim's apartment was any
indication, it wouldn't buy him an extra inch when the
cards were down.

"I need some help, Dray. See if you can pull some cash
out of our account for me. A couple grand."

"I'll do it first thing. Hell, I'm spending the morning
running around to banks, not like it's out of my way."

"Thank you."

"I'm your wife, stupid. It's part of the deal."

The sheets smelled of dust, and the pillow was so soft
his head parted the feathers, angling uncomfortably to the
mattress.

He awoke with a cramp that stretched from his neck
down through his rib cage. The showerhead coughed and
spit lukewarm water. A swirl of stray hairs clogged the
drain. The towel was so small Tim had to strain his shoulders to dry his back.

He took his time determining that the area was clear before approaching the Acura, which was parked where he'd left it, several blocks from his old building. He drove it swiftly out of the immediate area, pulled into an isolated parking lot, and wanded the car down with an RF emitter he pulled from the war bag in the trunk in case a transponder had been installed. To quell his concerns, he took apart the wand, in case the ESU geeks had installed a device within the emitter itself, a move he might have pulled on one of his better days. Nothing.

He wasn't surprised the car was clean—there was nothing to link the Acura to him, his now-defunct false identity, or the apartment building—but at this stage of the game, reassurance was a needed ally.

Once on the freeway, he was careful to obey the speed limit. After parking a good five blocks away, Tim crept up on the house, surveying it from all angles.

Like a dog to his vomit.

In the driveway Mac tinkered under the hood of his car, greasy rag protruding from his back pocket. Palton and Guerrera were about thirty yards up the road at the curb, looking conspicuous as hell in an '89 Thunderbird that listed left. They were doing dick to avoid getting eye-fucked because they knew, as did Tim, that he'd be an idiot to come here. They were sitting on the house simply because most of the time, as a deputy marshal, that's just what you did—covered your bases and tried to stay awake.

Aside from the obvious detail out front, the house looked clear. Tim withdrew and reapproached through the back-yard, sliding through the rear door. The smell of stale pepperoni and fresh coffee. Blankets and bed pillow still on the couch—Mac, concerned friend with the ulterior motive. Two pizza boxes on a new Ikea coffee table. Tim stared at the impostor, probably the first of many. The master bedroom was empty. The coffee-table box sat in the middle of Ginny's room, discarded, making all too evident that no one lived in the space anymore.

Tim found Dray at the kitchen table, silhouetted against the drawn blinds. Before her sat a canary yellow file and Tim's boom box. A tape rasped lethargically in the player, the speakers emitting a grainy whisper that showed the recording had ended. Dray sat at an angle, hunched right as if recoiling from intense heat or bracing herself for a blow. One arm she'd wrapped around her stomach; the other clamped it tightly in place. Her face had gone white, save for her trembling lips, which were a wan red. She looked more or less as she had when she'd taken the news of Ginny's death from Bear, the instant before she'd hit her knees in the foyer.

Just beyond the knuckles of her quaking right fist gleamed the brass safety-deposit key.

He approached on numb legs, on deadened feet.

Her head pivoted like a robot's; her eyes pointed at him but took no note of his presence. Her hand extended to the boom box, pressed "stop," "rewind."

Tim turned aside the file's vivid cover. The public defender's interview notes were on the top. He scanned them quickly—same stabbing words.

*The victim was the client's "type."*

*Client claims to have taken an hour and a half with the body after death.*

He turned to the deflating fifth page, but in place of what he'd read before appeared: *Client claims he was contacted at night by a man at his residence. Man was well built, blond, mustached, wore a baseball cap pulled down low over his eyes. Client knows nothing else about the mystery man.*

*Or imaginary friend*—the PD's annotation slyly read.

*Client claims man showed him photos of the victim and*

*maps and schedules regarding the victim's movement from
school to home. Client was to kidnap victim, then take her
back to garage shack for a later sex "show." Client and
mystery man agreed on date and meeting time for "show."
Mystery man never appeared again.*

Another single-sentence scrawl in the margin. *Story
thin, no corroborative evidence—deafness stronger route
for prelim.*

A prickly rage was fighting its way north from Tim's
gut, forcing itself up his throat. It emerged in a horrified
exhale, something between a grunt and a cry.

Rayner had doctored the notes before giving them to
Ananberg to copy—knowing, perhaps, that she'd leak
them to Tim. Either way he'd never planned on Tim's seeing anything but the expurgated version that indicated that
Kindell had acted alone.

The glossy surveillance photograph underneath took
Tim's breath from his chest. A nighttime shot of Kindell,
leaving his shack wearing only a T-shirt, his naked thighs
stained with blood.

Ginny's blood.

Tim stepped back violently from the table and leaned
over, hands on his knees. He retched a few times, the muscles under his rib cage straining, but he brought nothing up.
Sweat fell from his brow, spotting the floor.

The tape deck clicked, signaling the end of the rewind.

Dray reached out, hit "play."

*"Hello?"* Rayner's voice.

*"This a secure line?"* Frenzied breathing. Panic. Robert.

*"Of course."*

Tim pictured the sleek recorder by the phone on
Rayner's nightstand, generating another insurance policy
that Rayner could lock away in a safety-deposit box.

*"He killed her. He fucking killed her."* Gagging noise.

*"Cut her to pieces, the fucking retard."* Robert's high agitation matched the description of the anonymous caller who reported Ginny's body's location.

Rayner's breathing quickened. He managed a single breathy word. *"No."*

*"The whole thing's fucked. I didn't—fuck—didn't sign on for a little girl to get . . . Christ, oh, Christ. He was just supposed to hold her here and wait. Not lay a finger on her."*

*"Calm down. Is Mitchell there?"*

The phone being fumbled, then Mitchell's voice, dead even. *"Yeah?"*

*"Did you leave any evidence behind?"*

*"No. We haven't even approached the shack. We're up on the road above the canyon, our staging point for the entry. When we got here, we saw him inside, through the binocs. He was already at work on the body."*

Dray emitted a little noise from deep inside her chest.

Robert in the background. *"He was supposed to do nothing to her."*

*"Quiet down,"* Mitchell hissed. Then, to Rayner, *"I figured our little rescue-and-execution plan was out the window, so we aborted the mission."* Rustling. *"Hang on, hang on. Here he comes. He's stepping out. Stork—get the lens on him."*

The click of a high-speed camera. Tim's eyes returned to Kindell's glossy, blood-smeared thighs, his throat constricting. The photo was date-stamped—February 3. The top one of a stack of at least twenty. Tim felt as though his heart had shattered, and any move he made caused the jagged edges to dig further into his insides.

Robert's voice in the background. *"God, oh, God. The sick motherfucker."*

*"Listen to me,"* Rayner said. *"The plan is off. Get the hell out of there."*

Mitchell's voice came, cool and sly like a knife. *"We can still use this. For the candidate."*

That's me, Tim thought. The candidate.

*"What are you talking about?"* Rayner asked.

Mitchell, already calculating, maintaining a bone-chilling serenity. *"Think about it. 'A strong and personal motivation'—isn't that what you said we'd need to flip him? Well, William, I'd say we've just been outdone."*

Rayner's tense breathing across the mouthpiece.

Robert's raised voice. *"We gotta tell Dumone."*

*"No,"* Mitchell said. *"He'd go ballistic that we even thought about doing something like this. Plus, we gotta keep him clean for the candidate. The way this worked out, we don't have to tell Dumone anything at all."*

The way this worked out, Tim thought. The way this worked out.

*"No one breathes a word of this to Dumone. He'd have our asses. Or to Ananberg."* The media-polished, in-charge Rayner, rearing his well-groomed head. *"This isn't what we planned, but Mitchell's correct. It's a tragedy, but we might as well bend it to serve our aims. Get the hell out of there, and we'll regroup in the morning, get a new strategy."*

*"Out,"* Mitchell said.

The tape continued to spin; the speakers kept up their staticky hiss.

Tim raised his eyes to Dray's, and they stared at each other, the world seeming to screech to a halt. There were just her bangs, damp-pasted to her forehead, the heat in his face, the pain—no, agony—in her eyes that he knew mirrored his. She cracked open her dry lips but took a moment to speak. When she did, the sound seemed to shatter the hypnotic spell of the whispering spool.

"You asked Dumone what they had to gain by killing Ginny," she said. "The answer's simple—you."

The door to the garage opened. Dray quickly hit the "stop" button on the tape deck and flipped the file shut, hiding the photo of Kindell. Mac came in, wrench hooked through a belt loop, T-shirt stretched tight across his chest. A stalactite of sweat stained the front collar just so, as if a wardrobe stylist had sprayed it on. He looked up and froze.

Tim nodded at him.

"Rack, you can't be here, man. People are . . . they're looking for you."

"I'm leaving."

"You're putting Dray at risk." His eyes shifted to Dray. "And what are you thinking?"

Dray's head went on warning tilt. "Mac—"

"You're an active deputy."

"Mac, don't push this," Dray said. "Leave us alone."

"No, I'm not gonna leave you alone. He's a wanted—"

"I'm asking you to give us a minute."

"This is idiotic, Dray. You can't harbor a suspect in your house."

Dray's eyes seemed to contract to shiny dark points. "Look, Mac. I appreciate your being here for me. But I'm talking to my husband right now, and I think it might be time for you to leave."

Mac's face loosened, his mouth hanging slightly ajar in post-slap shock. In his indignation his features had arranged themselves somehow more gracefully, providing a window into some private reserve of dignity.

He nodded once, slowly, then eased from the room with a near weightlessness, light and forward on his feet. A moment later his car turned over in the driveway and the whine of his engine rose and faded away.

Dray sighed, digging the heel of her hand into her forehead. "Well, if I know one thing about Mac, it's that he wouldn't sell you out. He's loyal to a fault."

"He has no reason to be loyal to me."

Her eyes picked over his face. "To me, Timothy."

Tim pulled the tape from the deck and tapped it against his palm. Mac's brief intrusion had forced them both to recover their composure; Tim was scared to open the file again, to see the photo of his daughter's blood smeared across pale thighs. His mind drifted to Robert's frenzied charge down the basement stairs at Debuffier's. Robert's agitated words back at Rayner's afterward: *People fuck up sometimes. No matter what happens, an operation can spin out of control. We've all had that happen.*

"It was a mission that went to shit," he said. "They were gonna bust in, shoot Kindell, and play the big heroes to me. I can hear the sales pitch—here's a guy who was gonna rape and kill your daughter, skated on three priors due to loopholes in the law. The guy was your neighbor, in a school zone, no one monitoring him. Except us. *We* saved your daughter's life, kept her from being raped. Not the law. Come see what we're about. We have a plan that's gonna open your eyes."

"Those animals," Dray said softly. "Even if it had gone right, can you imagine what it would have done to Ginny? Being kidnapped? Being held? Having a man shot before her eyes?" Steam was curling from the cup of coffee to her side, and she ran her hand through it. "No decency. There's just not a fucking ounce of decency in men who would take those risks with a little girl's life."

"No," Tim said. "There's not." He pulled a chair out and sat down heavily. It felt as if it had been months since he'd been off his feet. "They've been torturing me all this time, holding the case over my head, the accomplice. They knew all along. Having Kindell kidnap Ginny was just part of some . . . psychological equation Rayner was evolving to get me to join the Commission. And it worked."

"You'll find them," Dray said. "You'll make them pay for this."

"Yes," Tim said. "Yes."

She nodded at his face, the bandage's bulge under his T-shirt. "You're okay?"

He touched his shoulder gingerly. "Yeah, it was nothing."

She looked away, but not before he saw her relief. "Your face doesn't look like nothing."

"I wasn't planning on getting by on my looks."

Her lips pursed but did not form a smile. "At least you're realistic."

"I want you carrying all the time. Even in the house."

Dray raised her sweatshirt to reveal the Beretta tucked into her waistband. "I hope to hell they do come after me. But I have a feeling they're not gonna make it that easy."

"Probably not."

She hooked her hair back behind her ear, then stood and fingered the blinds. "You shouldn't have come here. You're too smart to pull this move."

"Let's be grateful they think so, too."

"They've been out there feigning competence since yesterday morning. I told them we don't talk anymore, but I think they knew I was lying."

"Why?"

She shrugged. "Not all men lack perception."

Tim handed her the tape. "Not a bad piece of leverage. A little creative editing by Rayner and it could hang all his accomplices."

"Or at least keep them in line." She took the tape and set it down quickly on the table, as if she didn't want it touching her flesh.

"I shouldn't stay long. I don't want to put you at risk. I didn't have anywhere else to go. I . . . I need that money."

"Of course. I pulled out a couple grand for you this morning. It's in the gun safe."

"Thank you."

They sat quietly, unsure of what needed to be said, hesitant because the next words would likely signal Tim's departure.

"I see you got a new coffee table. The box is, uh, in Ginny's . . ."

"I can't respect that room as hallowed ground forever. Living here, it puts you on a different timeline, maybe. At least for some things." She looked away quickly, and he saw her face set, mad and little-girl stubborn. He remembered that he didn't miss all parts of her. "You wouldn't know."

He let the remark skip off into inconsequentiality. "How's security on Dobbins?"

"No way they're getting at him. His hospital room is like Fort Knox. Where's Bowrick?"

Bowrick's confidential hold ending at midnight was another concern to add to his list. "They won't find him."

She took a sip of coffee, grimaced against the heat. "Why would the Mastersons stay here where everyone's looking?"

"They hate L.A. because their sister was killed here, they hate L.A. cops because they handled their sister's case poorly, and they hate the system here because the L.A. courts turned her killer free."

"Where's her killer now?"

"Shot to death."

"Hefty coincidence."

"That it is." Tim cracked his knuckles. "They have a

plan for the city. They have strong contacts here, know their way around. Plus the case files they stole—all L.A."

"Now their motive for killing Rayner is a lot clearer," Dray said. "Tying up loose ends. Keeping eyewitnesses off the books." Her chest expanded, and then she sighed deep and hard, as if expelling something from her body.

"Yeah. They know there's no hard evidence or charges would've been brought. They're mopping up."

Dray pulled her head back, as if she'd been struck. Exasperation and intensity colored her smooth cheeks. She spoke slowly, as if she were still trying to catch up to her thoughts. "There's another loose end they're gonna have to tie up."

Tim felt his mouth go dry, instantly. An ocean rushing in his ears. Realization. Alarm. Stress.

He was on his feet, down the hall.

He was pulling ammo from the gun safe into a backpack when he became aware of Dray in the doorway. The roll of cash he'd wedged in the back pocket of his jeans. Dray studied his hands, the ammo.

"Take your bulletproof vest," she said.

"It'll slow me down."

"May you die and come back a woman in Afghanistan."

He stood, slinging the backpack over one shoulder. He started out, but she shifted in the doorway, blocking him. Her arms were spread, clutching the jamb on either side, the sudden proximity of her face, her chest, recalling the moment before a hug. He could smell her jasmine lotion, could feel the heat coming off her flushed cheek. If he'd turned his head, his lips would have brushed against hers.

"You're taking the fucking vest," she said. "I'm not asking."

# 42

**WHEN TIM TURNED OFF GRIMES CANYON ROAD ONTO THE** snaking drive to the burned-down house, he felt a thrumming start in the void where his stomach should have been. He pulled to a stop on the overgrown concrete foundation where the house used to stand, dead weeds crackling beneath the wheels.

Ahead, the stand-alone garage stood at the base of the small eucalyptus grove. At night it conveyed a sort of dilapidated grandeur, like a forsaken Southern mansion, but in the bright and unflinching daylight, it looked pathetic and distinctly unmenacing. Tim pulled on his gloves, his bulletproof vest, then approached.

The dirt-clouded windows had grown almost opaque. The garage door creaked up on rusty coils. The first thing that struck him was the odor, damp and dirty, the smell of water left stagnant and then drained. The busted water pipe had deposited swirls of silt on the greasy concrete floor.

Same ratty couch. Same hole in the far wall, no longer plugged by Ginny's underwear. Same enveloping dankness.

But no Kindell.

The side table had been knocked over, the cheap particleboard splintered down the middle, throwing up spikes of wood. One of the couch's cushions had been upended, the fabric split across the front like a burst seam. Crusty yellow stuffing protruded from the rip. The lamp lay shattered on the floor, the bare lightbulb still miraculously intact.

The mark of a brief struggle.

Tim placed his gloved fingertips on a dark spot on the couch, then smeared the moisture off the leather onto the white Sheetrock of the rear wall so he could discern its true color. Blood red.

A carton of milk lay on its side on the counter, a thread-thin tendril of fluid leaking from the closed spout. Tim righted the carton. Almost empty. He stared at the pool of milk on the floor, about four feet in diameter. He watched its drowsy expansion, gauged it had been at it for at least half an hour.

They'd taken Kindell somewhere. If they were merely going to kill him, they would have done it here. Isolated, quiet, rural. The stand of eucalyptus would have gone a long way toward stifling a bullet's report.

There was another plan in the works.

As Tim headed out, a white seam in the freshly exposed couch-cushion stuffing caught his eye. He walked over and tugged on it. His daughter's sock emerged.

A tiny thing, not six inches heel to toe, a ring of circus-color polka dots around the top. His daughter's sock. Stowed away in a ripped cushion like a dirty magazine, a bag of pot, a wad of cash. In this place.

His legs were trembling, so he sat down on the couch, gripping the sock in both hands, thumbs pressed into the fabric. The small room did a drunken tilt, a jumble of sensations pressing in on him. A waft of paint thinner. Milk dripping from the counter. A tingling in the scab over his eye. The smell of the embalming table, of what had remained of his daughter at the end.

He pressed his hand to his forehead, and it came away moist. His knees shook, both of them, uncontrollably. He tried to stand but could not find the strength in his legs, so he sat again, clutching his daughter's sock, shaking not with rage but with an unmitigated longing to hold his daughter, a longing that ran deeper than sorrow or even pain. He had not been braced, had not anticipated the need to shield these vulnerabilities, and the tiny white sock with its foolish dots had soared right through his fissures and struck him deep.

After ten minutes or thirty, he made it out into the pounding sun, across the scorching foundation to his car. He sat for a moment, trying to even out his breathing.

He had some trouble getting the key into the slot. He turned over the engine and drove off.

On the freeway he picked up the pace, accelerating until the speedometer pushed ninety, putting miles between himself and the killer's shack. Both windows down, air conditioner blasting. It wasn't until he roared past the First Street exit that his breathing returned to normal.

He pulled over and called Dray, reaching her at the station.

"They took Kindell."

The pause seemed to stretch out forever, then it stretched some more.

Her laugh, when it came, sounded like a cough. "What are they doing with him?"

"I don't know. If I could just get a lock on one of their residences."

"Big 'if.' "

"I was almost there. I can't believe the Stork's car didn't pan out. If the damn footage was clearer, I could have gotten the plate number."

"Wait a minute. Footage. What footage?"

"The security recording. I found his car on a security tape I took from a video store."

"Was it day or night? When the footage was shot?"

"Night."

"What was the lighting?"

"What?"

"The lighting. How did you see the car?"

"I don't know. A streetlight, I think. Why does this matter?"

"Because, genius, if the streetlight was sodium-arc, it would make a blue car look black on film."

Tim's mouth moved, but nothing came out.

"Hello? Are you there?"

"How do you know that?"

"Security-systems Secret Service course at Beltville last spring. Did you forget that in addition to being a domestic goddess, I'm a highly proficient investigator?"

"You got half of that right."

"Go check the streetlight. I'll start running the blue PT Cruisers, call me with the confirm."

"I'm on my way."

Fortunately, the streetlight was offset a good ten feet from the Cinsational Video front door, so Tim could stand gawking up at it without risking being spotted by the kid he'd robbed Saturday morning. He hadn't considered the fact that it was difficult if not impossible to determine whether a streetlight housed a sodium-arc lamp during the day, when it was shut off. He'd pulled on a zippered jacket to hide his bulletproof vest, but his reflection in a passing bus's window showed he'd succeeded only in making himself look conspicuous *and* fat.

A kid in a black hooded sweatshirt zipped past him on a skateboard, regarding him curiously. Tim waited for him to round the corner, then withdrew his .357, cocked it, and shot out the light. A puff of white powder emerged as the gas released, and then shards of glass tinkled on the sidewalk.

Tim got back into his car and drove away, already dialing.

Dray picked up on the first ring.

"Yeah, it's sodium-arc all right."

Tim waited patiently in a corner booth at Denny's, a Grand Slam breakfast sweating on the plate in front of him, though it was dinnertime. He scanned the front page of a discarded Sunday paper—MARSHAL VOWS TO STOP VIGI-LANTE THREE—picking up misleading background information on the players. A crime hot line had been established for phone-in tips. An LAPD spokesperson believed that the Mastersons financed the operations, using the money they'd received as part of their considerable settlement from the tabloid that had published the crime-scene photos of their murdered sister.

Page two reported on a Baltimore car salesman who, inspired by the Lane and Debuffier executions, had shot two men attempting to hold him up. One of the muggers had been seventeen, the other was his fifteen-year-old brother.

Tim skipped to the obituaries. Sure enough there was Dumone, wearing his Boston City Class-A's, looking stern, imposing, and—as always—slightly smirky, as if he were in on a joke lost on the rest of humanity. The cause of death was listed as terminal lung cancer, not suicide, and there was no mention of his involvement with the Vigilante Three. Tim wondered how Dumone would have felt having his eulogy appear in a paper publicizing Baltimore car salesmen emulating Charles Bronson.

Flipping back to the front page, Tim studied the photos of the Vigilante Three. The Stork's, in all likelihood pulled from his FBI file, framed his rigid passport-style pose against a washed-out backdrop.

His moral apathy and keenness for money made him a hell of a recruitment candidate—Rayner and Dumone had proved that once already. The good thing about greed is that it's a clean motive. It makes people predictable. Robert and Mitchell, driven by emotion, were a bit tougher to keep a leash on.

Another ten minutes had passed, so Tim hit "redial" again. He could hear Dray typing in the background even as she spoke. "Deputy Rackley."

"Me again."

"The PT Cruiser comes in steel blue and patriot blue. Edward Davis, aka Danny Dunn, aka the Stork, has one in patriot blue. He picked a new alias for the registration— Joseph Hardy. Ha, *ha*. From the look of his driver's-license shot, Nancy Drew is more on the money."

Tim sat up sharply, pushing away the plate of ripped-up pancakes. "Address?"

"You were right about El Segundo. One forty-seven Orchard Oak Circle."

**43** SINCE THE STORK'S FACE HAD BEEN PLASTERED ON every TV and doorstep in the state, his fleeing in the past two days would have been difficult. His distinctive features made a disguise unlikely, and nothing Tim had come across suggested that his technical proficiency extended into facial disguise. Tim figured he was holed up in his safe house, waiting for the media's ADD to kick in. Then it would be back to reports of shark attacks or terrorist cells, and he'd be able to slip on a plane to somewhere with lots of sand and umbrellaed cocktails.

The house was isolated, as Tim had anticipated, located at the rear of a large lot covered with foliage. Positioned at the end of a three-house cul-de-sac, the Stork's place was set back in the shadow of a surprisingly steep hill, the un-welcome terrain of which had probably saved it from de-velopment. No address numbers nailed near the front door, adhered to the mailbox, or sprayed on the curb. The house to its right was for sale, the picture window looking in on a barren room, and a remodel had ravaged the house to the left, tearing it down to its pressure-treated skeleton.

Crouching beside a construction Dumpster, Tim used a compact pair of binoculars to scan the foliage in the front yard. At least two security lenses peered out from leafy cover, craning on thin metal necks that had been spray-painted camouflage green. He picked apart the yard sector by sector. Another camera resolved from the foliage, and two motion sensors. The windows were barred internally, and the oversize front door looked to be solid oak. A gate blocked the backyard from view; a position up the hill would permit him a clear angle to the rear of the house.

Dusk cast a graininess over the street, lending it the slight unfocus of gritty war footage and washed-out black-and-white photographs. Somewhere, miles away, the rumble of waves rose into audibility.

Tim plotted a path up the hill, around the back of the house. He moved swiftly and evenly, ducking remembered camera lines of sight and IR beams. He had to acrobat his way through crossing motion-sensor fields near the side of the house, then it was free movement up the hill. He'd snugged his gun back into the hip holster so as not to worry about slippage.

He lay on his stomach and studied the backyard in the dying light, disappointed that he'd left his night-vision goggles in the war bag in the Acura's trunk. The only good thing about the chest-high fence, topped with a Slinky of concertina wire, was that it adhered to residen-tial zoning heights. With matching iron bars, the rear windows appeared to be equally impenetrable as those to the front. A virtual colony of security cams angled toward the back door like attentive prairie dogs. He picked up a motion detector over the back door, an ominously quiet doghouse blanketed in shadow, dog shit on the kidney-shaped lawn.

Keeping a nervous eye out for Fido, he inched down the hill and zoomed in with the binocs on the back door, barely visible through the wide mesh of the security screen. Single pane framed with a thick wooden stile. Though he couldn't confirm it from this distance, it seemed the edges of the pane bore a dark strip, a Plexi-coating that would indicate bulletproof glass. A latch protector extended past the doorknob and overlapped the frame, guarding the bolt from a credit-card lift; that, and the visible hinges, meant the door was outswinging. The knob itself housed a series of locks with immense key slots, probably custom-made.

He would have expected nothing less from the Stork.

The bulletproof pane looked in on a laundry room and another locked door, this one solid. Two shiny circles on the second door suggested standard locks, probably pick-resistant Medecos. A shimmering of metal near the doorknob indicated a wraparound mag plate to reinforce against jimmying. Tim would've put money on both doors' having reinforced strikes, long screws to beef up the plates against a kick-in.

He certainly had his work cut out for him.

He was just pulling back when a light clicked on deeper within the house, revealing a dining table overburdened with keyboards and computer monitors and surrounded by a copper-mesh cage. The Stork shuffled into sight, wearing a pair of baby blue pajamas, entered the cage, and plopped down in front of the cluster of equipment.

Tim lay in the darkness, his eyes resting on this man

who had played a part in his daughter's dismemberment. He felt his heartbeat in his fingertips, his ears; his entire skin seemed to move to the heightened pulse. He pictured the Stork behind a telescopic lens, calmly focusing as Kindell stumbled out from his shack, Ginny's blood across his thighs to . . . what? Bay at the moon? Breathe the crisp air? Catch his breath for continued sawing? The Stork wouldn't have cared; he'd have taken apart his camera lovingly, nestled its parts in foam, collected his paycheck.

The Stork typed for a few moments, then paused to rub out knots in his cramped hands. Through the well-barred window, Tim briefly watched him resume work before withdrawing back up the hill.

It took him nearly ten minutes to extract without tripping any alarms or crossing any lenses. He sat in his car a few blocks away, plotting, regretting he'd given up dipping tobacco again, since he felt like working something over physically to mirror the activity in his head.

Though he was competent with a pick and a torsion wrench, he had none of the Stork's finesse or training. He didn't stand a chance against those locks.

Finesse would have to go out the window.

He paid cash at the Ace Hardware counter, spending most of what Dray had given him. The checkout woman, an old biddy with the rough hands of an inveterate gardener, whistled over a strapping coworker to help Tim get his purchases out to his car. Tim waved him off, loading up the equipment in an enormous black duffel bag he'd pulled from an overstuffed wire bin in Aisle 5.

"Must be a hell of a project." The woman's breath smelled of Polident.

Tim hefted the bag up on a shoulder. "Yes, indeed."

Moving along the prescribed path through the Stork's front yard was trickier with the bulky duffel in tow, especially in the full dark of night. There was no way he'd get through the dueling motion sensors at the side of the house, and he didn't have the patience or tools to size out a mirror to bounce the IR beam back on itself. Instead he pulled a small shaving mirror from the bag, shattered it, and deflected the beam with a shard momentarily so he could smear Vaseline over the housing.

After some tedious creeping and hauling, he reached his post in the hillside. The effort and the heavy vest left him damp with sweat. Down below, the Stork was still working away in his blue pajamas at the computer. He appeared to be talking to himself. After a few minutes Tim heard the shrill ring of a telephone, and the Stork picked up a cell phone from the table but seemed to get no response. He shook his head, realizing he'd grabbed the wrong line, and set the cell phone back down. Rising from his perch behind the monitors, he walked into the adjoining kitchen.

Tim checked the bag to make sure everything was accounted for and well arranged, then began a silent descent to the back fence. He clipped a small canister of mace to his belt, checked his gun, and removed a length of blanket insulation from the bag. The Stork was visible in the kitchen, sitting on a stool, sipping juice through a straw and leaning to talk into the speaker of a wall-mounted phone. He fussed the cap off a bottle and took a few pills, continuing to massage his arthritic hands as he spoke.

Taking a deep breath, Tim heaved the duffel over the fence. The grass cushioned its landing, but still he heard a startled movement within the doghouse. He unfurled the blanket insulation over the concertina wire and scrambled over the fence as a Doberman streaked toward him, snarling. He hit the ground, reaching for the mace as the dog took flight in a long snarling leap. He got off a blast and ducked the dog as it sailed into the cloud, growl already turning to whimper. The dog rolled on the ground, pawing at its eyes, emitting a drawn-out whine like a horse's whinny.

Tim shouldered the bag and began a jogging approach to the back door. He crowbar-torqued the security screen, which popped with a satisfying clang and swung out on its hinges. He dropped to a knee, pulling gear from the duffel. As he fitted his electric drill with a wide circular bit, he heard movement within—the Stork's scrambling approach.

The Stork pushed through the laundry-room door and stood, watching through the back-door window. "Mr. Rackley, I'm glad you found me, since I couldn't find you. Robert and Mitchell have gone completely out of their heads."

"Open up and let's have a talk."

"Somehow I've been implicated, but I—"

"I know you were involved. I know you picked the lock for them at Rhythm's."

"I was just going to say, Robert and Mitchell coerced me into helping them. I didn't want to, but threat of death and whatnot. I did it with a gun to my head. I told them I'd never help them again."

"I also know you were involved in my daughter's death."

The Stork's entire body sagged, his shoulders rolled forward, his head dipped. "That wasn't my idea. Or my choice. I tried to warn them off, told them it could only come to—"

"Where are they? Where'd they take Kindell?"

"I haven't been in touch with them. I swear, Mr. Rackley. I don't know where they are." The Stork's eyes went to the Doberman, still rolling on the lawn far away at the back fence. "W-what did you do to Trigger?" His breathing quickened. "God, my house, how did you . . . ?" He shuddered. "Why should I trust you any more than *them*?"

"It ends here, Stork. You come clean with me. And the authorities."

"I won't let you in. I won't be turned in." The Stork's squeaky voice did little to disguise his panic.

Tim raised the drill. With a grating whine, it eased through the bulletproof glass, leaving a neat hole the size of a coaster next to the handle side of the wood stile. Next he revved up a pistol-grip saber saw.

"You're making a terrible mistake!" the Stork screamed.

Tim released the trigger, let the noise from the hammering blade fade to silence.

"I have dirt on you, Mr. Rackley, or don't you care?" Drops of sweat ran down the Stork's cheeks, having originated somewhere high on his bald head. "You were the actual assassin. I was just the tech guy. If you turn me in, I spill, and your life is over, too."

Tim started the saw again, and the Stork stepped forward, shrieking, tripping over a neat row of shoes beside the washing machine. His face was approaching tomato red. Tim starting cutting a line up the bulletproof glass, which yielded easily. He hit the wood of the top rail, and the saw's buzz kicked into high. The blade had started to gum up; chain saws worked better on bulletproof glass, but they were significantly louder.

The Stork had pressed himself to the glass, inches away from Tim, pleading. Tim stopped the saw, changing the blade. "You helped set up my daughter's death. You sat back and *took pictures* as she was being cut to pieces. I'm coming in. I'm making you talk. And I'm not going to sleep or eat or pause until the three of you have answered for the role you played."

"Stop it! Oh, God, stop it!" The Stork pressed his hands and forehead to the bulletproof glass, leaving smudges. He was gasping now, the mist from his breath clouding the pane in splotches. His shoulders were shaking, his curiously flat nose a white stroke on his flushed face. He appeared to be crying. "I just want to be left alone. I can't go out anyways, not since you released my name to the press. I won't do anything. I won't even leave the house. I just want to live here alone."

Tim started the saw again and leaned forward.

The Stork's face flicker-changed back to its usual inscrutable blankness—his performance was over. He leaned back, pulled a Luger from the back of his pajama waistband, and fired through the drilled hole of the glass directly into Tim's upper stomach.

The force of the shot knocked Tim off the concrete step. He fell back another two paces and landed flat on the lawn. Despite the screaming pain, he forced a double roll to the side, putting him out of the limited range the hole permitted the Luger. He tried to cry out but could not, tried to suck air but could not.

His mouth open, he lurched and bobbed, his insides a dense knot of pain that permitted no breath. A guttural creaking emerged from his mouth, foreign to his own ears. He kicked and flopped like a fish on a boat deck. The Stork watched him with curiosity, occasionally knuckling his glasses back up into place.

"I wasn't about to permit you to go to the authorities once you knew where I lived, Mr. Rackley. Surely you understand."

Tim tried to fight his jacket off, still straining, still struggling, still locked up from neck to bowels. At once his insides spasmed and eased, and he drew in a hard cool breath and immediately fell to coughing. He pushed himself up on all fours, nearly hyperventilating, coughing and snorting and sucking air. Snot dangled from his nose, saliva from his lower lip. It felt as though someone had swung a wrecking ball into his gut.

Tim stood. The Stork watched with amazement.

Tim pulled off his jacket, grimacing to get each shoulder free, and the Stork saw for the first time the bulletproof vest beneath. His eyes bulged in a nearly comic show of fresh-started panic, and he emitted a weak scream. Turning, he ran back through the laundry-room door and slammed it. Tim heard bolts turning, chairs being slid.

He approached the door again with firm, angry footsteps. His throbbing stomach made itself known each second as he sawed down from the hole, through the bulletproof glass, through the bottom wooden rail. He kicked the door, and it parted, one half flying open, leaving a length of wooden stile, a thin strip of bulletproof glass, and the myriad locks perfectly in place in the doorjamb. He stepped through the gap, dragging his bag.

Three steps in, the solid laundry-room door stopped him. It was steel-reinforced, and both locks were Medecos, as Tim had guessed.

Behind it he heard the Stork's panicked movements. "I'm sorry. You alarmed me, though, you really alarmed me. I have money here, lots of money. In cash. That's how I keep it mostly. You can take . . . can take whatever."

Tim popped the circular bit off the drill and fitted a carbide tip. The Medecos featured fortified ball bearings and hardened-steel inserts, which would render a normal bit all but useless.

Tim gripped the doorknob, and a jolt of electricity

knocked him to the ground. He slid to a stop near the split back door, shaking his head, his tongue and teeth gone numb. He gripped his arm to stop it from shaking.

The clever bastard had wired an electric charge to the doorknob.

Tim stood up, leaning on the dryer until the spell of light-headedness passed. A faint nausea washed through him, then departed, leaving him only with the pain in his abdomen, a pulse that spread down to his bladder and up through his chest each time he inhaled.

The Stork had gone silent on the other side of the door.

Tim dug through the mound of footwear, tossing aside the Stork's tiny sneakers, a worn pair of loafers. A street-hiking boot at the bottom, layered with rubber and stained with red dust, would do the trick. Tim slid the drill handle into the boot, gripped it as best he could, and used a lace to tie down the trigger.

At the drill's renewed whine, the Stork's frantic pleading started again. "Just give me fifteen minutes, and I'll clear out of town. You'll never see me again. *Please.*"

Tim aimed the carbide tip into the cylinder core directly over the keyway. Sparks flew out in a continuous fire-cracker blaze as the drill progressed, eliminating the lock pins, bringing the tumblers and springs down out of place. When he paused to wipe his heated hands on his jeans, they left red smudges from the dirty rubber boot. Gripping the drill through the boot made for slow going; by the time he'd finished the second lock, the drill chuck was steaming and his forearms were cramped.

He drew his pistol and kicked the door. It banged in, sending a propped chair spinning into the dining room. A severed lamp cord ran from an electrical outlet, its end stripped and duct-taped to the doorknob.

No sign of the Stork.

Tim heard whimpering farther back in the house, so he moved through the dining room toward the rear hall, elbows locked, .357 extended. The house was cluttered. Three laundry baskets full of padlocks that had been shot and drilled. A row of key-cutting machines sitting side by side, each one a menacing confusion of arms, levers, teeth. Safety goggles hanging from buffing wheels. Soldering irons. Tackle boxes filled with switches and sockets and washers. A multi-antennaed apparatus with an oddly vital appearance.

Tim moved with extreme caution, assessing everything around him, looking for booby traps.

The Stork's voice echoed down the hall at him. "God, don't take me in. I couldn't last in prison, a guy like me. Not for a second." The words deteriorated back into unintelligibility.

A thin trip wire gleamed about eight inches off the hall floor, just before the turn. Tim took care in stepping over it.

The bathroom on the far side of the elbow was empty, as was the small opposing study. Tim sourced the faint moaning to the hall's terminus. Another locked door, this one solid-core wood. Tim flattened against the wall to the hinge side of the door. When he ventured a hand and knocked, the moaning flared up into a shriek.

"Please just go. I'm sorry I tried to shoot you, Mr. Rackley. I can't go with you and be arrested. I can't."

"Where did Robert and Mitchell take Kindell?"

"I won't say anything. I'm not going to go to jail. I won't go to jail. I swear I just—" His words cut off abruptly. Dead silence.

"Stork? Stork? *Stork!*"

No answer.

After another minute of silence, Tim shuffled his feet in place to see if he could draw fire. He smacked his heel against the door, but this brought no response either. His stomach ached. He might have broken a lower rib. The skin on the roof of his mouth still tingled from the shock. His shoulder throbbed.

He slid down the wall to a crouch, pistol dangling between his spread legs, and listened.

Complete silence.

He stood again, fighting away the pain, fighting for focus. Pivoting, he kicked the door just to the side of the knob. It did not give. He stumbled back a few steps, gripping his ankle, cursing. His foot hurt like hell.

He crept back down the hall, careful to avoid the trip wire, retrieved a pair of channel locks from his bag, and returned. Trying to keep his body to the side of the door, he gripped the knob in the vise and twisted hard, snapping the pins and raking through the cylinders. Then he flattened himself again against the hinge-side wall, willed away his various aches, and prepared for the pivot.

Take two.

This time the door gave with the force of the kick. He barged in, .357 sweeping left, then right.

The Stork was backed against the far wall, drawn up in a huddled ball beneath the window, the Luger on the floor before him. His legs were curled under him, an arm gripping a knee, one hand clutching his chest. His face was deep red, awash in drying sweat, his mouth slightly ajar. His glasses had come unhooked from one ear and sat crooked across his face.

Tim kicked the gun away, checked a pulse and got nothing but tranquil, clammy flesh. The Stork's feeble heart had given out.

Tim stood and regarded the room, a bizarre mishmash of

spinster antiques and old-fashioned toys. A quilted comforter draped over a wooden sleigh bed. A Silvertone windup record player sat on a varnished table beside a stack of old LPs, a pile of stray hundred-dollar bills, and a Lone Ranger tin lunch box with the lid open. The lunch box was filled with neatly banded hundreds.

Tim leaned to peer behind the sole print on the wall—capless Lou Gehrig, head bowed, the luckiest man on the face of the earth confronting the packed stands of Yankee Stadium—and caught the gleam of the steel wall safe behind. The view from the other side revealed wiring and plastic explosives. Thinking of his ART teammates, Tim found a Sharpie permanent marker in the nightstand drawer and wrote BOOBY TRAP in block letters on the wall with a big arrow pointing at the frame.

He cautiously slid open the closet door, revealing several hundred old children's lunch boxes, stacked floor to ceiling. He pulled the top one off—the Green Hornet and Kato—and opened it cautiously. Filled with cash, mostly fives and tens. The money by the record player Tim figured to be the latest payment, perhaps for the Stork's part in planning Tim's own assassination. Or for a murder still to come. Kindell.

The bathroom counter was barely visible beneath a blanket of pill bottles. A rubber ducky stared at Tim from the tub's rim. Strung up on the tile were dozens of photos, most of them surveillance shots of Kindell about his business—emerging from a supermarket, tying his shoes on a sidewalk, brushing out his garage shack like a suburbanite on a Sunday afternoon. Tim wondered which were shot before Ginny's death. He was overtaken with a fierce, fantastic urge—to travel back in time so he could fill Kindell's head with bullets before the calendar lurched forward to February 3.

A photo of Tim and Ginny at the monkey bars, her expression one of apprehension, his of affectionate impatience. She'd been gripping his hand tightly, as if in fear that the monkey bars would mount an assault. Next to it hung a shot of Ginny walking home from school, backpack snug on both shoulders, face downturned, lips pursed—she was whistling to herself, as she often did, lost in that reverie children her age seem to fall into when alone.

He stared at the picture, feeling his grief again thaw and resolve, his mind clicking and whirring, trying to contend with the colossal unfairness that Ginny, in her mere seven years, had been targeted and risked and ultimately dismembered because of Tim's own talent and recruitability. A pilot light of guilt flickered, ready to catch and blaze. How much responsibility did he, his training, his psychological profile, bear? How much of Ginny's death had to do with the traits and skills embedded in Tim's own character? Guilt could reach startling depths, he'd learned, even when not attached to fault.

He moved back down the hall, again stepping over the booby-trap wire, and into the dining room.

Gizmos and gadgets of all sorts lay about the floor in various stages of development and disuse. Tim recognized Betty, the conical digital-tone renderer, and Donna, the modified peeper. Betty had been altered, the keypad removed and a single Walkman earpiece inserted. Tim picked it up, inserted the earpiece, and swung the sound-gathering parabola around the dining room. He picked up nothing. He angled it through the open laundry-room and back doors, and the Doberman's panting, hot and slobbering, burst into his ear. He let out a startled yell and tugged the earpiece free, his heart racing. The Doberman was still lying out near the fence, nearly fifty yards away. Tim was regarding the long-range mike with renewed admiration when he became aware of Robert's sandpaper chuckle, feet away.

He dropped Betty, his .357 drawn before she hit the floor.

Robert's malicious laughter continued. Muscles tensed, weapon readied, Tim followed the sound toward the kitchen. He swung into the room, back pressed to the jamb, but there was nothing there, just an empty kitchen table, the Stork's cup of juice on the counter, the red light of the telephone.

Tim slowly realized that the laughter was issuing from the still-active speaker on the wall-mounted phone. His assault on the back door had interrupted the Stork's call.

Robert's abrasive voice boomed out into the kitchen, over what sounded like low-level radio static issuing from the line. "Something scare you, princess?"

Tim spoke loudly in the direction of the speakerphone. "I'm quaking in my stilettos." Talking compounded the throbbing in his stomach.

"You put on quite a show. It's like old-time radio. 'The Shadow knows.' I bet the Stork would have appreciated it. Did you kill him?"

"He's dead."

"I figured."

In the background Tim heard a distinctive, familiar chime rise out of the static. "You have Kindell."

"You're a quick study."

"Have you killed him?"

"Not yet."

The barely audible static from the speakerphone found resonance in the kitchen, the sudden depth of stereo sound. The matching murmur issued from the direction of the kitchen table. As Tim walked over, a radio-frequency scanner came into view on the seat of one of the chairs. The distinctive chime he'd overheard on the line—LAPD's dispatch prompt. He felt his stomach tighten but pulled his focus back to the conversation. "What are you going to do with him?"

"I'm gonna violate his constitutional guarantees. And hard."

A digital counter on the phone ticked off the length of the ongoing call: 17:23. The clock on the stove showed 10:44 P.M. Bowrick was safe only for a little more than an hour; then he'd likely be turned out of the clinic and put back on the street.

"You set Kindell up to kidnap my daughter."

The air left Robert; Tim heard it across the mouthpiece like a burst of static. The rustle of the phone being covered. The murmur of the brothers conversing.

"We didn't mean for it to go down that way."

"Yeah? Well, then, why don't you tell me how you meant for it to go down? Because, hey, maybe once I hear this, I'll just forgive you and we can all go home."

"We needed an executioner. We'd been waiting for months, almost a year, while Rayner tinkered with psychological profiles. Ananberg was being an uptight cunt. Dumone was . . . well, Dumone moves slow. Us and Rayner, we needed to get the plan in motion. The problem was, Rayner said, a guy with your profile wasn't likely to say yes to something like the Commission. Needed a more personal motivation. So we thought we'd give you a little shove."

"A shove."

"It was supposed to go down easy. Kindell picks up Virginia, we bust in, cap his ass before he so much as touches a hair on her head. We save her, deliver her back to you in secret. We tell you the system let a child molester off the hook three times and placed him right there in your sunny little neighborhood. We tell you he had designs on your little girl—designs that would have been fulfilled if things were just left up to the system. We tell you we're guys with a plan, and since that plan just saved your daughter's life, why don't you come to a meeting?"

"I'm overcome with gratitude and, after subsequent bonding, I join the Commission."

"Something like that."

*"You put my daughter in the hands of a convicted child molester."* The venom in Tim's voice must have set Robert back on his heels, because he took a few moments to respond.

"Look, I'm sorry it went down that way, but desperate times and all that. Rayner was looking at Kindell closely since he'd gotten off for his priors—the insanity-plea bullshit, a loophole that made him a potential Commission target even before Ginny. Rayner did the profile on him. He wasn't a killer. None of his priors took that turn. We thought we'd just approach him, say, 'Hey, here's a girl you might like. Grab her and keep an eye on her, don't do nothing till we show.'"

"Didn't work out that way, did it?"

"No it didn't. And after, we figured Kindell would wind up in jail. We were gonna try to use Ginny's death to pull you aboard, but when he got off because of the deafness . . . well, shit, that made you a sure thing. Hey, man, life gives you lemons . . ."

"Then you slowly win my trust, Rayner doctors up Kindell's case binder so I'm convinced Kindell acted alone, and we vote to execute him. I do the job. I clean up your mess, the one remaining witness."

"Right. Once we off Kindell, there's nothing linking us to Ginny. Or to anything around the Commission. It's just your word against ours."

They had no idea that Rayner had taped their call from Kindell's. A sound escaped Tim, a creaking, eerie laugh that caught him off guard.

"What's so fucking funny?"

"You've become just like them. This plan of yours, it led you to kill a girl. A seven-year-old girl."

"Don't put that shit on our heads." Robert's voice rose, to the verge of yelling. "We don't own what Kindell did. That wasn't what we wanted."

From the beginning Tim had tried to understand the Mastersons' odd mix of resentment toward Tim and horror over Ginny's death. The resentment was guilt gone bad; the horror was their own revulsion at having her blood on their hands. He recalled Mitchell's words on the telephone: *We were gonna cut you a break, leave you be. Part of us figures we owe you.*

"Well, Kindell's gonna pay now," Robert said. "We'll do him for you. It'll be a statement, even, to this hellhole of a city. A little . . ."

"—tribute—" Mitchell's muffled interjection.

"—for all the other pukes out there to see. The first step of the next phase, *our* phase. It'll say, 'We got him. And you're next, motherfucker.' "

"I can't let you do that."

Robert's voice was shot through with intensity and menace. "Are you really gonna fight to save the life of the man who killed your daughter? This piece of shit deserves to die."

Kindell's image came to Tim quickly and vividly, as it always did. The crop of fuzzy hair, so much like animal fur, capping the flat forehead. The wet, insensate eyes, devoid of emotional comprehension. He thought of the relief Kindell's absence from the world would afford him. At the moment he could imagine nothing more disagreeable than extending himself to save his life. "I happen to agree. But that call isn't ours to make."

"Oh? He's bleeding here in Mitch's hands. So tell me, whose call is it if it ain't ours?" He chuckled. "And lemme warn you while we're at it—we know you're double-dealing with the marshals. Any sign of any car, we cap Kindell and shoot our way out. And believe us, we'll know. We got our ears to the ground."

Tim looked at the radio scanner on the chair.

"You forget, Rackley, we surveilled you for the better part of a year. We know when you were toilet trained. We knew how you'd react when Ginny died, how to fold you right into the Commission. We predicted you and played you like a fucking board game. We go head-to-head, you're gonna lose. We *know* you, Rackley."

"Like you knew Kindell?"

"Better. We operated side by side with you. Next time we see you, we're gonna break it off in you."

"Vivid image."

"Don't get in the way of what we're accomplishing here."

"Your righteousness is a joke," Tim said. "And if you think I'm gonna leave this city at the mercy of you or your brother, you're even more deranged than I thought."

Robert let out a sharp hiss of disgust.

Tim's rage narrowed to a single point of calm, the eye of the hurricane. "I'm coming for you." He raised his pistol and shot the telephone. It shifted and crumpled a bit. No sparks, no flying shrapnel—it was far less satisfying than he'd anticipated. He stood a few minutes in the quiet kitchen, waiting for his anger to burn itself out.

Clicking through the radio scanner's settings confirmed his worst suspicions—the Stork had managed to get ahold not only of LAPD tactical frequencies but also those of the marshal duty-desk radio, which corresponded with all deputies in the field. The radio echo he'd heard over the telephone meant that the Masterson boys—wherever they were—were well apprised of in-progress law-enforcement movement throughout the city. He couldn't know if Bear's cell-phone frequency was also being monitored; for the time being he'd have to assume that any communication with the authorities would tip his hand.

Returning to the dining room, he finished glancing through some of the Stork's oddly animated inventions before turning his focus to the copper cage. No keyboard vibrations going anywhere through that thing.

He leaned over and stared at the bizarre jumble of words on the computer screen.

"What the hell?" he murmured.

Letters scrolled across the screen as if they'd been typed: *what the hell*

Tim found the outpointed microphone atop the monitor and spoke into it. "You're a speech-to-typing program."

The screen responded again: *you're a speech to typing program*

He scrolled up the screen. It had picked up the majority of his conversation with Robert in the kitchen, though only his own utterances.

*I'm quaking in my still echoes he's dead you have kindle*

The speakerphone must not have been loud enough for the mike to pick up Robert's responses.

He scanned up farther, taking in the Stork's frantic remarks to him through the bedroom door, the computer hypothesizing about unclear words: *please just go I'm sorry I tried two shoot you missed her rackety I can't go with you and bereft I can't*

Scrolling all the way to the top, Tim discovered that the Stork had turned on the speech-recognition software to compose a letter.

*Joseph Hardy*
*P.O. Box 4367*
*El Segundo, CA 90245*

*Dear Mister McArthur,*

*I do have an interest in your recent shipment of young adult original classics, particularly* Tom Swift and His Megascope Space Prober, *1962, and* Tom Swift and His Aquatomic Tracker, *1964. I am only interested if they are near mint or better. The last book you shipped to me,* The Radio Boys' First Wireless, *was badly yellowed hello hello Robert doughnut use this lie I tolled you the new foams are clear your second payment was off buy too hunter I counted it twine I'm out I doughnut car this has gotten crazy since mister rackety leek too the press I wow leaf my house you done need me for survey lands the money mint is clear at night good line of site done the kill on all side I'm not coming especially too night too much heat no surrey and even if Ida considerate it would cost you more than that hang on Jesus hang on mister rackety I'm glad you fund me since I could nut find you*

The computer approximation of the Stork's dialogue to Tim through the back door continued, winding up with *stork stork stork what the hell you're a speech to typing program.*

Clearly the software had to be guided with additional audio commands to render sentences meaningfully; the Stork had ceased overseeing it when he'd gone into the kitchen to answer the landline. The farther he'd been from the mike, the less faithfully the program had transcribed his inadvertently recorded dialogue. His speech impediment probably hadn't helped much either.

Tim picked up from *hello hello Robert,* trying to figure out the sentence breaks:

*doughnut use this lie I tolled you the new foams are clear*—so far, so good.

The Stork had reached for a cell phone first when the phone had rung in his house. Remembering that he'd set it back down on the table, Tim searched and found it behind a stack of discarded keyboards. He scanned through the programmed names. Only two: "R" and "M."

Pocketing the phone, Tim turned his attention back to the screen:

*your second payment was off buy too hunter I counted it twine I'm out I doughnut car this has gotten crazy since mister rackety leek too the press I wow leaf my house you done need me for survey lands*

Tim got stuck at *the money mint is clear at night*

He pulled a pad over and jotted down variations.

Money man. Money print. Munitions.

And the following sentence—*good line of site done the kill on all side*—was no clearer.

Good line of sight to the kill from all sides?

He dropped the pen and thumped the notepad in frustration, his hand leaving a dirty imprint. He decided to move on.

The next few transcribed sentences were much easier to interpret:

*I'm not coming especially too night too much heat no surrey and even if Ida considerate it would cost you more than that*

Tim scratched his hairline with the end of the pen. Whatever the specifics, Robert and Mitchell were planning to kill Kindell tonight. Tim reflexively glanced at his watch. 11:13 P.M. The Mastersons had presumably called the Stork because they were ready to enact the next step in their plan; Tim didn't have much time to intercept them.

The Stork's reaction to the sound of Tim's interruption followed next on the screen: *hang on Jesus hang on*

And then his first words to Tim: *mister rackety I'm glad you fund me since I could nut find you*

Tim returned to the first problem noun, "the money mint," no doubt the key.

What would be clear at night? Did the Stork mean "clear" as in "safe," or "clear" in the visual sense? Probably "safe," since in the sentence before he was arguing that he wasn't needed for surveillance. What would be clear at night? A place of business. A public place. An actual mint? A planned robbery didn't seem to fit. Done the kill. Down the hill? Money man clearance?

Tim studied the reddish mark he'd left on the notepad— the smudge of his palm, four finger streaks barely visible. The stain should have been a brownish mix of dirt and grease from the tools, but the dust that had come off on his hand from the Stork's boot had colored it almost auburn.

*money mint*

Where had he seen dirt that shade?

*done the kill*

*the money mint is clear at night*

The slap of delayed recognition. The buzz of adrenaline. Tim bolted to his feet, forgetting the aching in his stomach. The chair rolled back lazily across the room and hit the wall.

Robert tilted his face back and shot a stream of cigarette smoke at the moon, two patches of dirt coloring his denim jacket at the elbows.

*money mint.* Monument.

The monument is clear at night. Good line of sight down the hill on all sides.

*I'll tell you what would make a good memorial. One guilty and unconvicted fuck swinging from each branch.*

*That's what I'd like. That's the kind of memorial we oughta build for those victims.*

At tomorrow's first light of day, downtown L.A. would have a grim silhouette greeting it over the skyline.

*It'll be a statement, even, to this hellhole of a city. A little tribute for all the other pukes out there to see. The first step of the next phase,* our *phase.*

Working quickly, Tim defused the booby trap in the hall, cutting the trip wire and writing an immense warning on the floor with the Sharpie. He resisted the urge to spend time figuring out how to reach Bear through a secure line. Whatever chance he'd have of bringing this conflict to a nonviolent resolution—admittedly slim—would be lost with flashing lights and a marshals-LAPD barricade. A stealth approach was likely necessary to save Kindell's life.

On his way out, Tim stopped to retrieve his jacket. The Doberman approached him and nuzzled his hand shyly, its eyes red and submissive.

**44** TIM EASED DOWN THE TILED CORRIDOR AND SLID INTO Room 17, checking the door numerals against the crumpled slip of paper in his hand. Bowrick sat cross-legged in bed, blanket drawn around his shoulders like an Indian chieftain. He started, then pressed his hand to his chest, relief washing across his face. "Can't you ever knock like a normal person?"

Tim tapped his lips with his index figure and gestured for Bowrick to follow. They made their way out the back entrance, the silence broken only by the admitting nurse's humming in the lobby.

They'd driven two blocks before Bowrick spoke. "Man, you're just in time. Nurse Needlestick's been foaming at the mouth, wanting insurance cards, asking billing questions, all kinds of crap. For the forty-eight-hour hold, you're free and clear, then they Grand Inquisition your ass." He glanced up as a green freeway sign floated overhead. "Where we going?"

"You still have your Monument Hill access-control card?"

Bowrick fumbled his key chain out of his pocket and held up the card.

"The two guys who tried to kill you are there. They've got a hostage, who they're planning to hang from the tree. I'm gonna surprise them. I need you to brief me on the monument."

Bowrick let out a pensive whistle, then chewed his bottom lip and picked at the scab on his arm. "Only way in is the front gate, 'cause the fence is high and they run an electric current across the top. That's the bad news. The good news is, the gate's out of view from the monument and quiet when it opens. Steer clear of the dirt path—you can see it pretty well from up top. Just east of it is the most brush cover, and it's a steeper approach, so it'll keep you pretty well hidden."

"How about the monument? How do you get up on it? Platform elevator or anything?"

"Nope. Climb the scaffolding, that's all. On the back side, there's some two-by-fours in place like a ladder. They use pulleys to hoist shit up, drop-tubes to junk stuff from up high."

"What kind of equipment is available? That can be used as weapons?"

"Mostly locked up at night. Probably a few hammers lying around. Oh—and a sandblaster. That fucker'll strafe your ass, lift skin. Then there's the usual suspects—steel plates, boards, nails. I'll show you as we go."

"You're gonna stay down the hill. I've gone through too much effort for you to get killed now."

"Why would you care?" His tone, sharp and little-boy bitter, cut through the collaborative mood they'd briefly established. He shifted in his seat, his face taking on a reddish hue Tim usually associated with crying. "Answer me. You've dragged me into enough because of all this. I've gone along with all your crazy shit. I want to know."

Tim fought away the first responses that came, knowing Bowrick deserved something more. "Look." He moistened his lips. "When I got to your house to kill you, when I saw you, I felt like I was looking into a mirror."

Bowrick's eyes shifted across the dash. "A mirror. Right."

"Look at me. Don't look down, away. That's just arrogance."

Bowrick held his gaze, though his face paled and his hands fidgeted in his lap.

"You think you're so bad nobody else can look you in the eye. Well, I can. We've both killed people for the same reasons. And I see that you're at the beginning of a process that just might be redemption. And I'm betting on that."

"What if I don't want that responsibility?"

"If you screw up, I can always come back and shoot you later."

Bowrick let out a short stutter of a laugh. His grin faded when he saw Tim wasn't smiling. "Okay." He nodded, his pale face flecked red with acne. "Redemption. Hell. I never had anything like this I'm supposed to carry until now."

"And?"

"That's fine by me. But you better keep studying it, too. Redemption. Because if you're just gonna look at me and think, 'Hell, that kid ain't as *bad* as I've been convincing myself, so maybe I'm not either,' then, shit, you haven't learned a damn thing. It's a *path* not a status." He let out a jerky breath. "And I don't know shit about redemption, but I been walking that path long enough to know you gotta keep walking."

They came around a bank in the freeway, and there it was, its dark silhouette visible even against the black sky, overlooking both downtown and the 101 like a guardian angel. They reached the base of Monument Hill within minutes, left the car on the street, and crept to the gate. Bowrick flashed his access-control card at the pad, and the gate whirred slowly open. They slipped inside and vectored east of the path, Bowrick leading, Tim clutching his binoculars so they wouldn't make noise brushing against his chest. He'd taken Betty from the collection of tech treats in the Stork's dining room, and he held her respectfully at his side, the earpiece coiled around her handle. The Stork had been correct about one thing: There was a good line of sight down the hill on all sides.

Bowrick extended his hand like a shark fin, tracing the route Tim should take up the rugged hillside. Tim nodded, then handed him the car keys and the Nokia, catching his eye so his meaning was conveyed. Gesturing Bowrick to stay put, he began his cautious approach. After a while he bellied back toward the path, forging through a stand of chaparral that blocked his vantage, the speedloaders in his pocket digging into his thigh.

He emerged about a hundred yards from the hilltop. Up ahead loomed the monument, now a complete tree, the metal hide having been laid over the skeletal supports of the tree's final branches. It remained ensconced within the web of scaffolding, a harmony of primitive planes and angles, a rudimentary form eager to emerge and shake off its shell. On the plateau at the monument's base sat a Ford Expedition and a Lincoln, parked nose to nose, visible between stacks of metal sheets. Though no one was in evidence, Tim discerned the faint murmur of voices. The uphill breeze quickened, just slightly, but enough to overpower any sound from the hilltop. He aimed Betty upslope in the direction of the cars, but she picked up little aside from the rumbling of wind across the parabola.

One of the Mastersons stepped into view between two tall piles of metal, and then the other. The dark figures were unmistakable, the swollen chests, the hard taper of the sides, all top-heavy muscle and bellicose posture. The first put his foot up on a sawhorse and lit a cigarette, arm bent across the raised knee. Through the binoculars Tim watched the ribbon of smoke unspool from the dark face. The glowing point of the butt lowered; the mouths moved in conversation. The mood of the twin shadows was stern, focused, decisive.

One pulled open the trunk of the Expedition and yanked a bound man to the edge of the tailgate.

Kindell.

Gripping him with a fistful of fabric at the shoulder blades and a clench of the belt, the man steeled his muscles. Kindell remained limp and contracted, hands bound behind his back, knees curled to his stomach. His captor tugged him hard from the tailgate, letting him drop the four feet to the dirt, doing nothing to break his fall.

Kindell landed flat on his chest and face. Despite the breeze, Betty picked up his pained gasping.

Robert and Mitchell were discussing something. Beneath their voices Tim made out a few spats of radioed correspondence from the service desk officer, in all likelihood issuing from a portable radio that was a counterpart to the one in the Stork's kitchen.

Through the earpiece Tim heard ". . . under wraps until . . . then come back . . ."

The first shadow had his foot resting on Kindell's back, as naturally as it had rested atop the sawhorse a few minutes ago. They seemed to arrive at some conclusion, for the second figure picked up Kindell and, swinging him once to pick up momentum, tossed him into the trunk of the Lincoln. He slammed the lid. Tim watched closely—no sign of either Masterson setting a booby trap in the trunk.

The two turned and disappeared into the maze of pallets and junked wood.

Tim crept out from cover and inched toward the two cars, but it was extremely slow going since the sawhorses and heaps of building materials concealed myriad hiding places, and he had to zigzag back and forth to ensure he wasn't leaving open a vulnerable angle. He reached the brink of the plateau and lay still in the waving foxtails, taking in the area in a long, slow sweep of the parabolic mike, earpiece snug in place, his right hand firm-gripping the .357. He got nothing back from Betty but a tinny whimpering from the Lincoln's trunk.

He popped up and did a quick run to the nearest cover, diving behind a mound of jagged metal refuse, the bulletproof vest and clay-red dirt not softening his fall enough to keep pain from screaming through his stomach.

Still no sign of Robert or Mitchell. Plastic drop cloths fluttered everywhere—between stacked metal planes, beneath sawhorse legs, around corded bundles of boards. Tim scanned up the dark monument with the binocs, but it was hard to make out much more than the tree's outline through the scaffolding. He could see the open hatch at the base of the trunk where the Sky-Tracker spotlight had been slid into the tree.

He low-crawled to a rusting sandblaster about ten yards

from the two vehicles, close enough that he could hear Kindell's desperate thumping in the car trunk. Again Tim surveyed the plateau, his eyes picking through the heaps of gnarled metal and discarded cuttings, the resting machinery, the boxy rise of scaffolding.

Kindell in the car trunk could very well be a baited trap. Tim rustled the Stork's new Nextel from his pocket. Since Mitchell, as a demolition expert, was accustomed to keeping his cell phones turned off, Tim clicked the preset number to "R," readied Betty, and hit "dial." The faint chirping ring of a phone was immediately audible, and Tim fanned the parabolic mike back and forth, searching for the strongest signal. The cone climbed the trunk of the tree, fanned out over one of the branches. Robert was not visible, because the wooden platform of the scaffolding cut off almost the entire branch from view, but Tim got a strong ring through the earpiece. He figured Robert was probably up there preparing a noose for Kindell.

The expected rough voice answered. "Robert."

Tim clicked the phone shut.

Robert appeared at the edge of the branch scaffolding, as Tim hoped he might. Raising his fingers to his mouth, Robert whistled a single harsh note. There was movement to the side of the monument, and then Mitchell's head poked up from a throw of scrubby brush; he'd been walking a surveillance patrol around the base of the monument while Robert readied the branch above.

Blocked from their view by the stacks of metal, Tim dashed over and tried to open the trunk of the Lincoln, but it was locked. The doors were locked as well—no getting to the trunk release without breaking a window. His efforts led to invigorated thumping in the trunk, and Kindell's muffled voice.

"Doan urt me. Please lee me be."

Kindell's loose, deaf enunciation brought fresh recollections, flooding Tim with revulsion.

He jogged back behind the sandblaster and aimed Betty again in Robert and Mitchell's direction, catching the tail end of their shouted discussion. "... on the Stork's phone ... keep an ear on the scanner ... get me Kindell ..."

Mitchell started for the vehicles, his Colt glinting. Tim, crouched behind the blaster, was almost directly in his path. Mitchell drew near, approaching the car, and banged on the trunk with the barrel of the .45. Kindell let out a shriek.

His face twisted with disdain, Mitchell dug in his pocket for the keys.

Tim braced himself, weapon up near his cheek, then stepped from cover. Mitchell caught sight of him breaking into the open, and at once both guns were up and aimed. Miraculously, neither one of them fired.

A Mexican standoff.

"Well," Mitchell said. "Now what?"

"You tell me."

The wind had picked up; Tim was pretty sure as long as no shots were fired Robert wouldn't hear them from his position up high in the tree.

They drew a little nearer, Mitchell's left hand supporting the hair-trigger .45 in his right. His eyes jerked to the monument, betraying his urge to yell for his brother. Hands regripping the pistol, Tim shook his head, and the look on Mitchell's face made clear he understood what the price would be for shouting. His thick hand was steady on the gun, his finger curled through the trigger guard. Tim pictured him sitting in a parked van watching Ginny leave Warren Elementary, his eyes calm, a notepad in his lap. Mitchell following her silently, shadowing her through the streets she took on her route home.

A Detroit cop, task-force member, explosive-ordnance tech. Stalking a seven-year-old girl who still used bunny ears to tie her shoes.

Mitchell's mustache broadened with his smile. "Don't suppose you want to drop the guns and go at it man to man."

"Not on your life," Tim said.

They circled each other slowly within the ring of metal stacks, blocked from the monument's view.

"Let me tell you this," Tim said. "I've fired nine shots in the line of duty, and they've all been hits. Eight of them have been kill shots." He paused, moistened his lips. "If we throw down, you have no chance of surviving."

Mitchell mused on that, his head bobbing. "You're right. I'm not a shooter."

He spread his arms wide, letting the gun dangle from his thumb. He tossed it to the left, aiming for the sandblaster. It bounced off the metal box, missing the "on" button by a few inches.

Mitchell's eyes went to the metal stack to his side. If anyone could lift a five-foot pane of half-inch steel by himself, it was Mitchell. Tim wasn't about to take any chances.

"On your knees. Arms wide. Turn around. Hands on your head now. That's right. Not a noise."

Tim slide-stepped in on him, both hands on the gun. At the last moment he saw that the toes of Mitchell's boots were curled rather than flat against the dirt.

Mitchell pivoted and sprang. Tim laced his hand through the .357 and hammered Mitchell across the face with a ball of fist and metal.

Bone crunched.

Mitchell staggered but did not drop. As he charged into Tim, his legs shoved against the ground, a linebacker gaining yards. He knocked Tim back into a stack of metal, jarring him, then the immense arms were a frenzied blur. The blows were even more devastating than Tim could have imagined. They were rapid and unremitting. They were car-crash powerful. They were rage and pain vented and embodied. Hunched protectively like a winded boxer on the ropes, Tim was wave-battered against the steel.

A haymaker brought him to his knees.

He'd have to shoot Mitchell or be killed. He brought the gun up, but then a shadow streaked toward Mitchell, flying up on his back, and Mitchell reeled, delivering a vicious elbow to the temple of his attacker. In the flash of an opening before Mitchell turned back, Tim delivered another gun-enforced blow, on the rise, directly between Mitchell's legs. Mitchell expelled a hard gust of air, and then a dry heave pulled him down into a lean. Tim rose, blood running freely into his eyes, and hammered the gun down across Mitchell's face.

Mitchell fell, his mouth open against the ground, his breath kicking up puffs of dirt. Bowrick stirred beside him, a lattice of broken veins coloring his left temple and upper cheek. Tim turned quickly, looking behind him for Robert's approach, but there was no sound save that of fluttering plastic and wind drawing across the plateau. Tim studied the monument but spotted no movement, no trembling of the scaffolding to indicate Robert's descent. Bowrick rolled over and shoved himself up on all fours, his forehead wrinkling with pain. He reached over, pulling Mitchell's gun from the holster, the barrel pointing at Mitchell's chest.

Tim tensed, dread locking the breath in his lungs.

Bowrick glanced over at him, their eyes holding for a moment, then he slid the gun into his jeans, sat back on his heels, and looked at Tim expectantly.

Tim gathered some cord from one of the wood stacks

and double-bound Mitchell's wrists behind his back, then his ankles. One of Mitchell's eyes stared up at him, a glossy animal organ, all pupil. Tim's first blow had broken his cheek badly; the skin sucked in beneath the eye like a drape pulled to an open window. Tim was gentle with the gag. He patted Mitchell down, pulling the car keys from his pocket.

Bowrick sat with his elbows resting on his knees, watching Tim work. He spoke in a harsh whisper. "Where's the guy they want to kill?"

Tim pointed at the trunk of the Lincoln.

"Why don't we get him out of there?"

Keeping his eyes on the monument, Tim crossed to Bowrick, lowering his voice so Mitchell couldn't hear. "Can't have him making noise. And he's unpredictable— we don't want him running around right now." He tossed Bowrick the keys. "Get the hostage clear. Don't open the trunk, don't talk to him. Neutral it down the hill, nice and quiet. The metal stacks'll block you from view part of the way down. Don't turn on the car until you're through the gate, then drive a few blocks, park somewhere out of sight, and stay alert. Keep the cell phone on. If you haven't heard from me in an hour, split, call Deputy Jowalski at the U.S. Marshals Service, and explain the mess I dragged you into. And this time don't come back, even if it is to save my ass."

Bowrick nodded, slid into the driver's seat, and pulled the door gently shut. The Lincoln began the solemn downhill roll, tires crackling softly on the dirt path, brake lights glowing in the night.

Tim sat for a moment and mopped the blood from his forehead. One of Mitchell's blows had opened up a seam just at his hairline; he'd have a scar on the left to match the rifle-butt wound from Kandahar. Another punch had struck his shoulder near the bullet-fragment wound; it had already swelled up. His torso felt like a nerve-filled skin bag holding rocks and razor blades. After a few moments the rush of blood into his eyes slowed, and he stood up, fighting off light-headedness.

He retrieved Betty and the Stork's phone and dialed Robert's number again. Betty sourced the ring to the same branch, hidden from view by the scaffolding.

Same gruff voice. "Robert."

Tim hung up. He circled the monument to the far side. If there was gunplay, Robert would have a tactical advantage firing down on him; there was no harder shot than one directly up.

The scaffolding made for easy climbing. Leaving Betty behind, Tim worked his way up as silently as he could, minding every creak and shift. When possible he climbed the metal branches, as they gave off less noise than the wood. Every few moments he'd pause and strain his ears, listening for Robert's movement, but the wind, especially as he got higher, drowned out most noise—a factor that also worked to his advantage. Metal plates were missing here and there, dark, empty gaps looking in on the hollow tree interior.

About fifty feet off the ground, he paused, leaning against the cool metal of the trunk, drawing a deep breath, and hooking his fingers into a few of the monument's myriad holes designed to beam out the spotlight's glow. From this angle he had a clear view of the dirt path. The Lincoln drifted silently through the gate. He saw the lights blink on as the engine turned over, and then it pulled away.

Tim inched his way up, hugging metal and wood, drawing a few splinters. He wound up on the platform supporting the branch opposite Robert's, about three feet lower. Crouching on a knee, he withdrew the Stork's phone from his pocket and dialed again. The phone's chirping ring sounded clear and loud, just on the far side of the trunk. Tim kept the call active, sliding the Stork's Nextel into his pocket. Double-handing his Smith & Wesson, he drew back to the far edge of his platform so he could get three steps of a running start.

He timed two deep breaths, then thundered into his run. The trunk brushed his shoulder as he leaped, shoving off the platform hard and flying across a five-foot break of open air. Beneath him the drop stretched down seventy feet, broken only by metal branches and wooden crossbeams.

He hit the edge of the opposing platform and rolled evenly across his back, popping to a high-kneel shooting stance, one knee down, one up, the thrust of the gun an extension of both elbow-locked arms.

About six feet off the platform, dangling from a noose looped over the scaffolding above, was Robert's Nextel. Ringing. It swayed gently, rocked by Tim's hard landing on the platform.

He felt his insides go slack, the rush of panic. Keeping both hands firmly on the .357, he shuffled two steps, careful not to trip over a stray two-by-four, and peered over the platform's edge. On the ground Robert sprinted across the plateau, directly at the monument, sliding a curved Gurkha knife back into a hip sheath. He was coming from the direction of the parked car and the stacks of metal. Tim knew before he raised his eyes that next he'd see Mitchell, staggering twenty yards behind Robert, working the freshly cut cord from around his wrists. Though Mitchell moved unevenly, dizzied from Tim's blows, his shoulders were firmed with rage, his legs moving in short, punching steps.

What alarmed Tim even more was that Mitchell had his black det bag looped over one shoulder.

Tim glanced down, trying to spot Robert again, but he had already disappeared underfoot. Before he had time to formulate a single coherent thought aside from the slapping awareness of how badly he'd been fooled, a reverberating clank announced the spotlight's activation. Blinding light filled the core of the tree, shot in thin beams from the holes of the trunk and branches. A gap between metal plates below threw light up against the bottom of the platform; it streamed around the sides like a gold, twinkling river.

Squinting against the brightness, Tim glanced over the edge of the platform and saw Robert stepping slowly backward, peering up at him through the scope of a McMillan .308.

A bullet cracked through wood, zinging past Tim's head and embedding in a beam overhead. Tim threw himself flat against the platform. A second bullet punched through the platform inches from his face, throwing a spray of splinters past his cheek. He rolled toward the trunk, splitting beams of light. Two more shots penetrated the platform inches from his spinning body and ricocheted off wood and metal. Tim froze near the trunk.

The ping of metal and then the slapped-meat sound of slug smacking skin. Tim's leg jerked as he heard the delayed report, and he cried out, more from shock than pain. His mouth cottoned instantly. Beams of light shot out from the tree branches all around him and through the bullet-riddled platform, one ray an inch off his nose, another just in front of the bend of his elbow; two he sensed rising between the split of his legs. He lay still, realizing that his movement made him detectable as he crossed over the fingers of light, making them blink out.

His thigh throbbed, numb and painless. He estimated that the bullet had entered just north of his right knee. When he heard movement down below, he risked rolling his head over to glance through one of the platform holes.

Robert, head down, chambered another round. In a clear

stretch of plateau about twenty yards from the monument, Mitchell was on a knee, pulling blocks of C4 from his det bag. From this distance the blood staining his face looked like oil.

Tim strained his eye back to where Robert had been, found him missing, and jerked away just as another bullet split the wood where his head had been, enlarging the hole he'd been looking through. A remarkable shot, particularly given the angle.

Tim froze.

The silence was nearly unbearable.

Another bullet broke through the wood; another beam of light sprang up like a fast-growing vine between his neck and shoulder.

The stray two-by-four, about five feet long, was just within reach of his right hand. With a grunt he shoved it a few inches forward. The far end of the board crossed a hole in the platform, quashing the thin beam of light, and quickly two bullets hammered through the wood on either side of the existing hole. Tim covered his head, waiting for the ricochets to stop.

What Tim had gleaned at Rhythm's indicated that Robert preferred a sitting shooting posture, an elevated tactical advantage, and a position offset right from a frontal view. Right now he was shooting from a standing position at a target directly overhead, and—despite those hindrances—firing with astounding accuracy. If Tim didn't get off this platform, he was going to get picked apart piece by piece.

The mouth of a tube, about three feet in diameter, faced him across the length of the platform. Designed as a flexible safety trash chute for workers to clear scraps of material, the tube wormed over the edge of the scaffolding and dropped to the ground. The sturdy canvas would never hold

Tim's weight, and even if it could, the nearly free-fall seventy-foot drop would spit him out almost directly at Robert's and Mitchell's feet.

Blood soaked his jeans around the bullet wound; it was only a matter of time before a few crimson drops made their way down one of the holes near his right leg and gave away his position.

Even if his leg wasn't injured, the tree trunk's diameter was too wide for him to James Bond down the interior, spread-eagling to slow the fall. He couldn't count on a rapid police response to such a remote site; even if the gunshots were audible over the rush of the freeway, at that distance they'd probably sound like little more than firecrackers. The only way off the monument was a tedious climb.

Tim shoved the two-by-four again to disrupt the light flow farther down the platform and risked a look through the hole near his head. Robert was repositioning himself. Mitchell had finished laying C4 around the tree trunk's base and was storming back to his det bag.

To buy a few seconds, Tim pressed his gun barrel to a hole near his hand and fired four times, blindly. Then he rolled to his back and shot once at the rope tying Robert's dangling Nextel to the scaffolding above. He hit the rope near the wood, pinching it off and causing the phone to drop straight down rather than swing off the platform's edge.

He timed a lunge, grabbing the phone and landing flat, arms and legs spread, barely missing the bullet holes in the platform, the loose two-by-four pressing hard into his shin. Two more shots hammered through the wood precisely where he'd been. Robert had now all but ventilated the platform; there was very little unpenetrated wood left on which Tim could lie without giving away his position. He removed the coarse rope from the phone and used it as a tourniquet for his leg. Another shot broke the wood beside him, forcing him to flatten against the platform again.

Breathing hard, his elbow bent to dodge the new beam of light, Tim lowered his hand and worked the Stork's phone from his pocket. With excruciating slowness he brought the two phones up to his chest, holding them side by side. Bullets continued to punch through the floor at intervals, pinging around the small cross-section of scaffolding.

He worked his foot over the two-by-four, pressing his toe against its end, then snapped his foot out. Right when the board slid off the platform's edge, drawing Robert's attention—Tim hoped—at least for a moment, he glanced through the hole to his right.

As he'd anticipated, Mitchell was still coming strong, the det bag looped over his shoulder and bouncing musically against his hip. He was heading for the C4 he'd left at the tree trunk's base, a coil of wire in one hand, a razor knife in the other, an electric blasting cap in his mouth.

Tim hit "redial" on the Stork's phone and tossed Robert's Nextel into the canvas tube. He heard it ring once on its way down. It whistled along the canvas as it fell, guided in toward the trash heap at the base of the monument.

A sharp crack as the electric blasting cap detonated, triggered by the ringing phone's RF pulse. A moment of perfect stillness, nothing but the wind whipping through the scaffolding, then a gut-wrenching wail.

Robert.

Tim rolled twice, sticking his head over the platform's edge. Directly below, Robert was genuflecting beside his brother's body. A spray of matter above the shoulders confirmed that Mitchell's head had been blown apart by the electric blasting cap.

Tim swung over the platform, gripping the edge to aid

his swing, and dropped ten feet to the one below. His right leg, weak and slick with blood, gave out, and he collapsed.

Robert roared down below, then bullets started hammering through the platform, sending chunks of wood flying. The gap between the metal plates in the trunk made the lower platform blindingly bright. Tim dragged himself to the visible section of trunk, lead flying up all around him, plunged his arm into the gap, and fired once, directly down the core of the tree.

A blast rocked the monument as the spotlight lamp exploded. The sharp flare of light disappeared at once, plunging everything into darkness.

Tim worked his way swiftly around to the far side of the tree. Smoke was seeping from the holes in the metal, the sluggish discharge recalling blood from wounds.

Robert continued to bellow down in the dark, firing randomly up at the branches and sky.

Tim hooked a toe on an opposing branch and pulled himself onto the far wall of scaffolding, then half fell, half slid down, catching splinters, moving quickly while the rifle reports covered the sound of his plunge and marked Robert's place across the monument.

The shooting stopped, either because the ammo had run out or because Robert was circling to Tim; either way the silence sat thick in the air like an unvented smell. Tim slid from the lowest metal branch, dropping six feet to the ground and bearing his weight on his left leg.

Fumbling out a speedloader, he refilled the wheel of his gun. Despite the makeshift tourniquet, blood had twisted down his jeans, engulfing his knee. His head swam for a moment, static obscuring his vision; he'd lost a lot of blood. He tried to run, but his right leg had gone numb, and he fell over, catching a mouthful of dirt. With the help of a sawhorse, he pulled himself back to his feet.

Robert broke into view, one-handing the .45 as it kicked and bucked, cording his forearm with muscle, muzzle flare lighting his face. His eyes showed too much white. Sheets of flesh pulled down from his jaw on either side, tight against twine-split muscle. He was roaring something, his lips loose and wet, his mustache a red slash above his stretching mouth.

Tim ran as best he could, threading through the scaffolding around the trunk's base, putting metal and wood between him and Robert. Robert was firing wildly; he was less skilled with a handgun. Tim could barely run with his bad leg; boards were flying past him on either side and overhead. He ducked and jumped and dodged. Lead sparked off metal, always just behind him, always just around the turn. He'd sprinted nearly 180 degrees around the trunk when he swung wide and turned, lining the sights. Robert appeared, gun leading around the curved turn and, still in dead sprint, Tim squeezed off a round.

Robert's .45, raised in front of his upper chest, caught the bullet with a clang of lead meeting steel. The barrel sparked, and Robert cried out as the gun tore from his hand.

Tim swung back just in time to see the thigh-high mound of refuse before him, and he ran into it full bore, nails and dust exploding. Shaving through the left side of the heap, he hit ground hard and slid a few feet, landing on his back with a brick pinching into his left hip. He looked up through the thickening cloud of stirred debris and saw, ten feet above him, the open bottom of the canvas tube staring down at him like a curious eye.

He sat up, .357 leveled. Despite his fall, he had the advantage now; his bullet had to have ruined Robert's .45.

Robert was standing perfectly still, about fifteen yards off, partly shielded by a stack of metal plates. Just watching him.

Tim's glance dropped from Robert's pink eyes, to his confident mouth—too confident for an unarmed man being gun-faced—to the rising globe of his biceps as his hand turned over, revealing the end of a remote detonator. Shifting farther behind the stack of plates so he was only a half man peering out, he nodded once at Tim, indicating something. Tim glanced down and realized that the brick pinching his hip was not a brick at all but a block of C4, the first of many spread around the monument's base at four-foot intervals.

Mitchell's body lay sprawled about ten feet to Tim's left, his det bag several feet closer where Robert had pulled it when he'd prepped the C4. Of course Robert would have primed the explosives—he'd still thought Tim was up in the monument.

Tim's head snapped up, and he fired once, but Robert anticipated his move, ducking behind the metal stack. The shot sparked off the steel. Tim braced himself for the explosion, but none came.

Instead came Robert's rough voice. "You took Mitch's head, you motherfucker. Took it clean off." The words wavered and blurred.

Tim glanced at Mitchell's body, a blur above the neck. Next to it lay Robert's rifle, partially buried in red dirt. A scattering of tools had fallen from Mitchell's bag. Spray-on glue. Needlenose wire clippers. The tiny shining cylinder of a nonelectric blasting cap, pushed into the earth. Tim picked up the blasting cap, rubbing its smooth side with his thumb.

LAPD would be here soon—the lit tree had to have been visible for miles—but Tim heard no sirens.

Robert's rifle—no bullets. The .45—out of commission.

He doesn't want to detonate the whole hundred-foot monument, Tim realized. He wants to shoot me, but he doesn't have any bullets left.

Tim turned the blasting cap in his hand and slid it down the bore of his .357, leading with the well end. It fitted barely, touching the metal on all sides. He needed something to jam it in place. He looked frantically around him for an appropriate-size object, knowing it was only a matter of seconds before Robert made his final demands. Nothing in the dirt around him. He leaned forward to dig through the mound of debris, and a spasm of pain racked his stomach.

The slug.

Tim's fingers scurried over the front of his bulletproof vest, finding the small mushroom of lead from the Stork's gun. A jagged little nine-millimeter.

It went hard down the gun, sharp edges digging grooves in the smooth metal bore. He used the tip of Mitchell's needlenose wire cutters to snug it in place. He lowered the .357 into his lap, praying that Robert wouldn't notice the altered weighting of the spiked barrel, since he was accustomed to a .45.

Robert's face resolved from the shadows on the far side of the stack of metal. "One click of this button and you're done. The only question is, do you want me to blow up this memorial with you?"

"No," Tim said. "I don't."

"Toss me your gun."

"Don't do this."

The detonator jerked up, clenched in Robert's hand beside his face. *"Toss me your fucking gun."*

Tim threw the gun. It landed in the dirt a few feet from Robert's boots. Robert stepped forward and took it, aiming at Tim with a shaking hand. The portable radio scanner swayed on his belt, long turned off. "Get up."

Tim struggled to his feet, favoring his left leg.

Robert's eyes pulled back to his brother's body. A tear

gathered on his lower lid but refused to fall. "I have a mind to take some time with you."

Tim staggered a bit to keep his balance on his good leg.

"But I'm not an animal like you. I wouldn't put your wife through the pain of having nothing left but a mangled corpse." With the gun Robert gestured to Tim's torso. "Take off your vest. I don't want to fuck up your face."

Tim pulled off his jacket and unstrapped his vest. The Velcro pulling loose sounded like cloth ripping. He dropped the vest in the dirt and faced the gun. From his angle he could see the scratches in the bore.

Robert beckoned him forward with the barrel, and Tim stepped from the cover of the monument, weaponless and bleeding and weak. The throw of ground outside the scaffolding seemed desert-barren. There was nothing to cut the wind.

"Was it you or Mitchell who met Kindell that night at his shack? Gave him the intel dump on Ginny . . . when she walked home, what route she took?" Tim's throat clogged with disgust. "Told him she was his 'type'?"

"Me," Robert said, his eyes red and morose. "It was me."

He pulled the trigger.

Tim dropped to a crouch, covering his head with his arms.

The blast was loud and surprisingly sharp, and when Tim looked up, Robert was gazing at him as if nothing had happened, his right arm extended as before, except his hand was blown off.

Robert's eyes found the splayed end of his stump, a pulled-weed tangle of roots, and then blood spurted from the left side of his neck where a piece of shrapnel had blazed a groove through his carotid artery. He fastened his good hand over the side of his neck but only succeeded in splitting the stream between his fingers.

Tim rose slowly and approached him.

Robert raised his injured arm again and stared at the wound, its gaping permanence, as if he still couldn't believe it. Blood streamed from his neck down his good hand, dripping from his elbow now. His eyes were wide and child-vulnerable, and Tim felt his breath catch in his throat.

Robert staggered back a step, his arm flaring for balance, and Tim took it and eased him to the ground. He stood over him, gazing down. Robert's legs and arms started jerking, and quickly he couldn't keep his hand pressed over the hole in his neck.

He bled out in the dirt.

Tim stood for a moment in the space between the sprawled bodies of the twins. His voice was steady by the time he called Bowrick. "It's clear. Come get me."

He pulled the Gurkha blade from Robert's sheath. As the Lincoln made its way up the hill, headlights glaring intrusively and throwing the bloody tableau into shadowy relief, Tim left Robert's body and limped over to meet it. Bowrick pulled to a stop, his elbow resting half out the window like a trucker's. He killed the engine, and the car sat dense and immobile in a swirl of reddish dust.

"Pop the trunk," Tim said.

Kindell had gone quiet, but at Tim's voice he started shifting again. The trunk yawned open, and there he was, curled between an empty gasoline can and the spare.

Kindell, who couldn't fix a fuse but could rape and slaughter. Kindell, who would forever own the privilege of seeing Ginny last, of being there when the light blinked out in her eyes. Kindell, the ultimate patsy.

"Lee me alone. Please lee me alone."

Bowrick was out of the car behind Tim now, arms crossed, watching.

Tim grabbed the rope binding Kindell at the wrists and ankles and hoisted him out. Kindell screamed as his shoulders stretched back in their sockets, then again as he hit ground. He strained to peer back over his shoulder, the clammy skin of his face quivering. His cheek was bruised, and one nostril was clogged with dirt.

He lay for a moment with his forehead touching the ground, saliva stringing from his lower lip. He was panting and making throat noises like an animal cornered after a grueling chase.

"Doan you urt me. Doan you dare."

Tim pulled the knife from his back pocket and crouched. Kindell let out a shriek and tried to wriggle away, but Tim pinned him with a knee between his shoulder blades.

He cut him loose and stood back up. Kindell continued to weep into the dirt.

"Get out of here," Tim said, though he knew Kindell couldn't hear him.

He shoved him with his foot, and Kindell looked up at him, fear finally draining from his face.

Tim enunciated clearly. "Get. Out. Of. Here."

Kindell scrambled to his feet and stood rubbing his wrists, disbelief doing a slow fade from his eyes. "Thank you. Thank you. You aved my life." He stumbled toward Tim, hands extended in gratitude. "I'm orry I illed your daughter."

Tim struck him hard in the face, his knuckles grinding teeth. Kindell yelped and went down. He lay panting, drooling blood, his eyes wide and unfocused. His front tooth hung by a bloody thread from his gums.

"Get the fuck out of here."

Kindell pushed himself to his feet and staggered a bit, staring blankly at Tim.

*"Get the fuck out of here!"* Tim took a menacing step

forward, and Kindell turned and scurried away. Tim watched his loping, irregular run, watched him trip once or twice on his way down the hill. A few moments after Kindell disappeared, he realized he was shivering, so he retrieved his jacket from the ground.

When he walked back, Bowrick stood watching him, his face impassive. "That guy killed your daughter?"

"Yes."

Bowrick bounced his head in a nod. "If you'd have killed him, would it have felt good?"

"I don't know."

Bowrick spread his arms—an ironic suggestion of martyrdom and self-display—then let them fall. He hooked his thumbs in his pockets, and he and Tim stood squared off, like adversaries or lovers, the dust still settling around them, letting the silence work on their thoughts.

Now, finally, came the distant scream of approaching sirens, and far down on the freeway Tim could see the glittering approach of blue and red lights, LAPD all the way.

Bowrick walked over and got into the passenger seat of the Lincoln, where he sat patiently. Tim looked at the spilled bodies on the dirt, the monument.

He climbed into the driver's seat and spun around in the plateau, throwing dust and pebbles. His headlights flashed past the boulder at the monument's base. The quotation chiseled into its flat side was now complete:

AND THE LEAVES OF THE TREE WERE FOR THE HEALING OF NATIONS. REVELATION 22:2.

# 45

**TIM WAS GRATEFUL THE MASTERSONS HAD CHOSEN A**
Lincoln, since there was no way he could have
worked a clutch and the gas with one good leg.
He coasted onto the freeway well before LAPD closed in
on Monument Hill. The faintest edge of gold peeked above
the horizon, enhanced by the inland smog.

Bowrick rested Mitchell's .45 in his lap. Tim took it and
slid it into his hip holster. Its weight on his hip was comforting. After making the mistake of glancing at his reflection once, he did his best to avoid the rearview mirror.

Fighting pain and light-headedness, he kept both hands
on the wheel and his eyes on the road.

Finally he eased to the curb and parked. Pulling his remaining money from his pocket—four hundreds—he
handed it to Bowrick.

Bowrick folded the cash into a pocket. "Thanks."

"I'm not your guardian angel. I'm not your big brother.
I'm not gonna be the godfather to your kid. I don't care
about your problems or your issues. But if you're ever in
trouble—I mean *real trouble*—you find me. You're not
gonna slip up. Not after all this."

He got out and limped through Fletcher Bowron Square
Mall, drawing strange looks from a few early-morning
suits. Blood and sweat had left his shirt warm and sodden.
Bowrick trudged silently a few steps back, one leg dragging
behind, head lowered, hands shoved into his pockets. After
a moment he sped up, his posture straightening, to walk by
Tim's side.

Passing under the tile mural, they entered the Federal Building. The security guard at the entrance lowered his cup of coffee, his face blank with disbelief. "Deputy Rackley, are you . . . ?"

They walked past him. Thomas and Freed were bullshitting in the lobby, Freed thumbnailing a stain out of his Italian tie. Their faces pivoted wide-eyed at Tim's approach. Tim grabbed Bowrick's arm, presenting him. "This is Terrill Bowrick. I blew his cover. You help him."

He left them in stunned silence.

Blood had worked its way down Tim's leg into his shoe; it squished when he walked. He left bloody footprints on the tile of the second floor, all rights, a neat line of paisley.

A secretary flattened herself against the wall, clutching a stack of papers to her chest.

Tim pulled the .45 from his holster and dropped the magazine. It bounced on the floor. He shucked the slide, letting the round spin and rattle to a stop on the tile. Holding the unloaded gun limply by the barrel, he carried it away from his body, upside down, pointed innocuously into his hand. He'd left his jacket in the elevator so he could show his empty holster.

When he pushed through the doors into the offices, the deputies' heads snapped up. From the smell of coffee and sweat, they were pulling a double shift. Maybeck's face went pale; Denley froze in a half crouch above his desk; Miller peered at him above a cubicle wall.

Tim walked into Bear's office, a small white box that recalled an unfurnished college dorm room more than anything else. Bear was poring over a stack of crime-scene photos from Rhythm's house, a head-wound close-up on top. When he looked up, his shiny cheeks took a moment to still from the movement.

Tim set the .45 on Bear's desk and sat down.

Bear nodded, as if in response to something, then re-moved a fat brick of a tape recorder from a drawer, set it on his desk, and turned it on. He hit a button on his phone and spoke into the speaker. "Yeah, Janice, can you send him over? Please tell him I have ex–Deputy Rackley in custody."

He and Tim stared at each other.

Finally Bear said, "I got the dog. He pissed on my car-pet."

"The way you keep your place, I don't blame him."

Bear nodded at Tim's leg. "You need medical attention?"

"Yes, but not immediately."

They stared at each other some more. Bear rubbed his eyes, the skin moving with his fingers. The wait was excru-ciating.

Minutes later Marshal Tannino appeared, cutting off a few deputies pretending not to gawk at the open doorway. He stepped inside, closed the door behind him, and locked it.

Bear indicated Tim's leg. "He might need medical atten-tion."

"Fuck medical attention."

"I'm fine, Marshal."

Tannino leaned against the file cabinet and crossed his arms, the glossy fabric of his suit jacket bunching at his shoulders. His eyes picked over Tim's badly scabbed face, his soggy shirt, the blood-stiffened leg of his jeans. "What surprise do you have for us now? I'm guessing it has to do with a phone call I just got from Chief Bratton about two bodies found up on Monument Hill."

Tim started to speak, but Tannino's hand flashed up an-grily, his gold ring glittering. "Wait. Just *wait*. I heard a full account of your dinner with Bear on the twenty-eighth of February, which I *still refuse to believe*. . . ." He paused, regaining his composure. "So maybe you'd better take this one from the top, because I'm gonna have to hear with my own two ears how my best deputy managed to land himself and this office in a pool of shit so deep it makes the Rampart scandal look like a small-claims dispute."

Tim started from the beginning, reiterating what he'd told Bear at Yamashiro. He told how the Commission had plotted the initial executions and how the Mastersons had gone on the warpath. He told how he'd discovered their role in Ginny's death, how he'd tracked them, and how they'd died, ending up with his freeing Kindell and driving down here to turn himself in.

A remarkably awkward silence punctuated the end of his story. Bear rearranged the photos on his desk. Tannino ran a hand through his dense hair and studied his knockoff loafers.

Finally Tim said, "Marshal, sir, my leg's going numb."

Tannino looked up at Bear, ignoring Tim. "Call the paramedics. Have him brought to County. Book him there." He walked out, closing the door quietly behind him.

His face drawn and weary, Bear picked up the phone and called for an ambulance.

**46** A THREE-DAY STINT AT THE USC MEDICAL CENTER JAIL
Ward got Tim's leg back in working order. The bullet had missed all major vessels, which Tim had already surmised from the fact that he hadn't bled out on Monument Hill. His right seventh and eighth ribs were bruised but not broken.

Since Robert's and Mitchell's deaths had taken place on Monument Hill, they charged him with crime committed on federal property to keep the case, murders and all, in their backyard rather than turning it over to the state courts. Plus, Tim's confrontation with Bear at Yamashiro was filed as assaulting a federal employee, another federal hook. The appointed PD pled him not guilty at the postindictment arraignment; Tim watched the proceedings glumly from a wheelchair.

In the news Dumone's name was mentioned only tangentially; evidently the "Vigilante Four" didn't have the same ring. The nature of Tim's involvement was kept under tight wraps, though that only seemed to whet the appetites of reporters and journalists.

Tim's new temporary residence, the Metropolitan Detention Center, was an adjunct to the Roybal Building, part of the cluster of buildings where he used to report to work. A high-rise with slit windows like squinting eyes, the detention area was cold and harshly lit, the lowest loop of Tim's inferno. Since he was a former law-enforcement officer, they celled him separately on Eight North, not leaving him to fend for himself in the general population. His ward in the Special Housing Unit, consecrated by the likes of Buford Furrow, who'd shot up the North Valley Jewish Community Center, and Topo, Mexican mafia godfather, was bare and clean. A single bed and an unlidded stainless-steel toilet. No hot water. The ceiling was low, so he soon acquired a stoop.

He wore a blue jumpsuit, a green windbreaker, and cheap plastic sandals that creaked. At 11:00 A.M. he had an hour for exercise, during which he could throw some weights around in the tiny pen or play basketball. Solitary H-O-R-S-E was less than invigorating; he usually just lifted and rehabbed his injured leg.

The federal guideline for first-degree murder was life to death. Federal guidelines, as that drunken public defender had pointed out to Tim, were notoriously inflexible. By his own count, Tim was up on at least three counts of murder one and implicated in three other deaths, not to mention the laundry list of additional felonies he'd picked up along the way, including obstruction of justice, conspiracy to commit murder, assault of a federal agent—to wit, a United States deputy marshal—illegal possession of firearms, and illegal possession of explosives. Tim figured he'd better get used to his current lifestyle. Frozen 7-Eleven burritos twice a day for the rest of his life.

A trial date had been set, he was told, for May 2, which gave him seventy-eight days.

The second week the congenial corrections officer politely took Tim from his cell and led him to the visitor area. Dray was seated when he entered the room, regarding him through the shatterproof glass.

She picked up the phone, and Tim followed suit.

"The photos," she said. "Those awful photos. Of Kindell. With Ginny. I turned them over to Delaney."

Tim chewed the inside of his cheek. "They won't be admissible. I obtained them illegally."

"Doesn't matter. I'm the peace officer, and I obtained them legally. From a civilian. You."

Tim's mouth moved, but no sound came out.

"The case is reopened. The arraignment was this morning. Prelim's in five months—the PD's scared, so he's taking his time this go-around. Aging the case."

Tim felt a tear swell at the brink of his eye. It fell, trailing down his cheek, dangling from the line of his jaw until he swiped it off with his shoulder.

They stared at each other for a moment through glass and embedded chicken wire.

"I forgive you," she said.

"For what?"

"Everything."

"Thank you."

Her eyes were starting to water, too. She nodded, pressed a hand to the glass, and walked out.

The COs offered him books and magazines, but Tim passed his days lying on his bed, reflecting quietly. They let him stretch his workout time in the exercise room to a few hours a day, which helped cut through some of his despondency. He ate poorly and slept well. He spent a lot of time thinking about his murdered daughter.

Lying on the cracked vinyl pad of the bench press one day, he finally had it—a single pure memory of Ginny, not of the loss of her, just her, untainted by rage or hurt or pain, laughing openmouthed. She'd gotten into a pomegranate; her chin was stained, and her happiness, even recollected, was contagious.

The day before his pretrial motion, the corrections officer tapped gently on his door. "Rack, wake up, buddy. Your new lawyer needs to see you."

Tim's attorney, a weary man with droopy features, had gone on a fishing trip to Alaska and elected never to return. Another PD burnout to add to the ash heap.

"I don't want to meet my lawyer."

"You have to. Come on now, you'll get me in trouble."

Tim rose and rubbed the sleep from his eyes. He splashed cold water over his face, smoothed down his hair, and brushed his teeth with a rubber-handled toothbrush. Pausing at the door, he regarded his blue jumpsuit. "How do I look, Bobby?"

The CO smiled. "I keep saying. It's a good color for you."

Tim was led down a hall into a dark conference room with no windows save a tiny square of shatterproof glass in the door. Bobby nodded reassuringly and opened the door for him.

Tannino was sitting at the head of the table, hands laced. In a neat row to his left sat Joel Post, the U.S. Attorney for the central district, Chance Andrews, the presiding federal district judge, and Dennis Reed, the Internal Affairs inspector who'd stuck up for Tim on his shooting review board. Bear stood shouldered up against the wall, one foot crossing his shin and pointing down into the concrete. Opposite them all sat Richard, the public defender Tim had protected from the bouncer that night in the club off Traction.

The door swung shut behind Tim. He made no move to the table.

"I hope one of you brought a cake with a file in it."

Tannino unfolded his hands, then refolded them, his face maintaining its unamused cast.

"The thing is . . ." Bear shuffled a bit against the wall, not quite making eye contact. "The thing is, I forgot to read you your Miranda rights."

Post leaned back in his chair, emitting a barely audible sigh.

Tim let out a short bark of a laugh. "I can give you my statement again."

"As your new court-appointed defense attorney, I would strenuously advise against that," Richard said.

"You're my . . . ?"

Richard nodded.

"This is ridiculous." He raised his voice to talk over Richard's objections. "I wasn't even in official custody yet in Bear's office—he didn't have to read me my rights."

Richard was standing, his face red and impassioned. "You were *clearly* in custody. There was a warrant out for you. You turned yourself in. You were not free to leave. They tape-recorded Deputy Jowalski's intercom call to Marshal Tannino's office claiming you were in custody, and when the marshal came over to take your account, he closed and locked the door. You were then held for questioning, even denied medical attention."

Tannino regarded Richard as he might the remains of a cockroach smeared in the tread of his loafers.

"How about my conversation with Bear at Yamashiro?" Tim said. "That's certainly fair game."

"That conversation is covered under attorney-client privilege," Richard said.

"Excuse me?"

"George Jowalski became a member of the bar in good standing on November 15 last year. In fact, Your Honor"— Richard nodded at Chance Andrews—"I believe you swore him in that day yourself."

Andrews, an old-school justice with a leathery, venerable face, tugged uncomfortably at his cuffs. It occurred to Tim he'd never seen Andrews out of his robes.

Richard didn't dare smile, but his face showed he was enjoying himself tremendously. "Mr. Jowalski confirmed for me in an interview that on the fifteenth of February he agreed to represent you if your shooting review board led to a criminal trial. All future dialogue that you had with Mr. Jowalski regarding criminal matters would be covered under attorney-client privilege, and therefore he cannot testify regarding your consultation in a court of law. Your discussion can't be admitted. Anyone else's knowledge of it from Mr. Jowalski is hearsay. Then, because of Mr. Jowalski's status as a deputy marshal, we have fruit of a poisonous tree—"

"Attorney-client privilege," Tannino muttered. "I don't know how they dig up this stuff. Like pigs rooting for truffles."

Richard gave a self-assured little nod.

It took a moment for Tim to speak through his shock. "Well, I'm willing to come clean again. Let's do it now."

Andrews cleared his throat. "I'm afraid it's not that easy, son."

"What are you saying?"

Post pressed both hands on the table, palms down, as if readying to do a push-up. "What we're saying is, we're having a tough time finding independent evidence."

"What?"

"We need independent corroboration of your account. Robert and Mitchell Masterson are dead, as are Eddie Davis, William Rayner, and Jenna Ananberg. The only accounts we have from potential victims Bowrick and Dobbins are of you acting in a protective capacity. Even the kid at the video store doesn't want to press charges. He says you were polite, never pulled a gun on him, and he told you you could have the security videos. He's a bit shaken up and just wants to put the episode behind him."

"You certainly knew how to go about things to cover your ass," Tannino said.

Post continued, "We have no witnesses to put you with any of the Vigilante Three before the Dobbins event and no direct evidence, no eyewitness testimony, no physical evidence, and no forensic evidence—ballistic or DNA—tying you to the Lane earpiece bomb or the Debuffier assault. Hell, we can't even link your gun to any bullets fired anywhere because the bore is blown apart. The files we recovered at Rayner's office indicate you were being illegally spied on—that's all."

"Oh, come on," Tim said. "Run some interrogations

around KCOM—someone will be able to recognize me despite the disguise. Maybe the guard who frisked me by the loading dock—"

Richard was on his feet again, yelling. "You are *not* supposed to help build the case against yourself."

"But we all know I'm telling the truth about my involvement."

Post raised his hands, then let them fall into his lap. "It's not what happened. . . ."

Andrews cocked his head, somber eyes on Tim. "It's what you can prove."

"Even *with* evidence there'd be a good chance you'd skate on charges," Post said. "Since Lane was planning to unleash sarin nerve gas after his interview, you could argue defense of others."

"I didn't have prior knowl—"

"My client has no comment on that matter," Richard said.

"At Debuffier's house you weren't even the shooter, and that was *clear* defense of others," Post said. "And you didn't go through with Bowrick."

"Fine. How about the Stork's house? The Mastersons at Monument Hill? You have plenty of evidence. I had their blood all over my shirt."

"Eddie Davis died of a heart attack."

"You could argue the felony-murder rule."

"Mr. Rackley," Richard said. "Shut up, please."

Andrews said, "Mitchell Masterson was clear self-defense, and Robert Masterson . . . well, even in my infinite legal wisdom, I don't know if there's a case to be filed for someone having a booby-trapped gun blow up while attempting to commit murder."

Tim held up his hands. "Wait, wait, wait."

"Plus, we'd have mitigating emotional circumstances to fall back on, due to your daughter's death," Richard said.

"Maybe even post-traumatic stress disorder or temporary insanity."

*"No,"* Tim said. "Absolutely not. I knew what I was doing. I was just wrong."

Tannino finally raised his dark brown eyes. "You are so goddamned stubborn, Rackley."

"Plus," Richard continued, "you're a citizen in good standing, you turned yourself in and cooperated with authorities in helping alleviate the threat of the Vigilante Three."

"Cooperated," Tannino muttered. "Hardly."

"Throw that on top of your daughter's murder and the fact that several of the deceased *conspired* to kill your daughter, and our jury-sympathy factor is through the roof."

Tim glanced at Reed. "And this is fine with you?"

"Just because I'm IA doesn't mean I like to see the service get a black eye when it's not necessary. The Rampart case set LAPD back ten years in the eyes of the public. We're not covering something up—there's just sparse legal ground to stand on here."

"Hanging everything on the other members of the Commission doesn't seem fair."

"Don't you fucking worry about fair," Tannino said.

"The homicides are shit cases, son," Andrews said. "Take it from me."

"In light of insufficient evidence and a lack of independent corroboration, I have to decline to prosecute the homicides," Post said. "I'm sorry."

"We'd like to cut a deal," Richard said.

"What deal?"

"Plead you out with a misdemeanor—1361, malicious mischief. They can prove *that*." Richard recoiled a bit from Post's glare.

"What's the sentence?"

"Time served."

Tim's jaw literally dropped. "So I just go free?"

"It's not like anyone's concerned with recidivism here."

Post said, "Despite the various levels of contempt in which we hold you—and they are various—we all do agree on one thing. You're not worth the space in our prison system."

"We're not gonna make it easy for you and send you away for ninety years." Andrews extended a knobby finger and pointed at the far wall, a gesture intended to indicate the awaiting world. "Out there, however, are hundreds of cameras representing international media organizations. The wolves. They want answers."

"But you walk," Bear said.

Tim finally sat down. "The system's not supposed to work this way."

"Do us a favor this time, Mr. Rackley," Reed said. "*Don't* do anything about it."

Tannino stood up and placed his knuckles flat against the table. "Here's what your future looks like, Rackley. Tomorrow in court you plead to this *misdemeanor*"—he spat out the word—"and you skate. It goes without saying that we're gonna keep you on a very tight leash, keep an eye on you. If you step even an inch out of line, we'll hammer you. Any part of this unclear?"

"No, Marshal."

"Don't call me 'Marshal.'" On his way to the door Tannino shook his head, muttering under his breath. "A Medal of Valor winner. For the love of Mary."

The others filed out, Richard pausing to shake Tim's hand. Only Bear remained. They had a tough time making eye contact but finally did.

"Did you do that on purpose? Forget to read me my rights?"

"Nah." Bear shook his head. "But if I did, I wouldn't tell you anyway." His shirt was rumpled as always, and Tim thought he detected a splotch of salsa beneath the too-short tie. "I brought you a suit for court. Have it out in the rig."

"I hope it's not one of yours."

It took a moment, but Bear returned his smile.

**47** THE READINESS CONFERENCE WENT SO QUICKLY THAT Tim barely kept up with the proceedings. Though sawhorses and cops were keeping throngs of press at bay on Main Street, inside it was a remarkably unimpressive affair; he was shoehorned between an Argentine drug dealer and a Bel Air madam with reputed mob connections and two-inch lashes. Though he smelled distinctly of tequila, Richard proved capable and articulate counsel.

Tim barely rose to his feet before Judge Andrews pronounced, "You are free to go."

As he headed down the center aisle toward the courtroom doors, he was enfolded in an incredible loneliness. For the past several months, he'd been focused on one crisis after another, all of them immediate. Now he had the rest of his life to face. The events of the past forty-eight hours still hadn't taken on a reality; it was inconceivable that he could be walking away.

The clamor of media rose as he stepped through the doors—glinting lenses, flashing bulbs, shouted questions. An army of reporters documenting his going free due to precisely those types of technicalities he'd committed such violence to protest. With some effort, police held their line at the sawhorses.

Tim continued down the marble courtroom steps, his eyes on the Federal Building standing tall and proud across the square.

When he glanced down, he saw Dray standing in the apron of calm at the base of the stairs, a twenty-meter stretch of sanity before the held-back horde. She was wearing the yellow dress with tiny blue flowers, the dress she'd worn the first time they'd met. He drew nearer, his pace slowed with disbelief, and saw that she was wearing her ring—no rock, no inscription, the plain, worn, twelve-karat band he'd given her on bended knee back when he couldn't afford anything more.

The din seemed to recede—the scrape of cable on concrete, the babble into microphones, the strident queries—fading into inconsequentiality.

He paused a few feet from her, regarding her, unable to speak. The wind kicked up, blowing a strand of hair across her eye, and she left it.

"Timothy Rackley," she said.

He stepped forward and embraced her. She smelled like jasmine and lotion and a touch of gunpowder around the hands. She smelled like her.

She pulled back her head and regarded him, hand on his cheek.

"Let's get you home," she said.

Specifics of bomb construction and cell-phone tracking have been altered in the interest of public safety. Also, please don't run with scissors.

# ACKNOWLEDGMENTS

I wish to express my gratitude to: Michael Morrison, my patron, for his continued faith and focus; Richard Pine, from whose expertise I have benefitted enormously; the Guma, for buying two and selling two; Marc H. Glick and Stephen F. Breimer, my from-the-gates backwatchers, who are the soothing white noise to all foreground static; Jess Taylor, my Reader, who lends me (fervidly insists upon?) brilliant editorial suggestions between close encounters of a Third World kind; Meaghan Dowling, my editor, for not just inheriting me, but adopting me; that whirlwind of competence I have come to know as Lisa Gallagher; Libby Jordan, for her energy and support; Tom Strickler, Adriana Alberghetti, Brian Lipson, and Dawn Saltzman at Endeavor; Lori Andiman, for representing me around the world; Carol Topping, for launching me on the web; Suzanne Balaban, for her enormous enthusiasm; Debbie Stier, for overseeing my publicity; Rome Quezada, for keeping everything rolling; and my entire team at William Morrow, from the dedicated sales reps to the brilliant marketeers.

I benefitted immensely from the generous contributions of my expert consultants, including: Sean Newlin, Deputy U.S. Marshal, Southern District of Illinois; Richard Kim, Los Angeles County Deputy Public Defender; Tony Perez, former U.S. Marshal for Central District, California—an absolute inspiration; Pat Espinoza, Deputy District Attorney; Tim Miller, Supervisory Deputy Arrest Response Team and Explosive Detection Canine Team; Brian Salt, Deputy U.S. Marshal Supervisor; Scott Badgley, former U.S. Army Ranger; Morrie the locksmith; Mike Goldsmith, former Customs Senior Field Agent, current Executive Director of the National Wilderness Training Center; Eric Hintz, criminal defense attorney; Matthew Collins, Special Agent, ATF, former Deputy U.S. Marshal; Steve Petillo, Palo Alto Police, retired; Deputy Phil Wang of the Los Angeles County Sheriff Department; and Tim Tofaute, former member of SEAL Teams FIVE and EIGHT, and of the Naval Strike Warfare Center, who always takes the time to expound on bullets and bar brawls.

Always and of course I appreciate the booksellers and librarians, as well as Pam Pfeifer, my parents, and Gary and Karen Messing—great supporters and readers, the whole lot of them.

Above all else, I'm thankful for Delinah Raya Blake, who makes all bad things good and all good things magnificent.

If you enjoyed
**THE KILL CLAUSE**
You'll love the following excerpt from
**THE PROGRAM**
Available at bookstores now
from William Morrow

**DRAY WALKED BRISKLY THROUGH THE KITCHEN AND** entry, wiping barbecue sauce on her olive sheriff's-department-issue pants, which she still hadn't had time to change out of. She pulled open the front door, and the image hit her like a truck—husky detective in a cheap suit thumbing a bound notepad, dark Crown Vic idling curbside behind him, partner waiting in the passenger seat, taking a pass on the advise-next-of-kin.

The detective crowded the door, imposing and cocky, which further added to her disorientation. "Andrea Rackley? Mrs. Tim Rackley?"

Ears ringing, she shook her head hard. "No." She took a step back and leaned on the entry table, displacing a tealight holder that rolled off the edge, shattering on the tile. *"No."*

The man's forehead creased. "Are you all right, ma'am?"

"I just talked to him. He was in the car, heading home. He was fine."

"Excuse me? I'm not sure what you . . ."

He lowered his pad, which she saw was not a detective's notepad but a PalmPilot encased in fine leather. Her darting eyes took in that his suit was not cheap but a fine cashmere, the car was in fact a maroon Mercedes S-class and the partner was not a partner at all but a woman with a wan face, waiting behind like a well-trained dog.

The flood of relief was accompanied by a torrent of sentence fragments even she couldn't keep up with. "You don't come to the door of a law-enforcement family all somber asking for a next-of-kin ID already lost someone in the family my *God*—"

She leaned shakily against the wall, catching her breath. A draft sucked the doorknob from her grasp. Startled, the man skipped back, lost his footing at the step, and spilled backward, landing hard on his affluent ass.

Dray had a split second to note the pain and alarm register in the wide ovals of his eyes before the door slammed shut.

Tim stifled a yawn as he pulled into his cul-de-sac, the starch-stiff security-guard monkey suit itching him at the collar and cuffs. His baton sat heavy on his equipment belt, along with a low-tech portable the size of a Cracker Jack box, which seemed like a toy company's idea of a radio rather than the thing itself. A big comedown from his beloved Smith & Wesson .357 and the sleek Racals he'd used as a deputy U.S. marshal before his own shitty judgment in the wake of his daughter's violent death had forced him from the Service.

Yesterday he'd chased down a teen vandal at the facility where he worked on the northern lip of Simi Valley. The pursuit represented the second time he'd broken a sweat in the eleven months he'd been guarding RightWay Steel Co.'s storage warehouses; the first had been unglamorously instigated by a roadside-stand enchilada *mole* he'd injudiciously wolfed down on a lunch break. Eleven years as an Army Ranger, three kicking in doors with the U.S. Marshals Service warrant squad, and now he was a locker-room commando with a diminished paycheck. His current coworkers got winded bending over to tie their shoes, which seemed to come undone with such alarming frequency that he'd spent the majority of the monotonous morning debating whether to volunteer proficiency training on the matter. The old man's groan he'd inadvertently emitted while stooping to pick up a dropped key outside Warehouse Five had leached the superiority right out of him, and he'd spent the afternoon valiantly refraining from doughnuts.

He was reminding himself that he should be grateful for *any* work when movement on his walkway drew his attention. A man stood appraising his suit, dusting off the pant legs as if he'd just taken a spill.

Tim accelerated sharply, almost clipping a parked Navigator with tinted windows. He pulled into his driveway and hopped out as the man smoothed his clothes back into place. A woman had climbed out of the Mercedes at the curb and was standing meekly at the end of the walk.

Tim approached the man, keeping the woman in his field of vision. "Who are you? Press?"

The man held up his hands as if conceding defeat. He still hadn't caught his breath. "I'm here to . . . speak with . . . Tim Rackley. Marshal Tannino gave me your address."

The mention of his former boss stopped Tim dead on the lawn. He and Tannino hadn't spoken for the better part of a year; they'd been very close when Tim worked under his supervision, but Tim last saw him in the midst of a storm of controversy Tim had brought down on himself and the Service.

"Oh," Tim said. "I'm sorry. Why don't you come in?"

The man patted the seat of his pants, wet with runoff from the sprinklers. He glanced at the door nervously. "Truth be told," he said, "I'm a bit afraid of your wife."

▓ The kitchen smelled sharply of burned chicken. Dray had forsaken her corn on the cob for a three-finger pour of vodka. "I'm sorry. Something about it—the knock, his expression—put me back there, the night Bear came to tell us about Ginny." She set her glass down firmly on the stack of overdue bills at the counter's edge.

He ran his fingers through her hair and let them rest on her shoulders. She leaned into him, face at his neck.

"I thought my heart would just give out there at the door. Good-bye, Andrea, hasta la vista, sayonara, I've fallen and can't get up."

Her voice was raised and, Tim was fairly certain, audible to the couple sitting on the couch one room over.

"He's a friend of the marshal's," Tim said softly. "Let's sit down, see what he wants. Deal?"

Dray finished her vodka in a gulp. "Deal."

They shook hands and headed into the living room, Dray refilling her glass on the way.

The woman sat on the couch, a gold cross glittering against her sweater. The man stood at the sliding glass doors facing the backyard, hands clasped behind his back, his stoic posture undercut by the moist patch of trouser plastered to his rear end. He pivoted as if just taking note of their entrance and nodded severely. "Let's start over." He extended a big, rough hand. "Will Henning. My wife, Emma."

Tim shook his hand, but Dray stood where she was, arms crossed. Copies of *The Lovely Bones*, gifted eight or so times by well-intentioned acquaintances, occupied the shelf behind her, the bluish stack accentuating her light hair. "What can we help you with?"

Will pulled a fat wallet from his back pocket, flipped it open, and withdrew a snapshot from the fold. He gestured impatiently for Tim to take it, his face averted as if he didn't want Tim to read the pain in it. A posed high-school-graduation photo of a girl. Pretty but awkward. A bit of an overbite, front tooth slightly angled, mournful green-gray eyes that were almost impossibly big and beautiful. Straight, shoulder-length hair that shagged out at the edges. Her neck was too thin for her head, lending her a certain fragility. Understated chin, full cheeks. The kind of face Tim had seen described as "heart-shaped" on fugitive identifiers; the term had stuck because he'd never before found it to make sense.

Tim's eyes pulled to the much-publicized school photo of Ginny on the mantel. Her second-grade year. And her last.

"I'm so sorry," Tim said. "When was she killed?"

Over on the couch, Emma made a little gasp. Her first peep.

Will took the picture back from Tim abruptly, casting a protective eye over at his wife. "She's not dead. At least we hope not. She's . . . well, sort of missing. Except she's eighteen—"

"Nineteen," Emma said. "Just turned."

"Right, nineteen. Since she's not a minor, we have no legal recourse. She's gotten herself in with one of these cults. Not like the Jehovah's Witnesses, but one of those creepy, mind-control, self-help deals. Except more dangerous."

Tim said, "Have you tried—"

"The goddamn cops have been useless. Won't even file a missing person's. We've tried every law-enforcement agency—FBI, CIA, LAPD—but there are virtually no resources devoted to cults. No one cares unless they turn Waco."

"Her name," Tim said.

"Leah. She's my stepdaughter, from Emma's first marriage. Her real father died of stomach cancer when she was four."

"She was a student at Pepperdine." Emma's voice was brittle and slightly hoarse, as if she had to strain to reach audibility.

Tim's eyes returned to Emma's cross pendant, this time making out Jesus' tiny hanging form.

"Three months ago we got a phone call from her roommate. She said Leah had dropped out. She said she was in a cult, that we'd better find her or we'd never see her again."

"She came home once," Will said. "March thirteenth, out of the blue. My men and I tried to reason with her but she . . . uh, escaped out the bathroom window, and we haven't seen or heard from her since."

He was the kind of man who had men.

"I'm sorry," Dray said. "I don't mean to be rude, and I understand how painful this is for you, but what does this have to do with Tim?"

Will looked to Tim. "We're familiar with your . . . work. Marco—Marshal Tannino—confirmed that you were a brilliant investigator. He said you used to be a great deputy—" He caught himself. "I'm sorry, I didn't mean it that way."

Tim shrugged. "That's okay. I'm not a deputy marshal anymore." The edge in his voice undercut his casual tone.

"We need our daughter back. We don't care how it's done, and we won't ask any questions. She doesn't have to be happy about it—she just needs to be home so we can get her the help she needs. We want you to do it. Say, for ten grand a week."

Dray's eyebrows raised, but she gave Tim the slightest head shake, matching, as usual, his own reaction.

Tim said, "I don't have a PI license, and I'm not affiliated with any law-enforcement agency. I got myself into some trouble about a year back, with a vigilante group— maybe you read about it in the papers?"

Will nodded vigorously. "I like your style. I think it was a great thing you tried to do."

"Well, I don't."

"What would make you say yes?"

Tim laughed, a single note. "If I could follow the trail legally."

"We could arrange that."

Tim opened his mouth, then closed it. His brow furrowed; his head pulled to the side. "I'm sorry, who exactly are you?"

"Will Henning." He waited for recognition to dawn. It did not. "Sound and Fury Pictures."

Tim and Dray exchanged a blank glance, and then Tim shrugged apologetically.

"*The Sleeper Cell. Live Wire. The Third Shooter.* Little art-house flicks like that."

"I'm sorry . . ." Dray said. "You wrote those movies?"

"I'm not a *writer.* I produced them. My films have grossed more than two billion dollars worldwide. If I could get fifteen Blackhawk choppers landing in Getty Plaza on three days' notice, I certainly think I can orchestrate your redeputization." His steel gray eyes stayed fixed on Tim. A man used to getting his way.

"The marshal probably has his own opinion on the matter."

"He'd like to talk to you about some creative solutions in person." Tannino's business card magically appeared in Will's hand. Tim took it, running his thumb over the raised gold "Marshals" seal.

On the back, in Tannino's distinctive hand: *Rackley— tomorrow a.m. 7:00.*

Tim handed the card to Dray, who gave it a cursory glance, then tossed it on the coffee table. "Tell me about the cult," he said.

"I don't know a goddamn thing about it, not even its name. Considering the amount we've paid for information . . ." Will shook his head in disgust.

"How do they recruit?"

"We don't know that either, really. We talked to a few cult experts—deprogrammers or exit counselors or whatever they're calling themselves this month—and they coughed up some generalities. I guess a lot of cults prey on young kids, in college or just out. And they recruit rich kids." He grimaced. "They get them to turn over their money." He ran his hand through his hair, agitated. "Leah gave away a two-million-dollar future. Just gave it away. That money was for her first indie film, grad school, a house someday. I even bought her a forty-thousand-dollar car before college so she wouldn't have to dip into it. Now her money's gone, she's alienated her friends, her family"—he nodded at Emma, who sat passively, hands folded, forehead lined. "She has nothing, nowhere to go. I've sent her letters begging her to come home. Emma has sent articles about cults, what they do, how they work, but she's never responded. I tried to talk some sense into her when we had her that day, but she wouldn't listen." His face had colored; his tone was hard and driving. "I told her that she'd given away her whole future."

"You told a girl in a mind-control cult *that?*" Dray said.

"We're not here for family therapy. We're here to get our daughter back. And besides, what was I supposed to say? You try dealing with a teenage daughter who's got all the answers."

Dray took a gulp of her vodka. "I would love to."

Tim squeezed her hand, but Will just kept on talking. "Leah's trust fund is irrevocable—I set it up that way to maximize tax benefits. It turns over money to her every year, and there's nothing we can do to stop it. She gets another million when she turns twenty, another million every year after that until she's thirty. Those people are stealing my money."

"The car," Tim said. "She still has it?"

"Yes. It's a Lexus."

"Is it registered in your name or hers?"

Will thought for a moment, eyes on the ceiling, fingers fiddling with the catch on his gold watch. "Mine."

"Okay. When you leave here, file a report that it's been stolen. The cops will put out a BOLO on the car—a Be On the Lookout. If they pick her up, they can hold her, and we'll see about getting her released into your custody."

"Jesus." Will looked excitedly to his wife. "That's a brilliant idea."

"Did she tell you anything about the cult?"

"No. No names, no locations, no matter how hard we pressed."

"So how do you know it's a self-help cult?"

"From her buzzwords. They weren't religious. More about how she learned to 'tap her inner source' and 'own her weaknesses' and crap like that."

"She didn't mention any names?"

"No."

"What did she refer to the guru as? She must have mentioned the leader."

Will shook his head, but Emma said, "She called him the Teacher. Reverently, like that."

Her husband regarded her, brow furrowed. "She did?"

"You mentioned the cult was dangerous. Did you get any death threats?"

Will nodded. "Couple. Some punk called, said, 'Back off or we'll slice you up like the lamb you served for dinner last night.'" Emma raised a wan hand to her mouth, but

Will didn't take note. "Creative little threat, letting us know they had eyes on us. I'm used to threats and bull-shit—thirty-four years in Hollywood—but I don't like be-ing pushed around. I didn't realize how serious it was until our investigator went missing. Then we got another call: 'You're next.' They probably figured if they hurt Leah, they'd be killing the golden goose, but us, hey. We're ex-pendable."

"Who was the investigator?"

"A PI. Former chief of security for Warner. My men hired him out of Beverly Hills."

Tim's mind reversed, drawn by the pull of a buried in-stinct. "The same men parked up at the mouth of the cul-de-sac in a Lincoln Navigator with tinted windows, license starts with 9VLU?"

Will stared at him for a long time, eyebrows raised, mouth slightly ajar. He finally sat. "Yes. The same men."

Tim crossed the room and grabbed the pen and notepad by the telephone. "Go on."

"Short little nervous guy, the PI was—Danny Katanga."

"And he was killed?"

"Disappeared. Last week. He must have been making some headway." Will let out a grumbly sigh. "That's when we decided to go to Tannino."

"We've had no word from Leah at all since she left," Emma said.

Will said, "I keep writing letters, hoping, but nothing."

"How can you send her articles and letters when you don't know where she is?"

"She left a P.O.-box number on our answering machine right after she first disappeared, so we could forward her mail—probably so she could keep getting her financial pa-perwork. We figure it's a holding box for the entire cult."

"Do any of your letters get returned?"

"No," Emma said. "They go through. To somewhere."

"Where's the post office?"

Will said, "Someplace in the North Valley. We tried to look into it—do you have any idea how difficult it is to squeeze information out of the United States Postal Service? We talked to some postal inspector, he acted like he was guarding the recipe for Coke or some horseshit. We finally sent Katanga to stake out the box, but the post office crawled up his ass about invasion of privacy, so he had to watch from the parking lot. He sat in his car for a few days with binoculars, but she never showed up. The cult's wise to it—they probably send someone different each time to pick up the mail. If they pick it up at all."

"I'll need that address."

"I'll have my assistant call Marco with it first thing tomorrow. Watch yourself with that postal inspector—I'm not kidding. He'll open you up a new one."

Tim jotted a few notes. "Did you record any of the threatening phone calls?"

"No. We managed to trace the second call back to a pay phone in Van Nuys. Nothing came of it."

"I'll want that information, too." Tim flipped through his notes. "What's Leah's last name?" Off the Hennings' blank stares, Tim added, "You said she was from Emma's first marriage?"

"She has my name. I adopted her legally when she was six. She's my stepdaughter, but I make no distinction between her and my own daughter." Will cleared his throat. "I may have progressed a bit foolhardy out of the gate. Wasn't sure what we were dealing with, so I came out swinging. In retrospect that may not have been the best plan of action." He had a habit, Tim observed, of holding his own conversation, undeterred by interjections. "I had my men post these around town. We got nothing but a bunch of nowhere leads." He pulled a flyer from his back pocket and smoothed out its folds on his knee before handing it to Tim. The same photo of Leah, beneath which was written, *$10,000 reward for information on the whereabouts of this girl, Leah Elizabeth Henning. Persons wishing to remain anonymous should tear this flyer in half, transmit one half with the info submitted, and save the remaining half to be matched later.* Leah's identifiers and contact information followed.

Tim thought he detected the faint tracings of pride in Will's face, probably from the *Dragnet* wording on the flyer he and his men had cooked up.

Tim turned the flyer over, unimpressed. "So now everyone in the cult knows you're after her, that you're the enemy. That's quite a mess."

"That's why we need you to clean it up. And why we'll pay you well to do it." Will enclosed one large fist in his other hand, bringing them to rest against his belly.

"We have to back off now." Emma shot a loving look at Will, which he returned. "We just had our first baby together. I won't have her be put in harm's way."

"And we're very concerned for Leah," Will said. "Who knows what they'll do to her? If they let her go, she can reveal secrets about them, maybe even try to get her money back. They need her either loyal or dead." He rubbed his eyes, wrinkling the skin around them. "They've convinced me they mean serious business. That's why we need you to poke around, quietly. Someone who can't be traced back to us or to her this time."

"What made Leah take off? When she came home that day?"

Emma rustled uncomfortably, and Will looked sharply away. "They're inside her head. She was insane, convinced we were persecuting her. She played around on my computer and managed to find all the e-mails I'd been sending out to cops and the like."

"She's a whiz with computers." Profound sadness undercut Emma's proud smile. "She was studying computer science. A straight-A student before she . . ." The scattering of pale freckles across her cheeks was visible only if the light hit her the right way. "To go through something like this, as parents, you have no idea."

Dray stiffened. Taking note, Emma shifted, noticing the framed picture of Ginny on the mantel. Mortified, she flushed, her eyes moistening. "Of course you do. I am . . . so terribly sorry."

She dug in her purse for Kleenex, tears running. Tim located a box and offered it to her. Will laid a thick arm across her shoulders and gathered her in. He kissed the top of her head gently. The two couples sat quietly in the room as Emma dabbed her eyes.

"It's terrible for me to cry here, after what you've been through," she said. "It's just so awful knowing she's out there, with these people. She wasn't herself when we saw her. It was like she'd been replaced by another person. She wore a filthy T-shirt, and she had a rash across her chest, bruises up the backs of her arms, open sores around her ankles. God knows what they've done to her. God knows what they're doing to her. Day after day." She pressed the balled tissue to her lips to still them. "How are we supposed to live with that uncertainty? As parents?" She made a strangled noise deep in her throat, something between a gasp and a cry.

Dray's face reddened with emotion; she looked away.

Will gazed tenderly at Leah's photo before leaning forward and setting it on the coffee table. "She was a damn good kid."

Dray said, "Maybe she still is."

Tim studied the picture, noticing for the first time it was worn around the edges, one corner faded by Will's thumb from being removed countless times from the billfold.

"I'll help your daughter," Tim said.